THE
ABLES

Turner Publishing Company
Nashville, Tennessee
www.turnerpublishing.com

This is a work of fiction. All the characters and events portrayed in this book
are either products of the author's imagination or are used fictitiously.

Cover design: Callie Lawson
Book design: Karen Sheets de Gracia

Library of Congress Cataloging-in-Publication Data Upon Request

9781684423378 Hardcover
9781684423361 Paperback
9781684423385 eBook

Printed in the United States of America
19 20 21 22   10 9 8 7 6 5 4 3 2 1

THE
ABLES

J EREMY S COTT

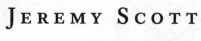

T URNER

PUBLISHING COMPANY

PROLOGUE

Those of you with sight are going to have to bear with me, at least for a while. There's only so much a blind person can give you in the way of visual detail. To be clear, I didn't even see much of what I'm about to tell you. Thankfully, with a story like this one, there are plenty of nonvisual details to go around.

Even though my eyes don't work—they never have—I've been a witness to some pretty fantastic things. Some horrible, some wonderful.

There's another world tucked right inside the world you know. You've seen only flashes of it, enough to get some conspiracy theories going, but not enough to serve as hard evidence. It is a world where amazing things are done every day by ordinary-looking people.

And I'm going to show it to you.

There are some secrets you just don't tell, and this story is full of them. The truth is about to come out soon enough anyway, and it won't be very long at all before the whole world can see what has been hidden for centuries.

For a good portion of this tale, you'll have to rely on the information I gleaned through nonvisual means as well as the eyewitness accounts of my friends. Don't worry; I'll do my best to compensate for my lack of vision with my other four senses.

I've been doing that all my life. You'd be surprised what I can tell about a person or a thing just by listening, smelling, or touching. Open your mind to the possibilities, and maybe you'll see some interesting things along the way as well.

I used to be just like you—reading stories about regular people doing incredible things. Then I found myself smack in the middle of such a story. I learned a few things about myself through the experience . . . and about others. Things that might be helpful to someone like you, someone about to find their world turned upside down, as mine was.

So if you believe in the unbelievable, as I have a feeling you do, read on.

PART 1
SUMMER

THE TALK

I was twelve years old when my father had "the talk" with me, and it was the single greatest moment of my life. It didn't start out too well, but it turned around pretty quickly. To say that it was a turning point for me personally would be an understatement of the highest order.

Twelve is a bit old for "the talk." I had picked up most of what I figured I would ever need to know just by listening to other people. Honestly, I had long since congratulated myself on being one of the lucky few whose parents didn't feel the need to sit down and explain where babies come from. *Surely that talk would have come before now.* I thought I was free and clear.

I suspected something was up almost as soon as Dad said word one.

"Son . . ."

There were exactly three levels of seriousness in the talks my father would have with my brother and me while we were growing up: "Somewhat Serious," "Normal Serious," and "Super Serious." Each variety had its own tip-off word, right at the start of his first sentence. If he opened with our nickname—Phil for me and Pat for my brother—it was a "Somewhat Serious" chat. Which meant we didn't have to stop what we were doing and turn our heads in his direction so long as we actually heard what he said and successfully repeated it back to him.

Lectures opening with our full first names, or first and last names together, were of the "Normal Serious" variety. Stop what you're doing, and turn and listen. There's probably some new rule you have to follow after this conversation is completed. This variety almost always has the lingering potential to escalate, so tread carefully.

Speeches that started with "son"—well, you can only hold on for dear life. Either you've screwed up in spectacular fashion and are about to receive the punishment of a lifetime or you're moving to another state. Or someone died. Also, the length of the pause between the word "son" and the rest of the lesson was directly proportional to the severity of the impending matter. In my entire life, my father had started exactly five conversations with me in this manner. It was the one trick he pulled out for only the most devastating announcements.

"Son . . ." he said.

I was reading a book—*Moby-Dick*, because the classics were the easiest to find in braille, though we'd also managed to find a handful of braille comic books over the years. Almost instantly, I felt my stomach drop. Dad had walked into the room somewhat casually from the sound of it, hands in the pockets of his suit pants; he always wore dress pants, *always*, without exception. He was just standing there, I guess, hanging out for a few moments before dropping the bomb.

"Let's go for a drive. What do you say?"

I said what any twelve-year-old would say in response to the most loaded question in the universe, "Um, sure . . . okay. I guess." I didn't know what I was in for, but I was pretty sure I wasn't going to enjoy it.

"Great," he said, in somewhat of a forced manner. "I'll get the keys."

As he turned and went for his keys, my mind raced. If someone had died, he would have been acting more upset. There was definitely something strange about his demeanor, but it wasn't sadness. Nervousness, maybe? He was acting weird, for sure. But not "your grandma's dead" weird. Plus, my grandma was already dead—all my grandparents were.

We weren't moving to a new city again, because we'd only just gotten here. Our family had been residents of Freepoint for exactly five weeks.

A horrifying thought hit me as I mentally ticked off any and every possible reason for the upcoming chat of doom: I was about to have to endure "the talk." After flying through several other ideas, nothing else seemed to hold any weight at all except for this theory. Dad and I had never had "the talk." And he was nervous!

As the reality of my fate set in, I basically wanted to die. I would rather have had to endure a thousand days of being grounded than listen to my father talk to me about sex. I imagined it would be awful, and I was certain it would be far worse than I could imagine.

As we reached the door that led from the kitchen to the garage, my mother and little brother came into the room from the hallway. Without saying a word, my mother reached out and squeezed my shoulder, and I could tell she was smiling at me. *Oh crap*, I thought, *this really is "the talk."*

"Get off the counter!" she screamed at Patrick, her hand still on my upper arm. Mom had mastered the art of yelling at one child while talking to the other about something completely different.

"I love you," she said softly. "Patrick, I'm going to count to three," she warned sharply without turning her head. She had also mastered the art of seeing things peripherally, sometimes even demonstrating the ability to know about things that were going on in completely different rooms.

Mom released my shoulder and turned to scramble after Patrick. Dad and I turned and headed into the garage. I could still hear her shouting at him as we climbed into the SUV.

Patrick was eleven going on four. The older he got, the more hyperactive he became. He was born just fifteen months after I was, and even without having had a sex talk from my parents, I knew that meant they hadn't wasted any time. Some days, our proximity in age made Pat and I inseparable best friends. Other days, his boundless energy and my lack of sight made us both more interested in avoiding each other.

Once Dad and I were on the road, I started to feel sick. I knew I was in for an emotionally scarring experience, so I figured it would be best to get it over with as soon as possible. "So . . . where we goin', Dad?" I asked. I had tried to act casual, but I wasn't remotely convincing.

"Well, do you remember Mr. Charles?" he asked.

I pondered the name. "The old man you keep inviting over for dinner?" There was this super-old guy who'd been over to the house once or twice since we'd moved to Freepoint. He seemed nice enough, I suppose, but terribly quiet. Some nights he didn't say a word. I often wondered what he and Dad even had in common. I guess maybe he reminded my father of his own father, who had died before I was born. Either way, the old man creeped me out.

"That's the one," Dad said. He actually seemed impressed that I knew who he was talking about. "Well, Mr. Charles has a farm just outside of town a ways, and I thought we'd go take a walk around the place."

"We're going to take a walk at a farm?" I blurted out before I could really stop myself, my own skepticism hanging noticeably in the air.

"Uh-huh."

Defeated—and still nauseous—I punched the button to change the radio station to one I liked, turned up the volume a bit, and slouched back into the passenger seat with my arms crossed.

This is the kind of thing that could scar me for life. I am way too old for this. I'm having the birds and bees talk with my father a good year or more later than I should be for such a thing . . . and we're going to a farm to have the talk so we can be in the company of actual birds and bees! Wonderful. At least I won't have to see his face when he does it. That would be even more awkward. Poor Patrick, he's so screwed.

Freepoint is a small town, maybe nine or ten thousand people. There are only a few stoplights and just one grocery store—the Freepoint Grocery. Everything in town had similarly creative names. There was the Freepoint Bank. The Freepoint Diner. The Freepoint Convenience Mart.

It was a far cry from our borough in New York City. I'm not sure we could have moved to a place that was less like our previous home. We'd been in Freepoint just a handful of weeks. In just one day, I would be starting at Freepoint High—a combination middle school and high school, spanning grades seven through twelve. Pat was still one year behind me, which meant that he would be headed to Freepoint Elementary. He had thrown several tantrums about it. In New York, a sixth grader would at least be in middle school, not elementary.

It didn't take a person too long to get from one end of Freepoint to the other, usually just five minutes or so, at least by car. After a couple songs on the radio, we'd already gone beyond the streets I knew by sound and feel to the outskirts of town.

Eventually, the car pulled down a long gravel driveway and came to a stop. Dad turned off the engine and removed the keys. We sat in silence for a few seconds. Finally he spoke. "Well . . . we're here. Let's go stretch our legs a bit."

If we have to. "Okay," I said.

We got out and Dad led me around to the back of the house, where I heard him yell hello to Mr. Charles, who was either dead or simply not listening because there was no response. I heard some chickens clucking and fluttering around and a dog barking in the distance. We kept on through what seemed like a much bigger backyard than ours and continued on out into the fields.

"On your left is a *huge* cornfield, and on your right, another one just as big. We're walking down a grass path between the two, and the corn is taller than I am." My father—my whole family, for that matter, even Patrick—was very good about setting the scene for me when we went someplace new to help me visualize the surroundings. I always thought it was the kindest gesture, and I say that without an ounce of sarcasm. "There are over seventeen acres of farmland here." We came to a stop. "There's a picnic table here under giant twin oak trees. Let's have a seat," he said.

We sat on the table surface itself with our feet on the bench, facing out over the cornfield. My father began to sigh here and there, and I could hear him fidgeting considerably. For the first time, I wondered how he must be feeling, realizing that the thought of having to have this conversation couldn't be any more appealing to him than it was to me.

A healthy breeze was blowing, rustling the oak leaves and the tops of the cornstalks. The dog in the distance continued to bark but sounded much farther away now. And aside from that, it was silent. Eerie, even. When you pay as much attention to sound as I do, true silence, or anything close, is a rarity. You can almost always hear *something* if you really want to.

"Son . . ." he said for the second time in an hour, which was followed by the single longest post-"son" pause in the twelve-year history of my father's big talks. It seemed like nearly a whole minute or two of pause. "Son," he said again, as though trying to jog himself into speaking, "I wanted to bring you out here today so we could have a conversation."

Aw, crap! I knew it. Please get this over with quickly.

"It's not an easy conversation to have."

Imagine how I feel.

"But it's an important conversation to have. And one that every kid in this town will have to have with his or her father or mother at some point. And, to be honest, it's a little overdue. I probably waited several months too long to have this talk. I guess I didn't want to admit that you're growing into a young man now."

Kill me. Just kill me.

"Life goes by so quickly, as you'll learn, and I just wasn't ready for this moment like I hoped I'd be."

Oh, for the love of—

"But you're old enough now that you need to be aware of how some things work. I can't stop you from growing up, but I can protect you and help guide you into making smart decisions. But to make those smart decisions, you need information."

I'm pretty sure most of this was regurgitated from a parenting advice book he must have read. Or an after-school special. My father never talked like this, and it made the whole scene all the more unsettling to me.

I decided to put us both out of our misery, or at least attempt to. "Dad, I know what you're going to say. I know what you want to talk about. You don't have to say anything because I already know everything about it."

"You do?" he asked, incredulously, the same way he did whenever I told him I knew who the killer was ten minutes into one of those cop shows. I didn't have to see him to know he was definitely grinning ear to ear.

"I do," I said boldly and authoritatively. It was the truth, for the most part. I had the general idea. The rest I could fill in with trial and error.

"Phillip, I know kids in the neighborhood talk, and that there are whispers"—*Whispers? How long ago was it that you were a twelve-year-old kid?*—"but I seriously doubt that you know what we're here to talk about." His tone was different now, suddenly much more at ease. It was almost as though my overconfidence had melted his nerves away and broken the ice for him a bit.

He paused briefly. "Besides, I have a duty as your father to explain things to you, even if it's not going to be easy. To dispel the misinformation you might have overheard. So . . . to that end . . . let's get this over with."

Yes, let's do.

"You're twelve now. You're starting seventh grade tomorrow. New school. You'll be a man soon. And your mother and I think that it's time for you to know more—a lot more—about . . ."

He let a moment of silence pass for effect—the P. T. Barnum of father-son sex talks. He sighed an overexaggerated sigh, the kind of sigh you let out right before saying something you can never take back, and finished his sentence.

". . . your superpowers."

$$\frac{\textbf{\textit{\Large \lightning}}}{}$$

My father's sense of humor is notoriously hilarious to him alone. Most of it consisted of awful puns and unclever wordplay. If you asked him to make you a piece of toast, for example, he would point his finger at you, make a bug-zapper noise, and say "Poof! You're a piece of toast." He would typically deliver one of these stunning one-liners, most of which we heard at least once a week, and then follow it up with some good-natured chuckling. It was the most annoying thing ever.

I waited more than a few beats after his sentence ended but did not hear the usual chuckling. I thought perhaps he was stifling his laughter a bit longer than normal at this latest gag.

"My what?" I asked, somewhat annoyed. I was so geared up for some big punch line that I didn't even consider the possibility that he was being serious. Never even crossed my mind. This was supposed to be "the talk," and he was just prolonging it for his own entertainment. I was so sure of it I couldn't even process what he was actually saying to me.

"Phillip," he said quietly, a smile in his voice, "you have the best hearing of anyone I've ever met. Do you seriously expect me to believe you didn't hear me?"

I thought about it for a moment. I did have fantastic hearing, mostly by virtue of being blind. They say the other senses pick up the slack when you lose one, and I found that to be 100 percent true.

And I had heard him say "your superpowers" just now, of that there could be no doubt. *But that couldn't actually mean that he's trying to tell me I have superpowers, right? Because that would be ridiculous.*

He broke my train of thought. "I'm here to tell you that your world will never be the same again. After today, your new journey will begin. Your journey to become . . . a custodian."

My brain was in limbo. I cocked my head to the side like a Labrador. My mind felt like pudding. Thoughts simply weren't coming to me. So I said something designed to buy me more time. "I'm going to be a janitor? What are you talking about, Dad?"

Now he chuckled. "This is not a joke, son, I promise you that. This is the most serious conversation you and I have ever had. And if you can just be open and listen, then I'll tell you what I'm talking about and why we had to keep it secret from you until now."

I simply nodded, not realizing the gravity of what I was agreeing to learn. *He said "superpowers," right?*

He spoke rapidly and nervously. "Superheroes, like the ones in your comic books—sort of—are real. They're real." He paused but then started right back up. "They stop criminals all over the world on a daily basis. Some fly and some have superstrength. There are thousands of various known superpowers, which you'll learn about in school this year. But I'm getting ahead of myself." He breathed deeply to reset his thoughts. "You'll have to forgive me. This is my first father-son superhero talk."

I nodded again, still not quite caught up. I was just nodding out of reflex. Much of what he was saying was slipping right past me while I mostly just heard the word "superhero" echoing around in my brain.

"You come from a long line of superheroes—called custodians—from your grandparents on back to your grandparents' great-great-great-grandparents. Your mother and I have powers. As far back as our family tree extends, it consists of bona fide heroes, people who had secret identities and superpowers and sacrificed their time and effort to help protect their fellow man. In Roman and Greek mythology, they called them gods. In comic books, they call them superheroes. But the two groups are of the same lineage.

"We are extremely careful, which is why you never hear about custodians on the news." Almost as an afterthought, he added, "There are some memory-related superpowers, and those have also helped to keep us under the radar for the most part.

"This town, Freepoint, is a custodian town. There are two more like it in the world. They are safe havens for heroes and those who support them. Everyone who lives here is either a custodian or what's known as human support—nonempowered individuals who assist and support the custodian community in a variety of very important ways." Another deep breath.

"We moved here for you, son. For you and your brother. We moved here so that you could go to high school with other boys and girls your age, all of whom are just now getting their powers like you are. So you can learn to use them safely and effectively and then go on to be a productive member of the custodian community." He paused for a moment. "Do you have any questions so far?"

I sat there silently for what felt like a very long time, slowly beginning to comprehend what he was telling me, even as I still struggled to believe it could possibly be the truth. My father was telling me that I had inherited superpowers and was about to go to a special high school for superheroes . . . in a special town for superheroes.

I sighed loudly in a manner that could have sounded only like relief, because that's what it was. "I thought you were going to talk to me about sex."

Dad's genuine laughter is a lot more pleasant to listen to than the goofy chuckle he fakes after all his puns, and it tore through the quiet farm air. "You thought I wanted to talk to you about sex?" he asked, spurting and choking each word through his guffaws. "That's the most hilarious thing I've ever heard," he gasped. "Oh dear, no!" His laughter was still going strong. "The last thing I want to talk to you about is sex!"

Another tidal wave of calm washed over me. I laughed too, nervously at first. Eventually we were both giggling together until he suddenly stopped for a moment. "I mean," he stammered, "unless you think you need to have a talk about . . ." The wave of calm rushed abruptly back out to sea.

"No," I blurted out, a bit more emphatically than necessary.

"Because," he continued, "I just assumed you would pick up most of what you'd need through the general course of your life, but if you *ever* have anything you want to ask me about—"

This time I cut him off. "Dad, it's fine! I'm cool. I'm good. Can we please just stop talking about this?"

"No wonder you've been acting so strangely. You thought this was the birds and the bees talk," he realized aloud, still chortling here and there.

"We did the birds and the bees in sixth-grade health class anyway," I informed him, still feeling a need to build a case against a lesson about sex.

"I thought so," he said knowingly.

We sat silently for a minute or two, my dad still enjoying the comedy of the situation and me basking in the knowledge that this was not, in fact, "the talk." It was a nice moment.

"Well then," he proclaimed, taking the conversational wheel again, "a conversation about how you have superpowers ought to be a nice surprise for you, shouldn't it?"

"Dad, I don't understand. But if you're talking about my enhanced hearing or whatever, I don't think that qualifies as a superpower."

"That's not what I'm talking about, Phillip." He put his hand on my shoulder. "I know this is a mountain of new information being thrown at you all at once, and I'm sorry it has to be that way. It's going to take some time to sink in, I know that. It was the same way when your grandpa had this talk with me—in this very spot, actually."

"Grandpa had superpowers?" I had never known the man, but my parents had told me that he was a kindly old gentleman who liked telling bad jokes—go figure—and that he had died in a car accident before I was born.

The lesson continued. "He did. My father had an ability called absorption, which allowed him to make use of the powers of other heroes nearby. He could lift an aircraft carrier over his head without breaking a sweat or run from here to Paris and back in ten seconds—as long as the right heroes were near him. He was, for a time, the most powerful hero in the world."

"So . . . he wasn't a traveling salesman?"

"No," he said with a chuckle. "No, your grandpa was one of the greatest custodians that ever lived. They called him the 'Everyman'—this was back when we still used silly monikers like 'Super Guy' and 'Awesome Man' and so forth. Today they just, you know, fight crime. We don't have costumes anymore. But your grandfather did. He wore the deepest-blue cape with silver trim." I instantly pictured a small blue-and-silver figurine my father had always kept in the glass cabinet in his office. It was a man holding a giant rock over his head. "He was one of the last superheroes that kept up with all the theatrical elements of fighting crime. He put more villains behind bars than all of his peers combined. And he was absolutely fearless about fighting crime."

It was clear these memories were as fresh as yesterday to my father. And he sounded incredibly proud.

A somber thought came over me. "He didn't die in a car crash, did he?"

I felt Dad's demeanor sag a bit. "No. He was killed in action. He was killed by one of the world's most notorious supervillains, named Artimus, one of the worst to ever live."

I could tell there was more to the story. A lot more. But he didn't seem to want to go into more detail.

I decided to steer the subject back to something less depressing. "And you got your powers from him?"

Dad's posture snapped back to normal as he climbed out of his moment of mourning. "That I did, correct. He and my mother."

"So you have the sharing power too?" I didn't know how it worked; I simply assumed you got the power from one of your parents.

"Sadly, no. Heroes have only a one in ten chance of inheriting the power of one of their parents. And my father's power was exceedingly rare. There have been only a handful of absorbers in recorded history. My powers are mental. Wait . . . let me back up a bit first," he said, getting animated. This had been bottled up inside him for years, and now he was finally able to share it with his son. "There are two kinds of superpowers: mental and physical. Some powers cross a bit into both categories. We call those hybrids, but those are pretty rare. Mental powers are, naturally, powers of the mind—things like mind reading, cognitive enhancement, supermemory. Physical powers are usually things like superstrength, flight, various members of the eye-beam family, and so on.

"There are more than two thousand known superpowers, and most of them aren't even very spectacular or exciting, like exceptional abilities in the area of math, science, and engineering. These heroes can do things on a whole other level from even the most intelligent nonempowered humans, able to do with their brains the kinds of things most folks need a computer for. Some custodians just have exceptional hand-eye coordination or hyperfast reflexes. The flashiest powers—x-ray vision or invisibility—those are actually more rare than you might think. Our family was pretty lucky. Blessed with good genes, I guess."

I had been pretty patient so far, but it was killing me. "What's *my* superpower, Dad?"

"Why, it's the same as mine, Phillip. Telekinesis."

Telekinesis. Telekinesis. What the heck is telekinesis? I raced frantically through the various storage cubbies in my brain, rummaging around for some previous memory or mention of that word, finding nothing. But I knew one thing: it sounded lame.

"What's telekinesis?" I asked nervously, assuming it was somehow related to the phone or the TV. I braced myself for the worst. *Please don't tell me I'm a human telephone.* This could happen only to me. Only I could find out at twelve that I have superpowers but then have them turn out to be something useless, like the ability to send radio signals.

"Telekinesis is the ability to move things with your mind." He hesitated, letting the definition sink in. "Just by thinking it, you could potentially send this picnic table hurtling across the cornfield."

"I'm pretty sure I can't move things with my mind, Dad. I'm sorry to disappoint you. I've tried it before, like a thousand times." I was dejected. What kid hasn't tried to move something with his brain? And like every other kid, I had never even sniffed success.

"Of course you tried it. Every kid ever born has tried it. You just couldn't do it because your powers weren't ready yet. You know that birds and bees stuff? I'm sure they talked to you in school about . . . you know . . . maturing and the body changes and—"

"Dad! Yes, okay? Geez."

"Well, it's kind of the same way with your powers. Most boys get their powers around eleven or twelve. You probably haven't tried to move something with your mind for several years. You probably gave up on it a long time ago, right?"

I nodded, realizing he was correct.

"You just have to overcome a few obstacles," he tacked on.

I wasn't sure what that meant. "Like . . . an initiation?"

He chuckled some more. "No, son. Like your blindness." He leaned in closer. "You see, telekinesis relies on your ability to know the intimate details of an object's dimensions in order for you to be able to move it mentally. Proximity—how far you are away from the object—plays a role as well, but it's not as important as how accurately you can judge its weight and length and shape. Typically, we telekinetics use our eyes to gain that knowledge of an object, to know every curve and corner. I could pick out an ear of corn over there in the field and have it in my hands at a moment's notice, but only because I can see it."

"Dad, you have to do it!" I knew he was going to do it before I even asked. He may be a dork, but I have the coolest dad in the world.

The late afternoon breeze had tempered, and it was as quiet as you would think a farm in the middle of nowhere would be. The only thing I heard was the sound of the vegetable smacking the palm of his hand. He reached over, opened my hand, and placed the corn in my grasp. I felt it up and down and was instantly sure that my father had just blown my mind. I was dumbfounded. Speechless.

Up until now, this was an entirely academic conversation—theoretical and abstract. Now, though, it just got real in a hurry.

Sensing my growing awe, Dad continued. "If you could see it—every kernel, every piece of husk and string—you'd have a mental picture good enough for your powers to send it flying back across the field. But even without your sight, your powers are still there. The more familiar you are with an object, the easier it will be for you to move it. You can acquire with touch, over time, what another telekinetic could see with his eyes in an instant. Put down the corn and get your phone out."

I did as instructed, setting the corn on the table beside me. I had a pretty swanky mobile device that had games and internet and a lot of other cool features a blind kid couldn't use, but it also had speech-to-text. I may not have been glued to it like most kids, but I'd used it enough to be very familiar with it.

"Roll it around in your hand. You've had that thing for nearly two years, Phillip. You know what all the buttons do, where they're located. You know how heavy the phone is and its shape."

He was right. It was like an extension of my hand.

"Now place it on the bench between your feet." Something in his tone changed as he shifted from father into trainer. This was one of those moments where I didn't realize the significance until much later.

Again, I did as he asked.

"Pay special attention to where the phone is on the bench—feel for your feet and the edges of the wood. Make sure you know which way the phone is facing and pointing." His voice was calm and smooth, like a meditation.

I felt around, using my fingers to get a "picture" of the phone's position. Dad kept on guiding me. "Hold your right hand out over the area where the phone is, straight out in front of you." I did.

We both sat there for a moment, anxious or excited or both. I know I was both.

"Now, I want you to pull up your mental picture of the phone. Remember how it's positioned. It hasn't moved. Everything about it is exactly the way you left it, just two feet below your hand. Concentrate on that image, son."

I wasn't about to start questioning him now. The man had just tractor-beamed an ear of corn into his hand, for crying out loud. I tried to focus on the phone . . . how it had felt in my hand . . . how it must have looked sitting down there on the picnic table bench. I tried to clear my mind of anything else.

"Now will it into your hand, son. I want you to silently picture the phone zipping up from the bench and into your hand." He kept encouraging me while I kept trying to figure out how to do what he was telling me to do. "Visualize it happening, and try and make it happen with just your focus alone. Just keep visualizing it over and over again."

I tried. I tried as hard as I knew how. But I had never moved something with my brain before. I didn't know how to flip that switch.

"You can do it, Phillip. I believe in you."

Several moments passed with me exerting every kind of willpower I could muster, but the phone refused to budge. I thought I felt a headache coming on. I began to realize that this was all a waste of time. My parents were wrong about me. I didn't have superpowers. I was just another normal, boring blind kid.

I gave up and felt his hand gently patting my shoulder almost instantly. I geared myself up for a pep talk about how it's going to take time and we'll keep trying—you know, all those encouraging things fathers usually say to their sons.

Instead, I got something else. "We're going to stay here as long as it takes for you to get it." He wasn't saying it in a mean way. This wasn't that threatening parental tone that the words might suggest. His voice was actually still completely soothing and loving. "Because I know you can do it."

I see, I thought. *He still thinks I just need to try harder.* I figured I would need to tell him just how hopeless I thought this was. "Dad, I really focused hard and the thing didn't budge. I don't want to disappoint you, but I really don't think it's going to happen anytime soon. How do you even know I have this power anyway?"

"Well, I know you have this power for a few reasons. First, it's genetic. We knew from the day you were born what your power was going to be. Every known power has a distinct genetic signature. It's in your DNA.

"Second, I know you have this power because I just know it. I feel it deep within me. You are my son, and when I look at you . . . I just know.

"And third—and perhaps most importantly—I know you have this power because you've used it before, and I saw you do it."

I had already believed him after the first point. It was pretty good. DNA is pretty strong evidence, from what little I knew about science. The second point was just sentimentality, which was fine with me, and it did make me feel good to hear him say it with such a sense of pride. But the third point threw me for a loop. I figured I would remember using my own superpower, particularly since I didn't know I had it until today.

Dad could sense my confusion. "Two mornings ago, I saw you hit the snooze button on your alarm clock by waving at it—from the far side of the bed." He paused briefly. "You weren't fully awake, sleeping soundly like you normally do. And your alarm was going off, so I came in to wake you, just in time to see you flop your arm in the general direction of the bedside table. Your hand was a good two feet away, but the button was pushed down . . . the alarm was turned off. And you rolled back over like it never happened. It's how I knew it was time to have this talk with you."

"Really?" I'm sure the truly great heroes had better quips at moments like this than I did.

"You can use your power, son, and you already have. So you don't have to worry about convincing yourself that you can. You just need to convince yourself that you already did. I'm not asking you to do anything new or anything you haven't already done before. It's just repeating a task." He stood up and stepped down from the bench, standing before me. "Now hold out your hand again."

I did.

"Your body already knows how to do this. Don't let your brain get in the way. Clear your mind of everything. There is no farm, there is no corn. There is nothing but you, this table, and your phone. It's not about telling the phone to move. Don't command the phone. Just visualize what you want to have happen. Imagine the successful outcome, and it will become the outcome. Don't try so hard this time."

I tried some deep breaths, pushing every thought out of my brain as best I could. I imagined the phone flying up from the bench into my hand and then imagined it again. Several beats passed as I strained and concentrated. I willed for that thing to move.

But it didn't. Nothing happened. My father had gone silent, probably not sure how to deal with my unexpected failure.

And with that fleeting thought, I lost my focus and gave up. I started to apologize as I moved my hand back to my right knee in defeat. "I'm sorry, Dad—" but that was all I got out before I heard the sound of the phone falling back to the bench.

I froze, in complete shock. "Was that what I think it was?" I inquired breathlessly.

"You had it almost a third of the way there," Dad confirmed, sounding like a beaming and proud father. "You didn't know? You had it moving at first and then you wavered, but you had it! You, my son, are going to make a fine telekinetic. You'll be able to pull it all the way to your hand in no time." He was gushing. It was as if all his poker buddies were standing around, with the spectacle he was making.

I was still in shock. *Did I really just move that thing?* People with sight really do take for granted the everyday assurance that comes from being able to see the things around you. The eyes are more trustworthy than the ears and nose alone, usually. I felt like I always had an extra layer of doubt beyond what most kids did, just from not having any visual confirmation of, well, anything.

I lifted my head up to my father in euphoria and spit out a brand-new revelation, the only thought I could find rumbling around between my temples, "I have the Force!"

"Yes, Phillip." He burst out laughing again and leaned in to hug me, much too hard. "Yes, you do indeed."

2

A NEW WORLD

I stood up in victory, arms in the air, and shouted, "I am a superhero!" I felt invigorated, unstoppable, free. I felt like I mattered.

Dad corrected me. "Custodian, son."

"Same difference, right?"

"I suppose," he allowed.

What followed was a series of questions the likes of which you normally hear only from five-year-olds, the kind where every answer leads to yet another question. It was the lightning round, my questions flying at him from all directions.

"How many people with superpowers are there in the world?"

"Thousands."

"How many are good guys?"

"More than half, but not enough. Some are neither good nor bad and simply choose to ignore their powers and live as normal humans."

"How many live here?"

"In Freepoint? Out of the nine thousand or so people living here, only about fifteen hundred, I believe, are custodians. Maybe two thousand. The rest are support."

"How many of them are bad?"

"Here? None. This is a safe zone for our kind. This is not a town where villains want to live."

"What about Bobby Simpkins?"

"Your friend from that camping trip?"

"Yeah."

"He does not have superpowers. His family is support. His dad works in our transport center, actually. He's a good guy."

"What's your real job?"

"Well, I was a crime-fighter in New York, busting robbers and other bad guys like my dad used to do. But now that we've moved here, I'm a protector."

"What's a protector?"

"A protector is a guardian of the city and its citizens. It's kind of like being a policeman of sorts."

"Wait a minute, I thought you said it was rare to have the same power as your parents," I said, just then recalling that part of his "introduction to superpowers" speech.

"That's right. It is. It's so rare that a lot of people at work think it's an omen."

"What kind of omen?" I asked hesitantly.

"That the child is special. Some of our greatest heroes in history have been sons or daughters who inherited a power identical to one of their parents. It happens only a few times every generation."

"So you're saying I'm special?"

"It's possible. In addition to inheriting my ability, you also have some genetic markers that suggest something about you or your abilities is unique."

"Genetic markers?"

"Your DNA looks like the DNA of every other telekinetic our scientists have ever seen, including mine . . . except in one or two small ways."

"Does it mean I'm flawed somehow?"

"No, son. All it means is that you are the first person alive to have these unique DNA markers. Until we see you grow up and mature, we don't really know what—if anything—they mean. Sometimes when this kind of thing is observed, the individual ends up with slightly enhanced abilities, and sometimes their abilities are slightly limited. Most of the time, these new markers like the ones in your DNA don't result in any noticeable change in abilities, personality, or development. You have to remember, while our gifted brothers and sisters have given us an edge in scientific and technological development over the nonempowered world, DNA is still a very new and exploding field for everyone, custodians and humans alike. There's just a lot we don't know for sure yet."

"I thought people got their DNA from their parents."

"They do. But the DNA of custodians behaves in odd ways. Sometimes the combination from two custodian parents results in recessive genes becoming dominant that have been dormant for generations . . . or genes we've never seen before at all. Despite all our advances in learning and knowledge, we still don't know much about how or why we exist . . . how we came about . . . how and why our DNA is different. Our 'race,' so to speak, is still a mystery even to us."

All this talk of DNA and family reminded me of a question I'd somehow failed to ask. "What about Mom?"

"What about Mom?" he asked playfully.

"What's her power?"

"Why don't you ask her yourself?"

I whined a little bit. "Can't you just tell me, Dad? I don't want to have to wait until we get home to find out."

"No, Phillip—I mean lift your head up and ask her yourself."

In that exact moment, I heard a strange noise. It was kind of like the sound a person makes when they're punched in the stomach, that "ooph" of air rushing out, only much faster. Or like the tiniest little explosion. I didn't think much of it until . . .

"Hello, dear." My mother's voice was unmistakable.

I jerked my head up. "Mom?" I'd lost track of the number of times my mind had been blown in the last hour or so.

"I guess you're having to process a lot of new information today, aren't you?"

I just nodded, still not sure how my mother got from the house to the cornfield or how long she'd been standing there.

"Well, why don't you ask me the question you wanted to ask me so I can get back to the house and make sure your brother isn't breaking everything?"

"Um . . ." I said, stalling, "Dad won't tell me what your superpower is."

"That didn't sound like a question to me," she scolded, reverting to mother mode long enough to give me a grammar lesson in the middle of my big superhero coming-of-age talk.

I rephrased, as all good sons do when they get an impromptu English lesson. "I was wondering, would you tell me what your superpower is, please?"

"That's much better," she said, a slight touch of humor in her tone. I heard her walk toward me. "Why don't you give your mother her first hug from her superhero son?"

My mother was completely ruining this moment for me by acting like my mother. *I just moved my phone with my brain, Mom. Do we really have to do hugs and kisses right now?*

I knew better than to actually say that, so I opened up my arms, shoulders saggy, and waited for this embarrassment to end. Thank God we were on a deserted farm.

She reached her arms around me and hugged me. She didn't have to bend down very far anymore; I'd grown a whole inch just since we moved here. I wrapped my arms around her and hugged her back, secretly kind of enjoying it.

She whispered in my ear without letting go of me. "My power is teleportation, Phillip, which means that I can go from one place to another in less than an instant."

I walked right into her little trap. "Like where?"

Ooph!

I heard that noise again and could instantly tell that we were no longer in the cornfield. "Like here in your own bedroom," I heard her whisper before she let me loose from her embrace. My nose told me that this was definitely my bedroom, as she had claimed. I could hear Patrick's cartoons blaring in the living room. Before I could acclimate to the new surroundings and comprehend what was going on, she grabbed my left hand and I heard that tiny explosion sound again.

Ooph!

And then I heard an unmistakable noise—the ocean.

Ever since I was a little kid, I'd loved the ocean. I would stand in the sand, right at the water's edge, and stare out into the sea for hours at a time. I couldn't see anything, obviously. But I could *feel* the ocean. And hear it. Smell it. And it seemed . . . enormous. Eternal. It may sound strange, but something about the infinite nature of the ocean just filled me with peace. With apologies to my loved ones, I never wanted to see anything in my life as badly as I wanted to see the ocean.

That day the waves were choppy. Mom and I were right up on top of them. A fine mist blew in our faces as the water clapped against the beach. "You know where we are, right?" she yelled over the roar of the surf. Like she even needed to ask.

"Yes!" I exclaimed. She knew how the ocean made me feel; that was why she'd brought me here. Only this time, I was as mesmerized by her abilities as I was by the ocean's might.

We were now at least a full day's drive from Freepoint, I knew that much. Maybe two. We had just traveled over seven or eight states in the span of a half-second. I decided then and there that teleporting was the coolest thing I'd ever heard of. Though I would never tell her, my mom earned some massive cool points that day.

Ooph!

The change in humidity was the first thing I noticed about this new location. Then the birds. Then the children playing. Then the sound of many car horns being honked. *Central Park!* My single favorite place in New York City had always been Central Park. Mom used to bring us several times a week to have picnics or go for a walk. She had always been very concerned about ensuring we got our fair share of exercise and fresh air in a metropolitan area as large as New York.

"How is this possible?" I asked in awe. "How can we go from here to there so quickly?"

"That's my gift, Phillip. Teleporting is like opening a door straight to another place on the planet. It's like skipping all the time and space in between. We're the reason heroes can live in Freepoint or one of our other two cities and still fight crime all over the globe."

"So . . . you're kind of like a superhero taxi?"

She laughed. Mom's genuine laughter could not have been more different from Dad's; it was much more melodic but every bit as pleasant to my ears. "I guess you could say that. I work at the transport center downtown. There are about thirty of us teleporters on staff there. And yes, we use our abilities to quickly get heroes to and from the various destinations their missions require. Without teleportation, Freepoint couldn't exist, and we'd all be scattered across the globe."

"How does it work? Do you have to be touching the person?" An avid science fiction fan, I was a bit of a stickler for details, particularly with regard to how things worked.

"That's right," she said, and I could hear the smile in her voice. "But it doesn't have to be a person."

"You can teleport other things!"

"Sure. Anything I can put my hand on. Or foot even."

"Like a car?"

"Uh-huh."

"A house?"

"Yeah, that too."

"An aircraft carrier?"

She laughed again. "I suppose so, yes. If I had to."

I just shook my head in awe.

"I've never had to teleport anything as big as an aircraft carrier, to be honest with you. But, yes, I do believe I could if I needed to." And with that, she grabbed my arm.

Ooph!

We were back in the cornfield.

"Dad, you're not going to believe where I've been," I bragged before realizing how dumb that must have sounded.

He humored me anyway. "I can't wait to hear all about it."

"Well, I'm sure Patrick has done something worthy of punishment by now. I'd better go inspect the damage," Mom said. And just like that—*ooph!*—she was gone. I could tell already that Mom's power was never going to get old.

Oh yeah, Patrick. "Dad, what's Patrick's power?"

He stood up from the table and walked the four steps to where I was standing. "This is where it's going to get very important for you to be able to keep a secret, because Patrick doesn't know about his powers any more than you knew about yours this morning. But your brother has superspeed."

"Like the Flash?"

"Yes. Just like that, actually. He can run, jump, move . . . anything physical with his body, he can do it as much as a thousand times faster than you or me."

Cool, I thought. I liked my brother for the most part. I know most people hate their kid brother for a large chunk of their childhood, but Patrick was pretty okay most of the time.

"Wait a minute," I said. "Is that why he's such a spaz all the time?"

"Don't call your brother a spaz, Phillip. It's not a nice word." He paused. "But yes, from what the doctors have told your mother and me, his hyperactivity is directly related to his powers. They won't really manifest for a while yet, we're told, but the seeds are there, already beginning to grow. And they come out that way because his body and his mind just aren't ready for them to come out any other way yet."

It actually made me like him even more to know that he was mostly not in control of his agitated behavior. I had assumed he was just a spaz.

"But you have to keep all of this from him, you understand? No practicing your powers when he's around, no talking about it, nothing. When the time's right, when he's ready, he'll have the same kind of talk you and I had here today. But until then, no matter what, you keep this to yourself, you hear?"

"Yeah, Dad. I will." I nodded. "So everyone in town is . . . 'in on it'?" I asked, not sure if I was using the right phrase. "You know . . . the whole superheroes-are-real thing?"

"Yeah," he said.

"Except for Patrick," I said, assuming.

"Except for Patrick and all the rest of the kids who haven't been told about their powers yet. Pretty much every kid gets his powers around the age of eleven or twelve, and for the most part, the heroes in town—even the teenagers—are pretty good about keeping the secret. It's kind of like Santa Claus out in the real world, I guess . . . how everyone knows not to spoil that for little kids. Does that make sense?"

It did. "Yeah."

"Only it's a lot more serious. Custodians view the act of informing children of their abilities as a sacred rite between the parent and the child—one they don't enjoy being robbed of. Besides, it's considered kind of uncool to go around using your powers in town anyway. We try pretty hard to keep the city looking and running like a normal city. We're in a remote location, but we do get some random visitors. Plus, it's good practice for when you're out in the real world as a grown-up hero, where keeping your powers a secret could be the difference between life and death."

The prospect of being an adult hero, out in the world fighting crime, was every bit as enticing as the word "death" was sobering.

"Now I think we'd better get headed home. You've got a lot to process."

"But Dad," I protested, "I have so many other questions! Can't we just stay here a little while longer?" I knew it wouldn't work. In all the times I'd ever tried the "but please, can't we just" approach to whining, it had never once worked.

"There'll be time for questions, Phillip," he reassured me as we started the long walk back to the car. "You have the rest your life to explore this new world. We'll be able to practice your powers together, and we can have a million conversations about being a custodian. We just can't do it all in one day."

I knew he was right, logically. But a twelve-year-old doesn't always prioritize logic. So I was bummed. But it took only a few steps for my brain to remind me that I was, at the very least, a person with superpowers. I had come out to the cornfield a young boy, but I was leaving it a superhero. Not every kid who dreams about such an event actually gets to have it come true. By the time we got to the driveway, my spirits were up again.

"Before we go home," my father said, "I'm going to give you something." He unlocked the doors with his remote, and we both climbed in.

"What?" I inquired eagerly.

He started the truck. "Your first superhero accessory." I could hear him reach into the center console compartment and pull his fist out with something in it. Then he swung his arm over toward me and said, "Go ahead. Take it."

I felt around his palm for a second and found a small circular object. I picked it up. It was heavy for its size and made of metal. Not much bigger than a silver dollar.

"There's a button on one side, son. But don't press it." It's a good thing he said the second part, as I was definitely about to press it. Thankfully, my father knows me well.

"How come?" I asked, curious to know why he would give me something I couldn't use.

"It's a radio call beacon. All active superheroes in the field have one. It's for emergencies. If you ever get into trouble, you push that button."

"And what will happen?" I wondered, rolling the device around in my hands.

"A teleporter will come. Your device is programmed to alert your mother. Wherever you may be in the world when you press that button, she'll know immediately that you're in trouble. And she'll also know where you are, thanks to the GPS chip inside. That means she can zap straight to you in the blink of an eye."

"Cool!" I couldn't hide my enjoyment of all this anymore. Superpowers, teleporting, homing beacons . . . it was like I woke up to find I was living inside one of my comic books!

"What I do want you to do with that thing, though," he said, throwing the truck in gear and pulling out, "is carry it with you all the time. Play with it. Feel it. Get to know it as intimately as you do your phone, okay?"

"Okay."

"And then, if you're ever separated from it for any reason, you'll be able to use your power to bring it to you."

This set off a small alarm in my head. "How far away can a telekinetic be from the object they want to move?"

"That depends," he said, pulling out onto the main road. "Some people have moved objects from several blocks away. A few have done it from even farther, a few miles. But there's no evidence of any limit. Some scientists think the only limit is the ability of the empowered person to focus. With enough focus, any distance can be overcome . . . or so goes the theory."

"What's the farthest you've ever been from an object you moved?"

"I guess a couple blocks, maybe. Nothing record-breaking."

I pondered that a moment as we bumped down the country road toward town, not really sure how to react. I wondered if my blindness might limit my own ability more than an able-bodied hero's. But I brushed it aside. I decided not to worry about the distance thing too much and to spend the rest of the evening enjoying this new life I was now living. "Dad, I do have one more question."

"Sure thing, bud."

"Why custodian?"

"What do you mean?"

"Of all the words to call ourselves, why are superheroes named after . . . janitors?"

He chuckled. "Janitor is only one of the definitions of the word 'custodian,' son, and became the most common only in the last few decades. Custodian can also mean caretaker. Back in colonial times, there were custodians of properties, custodians of estates, of people, even. It comes from a Latin word—*custos*—which literally translated means 'guard' or 'guardian.'"

"That's kind of cool," I allowed.

"The name for our people was chosen long, long ago, because it was and still is accurate. We are the guardians. The protectors of the people here on Earth. The custos, or custodians," he said with a grin. "And tomorrow, you'll start your journey to become one."

3

HIGH SCHOOL

Freepoint High School was literally a giant dome. Dad said the entire school—including the cafeteria, the gymnasium, the football field, the library, and all the classrooms—fit inside an enormous white dome. It was like an enclosed mini-city. From the outside, it probably looked like an extra-large professional sporting arena. The other new kids I met later in the day seemed plenty impressed by the dome, though its appeal was lost on me for obvious reasons.

I heard a few beeps and squawks in my ear as the other custodian device Dad had given me powered itself up and then . . .

Good morning. It's Monday, August 15, 7:59 a.m.

The voice was coming from the earpiece, and it scared the life out of me at first, despite the fact that I'd just knowingly turned on the earpiece for a navigation device. The voice was female and robotic.

You are standing outside the main office of Freepoint High, and your first class is about to begin. Please proceed to room 215. Turn to your left and walk approximately fifty paces.

Cool! I was instantly in love with the Personal Navigator. It was exactly the kind of wizardry that I expected the superpowered existence would come with. But my moment of wonder was interrupted by a sound that needed no explanation: the school bell.

I was late. I'd spent too much time taking in the sound of the hallway and fiddling with the Navigator device. *Great. Perfect.*

It is now 8:00 a.m. You are late for your first class. Please proceed to room 215. Turn to your left and walk approximately fifty paces.

I did. I practically ran. The hallways were empty, largely due to the fact that everyone else was already in class . . . on time. I was moving so quickly, I didn't even remember to count my steps.

After five more paces, turn right.

Before I could register the Personal Navigator's latest message, the school wall delivered it for me in very plain terms. I'd overshot my turn, and it was a dead end. By running and then losing count, I ended up taking a few paces too many.

It's not as though I've never run into something before. I was quite used to it, in fact. But I'd never hit a wall at a full run before. I bounced off the lockers and then hit the floor with a thud and a groan.

After a few seconds of heavy breathing and a mental inventory of my aches and pains, I lifted my head and slowly stood to my feet. I tried to shake it off.

Proceed ahead three hundred fifty paces. You are still tardy.

Crap! The pain took a back seat to more urgent matters, and I took off running again.

I ran for what seemed like ages. It was the longest I'd ever run in my life, of that I was sure. I wondered what the rest of the kids in the class would think. What would they whisper to each other about the idiot blind kid who couldn't even get to his first day of high school on time, who arrived sweaty and bruised?

In order to avoid a repeat of the last navigated turn, I slowed to a jog. Finally, when I was nearly out of energy, I heard the voice again.

In ten more paces, turn left.

I counted off ten steps and quickly did so.

Proceed twenty paces. The classroom is on your left.

Finally! I started taking deep breaths and walked toward the spot. Suddenly, I heard the voice again.

Obstruction in five paces! There is someone in your way. Obstruction!

I froze. I hadn't heard anyone approaching. I hadn't known my Personal Navigator long enough to really trust her, but I thought it couldn't hurt to speak up and make certain there really was a person in my path. "Hello?"

"Hello," I heard back almost immediately. "I see you have the Personal Navigator. Cool!"

"Yeah," I stammered, still confused. It sounded like someone my age, a male. "Are you a student?"

"Yeah. I'm in a wheelchair. What's wrong with you, besides the blindness, I mean." I knew his words weren't necessarily kind, but he'd uttered them in such a cheery manner that it was hard to be insulted.

"Nothing. Nothing that I know of. Except the blindness, that is."

"What's your power?"

"Telekinesis."

"Cool," he said, sounding like he meant it.

"Um, what's yours?" I inquired.

"Telepathy."

"Cool." I was equally impressed. "Were you just . . . sitting out here in the hallway?"

"Yeah," he admitted. "I hate the idea of being in this class."

"Right," I said, not having any idea what he meant but desperately wanting him to think I did.

"I'm Henry." He was pretty friendly for a stranger.

"I'm Phillip," I replied, being polite.

"Well, I guess we can tackle it together, then, right? I mean, you seem pretty normal."

I should have wondered why he said that, but I didn't. Instead I just agreed. "Sure."

"Well then, let me get out of your way and you can let us both in." I heard his voice moving from the left to the right as he gently rolled to the side to let me pass.

Obstruction cleared. Proceed four paces.

I stepped forward again, four times, and stopped one last time to compose myself.

You have arrived at room 215—Special Education.

What was that? And then realization suddenly rushed in. A blind kid . . . a kid in a wheelchair . . . the same classroom all day long . . . I had been placed in a class for disabled kids.

And for the first time ever, though not the last, I regretted being a custodian, having superpowers. I resented it. Because at school, at least, I wasn't a superhero after all, it seemed. I was an outcast.

You are now seven minutes late for class. Proceed through the door.

$$\lightning$$

"Phillip Sallinger?"

I could not believe that I was in a special education classroom. I was confused and angry. I had never felt so insulted in my short life. I was blind, not disabled. *There's a difference!*

Except for the fact that I actually *was* disabled. Blindness *is* a disability, whether I wanted to acknowledge it or not. Depends on whose viewpoint you take—no pun intended. I spent a lot of my earlier years denying that blindness even made me different at all.

But did my particular disability mean that I needed specialized learning? Surely it wasn't one that belonged grouped together with kids in wheelchairs, right? Heck, even in New York—in public school, no less—I'd been in regular classes. And I didn't even have a Personal Navigator to guide me around those places.

I was incensed. Had there been an error? Nearly a thousand gifted kids in this school, and I somehow got stuck in the remedial group.

"Phillip Sallinger?"

I heard her that time. I'd been so focused on my fury that I had tuned out everything around me. I wondered how many times she'd called my name before I'd noticed. The teacher had been in the middle of her first-day-of-school welcome speech and paused long enough for me to find my way to my seat in the center of the room. And then, after I sat down . . . well, I couldn't really remember what happened next. My mind was too busy racing to record anything.

And now my name was being called . . . repeatedly. Surely, everyone in class was staring at me. Snapping back to reality, I swiftly affirmed my presence in the classroom with a confident, "Here!" I had been through many first days of many new schools. I knew the roll-call drill.

Silence. Then some light giggling.

"Well," said the woman, "I'm certainly glad that you're here, and we welcome you here, but that's not what I asked."

Another smattering of giggles made its way around the room. *Wonderful.* The school day couldn't have been more than twenty minutes old, and I'd already embarrassed myself about five different ways.

"I'm sorry, ma'am," I offered meekly, "I was distracted. I didn't hear your question." I had learned long ago that honesty was almost always the fastest way out of a jam, even if it wasn't always the least embarrassing.

"When exactly did you tune out, then? Did you manage to hear any of what I said?"

I felt as though I was shrinking a bit. "No, ma'am. I'm sorry."

"Don't be sorry, Mr. Sallinger." She sounded sincere, like she meant it. "It's the first day of school, so I understand if some of you are a little . . . distracted." She sounded old, maybe a little cranky, and had a hint of a German accent. "But we weren't just taking roll. There are only eight of you in here. We can generally take roll just by looking. Calling out everyone's name to have them audibly respond would be a horrible waste of our precious time together. Plus, the rest of the class was present when you two came in tardy a few moments ago. No . . . we want to know more about *you.*"

"You mean, like, go around the room and tell your name and your favorite color?" I'd done that kind of get-to-know-you routine in other schools once or twice.

"Yes." I could tell she was smiling, which gave me some momentary relief. "I started us out by introducing myself. My name is Winifred Crouch, and I am your teacher. I have been graced with the ability to shape-shift, which means that I can disguise myself by altering my physical appearance. Then I suggested we go around the room, starting with you. That's all you missed, really." Her comments had the sound of someone only slightly exasperated to have to repeat themselves.

"We want to know not only about your interests and hobbies but also your powers . . . and your disability. You see, Mr. Sallinger, everyone in this room has a unique combination of ability and disability." I wouldn't say that she was speaking slowly, but she was definitely not in a hurry. "Some might say that this creates special challenges for you . . . hurdles for you to overcome. And that's probably true. Others—myself included—would suggest that maybe it also offers you special opportunities that most students within these walls will never have."

She continued, "But we'll never know exactly what the possibilities are until we get to know one another and get comfortable with one another. So, Phillip, why don't you kick things off, as I had originally intended."

"Okay. Well, I'm not sure what to say. I mean, I'm blind, obviously. So I can't see anything. And my power is telekinesis." I said all this quite matter-of-factly and without any enthusiasm, which I guess is how I say most things.

But there was an audible gasp among some of my fellow students. I could feel everyone's attention was focused on me, as though I'd just said something outrageous.

"Cool," I heard someone breathe.

My new teacher explained, "These kids aren't used to having a telekinetic in the class, Mr. Sallinger. That's one of the rarer powers. There are only a few in the entire school, I believe."

"Really?" I didn't know that. I mean, Dad had mentioned it was fairly rare, but I hadn't really thought about my power being something that other kids would think was cool. "I can barely use it," I said apologetically. "Since I can't see anything, it's really hard to make use of it properly." Almost as a throwaway comment, I added, "I guess that's why I'm in here."

After a long pause, the teacher decided to move on, much to my relief. "Okay, class, why don't we continue on? Thank you, Mr. Sallinger. Henry Gardner, let's hear from you at this time."

I was curious to hear Henry's story.

"I'm in a wheelchair because I was born crippled," he announced in that same straightforward manner he'd displayed in the hallway. His voice came from my left, one desk closer to the front of the room. "But I'm getting pretty good at getting around in this thing." He pounded on the wheelchair with his fists as he said it, beaming pride in his voice. "And I'm a mental, and my power is that I can read minds."

I was instantly surprised at the lack of oohs and aahs at this reveal. It was like they met a hundred mind readers a day. *They're bowled over by a blind kid's telekinesis but apathetic about reading people's minds? What's wrong with the kids at this school?* I was also struck by the notion that Henry's disability didn't really interfere with his powers at all, just his mobility. And yet the school had deemed him so disabled as to be "special." Maybe I wasn't the only kid who felt like he didn't belong in this classroom.

We continued around the room for several more minutes. Most of the stories were actually kind of heartbreaking—like Delilah's.

Delilah Darlington sat directly in front of me. She had superhearing, but she was also deaf. I thought it was the saddest thing I'd ever heard.

Delilah was the only person in the classroom whose power was 100 percent useless to her because of her disability. I couldn't use my power to the fullest extent, but I could still use it. Delilah was rendered totally normal by her disability . . . just a regular deaf girl in a high school full of superheroes. She had an interpreter with her, a pleasant enough woman named Mary, who translated Delilah's sign language for the rest of the class.

Behind Henry and directly to my left was Penelope Wilson. Penelope's power was unique: she could control the weather. She could make it rainy or sunny just by concentrating on it. Which is a pretty cool ability, but maybe not that well suited for crime fighting. It's not like you can foil all possible dastardly plans through the use of a strategic thunderstorm. You can really only turn that dastardly plan into one that's a little bit drearier. But it was still a very cool power.

Penelope's voice was high-pitched and squeaky, but she seemed very genuine and sweet. She explained her disability as an aversion to sunlight. There was an official name for it, but it had over six syllables, and I honestly couldn't remember four of them. But she said it made her skin pigmentation so unique that sunlight was very dangerous to her. She couldn't go too close to the windows on a really bright day—that's how bad it was. It was almost as though she had a superdisability. So the girl who could control the weather had to spend as much time as possible indoors. She even traveled to and from school with the help of a transporter like my mom.

Donnie Brooks sat behind Penelope and did not say a word. There was a teacher's aide, named Rebecca, who worked specifically with Donnie, and she did the talking for him. "Donnie has Down syndrome," she said, "which means that he kind of has the mind of a young child in the body of a grown man. He may look like a young man in his early twenties, but he's just fifteen years old." It was clear from her voice that Rebecca cared about Donnie very much. "Donnie is very friendly and lovable and is just a big teddy bear. Feel free to be friendly with him. He really enjoys company. He's kind of quiet, but he is listening."

I'm not going to lie; I was a little bit scared of Donnie. I wasn't sure why, but I was wary. I'd never met anyone with Down syndrome before, but I was pretty sure a fifteen-year-old in the body of a twenty-something-year-old was something worth being afraid of.

"What's Donnie's power?" The question came from Penelope, and I thought it was nice of her to make sure he didn't get left out of that part of the discussion.

"That's a complicated answer, young lady." The response came from old Mrs. Crouch. "Donnie's DNA has some extra pieces in it. That's what accounts for his Down syndrome. But those extra pieces also mutated the genes that relate to his powers. He might have superstrength or the ability to fly. But the truth is that we really don't know what his powers are. There's too much mutation to know. The sequence is unreadable."

Henry piped up. "Then how do you know he has any powers at all?" It was a valid point but kind of a snotty way to make it.

"Because the DNA of superhuman abilities is unmistakable, even when it is indefinable. Truth be known, we're not really human, technically. There are enough differences in our DNA to make humans and custodians separate species altogether. Anyone of our lineage would have unmistakable genetic markers, even if their powers weren't clear." Mrs. Crouch's voice was flat, almost dismissive, her knowledge of the facts obviously trumping Henry's. "Perhaps one day Mr. Brooks will show us what his powers are. Possibly we—and he—may never know. But that is no reason to prohibit him from seeking an education, and an education he shall have. At least on my watch. So welcome, Mr. Brooks."

The class gave their own halfhearted welcomes to Donnie, which consisted mostly of murmuring and a few grunts.

James Gregory was a teleporter. He sat in the front position of the third and final row of desks, which were on my right. James was energetic, almost fidgety, and he was the little businessman of the class. In fact, halfway through his self-introduction, he pointed out that we should see him after school if we had any interest in purchasing rides via his teleportation skills. He claimed he could take you anywhere in Freepoint. He even had business cards, which he handed out as he spoke. James was also blind, like me; unlike me, James had lost his sight in an accident at his father's lab as a young boy. This made it tough but not impossible for him to visualize the various locations he wanted to visit. He said he was a lot better at it than any adult ever gave him credit for.

As Mom had explained it to me, a teleporter needed some familiarity with the location they were attempting to travel to—not dissimilar from the way that I needed some familiarity with an object before I could move it with my brain. For instance, if a teleporter had been to a particular location before, it would be a snap to zap there again. But even when teleporting to a place they'd never been, most could spend a few moments with a picture or even a detailed description of the location and still successfully transport there. Some could even use latitude and longitude coordinates alone, without a physical description. Mom was apparently like this. But without the ability to see places or memories of places, James's powers were diminished, even if his entrepreneurial spirit was not. I reasoned that he would struggle to make the most of his power, just as I would, which made me want to be his friend.

Behind James, directly to my right, was Fred Wheeler. "Some people call me 'Freak-Out Freddie,'" he said, not nearly as excitedly as a name like that might suggest. Fred had a power I hadn't yet heard of: gigantism. He could grow to a size nearly three stories tall, also gaining the speed and strength expected of someone that large.

The problem for Freak-Out Freddie was his chronic asthma. It was pretty severe, and even a good brisk walk could leave him gasping for air. So as soon as he turned on his power and grew in height and strength to the size of a giant, he was so out of breath he couldn't move. Turning on his power made it useless.

He was like a human puffer fish; his size was all bark and no bite. Just another unlucky soul in a town full of people who'd hit the genetic lottery. Freddie had a pleasant quality to his voice and seemed quite likable. He spoke in even, measured sentences—like someone who'd learned long ago to take his time with most things in life.

Last but not least was Bentley Crittendon. Bentley had the name of a rich kid, which probably had something to do with the fact that his family was rich. Bentley was the son of one of the members of the board—Jurrious Crittendon—one of the oldest and longest-serving members of the custodian governing body. Bentley was as rich and privileged a kid as I would ever meet, which made his humility all the more refreshing. He seemed embarrassed about his name, his wealth, and his family's prominence. He had older brothers, but they were married or off at college, effectively making Bentley an only child.

Bentley was a mental who had elevated brain function, particularly in the areas of science and math. To hear him tell it, he was a junior mad scientist. He really had a distinct energy in his voice when talking about his powers. I wondered how sweet it would be if I could have elevated brain functions just during my math tests. I really hated math.

Bentley's disability, however, was something called ataxic cerebral palsy, a condition that caused him to have a poor sense of balance. He said he stumbled or fell pretty frequently and that he had some tremor-related side effects. His brain was advanced, but his body couldn't always perform even remedial tasks, like walking.

I'd had my share of falls in my time. And I knew what it meant to not be able to make your body do what your brain wanted it to. So I decided I wanted to be Bentley's friend as well.

Who am I kidding? I wanted to be friends with all of these people—except maybe Donnie, who didn't sound like an active participant in a friendship anyway. I just wanted friends. I wasn't picky. What few friends I'd managed to make in New York were obviously still in New York. I needed some Freepoint buddies, and fast. And it was looking like I was going to be spending most of my time with these people.

After the introductions, we dove right into actual school stuff. I was kind of relieved, though, really. Because school stuff helped me feel more normal and less like a freak. For almost three straight hours, Mrs. Crouch brought a volley of the most basic, boring schoolwork imaginable, full of introductory lessons on everything from math to grammar. It felt so much like a normal first day of school that she had almost managed to make me forget I was in a school for genetically advanced superhumans.

And then the lunch bell rang.

4

LUNCH

The Personal Navigator, which had seemed so space-aged just an hour ago, turned out to be actually quite useless in navigating the school hallways while they were filled with other students.

Obstruction! There is someone in your—

Obstruction! There is someone in your—

Obstruction! There is someone in your—

It was like a broken record.

Through a combination of determination and severe hunger, I managed to use my collapsible cane to tap my way along following the roar of the cafeteria. Four hundred students all eating at once creates an unmistakable sound, so I just kept tapping until I arrived.

The cafeteria itself had no doors but was just a gigantic open room alongside the hallway; no wonder I'd been able to hear it from so far away. I'd already decided to eat alone because I wouldn't be able to find my classmates even if I wanted to. And because it just seemed easier. And I was feeling a little sorry for myself.

I let the audio cues of the situation serve as my guide again. The highest concentration of students was near the front, so I navigated my way toward the far back corner.

My mother was a fantastic cook. But her job required her to start her workday much earlier than Dad. That left our school lunches in the not-so-capable hands of my father. So lunch was a sandwich, a bag of peanuts, and a fat-free pudding cup—which was fine by me. School food was a crapshoot. A sack lunch was a pretty safe bet.

The table itself was long and rectangular with benches attached, like an extra-large picnic table. It seemed like every other lunchroom table I'd ever known, with a hard Formica surface. I spread out my father's wholesome meal and ate in silence, wondering what Patrick's experience would be like next year on his first day. I assumed it would be far different than mine. Patrick was always a very popular and well-liked kid in whatever school he attended. He was the opposite of me in that way, I suppose. I always wondered how much his ability to see played a part in that difference between us.

The rest of the kids in the cafeteria carried on as high school kids do, talking a lot more than eating, it seemed. I daydreamed about what it would be like to be normal—to have sight. To not be different. It was my usual lunchtime ritual.

Don't get me wrong; I was fine with my disability. I'd made peace with it years earlier. But it was starting to feel like growing older only lengthened the list of things the rest of the kids my age could do that I could not. I couldn't just walk up to a table and introduce myself, because I couldn't even see where that table was. I couldn't play pickup baseball after school or have a paper route. I couldn't even solve math problems at the blackboard or take a normal test.

Nobody was really all that mean to me in my childhood. People hadn't picked on me for being blind or anything. I mean, sure, there were a few kids here and there, but that happens to everyone, right? My blindness wasn't causing me public shame; it was just holding me back. I could try to compensate in other ways all I wanted, but I would never be able to see, which meant there were a host of other things I'd never be able to do. In some ways, I would always be an outsider, no matter how hard the school or my parents tried to help level the playing field for me.

Sometime after the sandwich but before the peanuts were completely gone, I sensed someone approaching—a couple of someones, actually. I simply looked up and smiled. "Hello?"

"How did you know someone was here?" The voice was one I'd never heard before and sounded like it belonged to someone older than me, but it wasn't an adult. His tone suggested curiosity, not rudeness.

"I heard you," I replied.

"You have superhearing or something?" This guy obviously considered himself the stealthiest kid in the lunchroom because he seemed genuinely surprised I could have detected his approach. *Must not have much experience with the blind.*

"No. Just blindness." I wasn't afraid to converse with a stranger on my first day of high school, but I was definitely guarded. My problem wasn't shyness anyway. Most of the friendships I'd had in my life had been initiated by the other guy—because it's hard to walk up and talk to someone you can't see.

"You're new here, right?"

"Yeah. It's my first day." I felt stupid as soon as I said it. I mean, it was everyone's first day, really.

He didn't seem to pick up on it, though. "I'm Chad," he said in a friendly manner. "Chad Burke. And this is Steve Travers. What's your name?"

"I'm Phillip Sallinger," I replied.

The table rocked slightly. I knew that Chad was resting his foot on the opposite bench and was leaning with his arm on his knee. "Well, welcome to Freepoint, kid."

Steve finally spoke. "Yeah, man, welcome."

"So tell me, Phillip, what's your power?" Chad asked.

I had expected making friends to be a bit more difficult a task, as it had always been at regular schools, but this was turning out to be pretty easy. After all, every kid here had at least one shared interest: superpowers.

"I'm a telekinetic, actually." I probably sounded a little too proud. I paused then, expecting Chad and Steve to be every bit as impressed as my classmates had been.

And they were. Steve whistled—that high-pitched whistle people do when they're impressed—and then Chad said, "Wow. That's a pretty cool power, man!"

"No kidding, dude," Steve concurred. "You don't see too many telekinetics, do you?"

"No," Chad agreed. "You certainly don't."

Their chemistry was amazing, and I was buying it hook, line, and sinker.

"You know," Chad began before trailing off slightly, "I'm not sure I've ever seen that power in action before."

"Me neither," Steve added, playing his supporting role superbly.

And then Chad brought it home. "Say . . . I don't suppose you'd be willing to give us a little demonstration, would you?"

I was instantly hesitant, though not because I suspected anything was amiss. I just wasn't sure my powers were ready for showing off. These kids were probably used to some serious telekinesis folklore, people moving cars and trees and such. And that certainly wasn't me—though I briefly considered whether my father had ever moved a tree. "I don't know, guys. I'm not very good at it yet. It's hard to do when you can't see anything."

Chad wasn't going to be denied. "Don't be embarrassed, Phillip. I know you're not an expert yet. Heck, you should see how sloppy Steve still is with his powers, and he's in the ninth grade!" I heard Steve smack Chad on the arm. "No, I'm teasing, I'm teasing. Look, kid, everyone sucks with their powers at first. But you can move things with your mind, man! That's something I'll never be able to do, and I've never even seen someone do it."

Steve repeated his favorite line: "Me neither."

Chad said, "If you can use it—even a little bit—I'd sure like to see it."

"Yeah, me too," Steve added.

I was going to have enough trouble making friends my own age. How could I pass up this golden opportunity to impress some really friendly ninth graders? "Well," I admitted, "I am pretty good with this phone." I'd spent most of the night practicing my newly discovered powers instead of sleeping. I pulled my phone out of my pocket and set it on the table in front of me, face up.

"Yeah?" Chad asked excitedly.

Steve was equally enthused. "Let's see you move it! Come on, you know you want to."

I did want to. I wanted to show off and have a cool power and be the kid that other kids were jealous of. I wanted to fit in and be liked and show off my special abilities. So, naturally, I walked right into their trap.

"Okay. Give me a minute to concentrate." I moved my hand over the phone, my palm above it by a foot or so. I pictured the phone sitting on the table and then flying into my hand, exactly as Dad had taught me to. I kept visualizing it snapping up from the table and into my palm.

Only nothing happened.

"What's the matter?" asked Chad. "Can't you do it?"

I heard Steve start to snicker, but I thought he was just laughing because I couldn't move the phone, which would have been painful enough. But I still didn't realize there was any kind of conspiracy afoot.

"I don't know," I protested, suddenly worried that the moment was changing from the formation of a possible friendship into a life-defining moment of high school embarrassment. I didn't want to be the kid who couldn't use his powers. "I think I'm just nervous or something."

At this, Steve laughed out loud—I mean pure guffaws—and my head snapped in his direction in mortified shock.

But Chad was soothing and calming. "Don't mind him. Steve's a big jerk. He couldn't use his powers on the first day of school either, so don't let him get to you." His kindness was intoxicating, and it almost instantly distilled my anxiety. "Can you try it one more time . . . for me?"

I moved my head from Chad to Steve, which Chad noticed, reassuring me, "Don't worry about him. It's just you and me here." The funny thing is, I believed him. "Now, concentrate on moving that phone again. Just take a deep breath, relax, and you're all set."

And so I did. I breathed deeply, exhaled, and then focused back on the mental picture of the phone on the table. I blocked out everything but the thought of moving that phone. I'd done this dozens of times last night, and I would do it again right now, even if it killed me. Chad Burke was going to have his socks blown off, and then he was going to like me!

But the phone didn't move. Something was wrong. I wasn't sure how I could be experiencing so much stage fright.

Suddenly, without warning, I felt a quick burst of air, heard a small clicking sound on the table in front of me, and then there was a loud crash behind me as something shattered.

"You did it!" Chad exclaimed in faux excitement. "You moved it with your mind!" The mockery in his voice was thick now, replacing what had formerly been a genuine tone.

It took a second to register because it all went by so fast, but I knew in the pit of my stomach what had happened.

"Steve! Did you see that? This kid moved that phone with his brain! Smashed it right into that wall. That was amazing!"

Steve, as usual, agreed. "Totally awesome, man! He smashed it into a million little bits!"

"Why'd you smash your own phone, Phillip?" Chad had gone from my new best friend to the most evil person I'd ever known in about three seconds, and it cut deep. Gone was the genuine tone of voice and friendly demeanor. His words were now taunting and bitter, and I couldn't do anything but sit there in stunned silence.

Chad just continued. "Don't you know your own strength, you idiot? I mean, geez! All I wanted was to see you move it a little . . . you didn't have to obliterate it." Steve was roaring with laughter now. He was probably doubled over and crying in sheer joy.

"That's enough!" A new voice entered the discussion, this time a familiar one. It was Bentley, my classmate. And he sounded mad. "Why don't you pick on someone your own size?"

Good grief. In the history of high school, had that line ever worked? I was thankful for Bentley coming to my defense and equally relieved to hear his voice, but I was sure that line had never resulted in anything but more mockery. Things were about to get a whole lot worse.

But instead, I just heard Chad and Steve scamper off, as though Bentley had brandished a firearm or something. *How did a kid with cerebral palsy manage to sc—*

"You can't use powers in school, Phillip," Bentley declared.

"Yeah, it's an NPZ," said Henry, who I had not even realized was present. In the heat of the moment, I'd stopped paying attention to some of the subtle things my ears would usually key in on.

"What?" That was the only coherent thought I could find at the moment. I was still trying to figure out how a kid with a cane and a kid with a wheelchair scared off two ninth graders.

"The school is a no power zone," Henry stated in his trademark blunt fashion. "There's a blocker somewhere around here. Nobody can use their powers in this place."

"Those jerks were just messing with you," Bentley explained. "They do it every year to a new kid—at least that's what my brother said. They think it's hilarious. They find some seventh grader they think they can fool and then prank them into trying to use their powers. Then they laugh at them. It's pretty cruel, I think. And positively Cro-Magnon."

I was still a bit confused but was slowing catching up. The cafeteria was returning to its normal volume levels as everyone lost interest in the possible blind-kid fight. "Why would they do that?" It seemed unnecessarily evil to go so far in a lie just to get a chuckle.

"They're just mean. It's what older kids do, I guess," Bentley offered, not reassuringly. "I'm sorry we didn't get here sooner, but the lunch line was pretty long today."

"Wait a minute," I objected. "How in the world did you two manage to scare them off?" I was dying to know.

"Oh . . . I keep forgetting you can't see," Henry stated. *My, he is blunt, isn't he?* But at least he was honest; I had to give him that. "Donnie's with us."

I heard Bentley's cane as he propped it up against the table and sat down next to me. "Everyone's afraid of Donnie. Isn't that right, Donnie?"

I don't think Donnie gave Bentley any reaction, but he did sit down across from me, and I felt the table rock from his mammoth frame.

"I don't understand," I confessed. "Why would they be scared off by a guy who doesn't even know what his power is—no offense, Donnie." He again said nothing, so I simply hoped he had not taken offense, if he'd even heard and understood me.

"That's even scarier," Henry said like it was a fact. "Don't you think? I mean, if you were facing off with a supervillain, would you rather know for a fact that they could fly—in which case you could plan for that power and incorporate it into your attack—or not have any idea what danger you might be facing?"

"Besides," added Bentley, "whatever his powers are, he's definitely strong. Even regular humans with Down syndrome are strong. That's what my brother says. Those two wieners would run from Donnie even if he didn't have any powers at all. I know you haven't really seen him, but Donnie's a giant. He's, like, six feet tall. He's bigger than most of the teachers here."

As if I needed more reasons to be wary of Donnie.

But he had basically just saved my bacon, whether he knew it or not. I decided to cut him some slack while still keeping in the back of my mind the notion that he could crush me like a bug.

"How come Donnie was even with you?" I inquired.

"Oh, we can't get him to leave us alone, actually," Henry corrected me. "He followed me and Bentley all the way here from class. Then he followed us through the lunch line. Then he sat down next to us to eat. And when we saw you were in trouble, I guess he just followed us then too. It's like he's stalking us."

Bentley had a simpler explanation. "I think he's just lonely and wants to find some friends."

"Or that," Henry conceded.

"Well," I offered meekly, "thanks, you guys. Really. I really appreciate it. I still can't believe I *fell* for that crap!" I was mad at myself for being so naïve.

"I wouldn't worry about it. They'll find someone else to pick on, I'm sure." Bentley seemed so calm, so mature for someone my age. It was like he had an extra dose of wisdom or something.

Henry piped up. "The odds of running into them much during school are pretty slim, actually, since we're in our own classroom all day."

"Except that I have to share a lunch period with them every day for the rest of the year, Henry!" I was agitated, but I was also surprised that *that* bit of logic had escaped our little know-it-all friend. "How am I supposed to deal with that, huh?"

Henry didn't have a chance to answer. "Easy." It was Bentley, sounding pleased. "Just make sure you sit with us. Or, perhaps more importantly, make sure you sit with Donnie."

Donnie grunted slightly, just enough to make me wonder if he was paying more attention than I had assumed. Everyone smiled and chuckled at Donnie's possible contribution to the discussion.

"See," Bentley noted, "Donnie's got your back. And if he doesn't, we do."

"Great," I said sarcastically.

"Hey, how come you stopped wearing your Personal Navigator?" Henry asked.

Bentley perked up. "Personal Navigator?"

"Yeah, they give 'em to all the blind students, I think," Henry replied. Then I heard his voice turn back in my direction. "So why'd you quit wearing it?"

"Well," I explained, "I tried using it to find the cafeteria, but that thing's useless in a hallway crowded with people."

"Oh," Henry said dejectedly, "that's a bummer."

"That voice just kept shouting about obstructions. Honestly, it's a great little idea for a gadget, but it's not terribly practical in my brief experience."

"Don't worry," Henry said, "we'll show you the way back to class."

"Thanks," I said, meaning it.

"So, you're not going to use it?" Bentley asked cautiously.

"I can't see why I would. A couple more days and I'll know my way around this place, no problem. Plus, it's programmed to work only in the school, so it's pretty much useless to me."

"Do you mind if I have it?"

It seemed a little odd, but after thinking about it a moment, I didn't really have any objection to consider. "Sure," I said, fishing into my pocket to retrieve the device. "What do you want with it?"

"Oh, Arthur Stansbury—the inventor—is kind of a hero of mine," he said dismissively as he took it from my open palm. "I just want to tinker around with it." Then, as though that needed more explanation, he added, "I like to tinker with stuff."

5

SUPERHERO STUDIES

School went pretty smoothly the next couple weeks. I had one more encounter with Chad and Steve, a brief one. They caught me sitting alone while my classmates were still in the serving line, so they started yapping at me again about my super strong powers. But as soon as Donnie and the boys appeared, they scrammed. I made a mental note to never get on Donnie's bad side, because without him, I would be royally screwed.

Turned out that Chad was the son of the head of the board—the governing body for custodians—which meant that he got in exactly zero trouble for our little cafeteria incident. Even in the superhero world, people with powerful connections get a leg up. I probably would have been sour about it if I wasn't distracted by my own new group of pals.

Henry, Bentley, and I were becoming inseparable. We ate lunch together every day and had hit it off right from the start. James Gregory—the other blind kid from our class—had become a pretty regular addition to our lunchtime crew as well. The poor guy had been so worried about finding his way around on that first day that he'd eaten all by himself in the classroom. But now he was with us.

I have to admit, the actual schoolwork in this place was pretty awesome. Not the first half of the day, "the boring half," as I referred to it. That was math and English and the rest of the usual subjects. History was pretty cool, though, I suppose.

The truly awesome part about school kicked in after lunch when we had superhero studies, or Custodial Studies—its official name—which I simply called "the greatest class ever invented." It was as though school officials had taken a random polling sample to determine what the students wanted to learn and then just turned those survey answers into the curriculum. This class had my complete attention. Each day held some amazing revelation, sometimes several. For instance, I learned that there are documents far older than the Bible that talk about men with special abilities and powers.

Every Friday, for the last hour of the day, Mrs. Crouch would hold a superhero Q&A. Anything we wanted to ask about powers or heroes or villains. And for the most part, she answered every question.

During the first Friday Q&A, I had been content to simply listen. I got so caught up in hearing her answers to the other kids' questions, I didn't even ask one of my own. I just gaped in wonder and soaked it all in. But the second time around, I was a bit more comfortable in the environment and more familiar with the teacher and the students in the room. I wasn't going to stay on the sidelines again.

After some exceedingly boring questions about superhero politics from Bentley—God love him, no one could get more excited about mundane things than Bentley—Freddie managed to get Mrs. Crouch switched over to the subject of how NPZs work. I pictured a giant futuristic generator harnessing electromagnetic energy, but it turns out they're a lot less complicated than that. NPZs are caused by empowered people called blockers. The power that blockers have is to block out all powers within a certain area and range.

"What's the range?" No surprise that the question came from me since I spent most of my life acutely aware of distances and ranges.

"Well, Mr. Sallinger, it's different for everyone. Most powers vary slightly in their strength from hero to hero. You might ultimately be able to move larger or heavier objects with your telekinesis than your father, for instance. And it's the same with blocking. Most blockers project an NPZ that's roughly round in perimeter shape and maybe fifty to one hundred yards wide. Typically, they have to be pretty close to the area they want to block."

Henry piped up. "So you're telling me that there's a person sitting in a room somewhere in this building and that this person is creating the NPZ for the entire school?" He didn't sound much like he believed her, but I had quickly learned that Henry just always sounded that way. Know-it-alls are always skeptical of new information because they operate on the assumption that there is no information that is new to them.

"There is, Mr. Gardner," Mrs. Crouch responded, leaving out much of the added detail we'd all expected.

"Does that mean they never leave the school?" James wondered aloud. He was turning out to be a very sensible and levelheaded guy, even if he was a little too wrapped up in his teleporting business for a seventh grader. "Or does it mean that the school's not an NPZ at night?"

"The no-powers condition is dependent on this person's presence, and the school is still a no power zone at night, Mr. Gregory. He or she is a permanent resident here. It's a sacrifice, one made in order to provide security and protection for you and your fellow students and your families."

"So it's like the memory dude out in the real world?" This time it was Freddie again, who, judging by his tone, was quite impressed with himself for knowing about the memory dude. I must confess it was news to me, and I wanted to learn more.

"Yes, exactly, Mr. Wheeler." Mrs. Crouch appeared to be finished speaking on the subject of the memory dude, which simply wasn't going to work for me.

"Wait," I began. "What memory dude?" My father had made mention of some special memory-related powers that helped keep superheroes flying under the radar—sometimes literally—of the American public. But I wasn't sure if that was related to what Freddie was talking about or not.

Fred either assumed I had directed my question at him or just didn't care, because he answered before Mrs. Crouch could. "There's this guy that uses his powers to keep us hidden from the real world. You know, so they don't find out superheroes exist."

"Custodians, Mr. Wheeler, and that is correct. Paul Weatherby is his name, and he is probably the most powerful custodian among us. His mind is capable of perpetually shielding other heroes from the public. And that's how many of your parents stay safe and hidden from view."

This concept didn't make sense to me. And since we had only an hour a week to ask anything we wanted, I wasn't going to stop digging. "How does it work?"

"Well, Mr. Sallinger, the nature of what we do out in the real world—fighting crime and fighting other empowered individuals who have less-than-selfless motives—dictates that it often will take place in public, out in front of anyone who happens to see it. Mr. Weatherby is able to keep them from . . ." she paused, searching for her words, "remembering what they see." Then, as if sensing my lingering confusion, she added, "If custodians go zipping through the air in Manhattan, people are going to see them. Or if they slam a villain up against the Sears Tower, people are going to see it. But even though they see what's happening, the memory fades almost immediately, leaving a fuzzy, hazy shadow in its place. And that shadow is the end result of Mr. Weatherby's abilities. It's like the memory is never allowed to form or be stored by the brain in the first place, making it impossible to recall. Without him, we'd be placed in greater danger from the spotlight that comes naturally with what we do out there."

My mind always raced to the worst-case scenarios in life. "How many people like Paul Weatherby are there?" I was worried about my own memories. Could it be that I had been a witness to some amazing display of powers but had forgotten all about it due to some memory hacker like this guy?

Mrs. Crouch's demeanor changed slightly for just a hair of a second, and then she regained her composure. Most of the sighted kids probably didn't even notice it, but I could always tell with things like this. She didn't want to keep going down this road. "He is the only one."

There was a murmur in the room, which she quickly sought to quell.

"He is the only one strong enough, I should say. There are others with similar powers but at only a fraction of the range—able to blanket a small building, for example, but not the entire earth. None of the others are nearly strong enough to disguise *all* the heroes like he does. Throughout our history, there have been many with the more powerful version of this gift, but they always came from the same genealogy, the same family. Mr. Weatherby is simply the last of his line, and there is no one left for him to pass his power on to."

"Couldn't he just have kids?" Henry announced his plan as though it was the most obvious thing in the universe. He could have added the word "duh" at the end, and it would have fit the tone perfectly.

Another pause from Mrs. Crouch. "He had children once, Mr. Gardner. But they were killed."

The room went silent, and I now understood her apparent reluctance. The story she'd been asked to tell had a sad ending. Bentley didn't let the sober atmosphere disrupt his learning, though. "And when he dies?"

It was a question that didn't really need an answer, though we all hoped the obvious one was wrong. Mrs. Crouch, however, confirmed our fears. "Our actions and our cities will no longer be hidden."

For several beats, no one said a thing. Mrs. Crouch finally spoke again. "Let's call it a day on that subject, kids, and move on to something else. Surely someone else has a question about a different subject."

"What about Believers?" I blurted out, not waiting even a second for another kid to beat me to the punch. I knew this question would be a bit of a curveball, but I didn't care. I'd heard of the Believers twice since learning of my powers, both times merely overhearing the conversations of upperclassmen during lunch or in the hallway. They made the Believers sound like boogeymen, which made me want to learn more about them pronto.

"Believers," she simply repeated back at me, like she was weighing her response. "Well, Mr. Sallinger, I'd like to know if you'd be willing to tell me a little bit more about why you're asking—where you heard the term, that sort of thing. I'll answer your question, but I'd like to know what you know first."

"Well . . ." I began in my usual manner, "I've just heard other kids in school talking about them a couple times, is all."

Mrs. Crouch let out a long, deep breath. It struck me that I'd probably ruined her plan to lighten the mood when I simply changed one awkward subject for another. "A very long time ago . . ." she said haltingly, "before biblical times . . ." Another pause, though I couldn't tell if she was trying to choose her words carefully or was just being dramatic. "There is a story of an empowered man who had all the powers and abilities in one. He could fly and had superstrength. Every power you've ever heard of, this man supposedly had. In the more modern texts, he's called Elben. In some of our oldest historical records, he's referred to only as 'the one who can do all.'" Another huge pause ensued.

"Elben was the leader of the Haladites, an ancient army of evil that spread over two-thirds of the earth before they were defeated. The Haladites were the first group on record to attempt to use their powers collectively for selfish gain—sort of the godfathers of organized crime and modern supervillains. Together their combined powers overwhelmed the protectors of that era, who were unprepared for such a concentrated effort."

"How were the Haladites defeated?" Freddie asked.

"By perhaps the most famous group of custodians in history, an outfit known as the Ables. The Ables were the first group of custodians to band together for the good of the world, and of course, did so only in response to the rampaging Haladites. They were, quite literally, the only six good-hearted custodians left standing in the wake of Elben's march across Europe. In one of the most famous battles in our secret history, the Ables leveraged cunning and quick thinking to trick the Haladites into thinking their numbers were much larger than they really were.

"Confused and frightened, Elben's fearsome army panicked and scattered, and the Ables concentrated their abilities on the main villain himself, winning the day." She paused, perhaps considering whether to finish this particular story. "Convinced Elben's abilities posed a permanent threat to the entire planet's population, they executed him right then and there in a place we now refer to as the Bleeding Grounds."

Mrs. Crouch took a very deep breath before continuing.

"So, children, Believers is a word used to describe modern-day custodians who are part of a kind of order—an almost religious group that believes not only that the old-world stories are true but also that he's coming back."

I couldn't help but interject at that point. "What do you mean, 'coming back'?"

"In some of our texts, some of the oldest ones, there are prophesies. And one such prophecy suggests—according to some interpretations, not all—that 'the one who can do all' will return. That one day, the world will see another custodian with all the powers at once. The Believers treat this prophecy the way Christians treat the Bible or Muslims treat the Qur'an. They treat it like a religion."

"You mean they worship this Elben guy? The guy who might come back?" Bentley joined the discussion. It never took more than a few seconds for him to become interested in whatever the topic happened to be. He was the most voracious learner I'd ever met.

"Yes," Mrs. Crouch declared. "They essentially worship an individual who may or may not appear one day."

Everyone seemed deep in thought for a moment or two before Bentley spoke up again. "Do you believe the prophecies, Mrs. Crouch?"

She spoke so fast, she nearly cut him off. "Of course not," she said dismissively. "They're reading far too much into these texts. Some of them are just markings on the wall of a cave! They see what they want to see. They infer what they want to infer." For good measure, she added, "And I don't believe in reincarnation either."

This was a huge relief to me. I probably sighed out loud. Mrs. Crouch had just told me about the boogeyman but then instantly squashed him like a bug. I wanted to hug her.

"Now," she continued, "that's not to say the world will never see another multipowered individual. In fact, there are people with dual powers that we know of. They're rare, but they exist. Some people call them Jekyll-Hydes, because it's like two personalities. They have two powers, but most can use only one at a time, and it depends on their emotional and mental state."

Then she gave the boogeyman CPR, resuscitated him, and offered him a glass of water.

"Basic logic tells you it's possible for a person with all known powers to exist. It's just math and statistics. It's going to happen someday. It could well be millions of years from now, but even the rarest possibility sees its day in the sun."

As though sensing our fear—I can only assume that the other students were just as terrified of a multipowered monster rampaging through their bedrooms as I was—Mrs. Crouch decided to try and help ease the worry. "There are things just as scary as a man with many powers, kids, and maybe some things even scarier. There are powers that would send chills down your spine."

On further reflection, I decided perhaps her intention wasn't to make us feel better after all. Maybe she was trying to toughen us up or something.

"There are records of a woman in the first century who could turn into a black hole and suck up anything and everything around her that she wanted, sending them to some nothingness on the other side of the universe. In 500 BC, there was a man named Arbor, and everyone who ever touched him died instantly. There's a man alive today—in custody, mind you—that can melt people just by pointing at them."

This was getting worse by the second, at least as far as my future nightmares were concerned. Maybe Mrs. Crouch had a change of heart, and instead of easing away from the difficult topic, she'd decided to press forward? Maybe she was teaching us a lesson about being careful what we wished for with this Q&A stuff?

"I don't know how to tell you this gently, kids, but it's a scary world out there. Many of you will graduate and go on to Goodspeed, the capital city for custodians. You'll end up working in a job where people shooting guns at you is a regular occurrence. Villains are real. They exist. And some day, you will need to face them. The less time we spend easing you into that reality, the faster we can start training and preparing you for it.

"Yes, there are people out there who wish to destroy us, and some of them are fervent. Some of them are zealots, like the Believers. But there have always been such people, and there will always be such people.

"Yes, we may one day find ourselves without the secrecy and privacy we've come to cherish, and we'll have to decide—as a people—what risks are worth taking in the pursuit of fighting evil. And the world will change when that happens. But then, someday, not long after, the world will change again.

"The world changed for most of you just a few short weeks ago, when you went from ignorant bliss to knowing that superheroes are real. The world will change again several times in your lifetimes. And we will adjust and we will carry on and we will defeat the darkness. Because that's what heroes do.

"I wish it could all be roses, kids, but I'm doing you an injustice if I skip over the thorns."

6

THE SUPERSIM

There's something different in the sound of an entire student body filling the halls when they know the destination isn't a classroom. It's a touch more jovial an atmosphere, and my classmates and I were feeling it too.

It was a Monday during the fifth week of the school year, and we were on our way to our first convocation. During the first period of the day, normally reserved for homeroom, the entire student body was instead herded together into the gymnasium.

Except for the topic, it was like every other school assembly I'd ever attended. The students lined the bleachers, while the teachers all mingled around the basketball court. Most of our special ed class was all in one row together—the first row—with Henry and his wheelchair on the end.

The gym was cold—colder than the classroom, for sure—probably to help counter the rise in temperature that could be expected from cramming a thousand people into a room together. No one would be more acutely aware of the combined body odor of the room in a few minutes than me.

Judging from the way the sounds were reverberating throughout the room, I was pretty sure it was larger than any school gymnasium I'd ever set foot inside.

The guys and I were speculating on what the assembly topic would be. Bentley had his money on a rules crackdown. He'd heard about some vandalism problems. Actually, he'd overheard, perhaps even eavesdropped, while his dad was dining with some of his board buddies.

Henry was convinced it was something more exciting, like a school dance or something. I cannot emphasize enough how badly I hoped it was *not* about a school dance.

My theory, which I kept to myself, was a darker one. I was fearing the worst, as I tended to do. Some evil criminal had escaped superhero jail and was on the loose, I was fairly certain of it. Someone with a penchant for murdering middle schoolers, no doubt.

Before the debate could gain any traction, I heard feedback from the microphone and a gentle tap. And then I heard the voice of a scrawny old man—at least, that's what I guessed the owner of this voice looked like. It was nasally and high-pitched. "Check." More gentle tapping. "Check." He said the word as though it had two syllables, drawing it out as long as possible. "It's on?"

This is going to be the longest convocation of my life.

"Ladies and gentlemen, may I have your attention?" The rowdy crowd quieted just a hair but not all the way. "May I have your attention?" If he'd spoken louder on the second attempt, I couldn't tell, and I have pretty good ears. The crowd quieted another degree but was still plenty loud. He wasn't going to get anywhere with this technique.

So he tried a new word, one that made absolutely no sense to me: "Chelsey." Then, without warning, a loud and deep voice boomed throughout the gym. "I said, quiet!" It could have been God for all I knew. He sounded powerful and angry and absolutely everywhere.

"That's Principal Dempsey," Bentley whispered in my ear as the voice's echo started to wane. "He's what's called a broadcaster. He can manipulate sound waves!" He sounded pretty impressed.

I was still grappling with temporary deafness. *The first voice and the second voice belong to the same guy?*

Just out of curiosity, I asked, "Is he a scrawny, skinny little hundred-year-old guy?"

"Yeah, how'd you know?" Again, Bentley sounded impressed.

"Just a hunch." Another thought hit me. "How is he able to use his powers in the school if it's a no power zone?"

"Did you hear him say 'Chelsey'?"

I nodded.

"That's the call to lower the NPZ. He says it over a walkie-talkie, and the person controlling the NPZ knows to lower it."

"I'm guessing that person's name is Chelsey," I said matter-of-factly.

"Don't know," Bentley admitted. "No one knows who it is. That's why they do it that way, so that he or she can't be compromised. For all we know, Chelsey is just a code word. In fact, that's probably much more likely a possibility than the person actually being named Chelsey."

Principal Dempsey spoke again. "Chelsey." When the room was finally completely still, he continued in his normal speaking voice, which meant that his next sentence took forever. "Ladies and gentlemen, I'm going to bring up Coach Tripp to lead this assembly. And he's going to tell you about the SuperSim."

This set off a murmur of confusion among the students.

What on earth is a SuperSim?

"Calm down. Quiet down." Most of us didn't want to hear the "angry principal voice" again, so we shut it up fast this time. "Coach Tripp?"

I said a quick prayer that Coach Tripp was under sixty years old and able to speak at a more reasonable pace.

"Guys and girls, get ready to be excited, because you're going to love the Super Simulation, or as it is commonly known, the SuperSim." My prayers were answered. He sounded like a young man—younger than my father, at least—and his voice was filled with a friendly energy. "This year, after much debating in the various local governing bodies, the board has decided to reinstate an annual tradition that hasn't been followed in over twenty years."

Coach Tripp had my complete attention.

"We want you students to learn, to get an education. And we want you to socialize and be kids and have fun. But more than you may realize, we want you to be prepared for the life ahead of you should you choose to play the role of heroes. Therefore, in five weeks' time, we will be commencing the first of three Super Simulations, with the second two events taking place during second semester. The SuperSims are full-scale, citywide custodian simulations, where you'll have the chance to compete in teams to be the first to save the day."

The murmuring started up again, but Coach Tripp just kept going.

"The SuperSim is a huge event, guys. It requires the efforts of nearly the entire town to plan, stage, and execute a heroes-versus-villains scenario that you will then attempt to complete. There will be no taking turns. It's every team playing at once. There will be a list of instructions—we'll go over them in a moment—and then you'll get a handout and some ground rules, but we will not tell you a thing about the simulation itself. It'll be up to you and your team to discover the crimes, track down the perpetrators, and subdue them—just as if you were full-grown official custodians out in the real world. There will be multiple fake criminals and multiple fake crimes throughout Freepoint. The winning team gets a nice championship trophy and bragging rights they can keep forever."

Another burst of spontaneous discussion mixed with some applause swept over the student body. Once again, the coach just kept on talking. "I'm going to ask you guys to keep it down or else I'll end this thing right now." He sounded like he meant it but also like he didn't want to have to make good on the threat. I thought he was as excited at the prospect of this thing as we were. "You guys will have plenty of time to find your teams, and then you can talk and cheer all you want. But let me get through these instructions first," he said.

"Okay, here we go." I heard some papers rustling around on the lectern. "Participation in the SuperSim is optional. If, for some reason, you do not wish to join a team and take part, that is totally okay. If you do wish to be a part of it, you'll need to pick up one of the registration packets on that table over there by Mrs. Franklin on your way out. Inside, there's a permission slip. You cannot participate without your parents' permission. Let me repeat that. You cannot participate in the SuperSim without a signed parental consent form."

A parental consent form would be tough, considering my mother's tendency to be overprotective of me. But I knew my father wanted to nurture the little hero in me, so maybe he would be okay with it.

"Teams must have at least four members and can have no more than seven. You are allowed to name your team, but please keep it clean, guys. I reserve the right to refuse any inappropriate team names. Students are encouraged to choose their teammates wisely. Consider joining up with kids who have powers that complement yours, not just your friends. Think about all the possible scenarios you might encounter. You'll want to be ready for as much as possible.

Let's see here, what else? The event shall be timed. If there are no criminals apprehended within the allotted time, then there are no winners. However, each fictional crime and criminal will be assigned a point value by order of their difficulty. The team with the most points accrued by the end of the simulation event shall be the champions."

I had a feeling this thing was going to be amazing. My mind was already racing at the chance to compete in a citywide supervillain scavenger hunt. *Whom should I be on a team with?*

"Now then, there are some rules as well."

As a group, we were nearly ready to burst. You could feel it in the air; I could, at least. There was so much pent-up excitement, it was palpable.

"The officials in the SuperSim will be faculty members of this school and other adults from Freepoint. They will be highly visible throughout town, and their word is final—on everything. If they tell you you're disqualified, you are disqualified. If they tell you to stop doing something, you'd better stop. They are the referees of this simulation."

"Rule number two. No using your powers against other students or student teams. Period. This is a zero-tolerance policy. If you use your abilities against each other, you will not only be disqualified, you'll be suspended from school, and you'll probably face charges in city court as well." Offhandedly, he added, "Not to mention the officials will likely prevent you from doing it anyway if you try it anywhere near their line of sight."

"Similarly, there is to be no sabotage of other teams or impedance to their progress in any way. This is you against the villains, okay? Not you against each other. We can have more than one winner here."

Enough, already!

"Rule number three."

Oh, good grief.

"The simulation shall last exactly four hours in total."

Kind of like this assembly.

"At the conclusion of the time allotted, the success scores will be tallied and the trophy awarded to the team that earns the most points."

They have to make a rule for that?

"Rule four. No unnecessary damage to property in the city. Again, guys, the officials will be out and about, highly visible and always watching. Don't think you can get away with mischief here. You'll ruin it for everyone, and you'll only get busted for it in the end."

It sounded like he was wrapping it up. I definitely wanted him to be wrapping up.

"That's about it, I guess."

Praise the Lord.

"Everyone's going to get one of these packets. It's got the instructions and rules, the parental consent form, and we've got an FAQ here as well. It's full of useful and important information. The sign-up form is also in the packet. We'll start accepting these tomorrow morning. You can bring them to the main office. You can ask any one of your teachers for more information if you have questions."

The students began to stir a bit, sensing their release was imminent. They were probably all itching at the chance to start talking about this thing with their friends. I know I was.

The coach's voice missed the microphone just enough to let me know he had his head turned to the side as he said, "Do we have anything else?" He was most likely looking at Principal Dempsey or the other teachers. Or both. "Okay," he said, now facing the microphone directly again, "you are dismissed."

We rose, almost in unison, with an instantaneous thunder of conversation. Someone must have noticed what time it was and that the entire assembly had lasted only about twenty minutes, because Coach Tripp shouted over the noise, saying, "Go back to your homeroom classrooms. Homeroom!" Other teachers echoed the instructions to the students nearest them as we all shuffled together toward the exit doors.

My mind was racing on overdrive. I heard bits and pieces of the conversations happening around me as I inched forward with the masses. One kid to my left said something about wearing capes, and one of his buddies suggested masks. A girl that moved past me quickly said the word "compact," but I'm pretty sure she was talking about her makeup. The thought struck me that she could have been talking about having the power to make herself really tiny, which could be useful in certain hero-type situations. But it was probably the makeup.

These two guys behind me were clearly the two nerdiest kids in the universe. And you know you're a nerd when even I think you're one. One of them said he was a grower—he could cause plants and trees to grow with a wave of his hand. An excellent power, but maybe not great for catching villains. The poor guy swore there were stories of growers capturing criminals with strategic tree placement. His friend wasn't in much better shape, I'm afraid, with the special ability to do impossible math in his head. Again, a useful skill, but it's not one that's particularly handy for crime fighting. They were struggling to come up with names of kids they thought might consider joining their team, and I felt a bit sorry for them.

But I wouldn't have that problem.

I turned to Bentley and Henry, who were on my right. "Okay guys, whom are we gonna get?"

Bentley simply asked, "What?"

"Whom should we get on our team?"

There was a pause as we reached the doorway, and I felt the SuperSim registration packet get placed in my hand by whoever was passing them out. My entire life, I've just been taking whatever people hand me on my way in and out of places without really knowing who they are or what I'm accepting. It could be nuclear launch codes or a map to buried treasure, but I'd still just take it and hand it over to Mom when I got home.

"Oh, I don't know. How about Chad Burke?" He was being a smart aleck.

"Ha ha, Bentley. Very funny." I wasn't amused. "Seriously, we can have seven. Do we even know that many kids?"

This time it was Henry who responded. "Let me ask you something." He started out calm but quickly ramped things up with an emphatic, "Are you crazy?"

"What?"

"Why in the world would you think we should enter this thing?" He sounded so exasperated. "We wouldn't stand a chance!"

"Why not?" I didn't understand his reaction at all. Didn't every one of us want to play superhero?

Henry practically shouted, "Look at us! We're disabled, Phillip! I'm in a freaking wheelchair, man, and you can't see. We don't stand a chance against able-bodied kids. Why would I want to embarrass myself by coming in last at a superhero contest?"

Bentley tried to play the mediator. "I think what Henry's trying to say"—he paused, realizing it was a tough job—"is that you're crazy, Phillip. And we would get our butts kicked."

"Why? I don't get it, guys. We can do anything these other kids can do."

Henry chimed in again. "Except walk, see, or stand still." Henry was a real downer sometimes, even though it was obvious he didn't always mean to be. He was just blunt. Sometimes he was also pessimistic, which created a combination that didn't always save room for people's feelings.

"I can't see, but you can. You can't walk, but I can. Haven't you been listening to anything Mrs. Crouch has been saying? We can work together to overcome our disadvantages."

"Disabilities," Henry corrected me. "And you sound like a coach giving a pep talk before the big game in some terrible cheesy movie."

I ignored him and decided to concentrate on Bentley. "Bentley, you talk all the time about your little inventions." It was true. He had told us about the hours he spent tinkering and building things in his workshop, even though most of them never worked. One he talked about specifically was a remote control that he fitted with a thumb scanner so it wouldn't work if you didn't scan yourself first. He programmed the device to accept the thumbprint for everyone in his entire family except his older brothers. "What if you can get a couple working that might help us in the competition?"

"I don't know, Phillip."

I suspected he was just being modest and that he had some pretty amazing gadgets and gizmos down in that basement, but I was suddenly distracted by a small revelation. "We could get Donnie—everyone's scared of Donnie."

Nothing. I thought I heard Henry smack his forehead, but with all the ruckus in the hallway, there was no way to be sure.

"We can add James—hey, where's James?"

"I'm right here," James replied. He'd been there the whole time, just keeping quiet.

"James can transport, guys. And he knows this city like nobody else, don't you, James?"

"I can take us anywhere in town you want to go." He was giving his standard businessman speech more than he was actually showing interest in participating in the contest. He loved talking about how excellent his transport services were. He was quite the self-promoter.

"That's right. Anywhere in the city," I said, agreeing with him. "And with all my practicing, I can move certain items up to twenty or thirty feet already. Donnie's huge and intimidating. Bentley has gadgets." I was on a roll, building my case.

"Henry can read the villains' minds. Freddie is freaking indestructible, guys!" I paused before the conclusion. "If we can get one more kid . . . someone with superstrength or eye-beams of some sort . . . guys, we can do this. And even if we fail, it's not like we look bad. They already think we're losers. But if we show up . . . if we do well, even a little bit . . . maybe we win some respect."

We had reached the classroom. Everyone filed in without saying anything. I took my seat, optimistic that I had gotten through to them, that they would see this as the opportunity that it was instead of labeling it a land mine. I had never seen myself as a motivational speaker until now. I decided to let them stew for a few moments and started making mental notes of things to say to further support my argument.

But that didn't last very long.

Mrs. Crouch came into the room. Before she even made it to her desk, she'd crushed my dreams.

"Before any of you go getting your hopes up, you should know that special education students have been ruled ineligible for the SuperSim competition for your own safety and protection."

I let out an audible gasp of shock. "That's not fair," I began, ready to argue my case all over again.

But she shut me down. "Very few things are, Mr. Sallinger," she said with a tone that clearly indicated I could talk myself blue in the face, and it would be in vain. As she went around the room collecting the registration packets from us, I could practically feel Henry giving me an I-told-you-so look.

I spent all of the morning's lessons slouched in my desk, arms crossed, pouting in defeated silence.

7

EXPOSED

That evening after dinner, everyone was in the living room. Dad was in his easy chair, watching the national news and reading some work papers. Mom was doing a crossword puzzle, moving back and forth in her rocker. Patrick was on the couch with me, fiddling around with a handheld video game.

I sat with an open comic book in my lap, which I ignored, and contemplated how unfair it was that the school wouldn't let disabled kids participate in the SuperSim. I thought it was pretty wrong and wanted to say so, but I couldn't talk about it until Pat got sent to bed. I thought about picking a fight with him to get him in trouble so he would be sent to his room as punishment but decided against it. He got sent to his room enough on his own, so it would probably happen anyway, and there was always the risk of getting caught being the instigator.

I had been distracted the entire day by the SuperSim issue. I couldn't recall a single thing that Mrs. Crouch had talked about. I'd barely said a word at lunch. I was just depressed that I wasn't going to be able to participate. Another carrot dangled before me, only to be yanked away. *You have a superpower—oh yeah, you can barely use it. Also, there's an awesome superhero competition—but you're too fragile to compete.*

Ultimately, it wasn't the school I was upset with, though; it was my friends. I couldn't figure out why they were so scared. I mean, I knew we'd be underdogs and all that, but I didn't see any harm in trying. They did. And I felt a little betrayed.

The woman on the news started talking about an attempted bank robbery. I heard my father's newspaper rustle and could tell that he'd started watching the news story with his full attention. I wondered if he knew about that bank robbery. The anchor mentioned that the robbers used C-4, which any twelve-year-old kid who watches movies can tell you is explosive stuff. It sounded like the kind of thing an evil mastermind might plan and perpetrate. Dad could very well have been there, for all I knew, as part of the team that foiled the crime.

I longed for the day when Patrick was in the loop so we could talk openly at home about our powers.

The news story ended, and a new one about Congress began. Some kind of scandal. I was about to learn what kind of scandal when the phone rang, distracting me. Dad closed the leg rest on the easy chair, stood, and went to get the phone.

"Hello, Sallingers." It was his standard phone greeting, even if the caller ID revealed that the caller was someone he knew. "Why, yes, hang on one moment, will you?" I heard Dad walking back toward us and assumed the call was for Mom. Instead, I felt a tapping on my right shoulder.

I turned around to hear my dad say, "It's for you, son." It was the first phone call I'd received since we'd moved to Freepoint. I hadn't received many phone calls before we moved here either, frankly.

Who could be calling me?

As Dad handed me the phone, I lifted it to my ear and said a cautious, "Hello?"

"This is what I think we should do . . ."

I was instantly relieved. "Oh, hi, Bentley."

"We need to file an appeal." He was all business, with no time for pleasantries.

"A what?" I was still waiting for a hello.

"An appeal with the school board. That's the proper procedure." He was pretty excited and talking rather quickly. "If they won't let us compete, then that's illegal discrimination, and we can challenge the school's decision to bar us on the basis of the Americans with Disabilities Act."

Finally! He had come around. I was about to respond when I suddenly remembered my brother. "Hang on a second." I turned toward my dad. "I'm going to go take this in my bedroom, okay?"

"Sure, son."

I held the phone to my chest and made my way out of the living room, past the kitchen, and into my bedroom. I closed the door and returned to the conversation. "I thought you were against the SuperSim!"

Bentley explained, "I was. But I was just being scared. It's one thing to think about being a custodian some day in the future, but it's another thing entirely to actually go try to be one in only five weeks."

"So what changed your mind, then?"

"Your speech about working together, but not because it inspired me emotionally or anything—it really was pretty cheesy. But the logic of it just makes too much sense. You're right. Our powers and abilities can complement each other and make up for our disabilities. We're not any more or less able to stop crime."

"Well, okay then." I was beaming.

"That . . . and the fact that they told me I can't. I hate it when people tell me that I can't do something, Phillip. It makes me want to do it anyway and then shove it in their faces for doubting me."

"Do you really think we stand a chance with an appeal?" I was happy to have him on board, but I was skeptical of his plan's chances for success. It seemed a little extreme.

"Sure, why not? It's against the law to discriminate against disabled people just because of their disability. They have to let us participate."

"Can't you just ask your father to say something to someone? Isn't he, like, a bigwig on the board?"

"I asked him already," Bentley spat out in disgust. "He said his hands are tied, that it's not his decision. That a man in his position can't appear to be taking sides just because of his son. Buncha crap, if you ask me. He'd do it for Brad or Terry. But it's exactly what I expected him to say."

I sensed that this wasn't the first issue Bentley and his father had disagreed on. Judging by his tone, there seemed to be a history there.

"But we're just kids. Are we even allowed to file a school board appeal?" I honestly didn't know.

He sounded pretty sure, responding with a hearty, "Oh yeah. There's no age requirement. It's totally possible."

"How do you know?" It was an honest question.

"I just spent the last hour learning about the Freepoint school system."

Now, when a normal person says something like that, what they really mean is that they skimmed the important stuff and gained a cursory knowledge of a huge subject in sixty minutes' time. What Bentley meant, though, was that he'd just gained in one hour the experience and knowledge of someone who'd spent years learning on the job. He probably now knew more about the Freepoint school board bylaws than the president himself. That's just how his mind worked. He was a sponge for knowledge.

"In an hour?" I'd seen evidence of his superpowered learning abilities before in class, but this was something on a new level, and I was a little bit amazed.

"I got the basic gist, yeah. It's pretty simple. We file the paperwork with the proper office, and then the rest is easy. There are bylaws prohibiting the school from discriminating against students for any reason. I think we can make a pretty strong argument for our appeal by citing that rule."

"Your brain is amazing, Bentley, you know that? What I wouldn't give to be able to snap my fingers and gain enough knowledge to pass all the tests I'll ever see in school for the rest of my life."

"It's not all it's cracked up to be." He said it casually, with just a hint of sadness.

"Well, I hate to break it to you, but it's still just you and me. And we should probably make sure we can find a couple other guys to join our team to get to the four-person minimum before we go filing appeals and stuff."

"Henry's in. I called him before I called you."

"What?" I was incredulous. There was no way this was true. Henry had been adamant.

"Yeah, for real. He's in. I knew we'd need at least four people, so I didn't want to get your hopes up if I couldn't convince Henry. He said he'd been thinking all day about how cool it would be to actually fight crime. I believe his exact words were 'I'm already a fat kid in a wheelchair, what's a little more humiliation going to hurt me.'"

I was stunned. Henry wasn't exactly known for being persuaded to change his mind. But I wasn't ready to rejoice just yet.

"We still need more. Three's not enough, Bentley."

"So, then we get James, like you said. He seems pretty eager to please, and the teleportation will come in handy too. Or Freak-Out Fred. He's a pretty cool guy."

Bentley seemed to have it all figured out. And somehow, I was now the only one holding us back. But I wasn't about to wear that hat for long. "Then let's do it. What are we waiting for?"

"Okay. Monday, we'll start planning. We're going to need practice and planning sessions, though, Phillip. Lots. Most of us are still pretty raw with our abilities."

He was right, of course. I had gotten so wrapped up in the competition itself that I hadn't stopped to think about all the training we lacked. Even without disabilities, we were still babes in the world of superpowers.

"Right," I agreed. "Maybe we can all sleep over at someone's house— not mine, though. My brother's still not in the loop. I've almost told him on accident, like, six times. There's no way a whole group of kids hanging out here practicing powers is going to go unnoticed."

"We'll do it at my place. Or Henry's. No sweat. But we have to start soon. Most of these kids have a head start on us just because they're not handicapped. We're going to have to work twice as hard as they do to prepare—if not more." I could hear the excitement and determination in his voice. I'd created a monster.

"Okay. Maybe we can get together next weekend for our first group session?"

"Yeah, if not sooner. We have only five weeks."

I paused, suddenly apprehensive. "What if they don't let us compete, Bentley? What if we practice and rehearse and do all this work and they still won't let us play?" It seemed plausible to me that this scenario could happen. I guess my life experiences had turned me into a bit of a pessimist in these kinds of situations.

"They will, Phillip. Don't worry. Justice is on our side." He sounded so confident that my fears were nearly erased. Coming from someone like Bentley—someone smarter than everyone else in my life put together—the tone of certainty was comforting. "Besides, if they don't . . . screw 'em. We'll compete anyway." I already liked the original Bentley a great deal. But this new and improved Bentley—the one oozing confidence and bravado—was even better. Looking back, I'm reasonably sure that this is the moment I determined that Bentley would be a friend for life.

"Okay then."

"Okay then. See you Monday?"

"Yeah, see you Monday," I replied. The line went dead.

I leaned with my back against the bedroom door for a moment, taking it all in. Even earlier in the day, in the midst of trying to convince the guys to compete in the SuperSim, I hadn't actually thought much about the simulation as a real thing. It was abstract, some cool new thing on the horizon that I hoped to see someday. The way Christmas feels in July. But now that my friends had actually changed their minds to the point of even showing enthusiasm, well . . . the SuperSim was real now. It was going to happen. And it was a heavy moment for me. My first chance at acting like a real superhero was only weeks away, and those five weeks felt like about thirty seconds.

I returned to the living room, sat back down, and picked up the comic book I had been pretending to read, even less able to concentrate on it now than I had been before. I read and then reread the first frame of the comic several times, sliding my fingers over the tiny bumps on the page. I tried to dive into the story and leave the real world behind for a bit, but my memory wouldn't let me. I kept rolling over the conversation with Bentley in my head, still somewhat shocked at his 180-degree change of heart.

"Who was that on the phone, honey?" It was my mother, who always seemed to care as much about my social life as my father did about my homework and grades.

"Bentley. He's a kid in my class. One of my friends I told you about."

"What did he want?" I could tell she was still concentrating on the crossword even while quizzing me about the call. Something in her DNA allowed her to multitask like that, and it never ceased to amaze me. It was like a superpower unto itself.

"He wanted to talk about . . ." It occurred to me that I didn't have a handy lie ready, and yet clearly, I couldn't tell her the truth in front of Patrick. "A school project. We're on the same science fair team, and he had an idea for an experiment we could do."

Phew! Good save.

"Ooh, what kind of experiment?"

Dang! I hadn't thought that far ahead.

You never knew when Mom's string of peppered questions was going to end. And if you were lying, it always seemed never-ending.

"Um, well, he told me not to tell anyone about it yet. Keep it a secret." I had no real illusions that this feeble deflection would work.

Jeez, Mom, remember when you guys told me to keep this superhero stuff quiet in front of Patrick?

She went silent. She might have been weighing her response or puzzling over a particularly tricky crossword clue. Or maybe she realized there might be a good reason for my evasiveness. Eventually, she simply said, "I see."

And that appeared to be the end of it. Another mental sigh of relief.

The room fell silent except for the television. A commercial for bleach was wrapping up. I had no idea what bleach was used for, really, but there sure were an awful lot of commercials for it.

Again I attempted to clear my mind by returning to the comic. It was a Batman comic book, and he was pretty much my favorite superhero—well, he was until I learned that real superheroes existed. Of course, with comics in braille being a bit of a rarity, I didn't own very many, and I had read this one many times before. It was the famous issue where the Joker kills Robin. Pretty heavy stuff for a seventh grader. I'm pretty sure my parents never screened the comics before giving them to me, or they probably wouldn't have let me read this one.

After all the times I'd read this particular story, I practically had the entire thing memorized, which only made it tougher to focus. I decided to make one last attempt to immerse myself in the comic. I started from the beginning, the first frame. I placed my fingers on the page. But then something happened that was thoroughly unexpected, and all hope of concentrating on the comic went out the window.

The newscaster's voice suddenly shifted, taking on a more serious tone. "Excuse me. Ladies and gentlemen, we have breaking news. I'm just being told . . . We're going to interrupt our planned broadcast and send it out to the field immediately for News Channel 10's own Eric Fuller, who is live on the scene from Central Park in New York City."

I have to admit, I didn't typically pay all that much attention to the news. Who does at my age? But I was certain I had never heard anything like this. I was instantly alert. Maybe aliens had landed in Central Park.

"Thanks, Cindy." A man's voice. "Eric Fuller here in Central Park, where you can see a large crowd has gathered behind me, blocking the street and the intersection. Tonight, roughly ten minutes ago, I and many of these other citizens saw something . . . amazing."

He spoke with more than the usual amount of excitement for a news reporter, and it was obvious he was forcing himself to remain calm and professional.

"Earlier this evening, convicted murderer Calvin Creed escaped police custody during transport to the brand-new Islesworth Correctional Facility. A high-speed pursuit followed, eventually making its way here, to Central Park, where . . . he and his crew were stopped by a single man. The unknown man appeared as if out of thin air and was, well . . . flying."

He paused to let his words sink in with the viewers at home. And then, they did. *Wait a minute. Did he just—*

"Flying in over the park from the south side, this 'superman' then landed directly in front of the lead getaway car and stopped it dead in its tracks. Cindy . . . viewers at home . . . superheroes are evidently real, and there is at least one living among us here in New York City.

"Now, ladies and gentlemen, I'm sure many of you think I've gone off the deep end. But I assure you that I have just accurately recounted the events of this evening. And thankfully, you don't have to take my word for it, because News Channel 10 was on the scene. We were filming—this camera crew and I—a segment for a story on the city's plan to toughen up on crime in the park when we managed to capture this footage. No words can truly describe what you're about to see."

He went silent, but then I heard him again. "The mayor's office has repeatedly made Central Park crime a top priority throughout the—"

Suddenly he was cut off by the shriek of a woman who must have been standing nearby.

Ah, this is the footage from earlier, I realized.

Then there were more distant voices. I couldn't make them all out, but I did hear a few of them clearly. "What in the world?" "Eric!" "Oh God!"

More shouting and lots of commotion. Police sirens began sounding. I heard someone yell, "What the—" followed by a beep. Even a kid like me knows what that word was.

Then there was a sudden whooshing sound. It began quietly but rapidly grew in volume, like an oncoming train. Another loud scream. And then all the sounds started bleeding into one another. The voices, the screams, the sirens, the car horns—it all gathered into a hurricane of raw volume, capped off with a thunderous crash. And then it was over.

The whole thing lasted maybe thirty seconds from beginning to end.

"That was the scene here just about a half hour ago. And, as you can see, what happened defies all logic and common sense, and yet . . . that man was clearly flying. And those cars clearly crashed into him after he landed, crushing like soda cans around him. Once it was over, he glanced over the crowd and then leaped into the air and disappeared."

How is this possible? I thought about Paul Weatherby, the hero Mrs. Crouch had told us about. His power was supposed to shield heroes in the real world from view. But not only had this fellow tonight been seen, he'd been captured on film. I was suddenly filled with dread. Custodians weren't a secret any longer.

Patrick! I remembered my brother, and the fact that he was just as clueless as the rest of America had been five minutes ago. I thought that maybe it was possible he'd been so focused on his video game that he didn't even see or hear the news story. Not likely, but possible.

I heard the zapping sound our television made whenever it was turned on or off. I wasn't sure if it was Mom or Dad who had the remote. For a moment, no one said a thing. Then I got my answer about Patrick.

"Holy crap! Did you see that? Holy crap! That was amazing!" He jumped up from the couch, and I could tell that he was pacing back and forth, waving his hands in the air in excitement like a televangelist getting blessed—the way he did when he got that handheld video game last Christmas. "Dad, that was a real, live superhero! Did you see that, Dad? Mom?" He was losing it. "Oh my God, oh my God, oh my God—I can't believe it!"

I turned toward my dad. There were so many questions I wanted to ask: What did this mean? Who was the flying guy on the news? How come everyone could see him? What happened to Paul Weatherby?

But I couldn't ask any of them. I heard Mom doing her best to corral Patrick, and Dad didn't seem to be doing anything but just standing there. I suspected he was in shock. Finally, he reached out and put his hand on my shoulder. "Son, we'll have to talk about this later. Right now, I think I probably need to go into work."

Later that night, after Mom and Dad assumed I was fast asleep, they sat at the kitchen table talking about the events from the news story. Instead of sleeping, however, I was sitting at my bedroom door, blatantly eavesdropping on their every word.

Dad started off. "It was Frank Singleton."

"They're going to identify him, John. They're going to be able to tell who he was from that footage."

"I know." Dad sounded sad. "But there's nothing we can do about that now." I'd never heard the name Frank Singleton, but it sounded like Dad knew him on some level.

"How did this happen?" She sounded tired.

"The cloaker—Weatherby—there was some kind of attack on him. During the commotion, he lost track of controlling his powers. He's fine. He's back at it now. Everything's okay."

There was a brief lull in the conversation.

"Believers?" Mom asked.

"Who knows? They're the only group we know of that's sophisticated enough to break into that place and almost steal him out from under our noses, that's for sure."

"So the incident Frank took care of in the park just happened to coincide with the few minutes Weatherby wasn't doing his job?"

"Babe, it's New York. You remember what it's like there. There's always a crime to stop."

She sighed, appearing to agree with him.

It was odd listening in on them. Hearing them speak to each other the way they apparently do when we're not around was a unique experience. It was like they were a hair more relaxed with each other than they were in front of me. Not communicating as parent to parent but as husband and wife. I felt a little guilty for spying, but not enough to stop listening.

"And the others in the field have been warned?"

"They're on notice. Whoever went after Weatherby could be going after other heroes, especially the ones we value enough to put guards on. There's already been one other kidnapping."

This was news to Mom. "What!"

"We thought it was unrelated. Nathan Davis, a blocker from Goodspeed. Went missing a few days ago. But there were other circumstances involved there, and it seemed likely he'd just gone off on his own free will. Now we're not so sure."

"This isn't going to die down, John. It won't just blow over in a few weeks. For Pete's sake, they got Frank on film—in all his glory—doing the very thing we've worked so hard to keep hidden." She was clearly agitated. Concerned may be a better word.

"I know, honey, but there's nothing we can do. It's done. It's in the past. We can only make smart decisions moving forward." My father was nothing if not a practical, calculated man.

"What are we going to tell Patrick?" It was Dad.

Mom sighed heavily. "I don't know. Nothing, I guess. As far as he's concerned . . . this is all news to us just as it is to him."

"He's going to be going on about it for weeks," Dad reminded her.

"So will everyone in the country, John. The media isn't going to let something this juicy disappear from the headlines."

"I know," he told her.

"I thought Crittendon and his minions were making progress dealing with the US government," she whined.

"They are," Dad replied. "They just haven't finalized everything. Well, they're still in the early stages of that process. It's like foreign diplomacy, honey—it takes years."

"Well, we may not have years anymore," Mom said grimly. "Not after tonight. They could come for Weatherby again. But even if they don't, he's going to die someday soon, and we don't have any kind of plan in place whatsoever to deal with it."

"Well, I can only do so much, babe," he said in slight protest.

She paused. "I know, honey. I'm sorry. I'm just so worried about this world and what it holds for our boys."

"I am too." He sounded like he meant it. "I'm glad they didn't get him, but the mere fact that they tried has me concerned."

"Why?"

"Because it means . . . whoever it is . . . they're planning to do something big that they don't want anyone to remember."

That was the last I could hear of their words. I'm not sure if they just sat there in silence or if they were hugging or something.

A half a minute or so later, I heard their chairs scrape along the linoleum floor of the kitchen, which meant they were standing or shifting positions.

I heard Mom speak again. "I better go check on the kids."

And that was my cue. I darted back to the bed as fast as I could, jumping in and throwing the covers over my head, just in time to hear that familiar noise.

Ooph!

I held my breath so she wouldn't know I was awake, because I was young enough to still think that worked. I didn't want her to know that I'd been eavesdropping. It seemed like she stood there over the bed forever, even though I'm sure it was only a few seconds.

Ooph!

I finally exhaled, extremely relieved to have presumably pulled off the ruse.

But sleep wouldn't come quickly. My brain wouldn't shut itself down. Not since Dad had told me about my abilities had I been forced to process so much new information in a single day. Between the SuperSim assembly, finding out disabled kids were disqualified, Bentley's call, and then the news report . . . it had been a roller-coaster day.

I lay there on my back, facing the ceiling, contemplating what tomorrow would hold. *It could be almost anything,* I thought.

PART 2

FALL

8

THE GUESTHOUSE

Bentley's family was rich. I might have mentioned that before, but it's worth repeating. Jurrious Crittendon's position as a member of the governing body of the secret world of custodians apparently came with quite a salary.

How rich were they? Well, for starters, our sleepover was held in the guesthouse, which was a whole second house in the backyard behind the first house. In the guesthouse, there were three bedrooms, two bathrooms, a full kitchen, and a game room/home theater. It was bigger than my family's regular house.

The floors in the kitchen were made of marble or some kind of expensive stone, and the furniture was all made out of leather. There was a gigantic movie screen on the wall that everyone gushed about and three full rows of plush theater seats—that even had cup holders on the armrests! The game room had a pool table, a Ping-Pong table, and even a few old stand-up arcade games. I wanted to live there forever.

The Crittendon family's wealth was also apparent in the presence of hired help. Bentley said there were two maids, a nanny for Bentley's baby brother, a landscape guy, a butler, and a personal chef. And those were just the ones that were there every day.

We met Olivia, the nanny, when we first arrived. Thomas, the youngest of Bentley's three siblings, had already been put to bed, and Olivia was one of our chaperones for the first part of the evening. The other was Ted, the butler. Ted was actually Olivia's husband, I learned, and wasn't anything at all like what the movies had told me a butler was supposed to be. I was a little disappointed he wasn't ninety years old. Instead, Ted was a pretty young guy, maybe thirty or so. He was more than a butler, really, in that he actually helped Mr. Crittendon with a host of tasks and duties related to work and the home. He was more like a personal assistant, I guess. But he did answer the door when we arrived, and he called each of us "sir." He was peppy and wacky, and we liked him immediately.

His wife was lovely as well but very quiet and soft-spoken—the opposite of Ted.

Not once during my entire stay at Bentley's house did either of his parents make an appearance. I remember thinking that was a little strange, but I also knew they had to be very busy people.

And Bentley seemed right at home in the company of Ted and Olivia. There was a familiarity between them that suggested they spent plenty of time together. I couldn't help but wonder if some of the tension I'd sensed in Bentley regarding his father had a fairly common cause: maybe he just didn't get to see his dad all that much.

But I didn't have time to dwell on thoughts like that because there was entirely too much fun to be had and too much to talk about regarding the SuperSim.

Everyone was there: Bentley, Henry, James, Freddie, and me. And Donnie, of course. I'm sure he hadn't received many more sleepover invitations in his life than I had, so I was pretty confident he would enjoy himself.

We played Ping-Pong for a while—well, everyone but James and I played, even Henry. We ordered pizza from a place in Freepoint called Jack's, and it was quite possibly the best-tasting pizza I'd ever had. The whole night was fun. Everyone laughed and carried on like it was a party. It was one of the first such experiences of my life, actually. Between moving all the time and being blind, my life just hadn't produced many memorable social encounters with people my own age.

I was beginning to feel like I was part of a group. And I soaked it in.

After a couple hours of food and games, our adult chaperones turned in. They were staying in one of the guesthouse bedrooms for the night to keep us honest.

"Hey, you guys wanna see my workshop?" Bentley volunteered.

"You have your own workshop?" Henry asked.

"Sure. It's really just a spare room in the basement my dad let me turn into a workshop for building or tinkering with things."

"You mean like an inventor?" I asked, curious to know more about what an uber-genius like Bentley would attempt to invent.

"Yeah, sure. I guess. I don't know, I just build stuff. Most of it's junk . . . doesn't work. I started when I was younger, mostly just taking things apart to see how they worked. But it wasn't very long before I started trying to build my own things."

"Um," I said, clearing my throat, "I definitely want to go. Count me in." I was 100 percent on board with this little field trip, already dreaming of the laser guns and rockets I was sure Bentley was building.

"Yeah, me too. Let's see this workshop," Henry said, still acting a little skeptical.

Freddie and James didn't take any convincing after that, and Donnie never did. Bentley gave James some idea of where the room was in the main house and where that was in relation to our position. We all put our hands out in the center of the group, and then . . .

Ooph!

. . . we were there.

"That was awesome," Freddie giggled. Not everyone had a mother who could teleport, so it was the first trip for some.

"See, what did I tell you?" James bragged. Then, quietly to Bentley, he added, "This is the room, right?"

"Yes," Bentley said, a smile in his voice.

Everyone took in the room quietly for a few moments, while I wondered what it looked like. Henry was the first to speak. "Jeez, Louise, Bentley. This place is amazing!"

"Yeah, well, what can I say? My dad's loaded. I try my best not to make a big deal out of it."

"You do a fine job at that, because I had no freaking idea until tonight," Henry marveled. "You're, like, richer than the president!"

"I doubt that," Bentley said. "Anyway, this is it. Over in that corner is the chemistry setup. I play with electrical stuff over there." He was obviously giving a standing tour of the room, pointing out the various areas as he went. It was easy enough for me to tell which area was where just by how the direction of his voice changed as he moved his head.

He continued. "Robotics shares space in this corner over here with my woodworking stuff—I don't do much of that anymore. And then behind you is my brainstorming corner."

"Whoa," Freddie gasped, "you have a pinball machine?"

"It's the same one they have at Jack's," Bentley said, trying to make it seem less special.

But Freddie wasn't having it. "Yeah, but this one isn't at Jack's. This one is in your freaking house, man! That's incredible." He quickly paused to sneak in a puff of his inhaler before continuing. "Man, I don't think I'd ever get any work done if I had a pinball machine in my workshop."

"It's there only for when I need to take a break and get my mind off something for a while. That happens a lot, though," he added.

"So let's see some of these inventions already," I said, ready to get this show on the road.

"Oh no," Bentley said. "I never show anyone my inventions."

"What?" Henry was outraged. "You brought us all the way down here to show us where you invent stuff, but we don't get to see any of it? You gotta be kidding me!"

"They suck, honestly," Bentley argued. "Almost none of them work. It's embarrassing, okay?"

"Dude,"—for a twelve-year-old, the word "dude" can often be the most serious way to start a sentence—"you're a kid. You're twelve. I bet your failed inventions are better than most grown-ups' successes. Give yourself a break. You're supposed to be watching cartoons and playing flag football."

"Not with *my* legs," Bentley reminded us, somewhat somberly. It made me realize how left out he'd probably felt most of his life . . . just like me. Where I'd turned to comic books and stories, he'd turned to inventing and building things on his own. His inventions were probably more personal, more private than we had initially thought.

"Are there any that work that you'd let us see?" I asked, hoping for a compromise.

"Well, my eco-friendly bug zapper works," he said, suddenly less concerned. "I guess I could show you that one." He walked as briskly as he was able toward the sidewall, and I heard a door open. A few seconds later, the footsteps returned as he rejoined us in the center of the room. "Here it is."

I presume he held it up for the others to see while he spoke to point out the features. "It uses these little modified LED lights here, which I altered to mimic the same kind of light you see in a traditional bug zapper. But then, instead of zapping the bugs, I decided to let Mother Nature take care of them. So all we have here are these little light strips, which you apply to the corners and eaves of your house outside—you know, where spiders live. The moths and mosquitoes are attracted to the light and end up flying right into the spiderwebs. No mess, no fuss, all solar powered."

It sounded impressive, that's for sure.

"That's pretty, cool, I guess," Henry allowed, not sounding like he meant it. "What else you got?"

"Well, let's see," Bentley responded before walking back over to the closet again. It must have been a walk-in closet, because he went all the way in and closed the door, no doubt to keep us from following him. A moment later he returned.

"Robot fire hydrant," he declared joyously. A round of oohs and aahs followed from the sighted kids at a level appropriate for something called a robot fire hydrant. Any invention that started with the word "robot" was going to impress this audience.

"What does it do?" Freddie asked.

"Puts out fires, duh," Henry said.

"Actually, no. Putting out fires is the one thing it definitely does *not* do . . . It's actually started a few fires, to be honest. The fire hydrant is just a disguise. It's like a remote-controlled car, only instead of a car, it looks like an authentic fire hydrant—at only one-tenth the weight of a real hydrant."

"Why would anyone want a remote-controlled fire hydrant? It's not like they do anything special, you know, like a car or something."

"Well, it's designed for surveillance. The idea is that you could put a camera in there, and then it would be a pretty versatile thing, right? Because fire hydrants are everywhere, so it would never look out of place. And people never pay attention to those things, so there's little danger of anyone discovering the camera."

It probably wasn't the most specific surveillance device ever conceived, but I had to admit it had a certain level of coolness to it. I'd never really built anything in my life, and certainly never a working robot.

"So, it works?" Henry asked.

"Yeah, I just have to put a camera or microphone in there, and it's a fully functioning spy robot. The remote even functions up to one hundred yards away."

"Hmm," Henry said, not convinced it was cool.

"Hey," Bentley protested, "I made that thing when I was nine, okay? That's not too shabby, even if I do say so myself."

"I suppose," Henry admitted. "What else you got? What about some of the ones that don't work?"

"Oh, I have lots of stuff in that pile. A customizable digital bumper sticker, an electronic flower I was trying to make for my mom, about a half dozen versions of a time machine, and a toaster that's incapable of burning toast— except that it doesn't work properly, which basically makes it a normal toaster. There's a bunch more, but we won't be looking at any of those yet. I've already bent my rules enough for one night."

"Aw, man," Freddie groaned.

"No laser guns?" Henry asked hopefully.

"No, Henry, sorry," Bentley said. "No laser guns. Not yet, at least."

"Well, as long as you're considering it," Henry said, trying to find some optimism. "I guess that fly trap thing was pretty cool."

Bentley smiled—I could hear it in his voice. "Thanks, Henry, that really means a lot to me." Henry was a grouch, but as long as he was honestly trying to be nice, we tried to see the glass as half full, even if he frequently knocked it over. "Hey, you guys wanna see something really cool?"

When asked to an audience like this one, that was a question that required no answer.

⚡

Ooph!

We appeared inside a huge room—his father's office. The room had double-tall ceilings; that part I could tell for myself. Henry said later that nearly every visible surface was either wood or leather and that the room was what we might imagine Bruce Wayne's office looked like.

"I'm not supposed to be in here, but, well, what he doesn't know won't hurt him," Bentley declared, just a bit of his nervousness showing. "Anyway, there." He must have pointed, because the others all oohed and aahed a bit.

"What is it?" Freddie asked.

"It's the emergency call button to Goodspeed. If the city is ever in trouble, under attack or something, my dad can press that button and a bunch of reinforcements would be here in moments."

More impressed cooing.

"So it's like the Bat phone," I said casually.

"Oh my God, it *is* like the Bat phone," Henry exclaimed.

"I've never heard of this," James said flatly, almost mildly offended. "I never knew anything like this existed."

"Well, they don't publicize it," Bentley explained. "There are only three of these in the city, all at the homes of board members."

"So what happens if a board member resigns?" Sometimes I was just a slave to my innate desire to understand the reasons behind things. "Does he just have a useless button on his office wall the rest of his life? Do they install a new one at the new guy's house?"

"Honestly," Bentley said, "I don't think board members ever resign. I'm pretty sure it's a lifetime appointment."

"Jeez," Henry scoffed. "Sounds like a crappy job to me."

"Anything involving work seems like a crappy job to you," I joked.

"Hey!"

"Has anyone ever pushed it"—Freddie paused to refuel on his inhaler before finishing his thought—"on accident?"

"Man, I hope not," Bentley said. "I can tell you firsthand you don't want to make my father angry, that's for sure." This line of thinking prompted Bentley to get nervous again and insist we return to the guesthouse. "Come on, guys, I don't want to get caught."

"Well," Henry said, "this was pretty cool. Definitely saved the best part of the tour for last." Even when giving a compliment, Henry was kind of a jerk.

⚡

Back in the guesthouse, the conversation turned quickly to the SuperSim and the fast-approaching school board hearing.

We sat on the floor in our sleeping bags in a giant circle. It was like we were sitting around an imaginary campfire. Henry sat across from me, with Bentley on his right. Then James, me, Donnie, Freddie, and back to Henry.

Bentley was laying out the challenges ahead of us if we were even lucky enough to win the appeal. "One of the things I've been thinking about that we're going to have to overcome," he said, "is speed."

"Speed?" Henry asked.

"Yeah. We're not very fast."

"Ah," I said in agreement.

Bentley continued. "I have a hard enough time walking, let alone running. You're in a wheelchair, Henry. Donnie is . . . well, Donnie. James and Phillip might be able to run the best out of all of us, but they can't see where they're going. And Freddie's going to break down from an asthma attack as soon as he takes three steps." It was true, particularly the part about Freddie. He puffed on his inhaler just about as often as James talked about his transporter business. "We're not going to be able to get involved in any chases, you know?"

He was right, and it was something I hadn't considered. How could we catch criminals when we couldn't even run? I was about to do my usual thing of looking for the silver lining when Bentley interrupted. "Did you see that?"

"No," James and I deadpanned, almost in unison. That would become a staple joke for the two of us, and it never failed to make us laugh. We called it "blind humor."

"No, seriously—I think Donnie was just laughing at me."

"Donnie wasn't laughing at you, Bentley. He's not even paying attention to you," Henry said bluntly. "He's in his own little world, as usual."

"I think you're wrong," Bentley said curiously and slowly, like a scientist peering into a microscope at something interesting. "I think maybe Donnie's been paying more attention than we thought, haven't you, Donnie?"

"Yes." I nearly soiled my pants when Donnie answered verbally. I had only ever heard him say yes or no a few times in school, and then it was only to his teacher's aide—and almost always at inappropriate times, like in the middle of the teacher's lecture. But answering questions and speaking conversationally? This was a stunning development, and I gasped out loud before slapping my right hand over my mouth.

We talked to Donnie plenty—don't get me wrong. We would say something about Old Lady Crouch—that's what we called her, somewhat affectionately—and then turn to him and say things like "Isn't that right, Donnie?" We weren't sure he understood us, but we always wanted him to feel like he was part of the group.

But he had never answered us verbally. *Ever*. This was unprecedented. We were all stunned.

Bentley recovered and grabbed the reins again. "Donnie, what's so funny?"

Nothing. I could practically hear the gears in Bentley's brain turning. "Donnie . . . did you have something to add to our conversation?"

Again, nothing.

"Donnie, can you run?"

"Yes."

Holy crap! He did it again!

Somehow, it was even more remarkable the second time.

Donnie's disability left him with a mild speech impediment, and from what little I'd heard him speak, he seemed to slur his words a little bit. But there was no mistaking that he had answered in the affirmative and had done so in direct response to Bentley's question.

"Donnie," Bentley said carefully, "can you run fast?" There was no immediate response that I could hear. I wondered if the breakthrough moment with Donnie had ended just as abruptly as it had begun. Bentley tried again, speaking more deliberately. "If I asked you to go outside and race one of us around the guesthouse, would you win?"

Without warning, I felt Donnie bolt up to a standing position and leap away from the circle of sleeping bags.

"Donnie!" Bentley yelled.

"What the heck?" Henry exclaimed.

Before anyone could fully process what was happening, Donnie ran to the front door of the guesthouse and sprinted outside. He'd taken Bentley's question literally, not hypothetically. He had completely misunderstood the meaning of what he'd been asked and was now outside running around the house, absolutely trouncing all of us in a race none of us were running.

Bentley and Henry scrambled and chased after him, calling his name in a shouted whisper, trying to avoid waking Ted and Olivia. I wasn't sure what the guys were thinking taking off after Donnie like that because they were the least likely people I knew to catch up to anyone—outside of myself and James, that is. But there wasn't anyone else around that could go after him either.

James, Freddie, and I just sat there shrugging in disbelief. I wasn't about to go running anywhere in a house I barely knew. I shook my head trying to clear the cobwebs and get a grip on the situation. "Is he really outside racing around the guesthouse right now?" I was asking myself as much as anything, thinking out loud, but James answered anyway.

"I'm pretty sure he is, yeah."

"Wow." I couldn't believe it. I was still reeling from the fact that Donnie could understand direct sentences and questions. "I didn't know he could understand us that well." Right away, I started searching my memory for anything I might have said previously in his presence that could have been embarrassing or hurt his feelings. I couldn't think of anything, which was comforting.

"I don't know, Phillip. All Bentley did was ask if he could win a race, and Donnie thought that meant it was time to race—immediately. Maybe he understands us more than we thought, but I wouldn't say he understands us *well* . . . you know what I'm saying?"

James was right. I realized only in that moment how true it was that Donnie's mind wasn't as mature as his body. We'd been told that on the first day of school, but I guess I hadn't given much thought as to what it really meant.

After a few more moments of quiet, the front door burst open again, and in three great strides, Donnie reached his sleeping bag, plopping to the floor with a light thud. His breathing was quickened, but he wasn't gasping for breath or anything. And he just sat there, breathing rhythmically, as though nothing strange at all had just occurred.

I wanted to speak but couldn't think of anything to say. I was afraid of Donnie misunderstanding again and doing something unpredictable.

After a few seconds of the four of us just sitting there in stunned silence, I heard the door open again. Henry and Bentley entered, and they seemed relieved to see Donnie. "There you are," Bentley said with a sigh of relief. He used his cane as he made his way back to the circle, with Henry's wheelchair wheels squeaking behind him. They were both gassed, panting and wheezing from a level of physical exertion neither of them was used to.

"I guess we do have one person on our team after all who can run fast." Bentley paused before sitting back down to scold Donnie the way a loving father would. He spoke for all of us when he said, "You scared the crap out of me, Donnie, do you know that?"

"I win," Donnie said, beaming.

And that's when the entire group just lost it. It was one of those moments where the situation hits you just right, and you cannot help but laugh uncontrollably. "Yes, you did," Bentley managed to say between gasps. "You certainly did win, Donnie."

The giggling became infectious. Even Donnie started chuckling.

We laughed so loud and so long that we woke up Ted, who had to come out and tell us to quiet down and go to bed already. It struck me as humorous that it was ultimately the ruckus after the fact that woke up Ted, not the incident itself—not the sounds of the door opening and closing or kids running around the house outside, but the laughter.

We tried our best to calm down, and as Ted turned out the lights and headed back to his room, we all got situated in our sleeping bags and prepared to go to sleep. There was a bit more giggling and chatter for a few minutes, but it died down pretty quickly. It was later than I'd ever stayed up, and most everyone was exhausted.

As I lay there trying to fall asleep, I felt a new sense of responsibility for Donnie, and it was heavy. We all took care to look out for him and be inclusive with him, and we had already grown a bit protective of him from an emotional standpoint. But now, with a fresh demonstration of our influence over him, I began to worry for his physical safety.

What if he misunderstands us during the SuperSim and gets hurt?

I shuddered. Granted, any of us could be hurt during the SuperSim, but it wasn't quite the same with Donnie. I wasn't sure he had the same measure of free will that we did. He was participating as an extension of his loyalty to us, not because he wanted to play superhero or even understood what it was. He just wanted to belong.

I thought about how protective he was of us special ed kids at school— single-handedly keeping us bully free. Would that same instinct, combined with the newly discovered eagerness to please, cause Donnie to do something rash and get himself hurt in the SuperSim? It suddenly seemed like a very real possibility to me.

But then again, I did have a tendency to over worry. I was always seeing trouble where it likely didn't exist, which made it nearly impossible to tell the real dangers from the imaginary ones.

Just as I was finally quieting my mind and starting to drift to sleep, Henry whispered, "I win." And the unquenchable laughter started right up all over again.

9

THE SICK DAY

Our team was still barred from competing. We'd filed our appeal paperwork with the school board—the first legal step we could take—but had yet to have our day before the school board to state our case. We held a couple more get-togethers—strategy meetings, mostly—but it didn't seem to be helping very much. I think it was tough for us to give practice our full attention when we carried a secret fear we would lose the appeal.

Bentley seemed confident in our chances of winning, but I wasn't quite convinced. In truth, the hearing loomed large for me. Things usually had to be black and white for me to have any comfort, and our eligibility status for the SuperSim was anything but black and white. It was a muddled gray mess as far as I was concerned.

Despite Bentley's insistence that our rights were being infringed upon, I knew from Mrs. Crouch's Custodial Studies class that custodian law superseded American laws. I feared the school would simply deny our appeal on the grounds of doing so for our own protection, and that would be the end of it.

With the hearing now two days away, at least the worrying would soon come to an end.

It was so heavy on my mind that I didn't even notice that Donnie wasn't in school that Monday. He'd seemed fine on Friday at Bentley's sleepover—fine enough to spontaneously race around the house in his pajamas—but I guess he picked up a cold or something. But again, I didn't even notice he was missing.

My thoughts were consumed by the SuperSim and our planned defense of our petition.

My teachers blathered on about the usual stuff while I ran over contingency scenarios in my head. *What if they deny our appeal without hearing our arguments? What if they hear our arguments but deny us anyway? What if all this meeting and training and practicing we're doing leads to a big fat nothing?*

Looking back, it's easy to see that I was far too anxious for a seventh grader, and it wasn't going to get any better with what awaited me in life.

Bentley tried to reassure me at lunch. "Phillip, look, there's no way they're going to keep us from competing. It's discrimination, plain and simple. It's just the right thing to do—logically, morally, and legally."

"But that's a regular human law, Bentley," I argued for the hundredth time, "not a custodian law. There's no guarantee that they'll even care about anything else."

In my head, the school officials were ogres, evil trolls who took pleasure in denying us disabled kids any social enjoyment just out of sheer meanness. They were not ogres, obviously. In fact, I'm quite sure they were legitimately concerned about our safety. But at the time, I couldn't see them as anything other than another group of adults trying to keep a group of kids from having fun.

"What's the grounds for keeping us out, then?" Bentley challenged me, daring me to play the devil's advocate—a role I played quite naturally, as it turned out.

"Safety," I said plainly, as though the mere word itself would end the debate. "They're going to claim that we might get hurt." This was more than speculation; this was fact. My father had tried briefly to get us to reconsider fighting the school board, no doubt at Mom's request, and in doing so, told us a story.

It seems the SuperSim had been, in one form or another, a staple of the custodian high school experience for generations, going back to the very beginning. The first SuperSims happened centuries before the first Olympic Games in Greece. Custodian parents had long considered it a responsibility to prepare the future generations of crime-fighters and do-gooders with a series of tests and trials.

Until one kid ruined it all for everyone.

A boy named Samuel Meyers, who was blessed with the ability to fly, had been killed during a Freepoint SuperSim back in the early 1980s. The town had been rocked to its core, Dad said, especially given that Samuel was a disabled kid. Dad wasn't just regurgitating a story he'd been told. He was actually a student at the time and had even participated in that final SuperSim event.

Samuel Meyers had been blind, like James and me, but was competing on a team with able-bodied kids. His teammates had been tagged by the adult "villains" and were out of the competition, leaving Samuel the only remaining member of his team. In a last-ditch effort to help his team win the simulation, he had chosen to try and fly a hostage out of the center of the fight to safety.

It hadn't ended well. He knew the area, as any prepared blind person would, and shouldn't have had any trouble flying the short distance to the simulation safe zone—except for all the other people involved in the simulation. Samuel forgot about them. And a few of those other individuals also had the power of flight.

So Samuel had unwittingly hurled himself and his rescued hostage into the body of a high school senior who had been hovering overhead surveying the battle and barking out commands for his own team. All three of them went tumbling four stories to the ground below in a tangled flurry of arms and legs. Samuel and the other student had died from the injuries they received from the fall.

The "hostage" had been an adult who had the power of indestructibility—which I guess is why they chose her to play a hostage in the SuperSim—and had survived the fall just fine, at least physically.

The city officials and the board, crushed by the tragedy, had suspended the SuperSim indefinitely after that incident, and it hadn't returned in over twenty years.

"But more than that," I continued, "any of these kids could get hurt because of us. They're going to say we're a danger to ourselves and to our fellow students if we compete in the SuperSim. You know the story same as I do, Bentley. You were there when my dad told it." The news of our petition had spread through school rapidly, followed by the whispered retellings of the story of the blind boy who could fly and had caused both his own and another student's death. There were probably some students sitting around us right now who didn't think the special ed class ought to be competing.

"I heard the story. But that was an accident, Phillip. An accident can happen to any kid, whether he's disabled or not. Bottom line is it's not fair to keep us out, and we have to make them see that Wednesday night."

"So that's our case, then? Just show up at the hearing and say it's not fair and hope they change their minds? Should we roll around on the ground and throw a tantrum too? Do you think that would help?" I was getting frustrated at Bentley's persistent optimism, mostly because it conflicted horribly with my own growing pessimism.

"Well, not in so many words, I guess . . . but yeah. We're going to show them how unfair it is through legal evidence and personal conviction. We're going to overwhelm them with case law examples and hammer things home with the Americans with Disabilities Act." He certainly sounded fully prepared. "And shoot," he added, "if that doesn't work, we'll resort to some good old-fashioned begging. I'm certainly not above throwing a tantrum."

"Ha." I had to chuckle at that. "That'll work for sure," I said sarcastically before taking another emphatic bite of my sandwich.

"How do you think I got that Ping-Pong table?" Bentley replied wryly.

"I just want to have the whole thing over with already," Henry chimed in. "If we're out, then fine. I can go about being bitter and angry and then get back to my life. If we're in, then we can carry on with our practices without feeling like the whole thing is a waste of time."

Henry wasn't much for expending unnecessary effort, and I guess I wouldn't be either if I were in a wheelchair. But mostly I think he just didn't want to get his hopes up only to have them snuffed out, and I definitely could sympathize with that.

"It's not going to be a waste," I argued. "We have to learn somehow, especially with what happened on the news the other night. If they really do want us to be safe, they're going to have to let go of some of their fears and let us start learning how to use our powers."

I wanted to be a superhero more than anything. I felt like it finally gave me a purpose in life, one that I could be proud of. I wanted to contribute to this legacy and turn my previously boring life into something meaningful. As anxious as I was about the hearing, I wasn't about to let a silly high school simulation stop me from pursuing that goal.

"Maybe you're not supposed to even have powers." It was Chad's voice, forever burned into my memory from the run-in on that first day of school. I almost never forget a voice. He was behind James and me; Henry, Freddie, and Bentley were on the other side of the table. I kept my head down and tried not to move. "Maybe you're all a bunch of accidents—did you ever think of that?" He sounded bitter and angry and looking to pick a fight. I wondered how long he'd been standing there listening to our conversation.

And that was the moment I realized that Donnie wasn't in school that day. Because if he had been, Chad would never even have gotten this close to our table—let alone started harassing us. My stomach dropped with the realization that our gentle giant of a protector was absent.

"Yeah," Steve concurred. "You guys aren't cut out for this hero stuff, and you know it. So why are you trying to ruin everyone else's fun?"

"Leave us alone," Bentley muttered, clearly annoyed. He didn't sound as scared as I felt. He just seemed inconvenienced. But I knew Chad and Steve weren't going to miss their first opportunity to mess with us since the school year had begun. They wouldn't go away that easily.

"It's you who should be leaving us alone, cripple!" Chad spat, with venom in his voice. "Because I'm pretty sure the last time they let disabled freaks like you compete in the SuperSim, you ended up killing one of us normal kids. And maybe I'm not so sure I'm ready to put my life at risk by competing with you goons."

"Then maybe you should just bow out, Chad," Henry spat back, defiant as ever. "If you're so worried, maybe you should just let the real heroes participate."

The silence was deafening as I waited for Chad's next barb. And then, almost in a whisper, I heard his voice as he leaned his head down between James and me. "We're the real heroes, chump." He slapped the side of my head sharply. "You know how I know? How do I know, Steve?" His tone was even and calm, the way one might speak to a five-year-old when lecturing them.

"Because both your legs work?" Steve cackled. "Because you can see?"

"That's right. Because God didn't burden me with the kinds of imperfections he put on you guys. That's how I know who the real heroes are. If you were supposed to be heroes, you'd be able to use your powers properly." His calm manner of speaking made his words sound only more menacing.

And suddenly I felt myself standing, almost without my own permission. Between the memories of the smashed cell phone, the tension from the upcoming hearing, and this current verbal assault from Chad and Steve, I guess I snapped. "I'd like to see you outside of the no power zone, you big jerk, so I can show you just how well my powers work." I wasn't sure where the outburst came from. It was quite out of character for me. I was typically interested in *avoiding* conflict, not escalating it. But here I was, having risen up out of my seat to turn and face this idiot and fan his fire. I instantly regretted it.

My display of bravado was incredibly short-lived. No sooner had I gotten my sentence out and risen to a full standing position than I felt a pulverizing blow to my stomach.

Being punched in the stomach is something I wouldn't wish on anyone. It's awful. For the first few panicky seconds, it feels like you may never breathe again. Outside of Patrick, I'd never really been punched, and Patrick's punches were hardly representative of the general public.

But Chad had punched me quite thoroughly. It was a punch with a sense of purpose. It was as shocking as it was painful.

It forced the air out of my lungs like a vacuum, leaving me gasping as I stumbled backward. My limbs flailed in panic as I started to fall. On my way down, I banged my head against the lunch table, and that must have been when I blacked out.

I woke up almost immediately.

It definitely seemed immediate to me, at least. No sooner had I felt my body slumping to the ground and my skull slamming into the table than I was awake. But I had actually been out for a good sixty seconds or so, according to Bentley.

That was an odd thing to learn—that I'd lost an entire minute of my life in a blink. Just . . . gone. I would never get it back.

There was quite a commotion in the cafeteria. Fights in a high school always draw a crowd. Unfortunately for my bloodthirsty peers, this fight had ended before anyone even knew it was happening—and that included me.

"What happened?" I asked, a bit fuzzy on the details of how I ended up on the floor, though it was coming back to me slowly.

"You just got the crap beat out of you by Chad Burke, that's what happened," Henry said plainly, as though he was reading the world's most boring newspaper article.

"He punched me," I remembered. I tried to sit up, but a large hand held me down.

"Don't move, son. Stay there." It was a man's voice.

"Who's that?"

"Mr. Peterson."

Mr. Peterson was one of the senior teachers at the school. He must have been on lunch duty.

"Why shouldn't I move?" I asked, lying flat on my back, my arms stretched out alongside my body.

"I just want the nurse to check you out first, okay?" Mr. Peterson sounded about forty, but there was a worn quality to his voice, as though he'd been through this kind of thing many times before. He wasn't panicked nor was he completely calm. "What's your name, son?"

"Phillip Sallinger," I answered.

"What happened here?"

"He just got the crap beat out of him by Chad Burke, that's what happened." It was Henry again, giving a slightly more excited line reading for Mr. Peterson than he had for me.

"Did anyone else see this?"

A chorus of replies followed in the affirmative. Evidently, there had been several witnesses to Chad's sucker punch. Mr. Peterson stood up and started talking to some of the nearby students, getting their version of the story. I suddenly realized that Chad was going to be in some serious trouble over this, no matter who his father was. There was too much evidence against him. The thought brought a wide smile to my face.

"What are you grinning at?" It was Bentley.

"I just realized how lopsidedly I won that fight." I grinned.

Bentley sounded like he didn't think he heard me correctly when he responded, "Right. You really kicked his ass, Phil."

"He's delusional, Bentley. You know . . . cuckoo!" I could picture Henry drawing little circles with his finger by the side of his head as he said it.

"I'm not delusional," I stated. "Think about it. I may be lying on the floor of the cafeteria right now with a painful stomach and a searing headache, but I still come out ahead."

"How do you figure?"

"He just punched a blind kid in the stomach in front of a hundred witnesses. I mean, seriously, who punches a blind kid in the stomach? A coward, that's who. That's like shooting someone in the back in one of those Westerns. Nobody respects that. I don't think he gains any brownie points with his classmates by picking on a kid who can't see the fist coming. Plus, he's going to get suspended or expelled or something. If you think about it that way, who really ends up the loser in this situation?"

"You do," Henry declared, somewhat stunned that I could see it any other way. "You're lying on the ground with a stomach ache and a concussion, and he's probably off getting high fives from his buddies."

"I don't care about high fives, Henry."

"Phillip's got a point." Bentley had finally come around.

"It's not like they can embarrass me any more than they did the first day of school."

"Yeah," Henry countered. "Well, good luck getting him in any trouble, Phillip. His dad basically runs this whole custodian operation, you know."

"He can get his son out of smashing Phillip's phone," Bentley argued on my behalf, "but not this. This is too big, I think."

"Maybe," Henry allowed. "But I'll believe it when I see it."

"Me too," I joked.

"Ha!" It was James, excited to hear "blind humor" in the midst of a more serious situation. That kid had a way of staying out of a conversation until a random moment, usually after you'd forgotten he was around. I liked to think that he just didn't care much about the little debates Bentley and Henry and I had and instead used the time to plan more strategies for his fledgling transport business and come up with new marketing slogans.

The nurse arrived at that moment and was followed almost immediately by my mother. The school had called her pretty quickly, and she just zapped on over from wherever she happened to be driving at the time. She was a former nursing student herself, and she and the school nurse checked me out. I guess they determined that my neck wasn't broken because they finally let me stand up.

Mr. Peterson—who was surprisingly burly—carried me down the hall and then out to my mother's car. Mom drove me straight to the hospital to get checked out. I had to endure a few tests and a giant machine that the technician said typically made claustrophobic people nervous. I told him that it was hard for me to get too worked up about small spaces since I couldn't see my boundaries in any space. He still gave me a lollipop as a parting gift, and I accepted it, even though I hadn't really been all that scared.

After a couple hours at the hospital, the doctor gave me a clean bill of health and a bottle of extra-strength headache medicine. I would have a bump on my head for several days, he said, and he forbade me from going to school for at least one day to recuperate. But otherwise, I was going to be just fine.

Mom seemed relieved but still a little concerned. I guess that sort of thing comes naturally. We drove for a few minutes before she spoke. "Do you want to talk about what happened?" she asked cautiously.

The headache pills were a long way off from doing their job, and I was simply not in the mood to talk. "Not really."

She stopped at a stop sign and turned left. I knew we were only a mile or so from home just based on the turns she made. "The principal said that the other boy was teasing you and your friends," she said, trailing off for a second before continuing, "and that you stood up to him, so he punched you."

"Yeah," I said, corroborating Mr. Dempsey's account of the event.

"Well, whenever you want to talk about it, I'm here for you. But I just want you to know that I'm proud of you, honey, for standing up to those bullies." I normally hated it when she called me honey, but really, that was only when other people were around. When it was just the two of us, I secretly liked it.

It opened me up a tiny bit. "It really hurt," I said. I wasn't looking for sympathy but merely stating it as a surprising new fact.

She chuckled softly with pity. "Oh, Phillip, I bet it did. Do you need to take some of those pills the doctor prescribed?"

"No, no." I waved my hand in dismissal. "It doesn't hurt now. Well, it doesn't hurt nearly as much now that I took the ones he gave me at the office. I just meant . . . in general. Getting punched in the stomach hurts a lot more than you'd think it would."

"What makes you think I don't know?" she asked playfully.

"You've been punched in the stomach before?" It was tough to believe at first.

"Sure I have," she said, making one last turn onto our street. "And the face and the back and . . . well, I've been punched, kicked, or zapped in just about any place you can think of, son. It's all a part of the hero's job."

It was a tough idea for me to accept. The thought of my mother being punched in the stomach was uncomfortable. Painful, really. I didn't like it at all. This was my mother. How dare these people assault her? I'd come to grips with the fact that my parents had superpowers; in fact, I had witnessed them on display a number of times. But I hadn't really spent much time thinking of them as combatants.

Almost sensing my thoughts, Mom explained, "There's only one way to avoid being injured on the job as a custodian, Phillip, and that's to not become one in the first place. There *will* be bumps and bruises along the way. Granted, they won't always come from school bullies—they shouldn't *ever* come from school bullies—but they will come."

"How do you not die?" I asked. "I mean . . . I can take a punch to the stomach as a custodian, and now I've learned that firsthand. But how do you know the difference in scenarios between a punch in the stomach and a bullet to the head?"

"Goodness, I don't like hearing you talk like that. 'Bullet to the head'—is that from those comic books?" She didn't leave me any time to answer her before getting back on topic. "You don't know the difference, Phillip. That's the point. That's why you won't be fighting real crime until you're in college. It's a feeling you get—one you learn. And you trust your gut. But you're never sure." The car turned into the driveway, and I could hear the automatic garage door opening.

"I love you. I know I say that a lot," she added softly, "but you and your brother mean more to me than my own life itself. As your mother, I have to tell you this because it applies to your father and me and you and your brother, pretty much forever." The car pulled into the garage and came to a stop. "A hero is only a hero because he or she walks into that situation knowing full well they may not walk out. Whether they save the day or die trying, they're heroes because they make the sacrifice just by showing up."

I didn't respond verbally. And Mom seemed okay with that. It was a pretty heavy speech, after all. She turned off the car, and we went into the house without another word.

That night, Mom and Dad kept waking me up every hour or so, telling me they loved me and patting my head goodnight. I would learn the next day that they had been instructed to do so by the doctor as a way of making sure I didn't have a concussion. Apparently, they had to wake me up frequently to make sure that I could still wake up at all, which has a certain backward poetry to it, I think.

Normally, I would have eavesdropped on their conversation out in the kitchen—and I'm sure they had some interesting words to exchange about their helpless little blind boy—but the headache medicine Mom made me take before bed made me sleepy, and that night, I welcomed my dreams.

10

IN REVERSE

Bentley and Henry called the house the evening of the incident and begged my parents to let them stop by and visit me, but my folks had been too concerned with my getting enough rest. But considering that I was headed back to school on Wednesday and that the hearing was that same night, Mom and Dad spoiled me with a rare display of kindness: they let my two friends sleep over on the next night, Tuesday—a school night. We had to promise that we wouldn't use our powers around the house until after Patrick had gone to bed and that we wouldn't stay up too late. Both seemed like fair compromises to me.

We laughed and ate pizza—Jack's again, quickly becoming my favorite pizza ever, and I had lived in New York. Around eight thirty or so, Mom sent Patrick off to get cleaned up for bed. Not long after that, she and Dad retired to their room, leaving the three of us on our own in the living room. The second they disappeared down the hall, I breathed a sigh of relief.

I thought they'd never go to bed.

"I thought they'd never go to bed," Henry said in relief.

"I was just thinking that," I said, acknowledging the coincidence.

"I know," he replied, smiling.

It took a second to realize that he'd just used his powers on me. He had read my thoughts, the little bugger. I was impressed and surprised and offended all at the same time. "Hey," I said.

Henry started laughing. "Ha ha, I got you," he said, proud of himself.

"I have to be careful what I think when I'm around you. I keep forgetting you can read my mind."

"Do me, do me!" Bentley exclaimed excitedly.

There was a brief silence.

Then Henry spoke. "Man, that pizza was really good!"

"You're right!" And we all laughed some more.

"Wait, wait . . . do me again," I said, having just cooked up something hilarious.

Another quick pause while I concentrated on a specific thought, and he focused on reading it. He started reciting it before he'd finished it, just as I had hoped. "Henry is a doofus—hey, wait a minute!"

We all roared with stifled laughter, trying not to make too much noise. No laughter is harder to curb than the kind that occurs when you're supposed to be quiet. "That's not fair," Henry cried, chuckling despite himself.

After much snorting and giggling, we finally calmed down.

"Hey, Phillip, you know what's just occurred to me?" Bentley inquired.

"What's that?"

"I've never seen you use your powers."

He was right. The only "practices" we'd had for the SuperSim had ultimately turned into strategy sessions for the hearing.

Henry hadn't realized it either. "Oh yeah," he said. "How could we let it go this long without asking him to show us?"

"You're right," I agreed. "That's kind of funny." Most of the time we spent together was in the school, where powers were blocked.

"Well . . . show us," Bentley urged.

"Okay," I decided. I stood up and patted my hands around the couch until I found the remote control. I didn't watch much television, but I listened to plenty of it and had worked the controller many times. I knew the object well.

I extended the remote toward Bentley. "Here," I instructed. "Take this."

"Okay," he said cautiously.

"Hold it in your hands, with both your palms facing up, with the remote pointing at me."

"This is gonna be good," Henry muttered under his breath excitedly.

Bentley did as he was told. "Okay, done."

"Okay then." I stood up and walked over to the far living room wall near where my mother's crossword chair sat. That put me roughly nine or ten feet away from the guys. "You ready?"

"Yeah," Bentley stated.

"*Yeah*," Henry said enthusiastically.

"Here goes." I concentrated on the remote control, remembering its shape and the weight of it in my hands. Slowly, I stuck out my right arm, my hand open and facing Bentley. I visualized the object leaping out of his flattened hands and zipping through the air into my own. And then it happened, just as I had willed it to, snapping into my grasp with a loud "smack." I'd been practicing in my room every day with various objects and had gotten pretty good at this particular trick.

"Whoa!" Henry declared.

Bentley seemed equally impressed. "Holy cow, Phillip—that was amazing!"

"Really?" It seemed sort of old hat to me by now. Like a party trick. If only I was allowed to use it to shut my brother up.

"Are you kidding me? It's fantastic! Do it again."

I walked over and returned the remote to Bentley and then went back to the wall. It was even easier the second time, and I didn't have to concentrate nearly as hard. The remote again flew across the room and into my hand.

Smack.

"Outstanding!" Henry praised. "That is hands down one of the coolest things I've ever seen."

"How does it work, Phillip?" Bentley was by far the most inquisitive kid I'd ever known. He always wanted to know *more* about things, prodding with hows and whys and whens.

"Well, I guess I just focus on the object and try to picture it doing what I want it to do. And if my focus is good, it just happens." Then I added, "But I can do it only with objects I'm kind of familiar with."

"Why's that?"

It was odd to be in the position of teaching Bentley anything. "Because telekinesis requires me to know the general dimensions and weight of an object before I can move it. Sighted people, like my dad, can move things just by looking at them. They can actually see the dimensions with their eyes, and that also gives them an approximate reading on the weight. But since I can't do that, I usually have to familiarize myself with things by handling them."

"Man, that's too bad," Henry mourned, not meaning to be rude. "Imagine what you could do if you could see."

As usual, I wasn't offended by his accidental insult. "You're telling me, Henry," I agreed, "you're telling me."

"If you had my power, your blindness would barely even be a factor, you know? I don't really need my eyes at all to do what I do."

"I want to know more about how that works too," Bentley announced.

"Well, what do you want to know?" Henry said.

It was a mistake to be so open-ended with someone like Bentley. "Can you read every thought in a person's brain or just some of them? Can you do it selectively, person by person, or do you get everyone's thoughts at once? Can you turn it on and off whenever you want?"

Henry cut him off before Bentley could go any further. "Okay, okay—one question at a time, Bentley, jeez. Let's see . . . I can definitely do it selectively, and I can turn it on or off at will."

"Awesome." I exhaled. It was my turn to be in awe.

"But I can read only fully formed thoughts. Like, when you think to yourself in complete sentences. I can't see or hear fragments or the fleeting beginnings of thoughts that fade quickly away. And I can't read everything in your mind, only the current thought or picture."

"Picture?" Bentley asked, seeking more information.

"Yeah, you know . . . the visual. I can see what another person sees with their eyes or any fully formed thought they express."

"That's kind of amazing," Bentley admitted.

"And it's only in real time too. I can't access your memories or anything . . . unless your fully formed thought is about a memory, I guess."

"But how do you actually get that thought or picture? How do you turn it on, so to speak?" His questions could be relentless.

"I don't know," Henry said, trying to find the words to explain it. "It's sort of like reaching into your brain and plucking out the latest file, I suppose, like a giant mental hand. I just have to concentrate for a moment, like Phillip, and I kind of picture myself reaching into your brain to grab whatever's there on the forefront of your mind. And then I have it."

"But you can see actual pictures? Or just ideas and concepts?"

"Actual pictures. Tell you what, go around behind the couch where I can't see you, and look at something. I'll tell you what it is."

Bentley was excited to get a demonstration, and he slowly got up. He stumbled a bit at first but caught himself with the arm of the couch and then sauntered slowly around the sofa. I never knew what to do in those moments when his palsy caused him to trip or stagger. I was usually shocked at first, and by the time I realized I should help him, he had usually already recovered and moved on. He didn't seem to let it slow him down too much.

After a few moments he announced, "Okay, I'm ready."

It didn't take long at all for Henry to work his magic. "You're looking at a framed photograph on the kitchen counter. It has Phillip and Patrick in it, and Patrick is wearing a blue baseball cap. Phillip has on a red shirt and is smiling."

"That's freaking incredible," Bentley said. "You really do see the same thing I'm looking at!"

"Yeah," Henry said, like we shouldn't have needed any proof. "I told you I could."

Bentley returned to his sleeping bag and sat for a moment in silence. It was such an abrupt silence that it was clear his gears were turning, processing this new information about our powers.

I thought I'd try to fill the silence while he worked it over in his head. "Henry, I wish I could try it too, man, but I'm afraid I don't have any mental pictures for you to grab." It was a pretty bad joke, but if James had been there, it would have gotten at least one laugh, I'm sure.

Suddenly, Bentley spoke up. "Henry, I want to ask you a question."

"Okay."

"Have you ever tried it in reverse?"

"What?" Henry didn't understand, and frankly, neither did I.

"Have you ever tried to use your power in reverse?"

"What are you talking about, Bentley? You mean while backing up in a car?"

"No, Henry. I'm talking about your powers. You said it's like reaching your hand into someone's mind and grabbing the most recent image or thought, right?"

"Yeah," Henry answered, still not sure what Bentley was getting at.

"Then I'm asking if you've ever gone in the reverse . . . tried to reach your hand into someone's mind and drop something off instead of pick something up. Have you ever put a thought or a picture into someone's mind?"

That statement floored me. It was one of those moments where I realized just how accelerated and advanced Bentley's mental capacity was compared to mine. Not in a million years would I have thought to wonder if Henry's power could work backward. I was pretty bright, but I just didn't think like that. No one my age did except for Bentley.

"Well, no, I guess I haven't. Why?"

So Bentley explained, with enthusiasm and a growing energy. "Well, every power has a root definition. For Phillip, the most basic way to explain his ability is that he can move things by thinking about them. It's not that he has to feel them first—that's just how his disability augments his powers. His root power is the ability to move things. For Penelope, that girl in our class, it's that she can control the weather. Not that she can create tornados, which she can, or that she can call up thunderstorms, which she can. But simply that she can control weather. She could make it partly cloudy and a pleasant eighty degrees if she wanted to."

"I am so lost," Henry muttered.

"Me too," I agreed.

Bentley didn't slow down, though. "Now, Henry, it may be that your root definition is that you can pull out thoughts from other people's minds and that's it. Only taking. Or," he said dramatically, "it *could* be that your root power is simply the ability to reach inside someone's mind. And whether you take something or leave something is up to you. Now . . . we have Phillip here"—he patted me on the shoulder—"who, as it turns out, needs sight in order to fully maximize his powers. And we have you, who can reach inside people's minds and do things with images. What would happen, I wonder, if you were to try and reverse your power . . . to take an image from your own eyes and drop it into Phillip's brain?"

I swear to God, Bentley was the smartest person I ever knew.

11

THE HEARING

We spent the better part of an hour trying to make Bentley's theory a reality. Henry tried with all his might to turn his powers around and make them work the opposite direction, but nothing happened. But we were all convinced it was possible. Bentley made too much sense. His hypothesis was too sound.

I had protested at first, concerned that my blindness meant that I couldn't see images whatsoever, even ones from Henry's brain. But Bentley didn't think blindness worked like that. "Your brain's still capable of processing images," he explained, "but you just don't have any receivers. Your eyes don't work. You can't take in the signal of an image. See, the eyes just send what they capture to the brain for processing, and that's where the image is made. So even though you're without vision, if Henry's powers can serve as the signal carrier to your mind, you should be able to 'see' what he sees, so to speak."

So we tried, over and over again. But we never got anywhere. Nothing happened. And we had a hearing to rest up for, so we reluctantly went to bed.

That night, somewhat predictably, I dreamed about Henry sending me images from his eyes to my brain, and it was glorious. We were a well-oiled machine, chasing some bad guys through an alley. I saw whatever Henry saw and used those images to sharpen and strengthen my powers. Of course, it was just a dream, but I was throwing bodies against the wall and really flexing my superhero muscles.

We stumbled through the Sallinger morning routine like zombies. We'd stayed up too late laughing and trying to perfect our abilities. There is a reason that parents don't typically allow sleepovers on school nights, and we were finding that out firsthand. We were grumpy and tired. That feeling lasted well into the school day to the point that I began to have serious anxiety about our ability to focus and be alert for the hearing.

At lunch I learned that Chad Burke had been expelled from school. Freddie had all the latest gossip about it; that kid was a good listener, and his mother was the secretary to a well-connected board member. "Chad's father packed him up and shipped him off to Goodspeed." I heard his inhaler, then a deep exhale, and then, "He's going to live with his aunt and uncle. He was gone within twenty-four hours of the fight."

How about that?

Instead of using his position of authority to pull strings to get his son out of trouble, as I think we all expected, Mr. Burke had the opposite reaction. Embarrassed by his misbehaving son, who had a long history of troublemaking, he'd sent him somewhere out of sight and out of mind.

I enjoyed hearing the details of Chad's demise, I won't lie. I didn't feel even a little guilty about it. He'd twice singled me out for torment, for absolutely no reason whatsoever. Served him right. I was glad he was no longer a threat.

Donnie had returned to school Tuesday while I was home in bed recuperating. The guys had told him about what happened, though they couldn't be sure he'd followed what they were telling him. They did say he got a bit agitated and restless afterward. But he was his quiet, normal self by the time I returned.

"So, how does it all work?" I asked Bentley. "I've never been to one of these."

"Me neither," Bentley replied with a nervous laugh. "But from what I understand, it's a pretty straightforward affair. The school board is made up of seven members, and they sit up front facing the rest of the room. They'll ask us a bunch of questions, and we'll respond, and then they'll make a decision."

"You mean we don't even get to give an opening statement or anything, like on those TV court shows?" Henry sounded alarmed.

"No. They don't have opening statements. Just the petition that we turned in two weeks ago. They've already met and discussed it, and the hearing is our chance to answer any questions they have."

"That's messed up," Henry declared, shoving a bite of food in his mouth.

"It is," Bentley agreed. "But it's all we've got. We have to work our arguments into our answers."

"And you're going to do all the talking, right?" I was sure about one thing: I didn't want to do the talking. Public speaking was not my thing. Bentley, on the other hand, was eloquent, mature, and articulate. Plus, he knew the rules and the laws on the subject. He'd been studying for days.

"They can ask questions of anyone whose name is on the petition. That means me, you, Henry, James . . . any of us, even Donnie. Oh, and your dad."

My heart sank. "What? You didn't say anything about that!"

"Relax, Phillip, it'll be fine. He's the adult we got to sign our initial petition, that's all. We just have to all tell the truth and answer honestly, and we'll be fine. I'm telling you that this is just a formality. If the school board denies our petition, we'll file a lawsuit, and they aren't going to want us to sue because that's going to create a whole big mess and draw all kinds of attention to the matter. Believe me, this is going to be easy, guys. Besides, it's not like there's going to be some huge audience or anything. It's a school board hearing. Our families will probably be the only people there besides us and the board members. Relax. Everything's going to be fine. You'll see."

For the first time since I'd met him, Bentley was wrong.

There *was* an audience, and it was enormous. From our position in the front of the room, it sounded like there were three hundred people behind us. Henry said there were people standing all along the back wall because there weren't any seats left. Our little hearing was of interest to practically the whole town, much to our surprise. I hadn't dreamed that anyone aside from us would care about our quest. And yet, here they were.

The acoustics told me the meeting room had a much taller ceiling than most rooms. But the added space wasn't doing anything to help the temperature of the room. Hot to begin with, it had gotten only warmer with the collective body heat of the crowd.

I had a hard time believing that the typical school board meeting involved this kind of turnout. I had no idea why they were so interested in our little hearing and was soon struck by a new thought. *Are they here to support us or oppose us?*

"Could go either way," Henry said, as though I'd actually spoken my thoughts aloud. I turned my head in his direction to offer a scolding about how uncool it was to read minds without permission, but he quickly offered a humble apology. "Sorry, Phillip—nervous habit, I guess."

"Reading minds is your nervous habit? That's what you do when you're nervous?" It wasn't that I didn't believe him, because I did. It was just a strange thing to do when anxiety struck. Plus, I was a little jumpy.

"Well, whenever I get too worked up about something, my powers sometimes kind of go haywire a bit. They have a mind of their own. I didn't mean to do it, Phillip, honestly. It was an accident." He sounded very contrite, and I decided he was probably telling the truth.

That's when I realized how strange it was to hear Henry so freaked out. Henry usually spoke from a sense of confidence and assurance, even when he was completely faking it. I thought it would be a good idea to try and calm him down a bit, if only so he wouldn't make me more nervous. So, forgetting the pit in my own stomach, I offered my best encouragement. "Don't sweat it, man. Everything's going to be fine. There's nothing to be worried about. It's like Bentley said, the worst thing they can do—the worst possible outcome—is that they decide not to let us participate in the SuperSim. And they've already done that once, so . . . we won't be any worse off than we are already, you know?"

I'm not sure how I had evolved into the healer of the group. In all honesty, I never really belonged to any kind of peer group before, so maybe I was that way by nature and was only just now discovering it.

But I wasn't very good at it on this evening. I may have even made him feel worse. I felt him grip my arm, and he spoke in a crackled whisper as though on the verge of choking up. "I know. But it's too late, Phillip." I could tell that he was quivering and shaking a bit, and I thought for a moment he was having a panic attack, though I confess I had no idea what that actually meant.

"What do you mean?" I asked, trying to gently prod for more of an explanation.

"If they don't let us compete . . . I don't know what I'm going to do, because it's too late. It's too late, Phillip, and I couldn't help it. I already got my hopes up!" His voice wavered a bit. It was a rare moment of transparency for a guy like Henry, who didn't typically show much emotion.

I didn't begin to have the words to encourage him, though, so I opted for the truth. "I know, Henry. Me too." I grabbed his shoulder and squeezed—the way my father did when he was trying to make me feel better or hammer home a life lesson. "Me too."

It felt hollow. The newly awakened healer in me couldn't let it go at that, so I tried to tack on some kind of pick-me-up. "But whatever happens . . . we have each other, right? We're in this thing together, and we're not going down without a fight, right?"

Through his shivers, I heard Henry chuckling. "There you go again, Phillip, being all cheesy and stuff."

Then I laughed a bit. I had to admit, I was saying some pretty corny stuff.

"Could you squeeze a few more clichés in there?" Henry continued, the laughter now beginning to replace his anxiety, at least momentarily. "Let's see, we've got a 'we have each other,' a 'we're in this thing together,' and a 'not going down without a fight.' Good grief, Mr. Sallinger, I do believe that's three different clichés in one—"

Henry's moment of levity was cut short with the sound of a gavel piercing the air, and I jumped in my chair. The wooden hammer sounded four times sharply and then was followed by a voice.

"Uh, welcome everybody. This special meeting of the Freepoint School System's Board will now come to order." The voice was smooth and rich, with the deep twang of a Southern gentleman. It belonged to Octavius Tucker—the school board's president. He paused slightly before adding, "How's everyone doing out there tonight?"

Evidently, he preferred the hearings to be more casual and easygoing than we had been led to expect, and the audience seemed willing to go along with it. Many of them answered him out loud, each with their own variation on "good."

"That's mighty nice to hear, and I'm glad you're all in such good spirits." President Tucker's words were like molasses, slow and sugary. "Looking down the line here, I can see that all our board members are present and accounted for, so I guess we shall begin. Now . . . we have gathered here tonight to hear a petition to this board regarding the upcoming SuperSim training exercise." He spoke with the urgency of a tumbleweed. And while he was charming and obviously well-liked by the audience, there was something off about him to my ear. He sounded like a cross between a greasy car salesman and a kindly old preacher. He was probably a nice enough guy, but I wasn't totally sure about his motives. "Are the petitioners present?"

"They are, Mr. Tucker," my father answered on our behalf. No student was permitted to petition the school board without an adult sponsor; otherwise, kids would be overrunning the board meetings with all kinds of ridiculous challenges about gum-chewing rules and the like.

"And you might be . . ." Mr. Tucker said, implying that he expected my father to take it from there.

"John Sallinger, sir. My son, Phillip, is one of the petitioners."

"Very good, then, Mr. Sallinger." There was a bit of a pause, and I heard him shuffling some papers around. "You wouldn't happen to be related to Thomas Sallinger, would you?"

"He was my father, sir, yes," Dad responded. It was weird hearing my grandfather called by his name. Mom and Dad had always simply referred to him as "your grandfather" on the occasions when they had talked about him, which had been rare.

"Well, how 'bout that," the old man remarked, amused. "You know, I was a classmate of your father's."

"Is that right?" My dad was fantastic in these types of situations. He could have a polite conversation with anyone, in any situation, at any time. He was a talker. "I didn't know that," he said. But he did know, because he'd told me so on the drive to the hearing. "Your grandfather was a classmate of the school board president, did you know that?" he'd asked. He was only lying to be polite by claiming ignorance.

"Yeah, oh yeah. We had some pretty great adventures when we were in school, your father and I." He seemed genuinely tickled. Another brief pause. "It was tragic what happened."

Dad said nothing.

"But," Mr. Tucker continued, "he was a great man, your pops. A great, great man."

"Thank you, sir," he replied.

"Now, let's get back to the business at hand, shall we? Are the petitioners ready to give their opening statement?"

Opening statement?

The size of the crowd wasn't the only miscalculation Bentley had made, as we quickly learned the hard way that the school board no longer followed the old bylaws to the letter. I felt sick to my stomach almost instantly.

Opening statement? We didn't know there was an opening statement! Didn't I ask Bentley specifically about this?

My mind flew into action trying to wrestle up some quick solution to this new dilemma. *What could we say? How should we begin?* I could feel myself getting flushed. I wondered if the others were freaking out as much as I was. Tiny beads of sweat began to form at the top of my forehead, and for a second I wondered if I was about to faint. Our best and only chance to get to participate in the SuperSim was going down in flames because we hadn't bothered to come up with an opening statement. I silently screamed inside my thoughts—which I'm sure Henry heard.

And then Bentley saved the day again. Like a white knight charging in from out of nowhere to vanquish our foe, Bentley answered Mr. Tucker with confidence.

"Yes, sir. We are ready."

Wait . . . what?

Bentley had trouble shutting his mind off. He had trouble sleeping, which was an affliction I was familiar with as of late. And when he couldn't dream, he worked. He read and wrote and studied and created and invented, all just trying to occupy his overactive brain functions. The only problem he had with his powers, really, was that he couldn't seem to turn them off when he needed to.

And on a recent evening leading up to the hearing, as an exercise in formulating his arguments, Bentley had drafted an opening statement. He sat up late at night in his basement workshop and wrote one—several, actually— until he had perfected it. I just wish he'd told me about it before the hearing; he could have saved me a heart attack.

I slumped back into my chair with a sigh so loud the court stenographer probably added it to the transcript. It was hardly the last time Bentley would save my bacon.

He cleared his throat and then read a statement that surprised me with its eloquence. Words that were brand new to me but which had stewed in Bentley's soul for days poured forth like some kind of poetry. "Ladies and gentlemen of the Freepoint School Board, my name is Bentley Crittendon. I and my fellow petitioners are students at Freepoint High School and members of the special education class. We're each of us gifted with powers, just as nearly everyone in this room is. One of us can read minds. Another can grow several stories tall in an instant." He snapped his fingers for emphasis as he said it. "One of us is telekinetic!"

I don't even think he was reading it; he had it memorized.

"Yet each of us also has a disability. Blindness for some. Mobility issues for others, like me. But in truth we are hindered only by our determination and bound only by imagination." He sounded like a grown-up—a really smart grown-up.

"Now, we have collectively been barred from participation in the SuperSim competition, despite our status as active students in the school and despite our supernatural abilities. Our teachers and our principal will tell you they have made this decision in the best interest of our own safety. And, to their credit, I believe that is their motive. I believe they want to protect us and keep us from harm and are doing so with the best of intentions. However, there is no mathematical evidence to support the theory that disabled heroes are more prone to injury in action."

That was news to me, but if Bentley was quoting it in this setting, then that meant it was true. He wasn't just being dramatic. I bet he had the sources to back it up.

"In point of fact, ladies and gentlemen of the board, we have even seen some interesting developments in our abilities when working together to overcome our physical disadvantages. I'm not sure any of us here tonight can truly know the limits of what we're capable of together."

He was talking about the previous night and his suggestion that Henry should be able to send things into other peoples' brains as well as receive things from them. I wasn't sure why he said it since we actually hadn't seen any interesting developments whatsoever in that regard. *Is he just being argumentative, or are his convictions just that strong?*

"But the real truth—the real sad, hard truth—is that no matter what the intentions are, there is only one reason that we are not allowed to participate, and it's the fact that we're disabled."

He cleared his throat again and continued, gaining a bit of speed and volume as he came to the finish. "If I didn't have ataxic cerebral palsy, I wouldn't be in the special education class, and I would be free to compete. If Phillip could see, he wouldn't need to be here to petition for a chance to compete. Our disabilities are the root cause for the decision to keep us out of the simulation. And while I may not be able to stand up straight without a cane, I sure can think straight. Discrimination on the sole basis of a disability is not only illegal, it's illogical, immoral, and unfair! Thank you."

Before he could sit down a great roar went up from the crowd in attendance. They stood and applauded—some hollering and cheering. It was a little overwhelming. I got goose bumps. Whatever their convictions had been upon entering, the people were won over by the articulate and intelligent young Mr. Crittendon. I was beaming, and I'm sure Bentley was as well. I heard a cry of support from Henry, signaling that maybe he'd come out of his funk a bit. The whole team was clapping and yelling right along with the parents and townspeople. Bentley had rejuvenated our spirits with his rousing speech, and a wave of hope crashed over me.

If only the hearing had ended right there. Bentley would have ridden out of the town hall on the shoulders of adoring fans—mine included.

But it didn't end right there. And when it continued, the hearing took an abrupt turn for the worse. As it turned out, President Tucker wasn't quite as moved by the dramatic reading of a twelve-year-old kid as the spectators had been.

When the audience finally quieted down, he took a few moments to let the silence get uncomfortable before responding. "Well, young Mr. Crittendon, that was a whale of a tale, now, wasn't it? I commend you on your oratorical abilities, which are so clearly advanced beyond your years. You are quite the little spitfire, aren't you?"

There was a smattering of nervous laughter. Tucker's slow and consistent manner of speaking made it difficult to know the difference between sincerity and sarcasm.

"Unfortunately, my son, the school board answers only to the citizens of this fine city and to the governing board of superpowered individuals—known simply as 'the board' to you, no doubt, and the same board on which your father serves, I believe. Even if we wanted to," he said in mock-innocence that even I could detect, "we would not be permitted to bring matters of US national law into consideration in these proceedings. We are permitted only to interpret the laws that govern superpowered individuals, and those laws supersede all else. As such, your claim of discrimination on the basis of disability will not be a consideration for this board."

A round of mild boos went up from the crowd, as those who had been won over by Bentley's speech showed the school board their disappointment with this decision. But President Tucker cut them off straight away.

"I am not going to spend all evening babysitting those of you in the gallery. If you cannot be trusted to remain quiet and polite throughout this hearing, I will have you all removed."

The pin-drop silence of the entire room was all the proof he needed to know they had gotten the message. This was President Tucker's room, and he was very much in charge. I wondered what his powers were and if they commanded respect the way his mere presence did in this building.

"Very well, then. Now, removing the illegality of the matter from the discussion, we are left to consider whether the prohibition of these young people from the simulation events on the grounds of safety constitutes a breach of our moral code as a society. We will be solely focused on the concept of fairness. Is it fair to prevent these children from participating? Is it fair to the other students to potentially heighten the danger of the event by allowing these young people to compete even without full control of their abilities? These are the questions we will concentrate on for the remainder of this hearing."

"Mr. President," my father said, "if I might, I'd like to suggest that—"

Tucker interrupted him without giving him a chance to complete his sentence. "I do believe, Mr. Sallinger, that while adult sponsors are, in fact, required in order for a petition to be filed, there is nothing in our laws of procedure that permit you to argue the case on the behalf of your students. Don't make the mistake of thinking my affection for your father can be used to undermine these proceedings."

It was dismissive and rude, no matter how sweet the tone of voice delivering the message—the verbal equivalent of a slap in the face. He was telling my father to shut up and stay out of it, and it was so obvious that I wondered why he bothered coating the words in sugar.

I felt a touch of betrayal. The best argument we had going in our favor—that barring us from competition constituted a breach of our legal rights—had just been tossed out the window on a technicality. We'd barely gotten underway and the wind was already gone from our sails.

I was also insulted by the president's rather casual implication that our mere participation made the SuperSim more dangerous for the other kids, like it was already a given fact that disabled people equaled danger.

The deck seemed stacked against us.

What followed was a series of questions from the board so bland and harmless that it seemed designed, at least in part, as a mere façade. It was as though they were pretending to go through the motions so it wouldn't look like they'd already made up their minds—which they clearly had. Like seasoned boxers, they began to pummel us repeatedly with banality.

One of them would say something like, "What is your superpower?" And then another would say, "And what is the nature of your disability?" And finally a third board member would ask, "How does your disability limit the use of your powers?" And that would be it . . . next student, please.

On down the roster they went this way, starting with the row of team members behind us. One by one, the board members repeated the same boring questions—phrased the exact same way—in a coordinated attack designed to wear us down. It was like Chinese water torture . . . madness via repetition. There was no deviation in their line of questioning, no opening given to any of us to expound on our answers or explain our positions.

By the time they got to Henry, even the crowd was growing restless. I was waiting for President Tucker to dole out another reprimand to them, but instead he said simply, "And what is your power, Mr. Gardner?"

"I can read minds." Most of the other kids—like Freddie and James—had nervously given short but courteous answers like this one. But most of the others had also stopped at that point, whereas Henry was not content to follow the largely unwritten rules. "And it's not remotely affected by my disability," he added defiantly. It was his own personal little display of stubbornness to tack that last part onto there in a bit of civil protest. A show of defiance to what a sham this hearing had turned out to be. "I can do everything that any other mind reader can do."

"Except walk," Tucker said patronizingly, not missing a beat.

"Who cares if I can walk or not," Henry said sharply in retort, losing his cool a bit.

"Well, I do, young man," the old man said, his words dripping with sarcasm. "I'm concerned about an event of danger wherein you are unable to escape in time due to your mobility constraints. I am concerned only with the matter of your safety and the safety of those around you."

"I'm faster in this wheelchair than most humans using just their own legs," my friend shot back quietly but plenty loud enough to have been heard. And it was true. Henry was one with his wheelchair and had pretty much mastered its use. I had no doubt he was as mobile as any kid his age, short of confronting a staircase.

Tucker didn't seem swayed in the least. "And what if the enemy lies at the end of a dirt road or on the beach? How will you reach him to read his thoughts, Mr. Gardner?"

Looking back on it now, it's easy to see why my father was so upset at President Tucker after the hearing—and he was livid. The man was openly mocking Henry's disadvantage from behind the thinnest of veils and doing so from a position of authority. No amount of country charm could disguise the condescension behind his words.

"I'll get my friend James to teleport me there," Henry nearly shouted. It was shocking to hear, despite his reputation for speaking his mind. This was a kid so desperate to hang onto a dream that he was willing to talk back to one of the most powerful people in Freepoint in front of a huge audience.

Finally, Tucker shut Henry down. "I think you'd better reevaluate your tone of voice, young man, or you can spend the rest of the hearing outside in the hallway." It was the trump card the school board president held that had loomed over the entire hearing. He had all the power in this building, and we had none. He had only to flex his muscles to get the rest of us cowering.

"I think you'd better reevaluate your attitude, you sour old crank!"

I gasped but managed to cover my mouth immediately. As Henry's words sunk in, I was struck with the oddest sensation. I suddenly knew that he hadn't actually said what I had heard—not out loud, anyway. It's hard to describe to a sighted person, but my ears were just very well trained. And the voice I heard lobbing that insult back at President Tucker had not come from Henry's mouth. There was something different about the way his voice sounded, almost like he was far away.

No one else was reacting in shock to Henry's back talk.

In total, it took only about two seconds for me to realize that I had just heard Henry's thoughts.

And it took only a couple seconds more for me to realize what that meant—Henry's powers did work both ways! *Bentley was right!*

Henry must have been so agitated with Mr. Tucker and this sham of a hearing that he just stopped concentrating on his powers. He *had* said they tended to activate on their own during times of stress. That was the only explanation I could think of for why I'd just heard his thoughts. Maybe he'd been trying too hard the night before.

And I suddenly had an idea. Without thinking things through, and before I could stop myself, I leaped to my feet and shouted, "Your Honor—Your Grace . . . Mr. President, sir, may the petitioners have a moment to confer?" My mind was already three steps ahead, and I struggled to spit out the words.

I felt Bentley lean in closer on my right. "Phillip, what are you doing?"

"Sit down, Phillip," Henry snarled softly out of the corner of his mouth—this time actually speaking.

"I know what I'm doing," I reassured them, despite the fact that it was most certainly not true. "President Tucker? Will you grant the petitioners a moment to discuss things in private?"

I had no idea if this was allowed. I'd seen enough legal shows on television—or heard them, at least—to know that these kind of requests were common in a court of law, but this being my first school board meeting, I wasn't sure the same ground rules applied. I just knew I needed to talk to my teammates right away because I'd thought of a way to prove to the board that we were just as capable as the nondisabled students.

"I suppose so," President Tucker said with a sigh. "I don't see any harm with it. You have three minutes."

"Thank you, Your Honor, sir," I said graciously, putting an arm around both Bentley and Henry.

"He's not a judge, Phillip," Bentley reminded me as I pulled him in closer. "You don't have to call him 'Your Honor,' you know."

"Shut up," I said as politely as possible, knowing that time was of the essence.

We huddled together in private, just the three of us, as I rapidly explained how Henry's thoughts had found my brain just a moment earlier. I then laid out my idea for turning this hearing from a loss into a victory. They were skeptical—especially Henry, who did not yet trust his powers to come through in the clutch. But both agreed the hearing was a total loss to this point and that something dramatic was required in order to get the board's attention enough to sway their opinion to our favor.

I stood up out of the huddle, too nervous to be excited and too excited to be nervous. I felt my father's hand on my shoulder. "You sure you know what you're doing, big guy?" He spoke as my father, not our official petition sponsor.

"Yeah, I think so," I said. I'm sure he could tell I was faking confidence. "But it's not like things were going all that well to begin with, you know?" It had to be obvious to anyone with half a brain that the entire hearing had been a farce. Even if my idea constituted a parliamentary Hail Mary, it was the best shot we had against an otherwise certain defeat.

"Mr. President," I began.

"Are the young lads ready to continue again?" he asked, sounding like an impatient man who regretted having allowed us a brief conference.

"We are, sir," I replied dutifully. "And with the board's permission, I believe we can demonstrate that our disabilities do not impede our ability to use our powers."

He took a few seconds to contemplate my suggestion and then replied, "I assume this demonstration involves the use of superpowers, son?"

"Yes, sir," I said, "it does. But only briefly."

There was a great pause, and I could picture the various board members, hands over their microphones, whispering and muttering amongst themselves.

Finally the man in charge announced, "Very well, then, Mr. Sallinger. But you'd better be on your best behavior here. This board does not look kindly upon your generation's brand of funny business."

I knew what came next in the plan, but I still needed a beat to compose myself . . . and to say a few quick prayers in the hope that God was somehow real and would forgive my general ambivalence toward church up until this point in my life.

"President Tucker," I began, "I need you to choose an object near you. Like your gavel, for instance." I was shaking, and I gripped the table's edge between my fingers to try and steady my balance. "Would it be safe to assume I've never seen or handled your gavel prior to this evening?"

"It would, young man. I keep my gavel with me in my office whenever we're not in session. No one spends time with the president's gavel without also spending time with the president," he said with the charming precision of an oft-repeated campaign promise. Throughout the entire evening, from his opening pleasantries to his surprising reprimands, the speed of his sentences never increased. His Southern drawl remained steady.

"Very good, then, sir," I continued. "And . . . as you know, I'm a telekinetic, sir. But I'm also blind, which means that I can't see the things I need to see in order to take advantage of my abilities. I have to have spent time handling an object in order to be able move it with my powers." I swallowed, knowing there was no turning back. "And my good friend Henry, here, well . . . he can see just fine. And he's also telepathic."

"Young man, I do hope there is a point to all this, and more specifically, I do hope you'll be getting to it sooner rather than later. This board doesn't have all evening."

"Yes, sir," I said deferentially, momentarily distracted by the interruption. "We've . . . well, we've experimented a bit here and there with the possibility that Henry's form of telepathy might go in both directions. Well, sir . . . I guess what I'm saying is . . . that by combining our powers—"

"Mr. Sallinger," the old man warned, clearly losing patience with my rambling.

I cut the rest of my backstory and went straight for the big finale. "Sir, please pass the gavel to one of the other board members—it doesn't matter whom, just do it quietly and don't tell me who has it." My knees began to wobble, and for the first time, I started to worry that I might not pull this off.

"Okay, son," he said, letting me know he had done as requested.

"Okay then," I said, probably sounding as crazy as I felt. I raised my right arm in the air, my hand open and facing the board members.

And I waited for Henry to show me something.

And waited.

But nothing happened.

"Mr. Sallinger, have you fallen asleep?"

"No, Mr. President, I have not. Just . . . one second, please!" I turned and kicked at Henry's wheelchair with the side of my foot and let out a hushed plea. "Henry, go!"

"I'm trying," he whispered back at me.

"No, you idiot, don't try! Stop trying! Think about something else." I wondered if the board could hear us—they were several yards away, and we were whispering, but the room was awfully quiet.

Henry started to crack under the pressure. "Like what?" It sounded as though he might cry.

And then an unexpected inspiration hit me. "Think about what an idiot you are, you big idiot," I snarled at him with fake anger. I remembered how upset he had been at Mr. Tucker when he'd managed to send a thought to my brain and figured it was worth a shot to try and get him riled up again. I was out of options anyway. "Never mind, you stupid fool," I snapped. "I should've known you couldn't do it!"

I was no saint, mind you, but saying mean things to friends wasn't something I was practiced in. I winced inside at my own words, regretting them as soon as they'd come out of my mouth. But only for an instant.

Because my needling had worked. Suddenly an image flashed inside my head . . . a clearer picture than any image I had ever created from my own dreams or imagination. I saw a long wooden desk with the board members seated behind it. It was raised on a platform several feet above the floor, and they were looking down on us.

For only the slightest moment, I was tempted to just sit back and take it all in, drunk on the very notion that I was technically "seeing." It was the very first time in my life I had seen something not invented in my own mind, and it was beautiful! You've heard people talk of mountain vistas or life-altering sunsets, I'm sure, and this felt every bit as gorgeous to me, because it was . . . live. It was real. It was happening at this very minute, and I could see it.

But I knew there would be time for that later.

"I'm losing patience and interest, Mr. Sallinger." I got the feeling this would be my last warning.

It's tough to explain the picture I received from Henry. It wasn't like video. I wasn't able to see movement. He wasn't transmitting a live video feed to me but was sending something more like a simple still photograph. But I could still sort of hold Henry's image in my head for a while and search it for the one thing I really needed it for. I found the gavel in the hands of Mrs. Billings—I could see her nameplate too. She sat three positions to the right of President Tucker and held the item in front of her face loosely with both hands as she peered down at me behind her bifocals.

I focused in on the gavel and tried to block the rest of the picture from view. I concentrated as hard as I had ever concentrated in my life. I visualized it leaping forth from her grasp and flying straight into my outstretched hand.

And that's exactly what happened.

Before I knew what hit me, the gavel smacked into my open palm, as though I'd handled it all my life. The audience shared a collective gasp of surprise and awe.

And if I had simply sat back down in silence, if I had only let it end there, I would have been fine. I'm just certain of it. But for some reason—I'm still not sure what possessed me—I got it stuck in my head that sending the gavel back into the hands of Mrs. Billings would be the icing on the cake of my little visual demonstration.

I guess I got cocky.

It never even occurred to me to consider that Mrs. Billings and her hands may have moved since the time Henry's image had first been created or that she might not have the sharpest reflexes for a game of catch the heavy gavel.

I had considered the act of getting Henry to send me an image to be the hard part of my little plan and hadn't counted on my own hubris getting in the way. So I visualized the gavel leaving my hand and traveling the short distance back to Mrs. Billings's hands. I was still using the original image Henry sent me. That should have been the clue I needed—seeing Mrs. Billings behind the bench, *still holding the very gavel I was about to zap back over to her*!

But I didn't see it.

Mrs. Billings's hands were not in front of her face anymore. They were on her cheeks, where she'd placed them in surprise after seeing my powers in action. The poor woman had also leaned forward in her chair several inches to try and see me better. But not knowing these things, I tried to show off and sent the object flying back in her direction.

All I heard was a sickening thud—a sound that would clearly not be made by two hands gently catching a wooden hammer. The gavel hit her square in the face, and she flew back into her chair as the crowd cried in horror.

$$\lightning$$

After the pandemonium died down—and believe me, it was absolute bedlam when Mrs. Billings went down—I was escorted from the hearing and banished to the hallway. Henry, too, since he'd used his powers to aid my little accidental assault on a lovable old grandmother.

Two teachers from the school were sent to act as guardians, and they sat on a bench across the wide hallway from us. They were babysitters to the two of us troublemakers while the president tried to restore order and wrap up the hearing.

An ambulance was called. Ultimately, Mrs. Billings was given some ibuprofen and a heating pad, and that was it. She was going to be all right. The gavel hadn't broken the skin, and her forehead took the brunt of the blow. She even stayed on and continued participating in the hearing after a bit of a delay. She'd end up with some serious bruises, though, and a massive headache, I'm sure. And probably an innate mistrust of blind children for the rest of her days.

I was crushed.

The fact that I had just cost my teammates and myself a chance to compete in the SuperSim—not to mentioned I'd hurt someone and badly embarrassed myself in public—made this one of the low points of my life.

I wasn't crying. I wasn't panicking. I just sat there slumped down against the wall, dejected, feeling like the biggest worm in the entire world. I'd let everyone down. It didn't matter that I had been trying to hit a home run and win us the big game; what mattered was how spectacularly I'd struck out. All that was left was the formality of President Tucker announcing the board's decision. Hope had deserted me and left in its place a hollow isolation.

Henry wasn't speaking to me. We sat there, his wheelchair next to my regular folding chair, moping together in silence. I was pretty sure he wanted to strangle me, but I wasn't about to initiate a dialogue. Instead, I chose to berate myself in silence.

"I'm not sure I've ever seen such forlorn faces," said a voice—one that I instantly recognized as belonging to our teacher, Mrs. Crouch. I lifted my head to speak, but nothing came out. I was still in a great deal of shock.

I felt her sit down in the chair next to me and braced myself for a pep talk that was coming way too early. I wasn't ready to learn any life lessons yet.

"You know," she began, "superpowers are funny things, aren't they, boys? Sometimes they don't work quite the way you expect them to."

Again, she was met with silence. We were too caught up in our own depression to play our role in her little motivational moment. So she continued without us anyway.

"I know you're feeling pretty down right now, but I have an inkling that everything's going to work out all right, okay? Now why don't I go and see about this hearing real quick. You two hang in there." She patted my knee as she said it and then stood and walked away. I heard the giant oak door of the meeting hall swing open—the nervous sounds of a restless crowd pouring out temporarily before the door slammed shut again.

What was all that about? And why is Old Lady Crouch being so nice?

And again, Henry answered my thoughts with spoken words. "She's probably just trying to make us feel better. You know how adults are," he said matter-of-factly, like both our lives hadn't just been ruined.

I hesitated a moment and then figured I had nothing to lose by talking to Henry. "Nervous habit again?"

"No. I'm not nervous anymore. I was just reading your mind to see what you were thinking and to make sure you felt properly bad about what just happened." As usual, he didn't have any kind of meanness in his voice. He was just stating the facts plainly.

"I do, Henry," I said with no small measure of guilt. "I feel horrible!" And it was true. I did.

"I know, Phillip," he said. "I know you do."

It wasn't forgiveness, but it was something close. He didn't speak to me with anger, but it wasn't a verbal hug either. Maybe Henry wasn't yelling at me because he could hear me yelling at myself and thought I was doing a good enough job. I wanted to tell him how proud I was of the way he managed to place that image inside my mind, but it didn't feel like the right time for congratulations.

We carried on silently, in somber reflection, as we both contemplated life as shamed superheroes, as heroes too broken to be considered useful. I thought back to that day in the cornfield when Dad had first told me the big secret about our family and this town, and I decided I preferred life before the revelation. Since finding out I had superpowers, I'd been bullied, had my phone smashed, gotten punched in the stomach, had a concussion, and now had almost murdered a school board member while single-handedly ruining the reputation of disabled heroes everywhere.

However, unbeknownst to us, the hearing had taken a sharp turn for the positive the very moment Mrs. Crouch entered the meeting room. I didn't know it until later, when Bentley filled me in, but she had arrived just in the nick of time as the board was about to reconvene the meeting and announce their decision on our petition.

How I wish I could have seen it! To hear Bentley tell it, she was an angel sent from God himself.

As soon as President Tucker had banged the gavel and signaled the proceedings back into order—the very same gavel that I had moved with my powers—Mrs. Crouch spoke up from her position near the back of the room. She politely reminded the board of Article 12.1.A of the Freepoint Code of Conduct, which called for the school board to open any and every petition hearing to public comment before handing down a decision.

She wanted to address the board, and since she was citing their own rules of procedure, publicly and before the entire audience, President Tucker had no choice but to allow it.

Almost all of the school board members, as it turned out, were in the same age bracket; they were peers of Mrs. Crouch from her school days. And she'd come armed with enough ammunition, the kind of verbal napalm typically found only in movies, to defeat them all. She had some dirt, and she was ready to dish.

She stood before the board, but she addressed the crowd with her speech.

One by one, she named every single board member, followed by some specific story or fact about them that cast a new meaning on the hearing. For Alton Babbish, she recounted his own misadventures as a Freepoint High student, during which time he was suspended on no less than three occasions for blatant misuse of powers—one boy had ended up with a broken arm. Bentley said Babbish turned bright red and tried to bury his face behind his hand.

Cynthia Yearling was a board member whose current secretary was a disabled person named Sue Reed. Sue was a paraplegic but was blessed with the kind of advanced mind for mathematics that would make Bentley look dumb. And Mrs. Crouch told the entire crowd all about it.

Bob Vernor was the oldest member of the board, having served thirty years. One of his five grandchildren was a disabled hero who served in a field support role with the custodians' operation in Chicago. He'd won many medals and commendations.

On and on she went, rattling off a list of apparent hypocrisies among the board members. Each one had either gotten into trouble after an accident with their powers—as I had just done—or had some kind of connection to the disabled hero community.

By the time she got to Octavius Tucker, she'd already leveled more than enough evidence against the board to pressure their decision, but she didn't let that stop her. For Tucker, her story was truly a shocker—something only a person with intimate knowledge of a person would know. Octavius Tucker was himself a disabled person. He had scoliosis, and always had, and had kept it a secret most of his life. While it never interfered with his powers, it did affect his mobility, especially in old age.

Bentley said you could hear a pin drop when she was finished dissecting the board members. In a matter of minutes, Mrs. Crouch had managed to make every single board member feel guilty about their planned decision. They were speechless. And she used that silence to deliver her closing arguments.

Mrs. Crouch's closing comments made Bentley's earlier eloquence look downright Neanderthal in comparison. It was such a great speech that Bentley would later send a self-addressed, stamped envelope to the school board office requesting a transcript of the hearing so he could have a copy.

"Now, I realize that many of you might be feeling a little embarrassed right about now. One of your own peers has just aired some information about you that, while public in nature, is probably a little embarrassing considering the present circumstances. And you might think my aim is to discredit you or to make you look bad and lose face. But the opposite is really true. I am extremely proud of each and every one of you and think you are all model citizens in this society of heroes. Whatever your demons were in your youth, you've risen above them and gone on to have successful careers, making valuable contributions to this fine city. And those of you with connections to disabled individuals prove your heart's true nature every day simply by having those relationships.

"In fact, it is my love and respect for you that has led me to speak here today. Barring these children from competing in the simulation while many of you employ disabled individuals with powers is the very definition of incongruous. It flies in the face of logic. You simply cannot rule against this petition and then carry on tomorrow as you did yesterday, or you risk losing the credibility you have worked so hard to earn. If a disabled hero can serve in a field support role or as president of the school board, then how can we justify—as a community—telling these children they can't compete?" Bentley said her voice gradually picked up steam as she came to her conclusion.

"The choice is simple— either you believe in them, that they can become productive members of hero society . . . or you're just humoring them. And that would just be cruel! Thank you."

As she walked away from the board, the audience repeated the ovation they'd given for Bentley's opening statement, only twice as strong—Henry and I heard it clearly from the hallway outside. I knew immediately that something strange was afoot because the crowd had been on our side earlier. And our side had clearly lost. I could think of no reason for such a cheer to occur.

All I knew at the time was that the crowd was still hollering and clapping at full strength when Mrs. Crouch walked out of the room, turned, and moved briskly past us like she had some other appointments to keep. "See you tomorrow, gentlemen," she said as she walked away.

And that was that.

The hearing's spectators and participants spilled out into the vast hallway, and Bentley rushed to where Henry and I were sitting to tell us the good news. President Tucker had no choice but to relent or face a serious public relations nightmare—and he was up for reelection soon.

We'd won. We were in. We were going to be permitted to take part in the SuperSim.

Of course, that meant that now we had to actually go through with it.

12

COMPETITION

Sight. It's a difficult thing to describe, especially to someone who's had it all their life. The experience was a little different for James since he had, at one point in his life, actually had his sight before losing it in an accident.

In the days between the hearing and the SuperSim, Henry, James, and I practiced our new trick on our own quite a bit, fine-tuning and improving the patchwork system Bentley dreamed up to allow us blind kids the gift of sight. In no time, we were getting pretty good at it. Well, Henry had gotten pretty good at it; he was the one doing all the work. All James and I had to do was just sit there and receive the images he sent us.

One of our first positive achievements was dropping the need for a trigger. I no longer needed to goad Henry into anger in order for his powers to be reversible, which was a welcome change all around. He learned to activate his abilities in either direction at will, and it took only a few concentration exercises from Bentley.

Henry also greatly increased the speed at which the signal from his brain reached my own, which meant that the images were closer to real time. And he found a way to send them in frequent succession, like a pulse. It wasn't quite like a live video feed, but it was a far cry from the single still "photograph" I'd gotten in the school board hearing. I wasn't sure how much it would aid my powers, because there were still enough gaps in the pictures to keep me from truly knowing where everyone and everything was at every instant. If the bad guy was running away, for instance, I wasn't confident the staggered images would time out correctly for me to be able to use my abilities to stop him.

We practiced in the cornfield, in Henry's backyard, and even while just walking around town. He would pick an object around us and challenge James or me to move it in some way, using the visuals from his mind. There were some accidents along the way, though none as serious as the one at the hearing.

James knocked down a paperboy by mistake on one occasion. Poor guy had made the unfortunate decision to ride directly between our position and the trash can on the sidewalk, which just so happened to be the object Henry had challenged James to move. *Oops*.

I also broke a few windows, which pretty much tapped my already measly allowance. And one night this old lady on Harrison Street threatened to call the cops on us after I tried moving her cat. I admit that it wasn't one of my better choices, but it didn't work anyway. Cats are incredibly fast.

But all the ups and downs were worth it because we learned so much about our potential when working together . . . as well as our limitations. As an example, Henry's images were too slow for me to be able to move the cat. And they weren't quick enough for me to spot the cyclist James had nearly decapitated either. But stationary objects—those were no problem. I could even move something as large as a park bench. All I could really do was slide the bench across the ground, but Henry was still impressed.

I'd also managed to squeeze in some time to truly appreciate this new gift of "sight," such as it was. During the hearing it had been thrust upon me unexpectedly, in the heat of a stressful moment. But over the next few weeks, I was able to relax and enjoy the fact that I could finally see. My eyes were still broken, but I could see, at least as long as Henry was around. Bentley and Freddie worked on the plans for the SuperSim, while James and I were under strict orders to simply spend as much time as possible with Henry practicing our "sight."

The first thing I noticed was how wrong I'd been all my life about the relative size of things. Sure, through touch and acoustics, I had guessed pretty accurately at the size of my bed, my bedroom, and the refrigerator. But stop signs were way bigger than I'd expected. Stoplights, trees, various buildings, birds . . . anything I hadn't regularly put my hands on in life, I'd gotten all wrong.

Henry indulged me multiple times, bless his heart. I had him over for dinner one night so I could finally see what my family looked like. I had to hide it from Patrick, of course, even though my mom and dad both knew what was really going on. They made small talk with Henry while I gaped at how beautiful they all were.

I had assumed my mother was pretty, though I'm not sure why. Maybe every boy believes his mother is pretty. But I was wrong; she was beautiful. I'm sure some of my early experiences with this new ability were colored by the euphoria of simply putting visuals to my life around me, but she looked like a knockout to me. An angel. Brunette, hair down to her shoulders, with a small frame and the kindest eyes you've ever seen. She was nothing like I had envisioned and yet everything I expected her to be all at once. They all were.

My father was a very tall man, which I'd known previously but hadn't fully grasped. He had to duck under some of the doorframes in our house. I wondered if my inherited genes might help me grow as tall as he was. Would I be ducking under doorframes in the future?

Dad wore glasses with tiny lenses and had short brown hair. His nose was a little on the large side, but he was otherwise what I would imagine most women would call handsome. And skinny. His brain could move a tractor trailer, but his body was anything but buff.

My little brother was almost exactly what I had pictured. Blond, with braces. A wiry kid. Skinny as a pole. He had some freckles on his face and just the slightest amount of baby fat still in his cheeks.

Having sight for the first time was a bit like a drug to me. It was intoxicating. After she sent Patrick off to bed, my mother came over and gave me the biggest hug of my life while simultaneously bawling her eyes out. It was both heartwarming and a little awkward. She was so overcome with emotion in the moment that she could barely put a sentence together between sobs of joy. I caught the word "proud" and the word "love," and I'm fairly certain she mentioned how happy she was for me that I was finally able to see.

My dad, on the other hand, cracked one of his trademark cheesy jokes. He stuck out his hand for a handshake. "Nice to meet you, sir," he said, smirking at his own hilariousness. "My name's John, and, well, I'm your father." I didn't mind the cornball humor, though. Not this time.

Oh, and I got to see myself, of course. That was more than a little weird. I think most sighted individuals are so used to looking in the mirror that it's probably hard to imagine what seeing yourself for the first time would be like. I was me . . . but I was also a complete stranger. I was a fair bit skinnier than I had thought, which clearly ran in the family. And my haircut was a ridiculous embarrassment of disheveled brown locks. I wasn't particularly attractive, but I wasn't ugly either, which I scored as a win. Even though I'd run my hands over my own facial features hundreds of times before, I was still surprised at my own appearance and how it all came together. It was unsettling. I felt somewhat disembodied as I stared at myself through Henry's eyes. I wondered how people with sight could possibly stand to look at themselves in the mirror on a daily basis.

After dinner that night, the guys took me to see the beach. James teleported us to a spot where his family vacationed in North Carolina, and they all waited patiently while I finally took in the view. It was even more expansive and infinite to look at than it was to hear. I'd wanted to see a lot of things throughout my life, but I'd never wanted to see anything as badly as I wanted to see the ocean. And just a few months prior, it had been an impossible pipe dream.

But along with the awe-inspiring sights, this new gift also taught me a lot about the world and the little details I'd never known were there—things you don't really ever think about when you can't see. Like how bright the sun is on a particular day. Or whether your clothes match. Or how vivid and amazing the colors of autumn can be. Or the fact that Henry was black.

Some things just never occur to you when you're blind.

Race had never even been a consideration for me—it's easy to be color-blind when you're also regular-blind. The revelation didn't affect me either way, really, aside from its unexpectedness. The color of his skin was just another one of those details to which I'd never given much thought.

I thankfully got most of my slack-jawed awe out of the way prior to the SuperSim. By the time the event rolled around, I was fairly used to having occasional sight, such as it was. I'd gotten comfortable with it, and Henry and I had begun to work well together as a team.

⚡

"I can't believe how many teams there are," Bentley exclaimed. "I mean, I knew there were a lot of people dressed up today at school, but I didn't think there were this many."

We were standing in the Freepoint Circle Plaza, the general gathering place for all participants in the SuperSim. Circle Plaza was just a fancy name for the odd circular intersection in the center of town. Dad said it was called a roundabout. It was one of my most reliable landmarks. I could always tell when the car was holding the long left turn every driver had to make around the large statue of Lewis Freepoint that stood at the epicenter of the city. It's one of the many ways I was able to keep my sense of direction about me. It was nice to finally see what it looked like.

"People were dressed up at school today?" It was news to me.

"What?" Bentley asked, absentmindedly. "Oh yeah. You know how at regular high schools they let the football team dress up in their jerseys on the day of a game?"

I did not. "Um, no?"

"Well . . . they do. And, um, it's sort of like that. Kids in the SuperSim get to wear their costumes during school hours on the day of a SuperSim."

"You mean to tell me," I began, putting my mind around a new concept, "that all day long today, other kids were wearing capes and masks and stuff"—I paused, still in disbelief—"and nobody said a single word about it?"

"Yup," it was Henry, sounding like he was enjoying this a little bit.

"Yeah." Bentley this time.

"Don't you think that's a little weird?" I felt like I had a fair argument.

"Yup," Henry agreed.

Bentley tried to find a logical explanation. "I guess maybe it was such a public thing . . . such an obvious thing—I mean, to a person with sight, it was obvious. And maybe it was so obvious that it didn't need to be discussed?"

Nobody could instantly find a reasonable explanation for things the way Bentley could. I had to admit that he made a fair amount of sense. Why would people feel the need to talk about things that were blatantly obvious? *And yet I hear people talk about the weather all the time, and nothing could be more obvious than that.*

"I wonder what else I've missed out on knowing about just because it was so obvious to everyone else that no one bothered to mention it."

The group fell quiet, and for a moment I feared I'd dampened everyone's good spirits with my stupid self-pity.

"Mrs. Crouch's nose is pretty huge," Freddie suddenly offered, sneaking in a quick puff of his inhaler before continuing. "I bet you didn't know that. And I bet you no one talks about it either," he added.

That comment brought a roar of laughter from almost everyone.

"He's right, man," Henry said between snorts. "It's totally enormous!"

The mood lightened considerably after that. I was just about to launch into a story about a former piano teacher who had a giant nose when I was unintentionally interrupted by a stranger.

"Right on." The voice came from behind me. I heard a couple more voices echo his sentiments. Henry turned his head and looked up in time to see only the backs of their matching hooded superhero costumes, so he had no clue as to their identity. The jacket backs read "Vipers," which I found to be a pretty uninspired choice.

"Thanks," I said sheepishly for the hundredth time since the hearing.

I'd become a bit of a folk hero. I don't know how it happened, but somehow the little accident with my powers had made me a star. It must have been the shared bond between kids when it came to teachers, their common adversary. The entire school was still talking about it.

I'd gone from a blip on the high school radar to everybody's new best friend, almost overnight. The way the kids were fawning all over me, you would have thought I had mooned the principal or found an error on a teacher's test. I was *popular*. I didn't exist for the entire school year up until this moment, and suddenly, I was the center of attention. I was "that kid who nearly killed a teacher." I think even Chad Burke would probably have had a little more respect for me if he were still around.

By association, most of my friends were now considered pretty cool too. The girls would say things to Henry and Bentley like, "You were there?" and "What was it like?" These were the cheerleaders and the most popular girls in school, flirting with special ed kids. It was truly insane.

We were the underdogs who had taken on the school board—attacked the school board, literally—and won. We were the envy of every kid in town. Instead of being the joke, the disabled kids now had some street cred, even though we had come by it accidentally. And credibility was definitely important, especially for something like the SuperSim.

Many of the students who had joined teams for the event were taking it quite seriously. Some of them were like college fraternities, with chants and secret handshakes, the works. Across the circular patch of grass, there was a team in purple jumpsuits doing some kind of dance routine to pump themselves up. There had even been pledges and initiations for some of the more elite teams.

Most had picked out names for their teams as well as costumes.

"Those guys look ridiculous," Henry said softly as soon as the Vipers were safely out of range.

"Green boots, green pants, green hoods, and green jackets," I said, shaking my head.

Bentley agreed with my fashion take. "Entirely too much green. Plus, vipers aren't even green in real life."

"Ugh," Freddie said.

Our team had opted to go costume-free, much to my father's relief—he considered it silly to wear a special outfit just to fight crime, as most modern professional custodians did. But we did pick out a team name.

We'd discussed it over lunch about a week earlier, and it was agreed by all six of us that we wanted a name that was true to our identity and our spirit of teamwork. Well, to be honest, only five of us agreed on that. Donnie wasn't really the voting type. He raised his hand once in a while when everyone else did, but sometimes he'd just sit there and say nothing. We usually assumed he would let us know somehow if he ever had a strong opinion about something, though we had absolutely no evidence to suggest that.

Once we reached a group decision on the line of logic we wanted to follow to choose our team name, I knew immediately what it would be. I recalled Mrs. Crouch's Custodial Studies discussion and the original protectors who overcame their insufficient numbers to defeat the Haladites.

So we named ourselves the "Ables."

"Good luck, gimps," I heard suddenly. I didn't have to wait for Henry's images to know it was Steve Travers, Chad Burke's old partner in bullying crime.

"Get bent," Henry said. Donnie's presence made all the difference, of course, allowing Henry to cop an attitude with someone who could pretty much kill or injure Henry any way he wanted to in a one-on-one matchup.

Henry was looking at their team uniforms, which consisted of high-tech, lightweight body armor and chest plates emblazoned with the word "Punishers."

"You think you're hot stuff now that you won your little court case, is that it?"

"It's not really about what I think, Steve," Henry said. "But I do know that of all the pretty girls who have come up to talk to me tonight, the prettiest was probably Beth Franklin." He paused for effect. "Aren't you two"—another pause, feigning politeness—"I mean, isn't she your girlfriend?"

Steve said nothing, but it was obvious from his posture and expression that he was boiling within.

Henry kept hammering. "It's really about what other people think, you know? And Beth . . . she sure seemed to think I was pretty hot stuff. She was one of the ones asking for my autograph, right, Phillip?"

I didn't want to get involved in this kind of conversation at all, but thankfully, Steve didn't give me a chance to anyway.

"Yeah, you just keep thanking your lucky stars that Chad's not here and that your friend, the big man, is," Steve said, trying to sound more threatening than he actually did. "Or I would tear you to pieces."

"Get lost, Steve," I said, finally speaking up, if only to end it. "We don't want any trouble." Always trying to make peace. I would have made a good mediator.

"We'll see you little punks on the battlefield," he said, laughing. The rest of his team of upperclassmen jocks cackled as well, and they all turned their backs and pushed their way up to the front of the crowd.

"What a jerk," Henry muttered.

"Eh, he's nobody without his master," Bentley said flatly.

"Everybody's a nobody when Donnie's around. Isn't that right, buddy?" I asked.

Donnie made sort of a half grin. It was a common reaction for him.

"You totally owned him with that thing about his girlfriend, Henry," Freddie said, laughing.

"I also totally made that up," he replied, the sound of a mile-wide smile in his voice.

We all had a good laugh at that, and then we enjoyed another when Bentley pondered about the conversation Steve Travers would later have with the poor unsuspecting Beth Franklin.

"It's kind of chilly," Bentley observed flatly. It was getting colder, all right, with Halloween right around the corner. The leaves had started falling in earnest over the last week, crunching under my feet. Fall was in full swing, and the evening air was crisp.

I stood there in silence for a moment, watching the other teams via Henry's vision and marveling at how the temperature change between peoples' breaths and the night air allowed me to see little puffs of smoke as they exhaled.

We'd been briefed in full on the SuperSim proceedings multiple times in school over the last month. The rules were drilled into our heads. They were pretty simple rules, really: don't hurt anyone, don't sabotage, and don't cheat. That was basically it. The rest of what lay in store for us was a mystery. We were all left to discover and stop the fictional crimes throughout town on our own. There would be no maps, no list of instructions, no tips.

As we stood there shivering with a couple hundred other kids, I began to wonder if maybe there'd been some kind of delay. It seemed like it was taking a while to get things going, and the teams were understandably anxious.

Where are all the adults?

"They're probably already in their hiding spots, waiting for the signal." It was Henry, answering my brain's silent musings again. It was becoming a regular thing with him, but I was at least getting used to it. His powers let him listen in only on my completed thoughts—when I was thinking in complete sentences. As long as I was careful, I was able to avoid having him overhear any embarrassing or truly personal ideas. Plus, I sort of needed him to be actively using his powers if I wanted to see anything.

"You'd think I'd be used to having you inside my head by now, but it still catches me off guard sometimes," I said.

"I'm like a ninja," he replied, bragging just a little bit.

"Okay, folks," I heard a familiar voice say into a microphone, "we're ready to begin." It was Coach Tripp.

All the chatter came to a standstill.

"When I blow this air horn," he continued, "that's the signal to begin the competition. When you hear the air horn again, that's the signal that the SuperSim is over. Either time has expired or all the crimes have been thwarted. At the sound of that second air horn, you must—I repeat, *must*—stop everything you're doing and return here to Circle Plaza for a debrief and the awards ceremony. I think there will even be refreshments of some kind."

A brief cheer went up from the students, because kids who don't like refreshments pretty much don't exist. But we quieted down again to hear what Coach Tripp would say next.

Only instead of Coach Tripp's voice, we heard the air horn, which rang through the night air for a solid two seconds, loudly.

And then it was gone.

Everyone had been expecting the opening speech to continue, so the actual starting horn was a surprise. It caught most of the participants flat-footed. We all just kind of hung there in limbo for a moment before absolute madness erupted.

Voices went up in a chorus of shouts and commands. Orders were given and battle cries were raised. I think I even heard one group yell, "To arms."

Circle Plaza exploded with movement and sound as the teams hurried to enact the strategies and plans they'd drawn up. In a matter of seconds, the plaza was nearly empty.

"Where are they all going?" I asked no one in particular. Had I missed some announcement? Was there some obvious fact or strategy that we were foolishly overlooking?

Freddie weighed in, sounding as confused as I was. "Should we be running somewhere too, then?"

Henry echoed my thoughts. "They can't possibly know where the crimes are taking place."

We'd spent all our planning time discussing how we could collectively apprehend or stop a criminal; it wouldn't be easy, considering how many of our group's powers were mentally based abilities. We hadn't spent any time at all thinking about where or how to find the actual criminals. I guess we assumed that would be the easy part. We were so very wrong about that.

There was a loud scream in the distance, and it startled me. It sounded like a woman. As soon as I heard it, I realized an important fact: *every other team that took off running was already closer to that scream than we were.*

"That could be a crime," Henry shouted.

There wasn't time to waste critiquing our own lack of planning. Bentley jumped right into battle mode. "Phillip, can you tell roughly where that scream came from?" He was excited and speaking quickly, like someone who just drank six cups of coffee in three seconds.

"It was about four blocks west, but I'm pretty sure it was a student," I said. I was used to New York City noise, but the sound waves traveled a lot better in this quiet little town. My sensitive ears were one of my biggest assets on a team of misfits like this.

"Phillip, even if it's a student screaming, it could just as easily be a signal that there's something there we should check out," Bentley reminded me. "There could be some kind of clue or indication of another crime."

He was right, and I knew it. And thinking about it for even a few more seconds could cost us dearly. I nodded my affirmation. "Let's go, everyone. James, in the center. Maple and Grant, got it?"

James stepped to the middle of the group nodding as the rest of us gathered around, placing our hands on him. As soon as we were all touching some part of him—or the person in front of us who was touching him—I gave the command. "Now."

Ooph!

We arrived at the corner of Maple and Grant, but we were too late—way, way too late. The team from the plaza with the ugly green uniforms was standing between us and the action along with two other tardy teams—a group of high school girls in shiny silver getups and a team of kids our own age called the Cowboys. They were all wearing Western garb, which made about as much sense to me as going nude, but whatever.

Beyond them, we could see Steve Travers's team, with two criminals in custody. In the few seconds we were standing there taking it all in, two more teams arrived, only to find disappointment.

"Hey," Bentley said, "at least we know we can trust Phillip's hearing, right? You pretty much nailed the spot, just like that," he added, snapping his fingers.

"Come on, everyone, the night is still young." He was a natural optimist, and I wondered if he might even end up making a fine leader for our little crime-fighting unit. We'd need one soon enough, and none of us really fit the typical mold.

"Where should we go now?" James inquired.

"Yeah," Henry said, a touch of sarcasm in his words, "I don't hear any more screams."

The other teams were moving off—two of them disappeared into thin air, traveling by teleporter like we did.

"Where are they even going?" I asked. *What do they know that we don't?*

"Well," Bentley began, "it's a fair bet, just on basic mathematics, that there won't be any crimes anywhere in this direct vicinity since we just had one, right? So . . . we should definitely go . . . somewhere."

Another scream suddenly broke through the quiet night air, this time more of a yell. It was definitely a male voice.

I turned in Henry's general direction and thought some deliberate thoughts, hoping he'd be listening. *What was that you were saying about hearing more screams?* I smiled.

"Well, where was it, genius?" He shot back aloud, trying to conceal a slight grin.

I snapped into business mode. "Closer this time. James, center. Seventh and Haywood. Let's go, everyone!" My adrenaline was pumping.

Everyone scurried into our little circle, putting a hand on James's shoulder or jacket.

"Go!" I whispered.

Ooph!

Haywood Lane ran parallel to Grant Avenue, so we really moved only one block over and two blocks west. We were much earlier in relation to the crime but still too late. The Vipers beat us again and had already apprehended the bad guy—it was Mr. Henderson, one of the school's guidance counselors. He'd apparently been robbing the bank on the corner.

"Crap," Henry said. "Too late again."

"We're never going to apprehend a criminal by waiting for sounds and reacting," Bentley said.

"Why not?" I asked defensively. "With James's teleporting abilities, why can't we be just as fast on the draw as any other team?"

"Because there's already a team there, Phillip," he explained sadly, "causing the screaming in the first place. Think about it. A criminal's not going to go stand out in the street and scream or yell and draw attention to himself. A victim might scream, sure, but a lot of the sounds we're going to hear tonight are going to mean another team is already there. We're too late as soon as we hear it, you see?" He delivered it like bad news, because it was. He was right.

"Well, then how the heck are we supposed to find the crimes?" I asked, challenging the universe as much as Bentley's logic. "How are all these other teams doing it?"

"I don't know," he replied. "I can think of a hundred methods to use, but all of them require some kind of preparation or planning—or equipment. Without all that, we're just guessing."

We all stood around with slumped shoulders for a few seconds.

"You're a pretty smart guy, though, right?" I said. "We're all pretty smart, but you're a freaking genius."

"Yeah," he said, waiting for the other shoe to drop, perhaps expecting an insult.

"So your guesses are probably better than most people's well-thought-out plans, wouldn't you say?"

"Okay."

"He's right," Henry chimed in. "If your brain can't unlock a way to find some criminals, then no one's can."

"Think about this town, Bentley. Think about common crimes or cliché master plans." I was on a roll. Bentley's brain worked like a supercomputer when his powers were activated; I just needed to remind him. "Think about the types of places crimes happen. Think about the school and the board officials and what their desire for education might do to impact the kinds of crimes they choose to portray. Throw all that into that computer of a head of yours, and spit me out some options."

"Yeah," Henry cheered, like a fired-up athlete after a halftime pep talk.

"Let's brainstorm—which, for a guy like you, should be a brain hurricane," I said, smiling.

"Okay, okay," Bentley said, waving his hands in surrender. "All right. Give me a moment, okay?"

He closed his eyes to concentrate. We held our tongues and our breath while he put his powers to work. For several moments, it was completely silent. Everyone was staring at him expectantly; even I was staring, in my own way. Seeing through Henry's perspective sometimes impacted my body's natural movement. If he was leaning forward to see or hear something more clearly, I sometimes found myself mimicking the same body language without even realizing it.

Finally, Bentley opened his eyes and rattled off a rapid-fire list of information. "The Freepoint Bank—east location, Waveland. Dave's Diamond Outlet, Main Street. Boyle Chevrolet on Baily Boulevard. The Freepoint Teleportation Office, Wayne Drive. And City Hall, Main Street."

He'd thrown them all at us so quickly, I'd missed most of them after the bank. "Slower, slower," I pleaded.

He obliged, breathing a bit more heavily between statements, as though using his power had tired him out a bit. "The Freepoint Bank—east location, Waveland. Dave's Diamond Outlet, Main Street. Boyle Chevrolet on Baily Boulevard. The Freepoint Teleportation Office, Wayne Drive. And City Hall, Main Street."

He'd repeated the entire list word for word, and I wondered if anyone else noticed. His power, whatever it was and however it worked, was pretty awe-inspiring.

"Okay," I said, buying my brain a few seconds to process. Bentley had provided a pretty darn good list of possible targets for criminal activity in this community. "Are those in any particular order?"

"No," Bentley replied, sounding surprised. "You asked for brainstorming, not a weighted list." He was almost insulted, largely because he could easily have given them to me in order if he'd known that's what I wanted.

"That's fine. Really, it's okay, Bentley," I assured him. "You did an amazing job. Just tell me which one you think is the most likely target of all of them."

"I guess the bank, because the score"—he made air quotes with his fingers, an action I'd never known about before, though I instantly understood its meaning—"is the largest at the bank with all that money. But honestly, logic suggests someone has already beaten us to it, simply because it's one of the larger targets. Same with the jewelry store. Other teams would think of those, probably, just by thinking about robbery possibilities."

"Okay, that makes sense," I said. "What about the others, then?"

"I guess maybe the Teleportation Office," he concluded. "If you think about it, that place would be an attractive target to a real-world criminal."

He had a good point. The Teleportation Office and its staff would be a great asset in the hands of a criminal invading Freepoint, providing instant access to the city from literally anywhere on the planet, assuming any prisoner teleporters would cooperate.

"All right, then. It's settled." I decided for everyone, not stopping to wonder if that was selfish. "We're headed to my mom's workplace, which probably won't be awkward at all," I added with a gallon of sarcasm.

Everyone moved in closer together, without the rush, and made contact with James somehow.

"You know where it is, James?" I asked.

"You're asking a teleporter if he knows where the Teleportation Office is?" he challenged playfully.

"Right. Duh. Sorry. Everyone ready? Let's go, James."

Ooph!

We arrived on the street outside my mother's workplace. All the active custodians in town who needed to travel around the world for their work came to this building every morning for Mom or one of her coworkers to do the honors of playing instant cabdriver.

Henry looked around, taking in the scenery. Whether it was for my benefit or his own, I did not know.

This was the first time I'd ever seen the building, though I'd been inside several times. It was fairly nondescript. A two-story office building, with a few medium-sized trees around every corner. More impressive than the building was the parking lot, which was easily four or five times the size of the structure itself. It made sense to me, I figured, since it was essentially an airport of sorts—few employees and tons of customers who need to leave a car somewhere while they went to perform their work in another city.

We started walking toward the parking lot's entrance when suddenly, Mrs.

Foster, the school nurse, dropped in out of the sky. As a flier, she was a natural choice to fill the role of one of the SuperSim referees since her power enabled her to hover above the town and see a lot of the action at once.

"Sorry, children," she cooed like Glinda the Good Witch. "That building is off-limits and not part of the SuperSim competition."

"What?" Henry screeched, the way that all kids do when they're suddenly disappointed.

"I'm sorry," Mrs. Foster said again, with no change in the cheeriness of her tone. "There aren't any SuperSim crimes and criminals in there. The Teleportation Office is a twenty-four-hour operation, so we aren't able to use it."

"Well, there goes another one," I muttered, thinking about the two locations left on Bentley's list: City Hall and the Chevy dealership. "Are there any other locations like this that are off-limits?"

"Yes," she said, pausing to smile. For a moment I thought she might not continue. "City Hall—"

"Crap!" Henry bellowed in the background. His field of view shook wildly with his head, making me a little dizzy.

"Don't mind him. Please continue," I said, not wanting to get on her bad side while she was giving away free SuperSim information.

"City Hall, the school, the public library, residential homes, and a handful of other locations that are guarded but that I can't mention."

She'd just made our decision for us. "I guess we know where we're going, then, eh, boys?"

A round of dejected affirmatives came back. We all started moving back toward the street as Mrs. Foster floated lightly back up into the sky without a noise. "Good luck," she called softly as she went.

"So we come up with a killer list of amazing possible targets, and from that list of five, we're already down to one?" Henry wheeled toward James as the rest of us moved in as well.

"Yeah, that about sums it up," I confirmed.

"That sucks!"

"Okay, James."

Ooph!

We arrived at the Chevy dealership to find it deserted. Bright lights shone all around from above, illuminating the flashy vehicles in case that random late-night car buyer should come by. All we could hear was the hum of the lights, nothing else.

"It's empty," Bentley declared, dejected. "I thought for sure there'd be a criminal here."

"Maybe there was," Henry said, "only they already got caught."

"I don't see any signs of that kind of thing," Bentley said. Henry glanced at him, which allowed me to see how intently Bentley was looking around.

"Maybe we should hide," Freddie suggested with a bit of excitement.

"What?" Henry asked.

"You know, in case the criminals haven't been here yet, so we can jump out and catch them when they show up."

"That's a great plan," came the expected sarcastic response from Henry. "Let's spend the rest of this stupid SuperSim, in which we've accomplished nothing, hiding behind some cars and waiting!" By the end of his rant, he was nearly yelling. It was probably a step or two too far.

"Hey," I shot at Henry. "Take it easy."

"I'm sorry, it's just . . . a really dumb idea."

"I said, take it *easy*!"

"You take it *easy*," he called back.

"Guys . . ." Bentley tried to step in.

"Why do you have to be such a jerk all the time?"

"Guys." Bentley tried again, a bit louder.

"Why do you have to be so stupid all the time?" Henry had perfected a high-pitched imitation voice.

"That's really mature, Henry."

"*Guys!*"

"You wanna see mature?"

My vision suddenly disappeared. "What?" It took a moment for my brain to recover from the shock of losing it, but then I knew instantly what had happened. "Yep," I said angrily, "you were right. That was even more mature. You want a diaper change now too?"

"Don't think I won't kick your ass just because you're blind."

"Don't think I won't just push you down a big hill just because you're in a wheelchair."

"Will you shut up!" I didn't know Bentley had that kind of power in his voice, but that was a certified shout. And it worked. Both Henry and I instantly clammed up, stammering in surprise.

Before anyone could speak another word, we heard a muffled crash somewhere in the distance. Instinctively, we all scurried to hide behind the nearest car we could find. Whether he realized it or not, Henry started sending me images again, so I got to piggyback on his vision when he leaned around the back of the car to take a look down the street.

I couldn't see anything out of the ordinary. I saw a couple houses, a vacant lot, and down at the end of the block . . . the Freepoint Library. Henry looked to his right, at me and the rest of the gang. "What *was* that?" he whispered.

I shrugged, and so did Bentley.

"Was it a car crash?"

"I didn't hear any squealing tires or anything like that," I said.

"Quiet," Bentley barked. "It might happen again."

For several seconds, each of us peeked over and around the midsize red Chevy sedan, straining to see and hear something we weren't even sure was coming. But then, just as I was about to give up, another crash.

This time, since we'd been paying attention, we could tell it was coming from the library. There'd even been a quick flash of light along the southwest windows right when the crash occurred, and the sound had definitely come from that direction.

"That's not right," I said.

"That came from the library, didn't it?" James inquired.

"It did," Bentley confirmed.

"That's not right," I repeated. "That shouldn't be happening, right?"

"I think the library is off-limits too, guys." Henry said. "Whatever's going on in there, it's not part of the SuperSim, okay?"

My reply was admittedly simple. "So?"

"So, what," Henry retorted. "We can't score any points in there, man. It's a dead end, like everything else we've investigated tonight."

"Who cares about scoring points? What if there's really something shady going on in there?" I was intrigued by the possibility of an actual crime being committed. I wasn't scared by it, though I probably should have been.

"Even more reason to go the opposite direction, Phillip. Are you crazy? We're not crime-fighters. If there's an honest-to-God villain in there, he'd have a tougher time facing an army of kittens."

"All the adults are wrapped up in the SuperSim. If someone's in there stealing something or whatever, they'll never know about it."

"Phillip, in case you haven't noticed, we can't even catch a pretend criminal. We suck. We're little freaking kids! The SuperSim was one thing, but now you want to try and fight actual crime?"

"I have to side with Henry on this one," Bentley said, somewhat reluctantly. "I don't think it's a good idea at all. Firstly, it's against the rules to go in there. Secondly, there's probably not a crime . . . the janitor probably just spilled his mop bucket or something silly, and then we'd get in even more trouble for going in."

"I'm not talking about fighting crime or catching any criminals or anything. I'm just talking about . . . investigating. Checking it out a little . . . seeing if we can learn more information about whatever might be going on. You gotta admit you're curious, aren't you? Imagine how we'd look if we brought back a lead on a real crime in progress instead of a bunch of teachers in costumes."

In a bit of perfect timing from the universe, another loud crash sounded out, along with another flash of light.

I turned to Bentley to plead my case. "That ain't no mop bucket, Bentley."

He turned to Henry, then back to me. "We're not going over there, Phillip. It's a very, very bad idea."

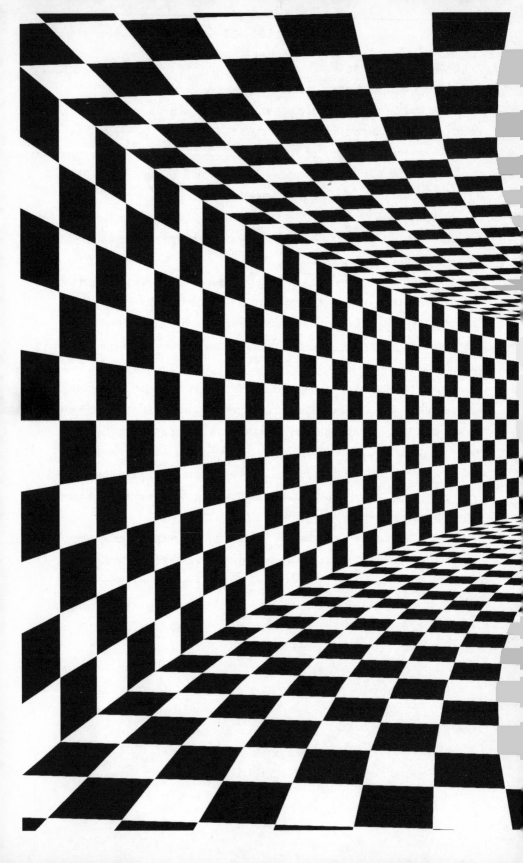

13

BOOK THIEF

"Shh. Be quiet," I mouthed, pointing at my teammate's shoes. The huge marble hallways would echo any sound we made.

It was only James, Henry, and me. I would have gone alone, but I needed James to get me inside without using the front door and Henry to let me see where I was going once I got there.

This is a very, very bad idea, Phillip. Henry had taken more arm-twisting than James, mostly because he was a big baby.

Shut up. I can't concentrate on listening if you're prattling on in my head.

The hallway was empty, with a series of dim orange lights around the edge of where the ceiling met the walls. At the end of the great hallway was a door, partly ajar, with a small light shining through the crack. The building seemed a few degrees warmer than it should be, which I assumed meant they had the thermostat set higher for the overnight hours.

We crept a few paces very slowly and with surprisingly little noise considering two of us were blind and one was in a wheelchair. It helped that the central hallway of the Freepoint Library was wide, and aside from an information desk in the very center, mostly empty. The main hallway ran approximately 120 feet or so, with various sections of the library—young adult, nonfiction, etc.—in spacious side rooms branching off here and there.

We'd been to the library a few times since moving to Freepoint, and I always enjoyed it. The building had an official, stately feel, with two-story-high ceilings and expensive marble floors. The acoustics reminded me of some of the Smithsonian museums we'd visited on our trip to Washington, DC.

Now that we were actually inside the building, we could hear more noises coming from the southeast corner, including a few muffled voices. James, Henry, and I stood as silently as possible, straining to hear more detail in the far-off noise. Bentley and the others remained outside, hiding in the bushes, keeping a lookout in case the bad guys made a break for it.

I took a couple soft steps forward. I could make out male voices only, but there were at least three distinct individuals talking.

If these aren't SuperSim villains, that means they're regular criminals, Phillip!

I'm aware! I just want to get close enough to hear a little better.

That's funny. I don't want to get any closer at all. I actually wouldn't mind getting a little farther away.

Shut up!

Another crash, only far louder now that we were inside the building. The rooms off the main hall could be quite large, with a patchwork of their own side rooms and hallways. There was no way to tell where inside that section the intruders actually were.

Who would wanna break into the library? What are they doing? I couldn't fathom any criminal activity in a place like this that would require something so loud.

Without any warning or indication anything was imminent, I lost my vision completely. It was there one second, then gone the next, replaced by the same black nothing I'd been staring at my entire life.

Henry, what did I do now? Why'd you stop sending me images?

Um . . . I didn't, Phillip. The lights just went out.

But why would the lights—

Footsteps. Unmistakable on marble floors such as these, and from the sound of it, coming from the doorway at the end of the hall. Click-clop, click-clop. The heel-then-toe rhythm continued for several paces until it reached a point that had to be near the unmanned information desk. Then . . . nothing. For a handful of seconds, I couldn't even hear anyone breathing besides the three of us kids. Usually, I can hear all sorts of things people think are silent.

We were frozen in place partway down the hall but still a good fifty feet or more from the sound of the last footsteps.

Who is that?

How the heck should I know, Henry? Just stay still! Maybe he heard something and came to check on it.

Click-clop, click-clop, click-clop. The steps suddenly picked up where they'd left off . . . and at a faster pace.

We're gonna die. Oh my God, we're all gonna die!

Calm down, Henry. I'm trying to think.

Click-clop, click-clop, click-clop, click-clop.

Oh God, oh God, oh God, oh God. Henry's tough talk had melted into fearful blubbering in a matter of seconds, and all it took were a few footsteps.

Click-clop, click-clop, click-clop, click-clop. The figure drew closer and closer. I began to think he might walk straight through us, until—

"Stop where you are!"

I wasn't sure where it had come from. I mean, I knew I was the one who'd said it, but I wasn't sure from which of the unexplored recesses down inside me it had come. It was a reaction, to be sure, and not born out of rational thinking. The eighty-five-pound weakling in me knew better than to challenge unseen adversaries during a break-in. I regretted it as soon as I'd said it, but it was obviously too late.

The footsteps slid to an abrupt stop midstep and then settled as the unknown figure adjusted to hearing my command.

I honestly didn't know if it was a man, woman, or werewolf, though I was at least finally close enough to hear the intruder's breathing. As we stood there exposed in the dark by my actions, my mind began to race through all the terrible individuals this could potentially be in front of us. After all, the SuperSim villains simply wouldn't be here. This had to be a real bad person of some kind, committing a real crime in a superhero town. And I'd gone from "just scoping things out" to direct confrontation with astonishing speed.

What the hell did you do that for? Henry seethed.

Well, to try and stop him, I guess. It worked, didn't it?

Well, now what do we do?

Why don't we just leave? It was James, with a helpful thought that none of us really expected an answer to, at least not from our assailant.

"Because then we'd never have the chance to get acquainted with one another, young James."

It was a man, and an older one at that, easily over sixty. His voice was warm, and he spoke with confidence. Prim and proper . . . almost a bit like a British accent, actually.

A quick scratching noise was followed by a bright flash of light, which dulled considerably right away. The light pulsed slightly as the man drew smoke from his pipe. The orange glow illuminated just enough of his face to assure me he was not, in fact, a werewolf.

He puffed a few times while the three of us stood there actively trying to avoid soiling our pants. In addition to surprising us by speaking, he'd also managed to read our minds.

His pipe finally lit, he continued speaking as his right hand shook the match in the air to put it out. "And I do so hate missing the opportunity to meet new people such as yourselves." He puffed twice more and said, "Shall we have some light, then?"

The hallway lights instantly returned to full strength, blinding us all in the process for a moment—well, blinding Henry at least. When he finally blinked the white spots away, what we saw before us was one of the least scary men I'd ever seen . . . except for the scar.

From top to bottom, a hideous scar split his face, rippling with texture and disgusting detail. It was as though something had cut his face in two, pulled the halves apart by a couple inches, and then froze everything in place. Other than that admittedly large detail, he looked like any other ordinary old man.

He was definitely someone's grandfather, and he dressed the part too. A tweed suit, complete with handsome leather patches on the elbows of the jacket. Instead of a tie, there was a scarf with a tiny silver medallion holding it in place. Atop his head sat a hat—also made out of tweed—with a bill in the front and another in the back. Henry would later tell the others the man resembled Sherlock Holmes, but with a mustache and a cane. I had no visual frame of reference for that analogy, but it seemed to help the other kids on the team.

"Now then, the proper way to begin when meeting new people is with formal introductions. Allow me to begin. My name is Mr. Finch." He removed his hat, wrapped his cane under his arm, and bowed. "Now, traditionally, you would introduce yourselves to me and bow in return. So why don't you begin, Mr. Gardner? Or would you prefer to start, Phillip?"

His voice was even and pleasant, not at all threatening in tone. But the intent of his words seemed less than friendly. We were old enough to know he was trying to intimidate us by showing he already knew who we were. And it was working, for me at least.

"You can't impress me with your tricks. Reading minds is easy." The cocky side of Henry was back now that he'd gotten a look at his opponent and evidently judged him weak and puny. Henry judged a lot of people to be weak and puny, considering his own appearance.

"It definitely is for me," Finch replied. He wasn't boasting, merely stating a fact. "But so are a lot of other things. Like breaking into the Freepoint Library. You know," he started, pausing briefly to draw more smoke, "I've never seen a more poorly guarded building in all my life." His arms went out at his sides, gesturing to the building's complete lack of security evidenced all around us. "It's almost as though the good people of Freepoint don't believe there's anything of value here, isn't it?"

It was true. There were no surveillance cameras, no security guards. There wasn't even an alarm system.

"We're here now, though, aren't we?" Henry bragged.

"My, you are feisty, aren't you?" He almost sounded impressed. "Well," he added, clearly wrapping things up, "now that we've made our acquaintance with one another, and Mr. Gardner is foaming at the mouth, I'll be heading back for what I came for. I do have a robbery to commit and evidence to erase. As for you three . . . I have no idea, but I wouldn't think it a wise idea to be hanging around a crime scene. Unlike me, you might leave a bit of evidence lying around. We'll meet each other again soon, I'm sure. I kind of like this town. I think I'll return."

"And what makes you think we're going to just let you go back to what you were doing? What makes you think we won't stop you and turn you in?" Henry was acting quite cocky, and I wondered if that would change the day we actually had to do the things he bragged about.

Finch smiled the way all adults do when they know something you don't, and with a wave of his hand said, "Because you're in Cleveland."

Wait, what?

Ooph!

I'd been to a lot of places in my young life—between our many moves and vacations, over a dozen states already. But I'd never been to Cleveland. So this trip, unplanned as it was, was at least a milestone of sorts.

We found ourselves in a parking lot of a supermarket. It appeared to have been abandoned for some time. There was a strong city smell in the air—the smell of millions of drivers on the road every day—and it reminded me of New York City.

We were definitely not in Freepoint anymore, and it made sense to assume the old man hadn't been lying about the destination. We were in Cleveland. The lone car in the lot was empty, though we had plenty of fluorescent light humming above our heads.

Why are they lighting up a parking lot for a business that doesn't exist anymore?

"What in the heck just happened?" Henry was freaking out a tiny bit.

"We teleported," James answered. "Probably to Cleveland, I'd say."

Henry sputtered, "I don't even know where Cleveland is!"

"It's in Ohio," James answered helpfully.

Henry just screamed.

"He didn't touch us, though, James," I protested. "How did he do that?"

"That I don't know. I've never seen anything like that before. I've never even heard of anything like that."

A car driving out on the main road slowed as it passed and then turned into the far entrance of the parking lot.

"We'd better get out of here," I said.

The car turned and slowly drove in our direction, headlights getting brighter by the second.

"Agreed," Henry said, nodding, as he rolled himself toward James and me.

The driver of the vehicle turned on a tremendously powerful spotlight attached to the window, causing Henry to squint.

Cops!

"James, the Freepoint Circle," I said sternly, placing my hand on his shoulder. "Go, buddy!"

I heard the officer say through his loudspeaker, "Don't move!"

But we were already gone.

⚡

"I can't believe this is happening!" I'd gone through frustration and anger and had settled firmly into despondence. It was a full-on "woe is me" moment.

The guys and I had gone back to the plaza, found some adults, and breathlessly told them about what had happened.

The SuperSim had ended while we were in Cleveland, and the teams were beginning to roll back into the center of town. Dad and a few of his protector buddies hightailed it over to the library but found nothing.

Dad said that not only did they not find Finch there when they arrived, but there was absolutely zero evidence anyone had been there at all.

Nothing was missing, broken, or out of place.

"Did you smell pipe smoke?" I was grasping at straws, but I needed something to hold onto.

"I don't know, Phillip. I didn't have that very specific piece of information when I was investigating. I suppose your man was smoking a pipe?" I'm pretty sure he wanted to strangle me. I had probably embarrassed him with his coworkers.

"Dad, you know that I'm telling the truth, right?"

He said nothing. Without Henry around, I couldn't see the visual cues that might provide a clue to his true mind-set. But there were plenty of audio-based nonverbal signals for me to pick up on. Like the heavy breathing directed down at the floor and the tapping of his finger on his arm.

"Of course we believe you, son." It was Mom, bringing a round of fresh-baked cookies to the table the way she used to do when Patrick's team lost a Little League game. "What's important is that you're okay."

"No, Mom," I blurted, "what's important is that everyone is gonna think we're a bunch of liars."

The chair screeched as she pulled it back from the table. Then she sat down and clasped my hands inside her own.

"Well, Phillip, are you a liar?"

"No!" I was offended she'd felt the need to ask.

"Then get over it." She let go of my hands, stood up, and headed back to the counter.

I didn't process what she'd said right away. "What?"

"I said get over it, son," she called over her shoulder. "Listen, if you want to be a superhero, you're going to have to get used to the idea of people saying bad things about you. It's part of the package. You can't please all of the people all of the time. And you wanna know what's worse than that? Sometimes you're actually going to be at fault. Sometimes you're going to make mistakes, so you'll have to stand up to the criticism that comes from them."

"But I didn't make a mistake, Mom."

"You didn't go into an off-limits building to go snooping around? Because that sounds like a pretty huge mistake right there." Mom was a conversational ninja, always doling out love with one sentence and a verbal spanking with the next. She'd been setting us boys up and knocking us down since we were toddlers.

"You're right," I moaned, because I'd learned long ago that parents want to hear they're right, even when they're wrong. "I shouldn't have gone into the library—but I'm not lying about what we saw in there!" I turned to the parent I was really trying to persuade. "Dad, I swear!"

Dad was still fuming silently in his chair, not having anything nice to say. His rate of breath was noticeably above normal.

"We believe you, son," Mom said warmly.

That wasn't so hard, was it?

"But that doesn't mean everyone else will. From what you're saying, you did the right thing, right up until you went inside that building instead of calling an adult for help. Let the world think what they want, because I promise you this, Phillip," she said as she turned and faced me to make sure I was paying attention, "they're going to anyway."

"That's not even close to fair, and you know it." I was struggling to understand why I had to just accept it and move on. If people were wrong and I was right, something ought to be done to point it out to them.

"If you're going to give up when things aren't fair, then you might as well just not even start down the path in the first place." She'd started washing the dishes by hand, despite the expensive dishwasher we owned—something that drove my father crazy. "We can't change everything that's not fair, Phillip. That's just not the world we live in."

I crossed my arms and remained quiet, not wanting to prolong the conversation any more than necessary, particularly since it wasn't remotely going my way.

"Now go wash up and get ready for bed. It's way past your bedtime."

4

I lay on my back on the bed, exhausted but nowhere near sleepy. The metal disc my father had given me—the direct-line emergency beacon—danced in the air above my head. I couldn't see it, but I pictured what I thought it looked like in my head as I used my powers to twirl it around absentmindedly and flip it end over end. It was something I'd started doing whenever I had trouble sleeping, which seemed to be common lately.

I could hear the usual sounds of Mom and Dad getting ready to go to bed. The TV was the first thing to go, then the lights in the hallway—they were fluorescent and gave off a nice deep hum when they were on, which you never really noticed until they were turned off. Usually my parents would be talking throughout this routine, but tonight they said nothing.

Mom pushed the last chair in under the table, making sure all four chairs were uniform in position, and then I heard two sets of footsteps come down the hallway.

Their bedroom was on the other side of mine, which meant we shared a wall. I crawled out of bed and crept into the closet, leaning my right ear up against the wall.

My hunch was right; they were talking. The voices were pretty muffled, but I could still make out what they were saying.

Mom sounded concerned. "First the kidnappings, and now this?"

There's been more than one kidnapping? That was news to me.

Mom continued. "Strangers showing up in our town confronting our children!"

"It's going to be fine, honey. From Phillip's description, this guy sounded like an old man . . . and a charming one, at that. I'm not convinced he's dangerous."

"An unknown man with superpowers shows up on the night of the first SuperSim and messes with your son's team, and you don't think he's dangerous?

What possible harmless reason could he have to do that? And with all this stuff in the news about superheroes . . . it's getting too dangerous out there for a mother, John."

"The board is still working very hard, honey, meeting with the government to try and figure out the best way to introduce our kind of people to the world. You have to realize how delicate a thing like this is going to be, right?"

"Well, while they fret over wording and who's going to be the boss of whom, we're seeing unprecedented criminal behavior in the form of attacks on our people and even in our own town."

Dad didn't have a quick reply, but after a moment he gave it a stab. "I think if he wanted to hurt them, he could have, Emily. But he didn't."

"I'm worried, John. We've lost two NPZ officers, Weatherby got attacked, and now this? Something feels very wrong to me."

NPZ officers? Was someone kidnapping heroes with no power zone abilities?

"The world is changing, Em," Dad said, with as soft a tone as I'd ever heard him use. "It's not going to be for Phillip and Patrick like it was for you and me."

"Just tell me you're looking into this."

"Of course we are, babe. And we're going to find those missing custodians and bring them back, okay? It's the agency's top priority."

"I know the kidnappings are a priority—I'm talking about our son being threatened."

"We'll look into this more too, honey, okay? But we don't really know what happened in there. We've got the word of our son, whom we trust and love, but who can't see."

"He can see when he's with Henry." I loved hearing Mom come to my defense.

"Sure, but he doesn't have a lot of experience with it, babe . . . with visual accuracy or visual memory."

"So you actually don't believe him, then?"

"No, I do. I do. One thing I can say is that Phillip's never been a liar. He's always been truthful with us. I just don't know that we can draw a lot of conclusions given two of our three witnesses are blind, and there's not really any evidence to support what they're saying."

"Well, regardless of what you really feel, your son thinks you don't believe him. I hope you're happy about that. Would it have killed you to tell him you believed him?"

Dad went silent at that. So silent I thought maybe I'd misheard something or the conversation had ended. I strained to hear better, smashing my head tighter against the wall.

"You're right," he said quietly. "I'll talk to him."

"Don't kiss me," I heard her say, scolding him. "You can kiss me in the morning, *after* you've talked to him." Her footsteps trailed off across the room, and I heard the door to their bathroom shut.

14

THE LIBRARY

I woke up that morning with a reputation hangover, instantly filled with embarrassment at the stories that were surely already circulating throughout town. I was more than happy for the distraction when Bentley called to invite me to a spontaneous lunch.

I was out the door and on my way to meet up with Bentley five minutes after I hung up the phone. It was getting cooler, though it was still plenty warm. Fall was moving in fast in this place, and a nice breeze kept the morning sun from being too hot while I walked.

Bentley had invited the rest of the gang too, of course, but only Henry had been able to make it on such short notice. We met up at Jack's Pizza. I'd eaten their takeout enough to know the food was good, and the downtown location made it central for all of us. The in-person Jack's experience was even better than the takeout. They had amazing breadsticks, with a zesty cheesy dipping sauce, as well as a wall of video games. It was kid heaven.

After a quick bite for energy—and three Mountain Dews for Henry—we got ready to leave. Oddly enough, we bumped into Mrs. Crouch on her way in. It was strange seeing her outside of the school environment, particularly in a place like Jack's, which catered more to people my age than to grandmothers.

"Oh, hi, Mrs. Crouch," I said, holding the door open for her. She entered, allowing Bentley and Henry to scoot by.

"Hello there, Mr. Sallinger," she said politely. "Mr. Gardner. Mr. Crittendon. What are you boys up to today?"

"We're going to be working on ideas for the next SuperSim," Bentley answered cheerily. "We didn't fare too well in the first one, you might have heard."

"Oh, yes. The library," she said, having obviously heard the story, like everyone in Freepoint.

"I don't really even mind doing poorly in the SuperSim," I said. "What I mind is being called liars."

"If you really want to prove you're not lying, young man," she said, just a hair shy of scolding me, "you're going to have to find some evidence."

"There isn't any evidence, though," I whined. "My dad and the other protectors couldn't find anything."

"Oh," Mrs. Crouch said, with her own brand of sarcasm infusing her words. "Well, I guess there's no point in looking further, then. I'm sure their five-minute late-night investigation was totally thorough."

The guys and I exchanged looks before I glanced back up at her and said, "Are you saying we should do our own investigation?"

Mrs. Crouch leaned down and smiled. "Not in the least. I'm merely saying . . . it is a *public* library." She looked up and across the street at the library. "Isn't it?" And with that, she turned and walked away. "Don't forget your math homework for Monday, boys," she called over her shoulder.

Henry watched her walking away and then looked over at the library before finally turning his gaze back to Bentley and me.

We hadn't considered investigating the library on our own—at least I hadn't. It never crossed my mind that Dad's buddies would have done a less than thorough job searching for clues. But, in hindsight, they'd come back awfully quick. They couldn't have spent more than a few minutes checking on our story and probably went into it thinking we were selling a whale tale anyway.

"Well, gentlemen, I'd say we have a change in plans," Bentley said, smiling ear to ear.

We stood in the hallway, in roughly the same spot we'd stood during the SuperSim, and took it all in. There was a gal at the information desk, speaking with two older ladies. A few other patrons moved through the great hallway, making their way to another section. At the far end of the hall was the main desk, where a small line of customers stood waiting to check out their selections.

The building was cooler this time, a more proper seventy-two degrees, give or take a degree. I was a borderline savant with guessing temperatures, though no one ever seemed to appreciate that gift.

It felt strange, like I could still hear the sound of Finch's footsteps and the echo of his overly polite voice.

"Come on," Bentley said, tapping me on the shoulder. "Let's go see what he was after."

We made our way through the hall to the door we'd seen open during the break-in. Henry looked up as we approached it. "'Resources and References'— oh man," he said. "No wonder I've never been in this section before. Nothing but encyclopedias and other boring crap in here."

"Hey," Bentley scolded, "encyclopedias are not boring." The main References Room was large, maybe the size of our school's cafeteria. Along the far wall was a gigantic array of Dewey decimal filing drawers. The center of the room was dotted with huge work tables, some even including little dividers for individual study sessions. Along the left wall were periodicals and encyclopedias. In the opposite corner of the room, an open doorway led to another hallway. "Let's go see what's down that hallway there," I said, pointing.

We zipped through the main References Room, a bit of adventure in the air.

"I'm calling it right now," Henry said, wheeling in front of us, providing my vision. "This guy's the most harmless criminal in history. I mean, what kind of a geezer nerd do you have to be to steal from the references section of the library? What's the most nefarious thing he could be up to, really? I mean, honestly."

"Hey, don't knock the references section so much. There's a lot of knowledge in this room. In fact, you could argue that pretty much all the knowledge in the world is contained in these materials."

"Bah!" Henry dismissed Bentley with a wave of his left hand, which then went right back to manning the wheel.

"You can learn how to build an atomic bomb using the references section of the library," Bentley said nonchalantly.

Henry stopped abruptly and turned his head. "Wait . . . really?"

"Sure," Bentley said, like it was common knowledge. "There are all sorts of nefarious things our man could have been up to. It's actually pretty scary if you think about it," he added, not sounding remotely scared.

"Jeez," Henry breathed. "Okay, so maybe he's not so harmless after all." He returned to wheeling himself forward as we went through the open doorway into the smaller hallway. Henry glanced up at the door as we passed. "Archives," Henry said in mock surprise, "of course. Even *older* encyclopedias and other boring books. Wonderful."

The Archives Room was nothing like the main references area; it contrasted sharply in almost every way. To begin with, it was round—an odd thing considering there were nothing but 90-degree angles and straight lines all around the building's exterior.

There were technically two stories to the room, with the domed second story mostly consisting of a half-level of shelves, accessible only by one of those permanent wheeled ladders in the center of the room. It was like a special little balcony just for books. The whole room couldn't have been more than fifteen feet across.

Where the main library was clean and classical, the Archives Room was cluttered and dusty. Cobwebs hung in all the corners. It appeared the word "archives" basically meant "stuff to be ignored forever."

Henry wasn't done sharing his unfiltered opinions. "Aw, man, this is a dead-end room."

"Not necessarily," Bentley countered, already a couple rungs up the ladder to investigate.

"Come on, Bentley," Henry continued. "This tiny room? This is what you think Sherlock was after?"

Bentley stopped climbing and looked down at Henry to make his point. "He has to have been after something in the references section. We can't really know what until we start crossing off possibilities." He returned to his climbing and in no time was slowly inching around the room inspecting the books.

I wasn't about to climb a ladder, and Henry wasn't either, so we began investigating what we could see on the main floor. It was impossible to investigate separately from Henry unless I was going to just feel my way around the room. I was pretty much stuck exploring whatever he was exploring if I wanted to see anything.

Henry started reading the titles of the old books on the shelves. Each one looked more antique than the last, though they were all pretty disgusting, covered with years of grime.

"*Maps of the Mountain Masters*," he said aloud as his powers let me read along with him.

"Okay," I said cautiously, wondering who the mountain masters were and why they'd allowed themselves to be called something so silly.

Henry merely gave it a hearty "Ha!"

"*The Right and True Synopsis of Rygren the Terrible*," he continued, calling out the next title he saw. "That . . . actually sounds pretty cool." He pulled the book out a tiny bit, marking it for later, I suppose, and then moved on to the next book.

"*The Sixteen Laws of Simon Smith*," he said, reading another book title.

"Ooh," Bentley said excitedly from above. "They have *The Sixteen Laws of Simon Smith*?" He poked his head down.

"Are you serious? You've heard of this book?"

"It's pretty fascinating, actually. In the sixth century, the leader of the superpowered people was Simon Smith, a man of deep religious faith. He believed that heroes were literally God's angels, and he set about rewriting the bulk of superhero law at the time from scratch. I'm definitely taking that book with me." With that, he popped his head back up and continued his own exploring.

Henry looked at me and delivered a complete thought. *That dude is seriously nerdy.* He pulled the book out to mark its place.

"Nothing but boring crap up here, for the most part," Bentley called down. "Mostly ledgers and old financial accounts, from the looks of it. A few books on songs."

Henry kept going. "*Elben's Wrath*—ooh, Bentley, I bet you want this one too, yeah?"

I shivered. I'd heard plenty of the scary superhero stories since starting school, but none of them gave me the creeps like the tales about Elben. No villain could ever be more frightening than an all-powerful one.

"Are you kidding?" Bentley taunted. "I have three copies of that one already."

The pictures from Henry bobbed back and forth brightly, indicating he was most likely mimicking and mocking Bentley's last statement. Then I saw his gaze turn to the wheeled ladder, which had just been rolled to a position right in front of the wheelchair. Henry looked at me, and I watched myself shake my head in an emphatic no, but he did it anyway.

Henry ripped his right arm down on his right wheel and pulled his left arm up on the left wheel, spinning the entire chair sharply to the left. The footrests banged into the ladder, sending it rolling several inches. Bentley was understandably not prepared for this and lost his footing. His feet slipped a few rungs, and he finally caught himself with his hands, avoiding falling all the way to the floor. But then, he slipped again.

The ladder shot out in a flash, and Bentley's limp body fell into the lap of someone who deserved it, Henry. The impact of Bentley's fall caused them to tumble over backward as the wheelchair capsized, sending them both scattering onto the floor.

Somewhere in the confusion, I lost my vision. Henry must have been jarred enough himself to stop sending what he was seeing. I was about to cry out in shock and alarm, fearing my friends were injured, when I began to hear laughter. It was Henry, enjoying the unexpected outcome of his little prank more than I would have expected him to.

"Ha ha ha ha. Oh man," he said, breathing heavily, "that was hilarious."

"Hilarious?" Bentley cried in offense. "You jerk. That freaking hurt, you idiot!"

That made Henry laugh even harder.

"I swear, Henry," Bentley warned without much believable machismo, "one of these days you're going to get it."

"Oh, and I suppose you're going to be the one to give it to me," Henry taunted playfully.

"Don't think I won't hit you just because you're in a wheelchair, buddy. Don't forget I'm a cripple, too, technically!"

I figured it was time to intervene. "Yeah, that's definitely a fight I'd pay to see, two crippled superheroes with mental superpowers going head-to-head

. . . sounds like a good time. Henry, why don't you stop laughing and get up off the floor." I reached out my hand, and thankfully, he grabbed it and started pulling.

Henry was a big kid, so I dug in my heels to gain leverage, and as his body began to rise up off the floor, my vision returned. I kept pulling until Henry was back in his chair, and that's when I realized something was off. "Wait a second," I said. "Go back down to the floor."

"But I just got back up here," he protested.

"I know, I know. I wanna see something," I explained.

"Phillip, you're blind."

"Not with you around, buddy, remember? Now . . . just go look closely at that center tile there. I want to check something out."

"Okay, okay. What the heck, lower me down."

I reached out my hands, and he grabbed them to lower himself back down to the floor. From there, he turned and used his arms to slide himself over to the center of the room, near the spot where he'd tumbled from his chair. He looked directly at the center tile, giving me a fine view of it, though that's not really what I wanted to see.

"Okay," he said skeptically, "what am I looking at?"

"Get closer. Put your face right down near it," I urged.

To my surprise, he obliged, and just as his face reached the point where his nose was nearly touching the floor, my vision disappeared again.

"There!" I shouted. "My vision is gone!"

"What?" Henry asked, lifting his head to look at me, returning my vision in the process.

"And now it's back," I said proudly. "Go back down."

Henry lowered his head toward the ground again, and at the same spot, my vision disappeared again. "And now it's gone again."

"What are you talking about, Phillip? I'm still sending you my vision."

"I'm sure you are," I said, smiling. "Do you realize what this means?"

He did not. "Um, you're a crazy person?"

But Bentley knew it instantly. "There's an NPZ down there!" His powers snapped into action. "There's gotta be a hidden room directly underneath this room."

"What?" Poor Henry was still playing catch-up. "What makes you say that?"

"Why else would there be an NPZ that only kicks in at floor level, huh?"

"How do you even know it's an NPZ?"

I fielded this one. "What else could it be, Henry? A break in the space-time continuum that disallows superpowers? Your abilities work everywhere else in this building except for right here in this room, near the floor. Bentley's right. There's a room down there. And what's more, I guarantee you that whatever Finch was after was in that room."

Henry rattled off a series of questions any one of us could have asked. "Do you think that's what the banging and crashing was? He was trying to get into the secret room? Do you think he succeeded?"

Bentley turned toward me and said, "There's only one way to find out."

15

HALLOWEEN

From that point forward, our team was about as dedicated to self-improvement as could be. After our dismal first performance, we had nowhere to go but up, but it would take practice and planning to get there.

We met every day at lunch to discuss SuperSim strategy. We met at Mr. Charles's cornfield twice a week in the evenings for practice. Heck, some Little League teams don't even practice that often. We even had a few weekend practices.

Not everyone on the team was able to make every practice. Freddie had piano lessons one night each week, and James's parents were pretty strict about "family time." But Henry, Bentley, and I never missed a practice.

We went through scenarios that tested my ability to use my powers to stop an opponent. We fine-tuned the video link between Henry and me by running drills. Bentley spent tons of time researching past SuperSims, looking for patterns and themes we could capitalize on. Our team was never going to be very intimidating. After my telekinesis, we had only James's teleporting and Freddie's gigantism as physical powers to play with.

We hadn't ever seen Freddie use his power. We imagined it would be intimidating and frightening to opponents, but he said there wouldn't be time. Once Freddie puffed up to full size, he almost immediately needed his inhaler . . . desperately. Bentley briefly talked about building a giant-sized inhaler for Freddie to use once he grew to his extraordinary size, but apparently the medicine they put in those things isn't exactly easy to come by in large quantities.

We still had no idea what Donnie's ability was, but he was huge and strong and certainly ran faster than average. He was the closest thing to a legitimate intimidator our team would ever have. But ultimately, he wasn't particularly well equipped to deal with bad guys one-on-one.

So the actual work of stopping the criminals with our powers would fall to Freddie, James, and me. We practiced using James as a bit of a kidnapper, where we would distract the villain somehow so that James could pop in and grab him, only to pop back out to a jail cell or squad car.

We practiced using my powers to disarm opponents, which seemed to work pretty well—particularly if the enemies in the next SuperSim ended up using ears of corn as weapons.

Had my powers been stronger, I would have been more help with restraining villains. I knew that other movers, like my father, had the ability to mentally lift an opponent up off the ground and suspend them in midair, though usually for only a few seconds. I couldn't do that kind of thing nor anything close to it. The maximum strength of my powers was little more than a Star Trek shield or force field. I could knock people down sometimes, but that was it. So, for me, we focused on using other objects as projectiles or ripping stolen goods from a thief's hands with my mind.

We were focused and dedicated, determined not to repeat our mistakes. There was only one thing that could slow us down or keep us from focusing on the next SuperSim competition: a holiday. Specifically, Halloween.

Halloween was easily my favorite holiday. I think it was the costumes, which might be strange for a blind kid to say. Costumes felt like disguises to me, and I guess that helped me feel less different, less disabled. Less me.

But the candy obviously didn't hurt either.

I loved how Halloween came and went in relatively tidy fashion. Not at all like Christmas, which takes its sweet time over two months of anticipation and buildup. Halloween just suddenly shows up one day, lets you prance around in a cape and a mask collecting milk chocolate and gummy bears, and then disappears as quickly as it'd come. No fuss, little mess. Maybe an upset stomach, but then things go right back to normal.

Mom, of course, preferred Christmas. She loved the two months of buildup, the decorating, the carols—she loved it all, and she savored it. She had this little Christmas village made up of miniature ceramic houses, and instead of putting the whole thing out in one evening like a normal person, my mother would put out one house every night for weeks and weeks until she broke out the final one on Christmas Eve. The whole thing seemed very unnecessary to me at the time, though I have since come to see the appeal.

Don't get me wrong. I loved Christmas, as any kid would. I just felt like the whole thing took too long to get going and then took too long to get over with. And all the truly great elements of Christmas were sandwiched into one or two days in the middle.

I also think the smells of the various holidays played a part in how I chose my favorites because that's simply the way I connected my memories to the events. I couldn't see the twinkling Christmas lights, but I could smell the gingerbread, the evergreen, and the peppermint.

And I think I liked the smells of Halloween the best. The smell of fall and spice and apple concoctions. I'm quite certain I could drink apple cider every day for the rest of my life and not grow tired of it.

Anyway, Halloween showed up—suddenly, as always—and our team was happy to take an evening off from studying and practicing in order to dress up in costumes and go get some candy. But we were still a team, and none of us really had many friends outside the group anyway, so we made arrangements to meet at Bentley's house so we could go trick-or-treating together.

Bentley dressed as Sherlock Holmes, one of his many "heroes of intellect." He had originally asked if I wanted to go as Watson and pair our costumes together around the same theme. But I reminded him that nobody knows what Watson looks like, which leaves little reason to dress up as him. A Halloween costume should be recognizable; at least, that was my rule. People shouldn't have to wonder who you're dressed as.

Henry told us he had a long history of incorporating his wheelchair into his costumes. On previous Halloweens, he'd gone as FDR, Professor X from *X-Men*, Stephen Hawking, and most of the other famous wheelchair-bound individuals, both real and fictional. This year he was paying tribute to some kind of documentary about wheelchair athletes who play a physical, hard-nosed form of basketball. I hadn't seen the movie, but his description made me want to. Henry was dressed in a basketball outfit with a fake goatee and some temporary tattoos on his arms.

Donnie was dressed in an all-white leisure suit from the 1970s, with a bright-blue button-up shirt under the jacket. He definitely looked odd. I wasn't sure if he'd picked out his own costume or if his parents had dressed him, and I had no idea what he was supposed to be. But I was impressed, nonetheless, as I'd expected him to show up in blue jeans and a polo shirt—the standard Donnie uniform.

Penelope, that weather-controlling girl from our class, showed up. I wasn't sure why since I'd assumed it was just an evening for the team to hang out together. She was dressed as some kind of cartoon princess. I didn't know which one it was, and I honestly didn't care. All the animated princess characters ran together for me, just as my various comic book heroes surely did for Penelope.

James couldn't make it, sadly. His parents were already frustrated with how much time he was spending with us, it seemed. They were a very close family and had begun to miss his company. So they insisted he spend the holiday with them. It sounded fair enough to me, I suppose, but a bit of a bummer.

The real disappointment with James not attending, aside from missing his cheerful company, was the fact that it torpedoed our master plan to get extra candy. We had intended to use James's ability to teleport as a way to help us hit more houses than we could ever hope to visit just by walking. We figured that each of us could triple our candy haul just by skipping the pesky task of shuffling from house to house. Bentley drew the whole thing up, and I swear it was a work of brilliance. He even had blueprints!

Sadly, it was not to be. James gave me a stack of his business cards and asked me to hand them out to the people at the houses we went to. I promised I would, but I didn't exactly keep that promise.

I waffled on my own choice in costume for a few days because I wanted it to be perfect. I thought about going Henry's route and picking a famous blind person to impersonate, maybe even a superhero like Daredevil. But that seemed a little too easy. And there just weren't very many famous blind people that I could think of outside of Stevie Wonder and that opera guy my mother was always listening to.

In the end, I decided my blindness didn't need to be reflected in my choice of costume. After all, I had recently gained the gift of sight, at least on certain occasions. Maybe wearing a blind man's costume wouldn't really be a very accurate reflection anymore anyway.

So I dressed in the same costume I did every year: Batman. Even though I knew that choice would keep my costume from being truly unique—there were at least thirty kids out in Freepoint that night dressed as the Caped Crusader—I had always felt a connection with the character.

We were allowed to go out for candy on Halloween night by ourselves, without parental supervision. It was a first for me. Of course, my most recent trick-or-treating experiences had been in New York City, which is not exactly a safe place to go out alone at night even if you're a forty-five-year-old man. But Freepoint was a much safer town, populated solely by good guys, supposedly. And we were all twelve or older. So none of the parents put up a fuss about it, though we all got a decent lecture on staying together and being careful and coming home on time—10:00 p.m. for me, also a first.

If they'd had a crystal ball, they probably would have banned us from trick-or-treating altogether. Forever.

Giddy and excited for a night of fun, we set off on our quest for sugar. Blind Batman, a hard-core basketballer, Sherlock Holmes, a Disney princess, and a large male disco dancer. We were quite the sight.

We hit the houses in Bentley's neighborhood first, mostly because they were all owned by rich people. It was simple math, really. More money equals better candy—so we thought. Unfortunately, we discovered that rich people don't really give out candy proportionate to their wealth. Not that we didn't do well. But we'd built it up too much in our minds ahead of time.

After covering the two neighborhoods nearest Bentley's, many of us had bags that were already full. Penelope was starting to whine about being tired, even though we'd been at it for only a couple hours, which made me glad she wasn't actually on our SuperSim team. Henry, Bentley, and I were willing to keep going, but after a few more houses near the center of town, Penelope's will gave out and she decided to call it a night.

For some reason, Bentley offered to walk her home . . . for safety, he said. I guessed maybe he was tired, and her exit gave him an opportunity to make his own.

I honestly didn't think anything of it. *She's a girl, she's scared, and it's Halloween*. It made perfect sense to me that she would need an escort, especially after all the "stay together" warnings from our folks. So we said our goodbyes, and then Henry, Donnie, and I forged ahead.

We hit maybe ten more houses and then decided to rest. At the corner of Wabash and Gregory, on a concrete staircase in front of a nice old lady's house—she'd just given each of us two king-size candy bars apiece!—we sat and took a breather. We ate some of our candy, both to boost our energy and to make more room in our bags, and compared our collections.

Wabash Avenue wasn't the busiest street for trick-or-treaters, but it wasn't empty either. There were a few groups of kids on the sidewalk opposite us moving to our left toward where we'd just been. And there was a trio of kids from behind us that had almost caught up to us while we rested.

Henry glanced around, allowing me to see our surroundings along with him. He panned his head left to right, taking in the scenery, and then back to the left again—all the while lecturing Donnie on the proper hierarchy of the various candies of the world. It was easy to lecture Donnie since he so rarely participated in conversations, but Henry had a habit of speechifying anyway.

He'd taken to sending me his images without even thinking about it, for the most part. It had become second nature in a very short span of time, though we were still working on smoothing out the pictures into something more like a true video stream.

"The king-size Reese's Cup is the king of all candies," Henry declared with authority. "It is the big dog, and it's not even close."

Donnie just nodded, taking a bite out of his own candy bar.

While Henry rambled on, showing off his extensive candy expertise, he continued panning his gaze. I wasn't sure if he was doing it for me or because it was dark, late at night, on Halloween. I took advantage of the view regardless. I studied the scene at the far right end of the street. Down the roadway, on every block, street lights illuminated the intersections going away from the center of Freepoint. A few trick-or-treaters were moving in our direction on our side of the street, about two blocks away. Across the street and closer, a couple more dressed-up kids were headed away from us.

Just before Henry panned back to the left again, something three blocks away caught my attention.

"Wait, wait, wait! Go back," I said quickly.

"What?" Henry asked, simultaneously turning his gaze back to the right.

"I thought I saw something."

It was silent for a few beats while both Henry and I took in the view.

"All I see is some old man way down there."

"Exactly."

"What?" Henry asked. "You recognize that guy? He's, like, a mile away."

I did recognize him. Well . . . I thought I did. There was something about the brisk-but-casual meter of his footsteps. I could even faintly hear them in the distance.

"Look at how he moves, Henry." The man was pretty far away and only a silhouette could be made out, but I could still see his movements as he slowly walked in the opposite direction. "See how his head bobs, ever so slightly." Everything about the way he moved was familiar.

"I don't know, Phillip," Henry said reluctantly. "All I see is a dark stick figure on a darker background. He's way too far away. I give up, man, who is it?"

Click-clop. It all started to come together for me.

"Is he smoking a pipe?" I burst out suddenly. "He is! Did you see that?"

"Holy crap," Henry breathed. He finally saw it.

I was utterly convinced now. The pipe had sealed it for me, though the footsteps should have. Even though a few weeks had passed, the memories from that encounter were still fresh. The man on the sidewalk three blocks away, walking away from us, was the same man we confronted in the library during the SuperSim.

We decided—rather hastily, I might add, now that I have the gift of hindsight—to follow this Mr. Finch and see if we could find out where he was going.

This was the man who had single-handedly ruined our reputation around town. The man who had made us look like idiots and fibbers. The man nobody else believed even existed. Of course we were going to go after him. There was zero debate.

But this wasn't a SuperSim. This was real, and I felt the corresponding chill come over me as I contemplated the possible danger.

Now it's important to note that Henry's wheelchair was relatively new; it had been a birthday present several weeks prior. It was just about the fanciest wheelchair in existence. It was built with tungsten and titanium for a super lightweight and maximum strength construction. And it was quiet as a mouse.

Staying on our side of the road, we crept slowly after our target. He was now four blocks ahead of us, but he wasn't in any hurry. Just taking a stroll through Freepoint, smoking his pipe, on Halloween.

Wabash Avenue, as it happens, is lined with tall oak trees. They're stationed like sentries, one in front of each house, out between the sidewalk and the road. They must have been planted generations ago because they towered over the houses and the telephone poles. Between the massive tree trunks and the parked cars, we were blessed to have many objects to hide behind as we went along. The old man was moving at such a leisurely pace, we were able to make up ground just by walking quickly.

After a block and a half, we could see him more clearly. He was wearing the same goofy hat and the same distinguished jacket. I had a sudden realization that for this one night, Bentley and Finch were both dressed like Sherlock Holmes.

Soon, we were close enough to hear him whistling.

The fact that we could hear him made me realize he could hear us too if we weren't careful. I held my finger to my closed lips to let Henry know to stay quiet. Henry craned his neck and peeked over the station wagon we were using as a bunker, and we both saw something unexpected. It didn't compute.

There was a second man walking with Finch. Where there had been only one mysterious old man just moments earlier, there were now two, walking side by side away from us. The new guy was shorter, with medium-dark hair and a long, flowing black cape. There was a second set of audible footsteps and a hushed murmur of covert conversation.

"What the . . ." Henry whispered. "Where did he come from?"

The temperature seemed to have dropped a few degrees as the cold wind started to gust.

"Were there two of them before, and we just didn't see the other guy?" I knew it was a long shot.

"No way, man," Henry confirmed. "We would have seen another guy."

"So he just appeared out of thin air?"

"Well, the old man did teleport the first time we met him, remember?"

"Geez," I said, exhaling in frustration. "What do we do now?"

"We keep following them, duh."

"I know that, I'm just saying . . . what if they split up? What if there are more of them?" *What if I'm starting to get a bad feeling about this?* I was, indeed, getting a bad feeling. What little we knew about this man made us curious to learn more, for certain, but it was also cause for hesitation. And fear. I was experiencing plenty of both.

"Don't worry about your bad feelings," he said, reading my mind as always. "We're superheroes, dude. You're going to have to get used to seeing crazy stuff. Now, we gotta go. They're getting too far ahead of us. We'll figure that stuff out as it comes, Phillip." And with that, he was off toward the next car up the block, using his arms to churn the wheels forward silently.

After another block of following them, the two men reached a corner and abruptly turned left. They were still two blocks ahead of us, and we were unprepared for the sudden change in direction.

"Crap," I exclaimed. I'm not sure why we just assumed they'd keep going in a straight line.

"Come on, let's cross the street," Henry urged.

We scampered across Wabash to the sidewalk our targets had just been on and then hurried toward the corner. The candy bags were starting to feel like dumbbells, and the muscles in my arms were beginning to burn. This time we ran, but we managed to do it without making much noise. There was a concrete retaining wall lining the yard of the corner house, and by ducking just the slightest bit, we were able to hide behind it as we moved. We reached the corner, stopping a few feet short of where the wall ended, and caught our breath.

After a few seconds, Henry slowly moved toward the edge of the wall and leaned his head around it to look down the street. The images I received from him were turned at an angle as he tilted his head. It was a strange feeling to have a first-person view of a peek around the corner without doing any of the actual peeking, like Henry was a personal periscope.

Unfortunately, a giant sagging tree branch hung low over the sidewalk about two houses down. We could see a foot or two through the leaves, but the total view was obstructed. The branch almost touched the sidewalk.

"Dang it," Henry sputtered. "What next?"

As he continued straining his neck left and right, trying to find some magical angle through the leaves that revealed a better view, I was struck with an epiphany: *Henry's right—you have superpowers, idiot!*

I concentrated on the drooping branch, focusing all my thoughts on it alone. Through the gift of Henry's eyesight, I was able to see my powers in action even though I was still physically around the corner of the concrete wall. The branch slowly lifted, sighing back into a position it must have held years before, upright and tall.

"Not bad, Phillip," Henry said, clearly impressed. "Not bad at all."

But the congratulatory moment passed immediately for us both as we saw what the tree had been obstructing. I instantly regretted having moved the branch, because now there were four figures moving away from us. The new additions had similar capes, and I noticed all four sets of footsteps were in perfect rhythm.

"What in the heck is going on?" I said in frustration as Henry pulled back from the corner. I let the tree branch drop back into its former position.

"I don't know, Phillip. Where are they all coming from?"

My bad feeling was coming back, this time much stronger. By this point, we were reaching the edge of town, having stayed on the trail for several blocks. We'd started out following one man and now were outnumbered two to one.

"Hey," he replied, playing devil's advocate, "We're not going to attack them. We're just following them. We're only trying to see where they're going, okay?"

"Yeah," I conceded, my lingering reluctance still showing.

"Look, don't you want to know what this guy's deal is? Who he is? What he's up to?"

"Of course I do!"

"Well, then you can't take your candy and go home just yet. We have to keep going. And they're getting away if we don't move soon."

He was right. I did want to know what was going on. Who was this guy? And why did he have so many caped-crusader helpers? It didn't make any sense to me at all. My curiosity got the best of my anxiety for the moment, and I nodded.

Henry stole another glance around the wall's edge, and I lifted the branch again, but this time, the men were gone. Disappeared. Poof. He stuck more of his head around the corner to get a better view, but there was no sign of them. He wheeled his chair completely out from behind the wall and looked long and hard down the sidewalk. Nothing.

"Where did they go?" he asked, turning his head back to me. When his eyes finally trained on my position, we both saw Finch standing right behind me.

16

FIRE

"Hello, again," he said simply. His voice was as friendly as his presence was creepy.

Instinct kicked in, which means we screamed like girls and ran away from the old man, rounding the corner we'd been hiding behind and taking off like our lives depended on it.

"Come on, Donnie," Henry yelled.

Donnie! I'd almost forgotten all about him. He'd been quiet, as usual, just creeping along behind Henry and me all throughout our attempts to play spy. I shuddered at the realization that I could so easily just forget about him. *But*, I reminded myself, *I am blind.*

In addition to being strong and stealthy, Henry's new wheelchair was also very fast, and it was a struggle to keep up with him. I tried my best to quickly memorize Henry's images, which he was still sending me, whether he knew it or not. It's not easy to look where you're going when your vision is twenty paces ahead of your feet. I stumbled and tripped as I ran, my cape flapping and snapping in the wind behind me. Donnie's hands were suddenly on me, steadying me as he ran alongside me.

I reached up and pulled off the cowl and cape, tossing them aside to decrease wind resistance. Also, I kind of didn't want to die in a full Batman costume. We ran and ran for two or three blocks without looking back. We were certain there were hundreds of caped weirdos and a kindly old gentlemen right on our heels, carrying pitchforks and tobacco pipes.

But when Henry finally stopped and whipped his gaze around, there was no one behind me. Another disappearing act.

We all gasped for air while Henry darted his eyes in every direction. It didn't appear as though we were being followed. As I watched the images from Henry, a wave of recognition came over me. "Hey," I said slowly, "I know where we are."

We were near Mr. Charles's farm—our practice field. Through all the evening's adventures, I hadn't realized we'd gone all the way to the edge of town. Just a block or so east, and we'd be at the tree line that marked the farm's north boundary.

"Yeah," Henry agreed. "Me too. Come on!" He turned and took off again, headed for the nearby familiar ground.

"Donnie," I yelled, waving my arm for him to follow.

By the time we reached the tree line, we were all gassed. But we kept running until we reached the cornfields, stopping fifty feet or so into the grass swath that ran between the two large plots.

Air seemed to be in short supply, and we all doubled over in fatigue as we gasped and panted, dropping our candy bags to the ground.

And through the sound of the deep breaths, the old man spoke. "It would seem to me," he said, "that running would not be a very effective strategy for you gentlemen at this point. It only wears you out, you see?"

Fear raced through me like a wave, starting from the tips of my fingers and toes. He sounded about thirty yards away, give or take, and the very fact that he was standing there was proof of his statement—it was futile to try and run away from him. He was a teleporter.

"Isn't it funny, don't you think, that after following me for several blocks— poorly, I might add—and then being frightened into a flight response . . . you still somehow ended up at the place I was headed to myself?"

"Well," Henry huffed, "we'd be happy to go somewhere else, then. Honestly . . . we don't really want to be around you anymore. I don't, at least." He inhaled another deep breath.

"That's certainly out of the question."

I felt like I should say something. I searched my brain for something confident and defiant. But I found nothing. I was terrified.

"Well," Finch said with a deep sigh, "I suppose you'd better come take a look at what I've been up to this time." With that, he turned and began walking slowly away from us. He got about ten paces before he stopped and turned back around. "Let's *go*, children! I have many things to attend to, and I can't spend all evening with you playing deer in the headlights."

Henry turned toward me and I toward him.

"If he wanted to kill us, he would have," I offered weakly.

"If he wanted to kill us *now*, he would have," Henry countered.

"Well, if he's going to kill us either way, I'm at least going to see what he's talking about." I turned and started walking. After a few steps I heard Henry sigh loudly and then begin following me.

"Come on, Donnie," Henry said.

Finch turned and continued down the patch of grass between cornfields toward a ridge fifty yards away, where the farmland dove into a valley. As we got closer to the ridge, I began to hear all kinds of noises—machinery, voices, concussive sounds. Something was lighting the valley enough to create a soft white glow just above the ridge. Little plumes of dust and smoke were scattered here and there, floating up as they disappeared into the night sky.

Eventually we reached the very edge, where Finch was waiting for us. And what we saw in the valley defied logic. Somehow, in the course of one evening, Finch's workers—all in black capes—had managed to carve out a huge chunk of earth, creating a cavity ten stories deep.

Henry moved his gaze around, and I counted at least fifty men and women, all standing completely still inside a crater the size of a sports arena in the middle of Mr. Charles's farm. *Where the heck is that guy? He's just going to let this happen?* They were spaced apart in uneven increments, but the overall effect was that they were arranged in some kind of symbol or pattern. In the middle of the giant hole in the ground stood a strange square machine standing on four squatty legs.

We stood in silence as Henry and I took it all in.

Finally, Finch spoke. "Are either of you familiar with the story of Elben?"

We were, and he knew it. Every kid knew the story of Elben, the ancient one of our kind who had possessed every power all at once and had nearly decimated the entire population of the planet. Hearing his name aloud was cause for a shudder, but from Finch's mouth, it rang out even more ominously.

"I see, then." Finch added unnecessarily, "I wonder, have you ever heard of the prophecy which foretells Elben's return?"

Again, both the question and his waiting for our answer were unnecessary.

The prophecy of the return of "the one who can do all" was considered by many to be a load of hogwash. My father, for instance, did not believe in it for even an instant. Nor did the pragmatic Mrs. Crouch. But a twelve-year-old boy can find a way to believe in even the most unlikely thing when it's scary enough.

"These men and women you see here have dedicated their lives to the belief that Elben is coming back. They, along with me, are Believers."

The hair on my arms began to stand up.

Finch continued. "You see, long before America existed—indeed, long before America was even discovered—this place, this city, this very *spot* was central to our people . . . *your* people."

The whirring of the giant machine in the center of the crater distracted all three of us, and we turned to see it lifting slowly off the ground. In the center, a huge boulder could be seen being pried from the dirt.

"'Be thee wary. Be thee watchful. Signs will appear but only to those looking.'" Finch was quoting the well-known ancient prophecy. He went back into kindly old teacher mode. "Elben is the only custodian in history to have every single known ability. And Freepoint . . . was his home. It wasn't called Freepoint, then, of course. But long before your parents gentrified this place into a heroes' town, it was home to a darker power. And though dormant, that power surges still today."

"So, you're digging up the bones of Elben for some kind of goat sacrifice, then?" It warmed my heart to see that Henry dished out his usual bluntness to enemies as well as friends, though I suspected it was just a defense mechanism to mask his own fear.

Finch just laughed. "Sort of. But no. Elben's instructions for his Believers require us to make a few . . . how shall I say . . . preparations just prior to his arrival." I immediately thought of my parents' hushed discussions about the Believers as well as the recent kidnappings.

"Elben does not and will not require resuscitation. In fact, he's already here. He's already been reborn. We just have to find out who he is, which we won't be able to do until he reveals himself at the appointed time. Until then," he paused, true excitement in his voice, "there is much to do."

"So you're like the leader of the Believers?" Despite all my better instincts, I felt myself relaxing slightly. Perhaps it was Finch's intoxicating tone that set me more at ease.

"Of *these* Believers, yes."

"For a second, there, I thought you were going to say you were Elben." Henry chuckled.

Finch smiled politely. "Oh, probably not."

I breathed a quiet sigh of relief.

"It's likely that I'm something different . . . entirely." He smiled strangely, then turned suddenly and called out to the workers below. "Time to wrap it up, boys. Get what we came for, and let's get out of here. Company is coming."

Company? Henry looked at me in confusion and then turned to see what the Believers were doing in response to Finch's command, but to my surprise—and his own, no doubt—they were gone. The mammoth hole in the ground was gone too, replaced by the peaceful cornfield that had been there prior to the hole's existence. No sound, no light, no indication whatsoever that they'd gone. In an instant, just like that . . . it was as if they'd never been there. *Had they even been there?*

"Ordinarily, we have two options in situations like this." Finch's voice was more serious than normal, with an edge I hadn't heard before. "Invite you into our clan of Believers or kill you." He stopped there to let those words sink in. "Now, obviously you're a little young to be Believers, and I'm not quite certain you'll be willing to just pretend tonight never happened." He was right on both counts. "So I'm left with a bit of a conundrum."

"Look," Henry said, exhausted. "If you're going to kill us, just freaking do it already. Honestly . . . we already had a long and tiring night before even running into you, and I don't think I have the patience for your games, okay?"

It's funny how a few minutes of calm conversation can relax a person who should still be very much on alert.

"I don't want to kill you, that's for certain. But unless you can guarantee me that you two can remain silent about the events here this evening, I'm afraid I can't let you go. The library . . . that was . . . something different. Not like this. This . . . we need you to keep to yourselves."

"Yeah, right," Henry scoffed. "Do you even have any idea how kids work? We can't keep quiet about anything, man, much less a plot to take over the world that starts with digging giant holes in cornfields!"

"So then, you understand my predicament."

"Should we even be afraid of you?"

"Uh, Henry," I offered, too late.

"You're not the bad guy, you're just some . . . lackey. And you already sent your Believer buddies away too. So exactly why should we even listen to you?"

"There is more than one evil in this world, young man." All trace of kindness and warmth had gone from his voice, replaced by a chilling tone. "Elben is . . . merely one of them. Powerful, sure. But far from the worst thing there is to fear on this earth. You'd do well to remember that, Mr. Gardner."

"Bah!" Henry waved his hand in contempt, grabbed his wheels, and spun around his wheelchair in dismissal. "Come on, guys. Let's get out of here. Grandpa's going to be preaching for a while, and I don't think he has anything more to say that we should listen to."

I warily turned to follow Henry and Donnie. Something inside me told me there was more to Finch than we currently knew and that the rest of what there was to learn about him would be all terrible. I wanted to get the heck out of this situation as quickly as possible, and Henry had managed to create the first legitimate opportunity to do so. Now that we'd turned away from Finch completely, I was hoping against hope that "out of sight, out of mind" would become more than just a saying.

I shuffled my feet through the grass, following the sound of Donnie's footsteps and Henry's wheelchair a few paces in front of me. I held my breath, waiting for a rebuke from Finch. For several steps, there was none. But any hope of easy escape vanished quickly.

Finch sighed audibly. "You guys are really going to make me do this?" We stopped, not turning around, and then continued walking. "I was really hoping to save the whole 'display of powers' thing for a little further down the road. And honestly, after Cleveland, I'm kind of surprised you aren't a little more wary of my abilities than you are."

Henry turned around, and following the images in my brain instinctively, so did I. "Ooh, you can read minds *and* teleport people! Some of the least scary powers there are, mister. And now that we know you have an army of Believer whatevers at your disposal, well . . . maybe I'm not so convinced you have any real powers yourself anyway, okay?"

Before he'd finished his sentence, a blast of red light shot out of Finch's eyes and scorched the ground near Henry's left wheel. It was the single loudest noise I'd ever heard in my life, a high-pitched static noise, and the sound alone stopped my heart for a couple beats. The grass sizzled in the silence.

Henry, maybe stop antagonizing the bad guy!

I'm sorry, I didn't know he had freaking eye-beams!

"That's not all I have, gentlemen. You see, I'm an absorber. But a unique one."

At this point, both Henry and I were afraid to do anything. I was personally still reeling from the ear-ringing eye-blaster we'd just witnessed in action.

Finch continued, as though sensing our fear and pouncing on it. "Most absorbers can use another custodian's power only while in proximity to that absorber. Thanks to . . . good fortune . . . I'm actually able to use absorbed powers for several hours after contact with the original custodian, so even though my friends have left us alone here tonight, I'll have full use of each of their powers for, oh, more than long enough to take care of the three of you."

If what he was saying was true, it changed everything we knew about how absorbers work, and that was already a rare enough power to begin with. It created some potential issues for crime-fighters and protectors like my father, that's for sure. But I wasn't thinking about that right now. Instead, I was thinking about survival.

Finch continued. "Some among our order even think that I could be the reincarnation of Elben, given the uniqueness of my abilities."

"So . . . are you?" Henry chirped.

Finch replied, "I have no idea." He cocked his head to the side, as though considering it. "Maybe I am him. Maybe I'm not. It's not for me—or you—to know . . . yet. All will be revealed at its appointed time. What should concern you at the moment is that my current power situation makes the question moot. So many powers at my disposal," he said, a smile in his words. "How to best place you into a proper state of awe?" His earlier friendly tone had morphed into a taunting one, much like Chad's voice had done that day in the cafeteria once he'd revealed his true intentions. "Should I levitate myself?" He lifted off the ground about two feet, hanging there like a hummingbird. "Or shall I rain down fire from the sky?"

Instinctively, Henry jerked his head up to the night sky. Several bright stars were visible, but no fireballs were present. After several seconds of nothing—actually, enough time went by that I began to wonder if Finch was just trying to distract us—I finally noticed one of the stars was moving left to right, ever so faintly. No sooner had I made this realization than the thing sped up rapidly and began to grow in size. It was coming right for us.

Before I could process any of this, the fireball ballooned, heat filled the air, and it thundered into the cornfield to our left with a furious crash. Flames immediately danced up the stalks and spread across the crop as though the entire field had been previously doused in gasoline.

Finch spoke again. "Shape-shifting?" Henry turned his wide eyes back toward the old man. In each of his open palms, a fireball appeared. In a blur he flung both into the cornfield on our right, repeating the instantaneous blaze from seconds earlier. He started to grow in height and size. Before we knew it, he was fifteen or twenty feet tall and entirely composed of loud, rippling tongues of fire. His shape began to change, and he morphed into something much more terrifying.

A bright blue flash of light flared behind us, but by the time Henry whipped his head around, there was nothing there, which is when we both realized Donnie was gone. *Donnie! What did he do to Donnie?*

We both turned back toward Finch to find our nightmare was very much still a reality.

I wasn't exactly accustomed to seeing fire. And through my distorted view of the surroundings, it looked like the cornfield around us was now completely engulfed in flames. The sharp rise in heat was intense. Fingers of bright orange fire danced off the tops of the stalks, crackling and hissing. I was terrified.

"Do you see that?" Henry's voice betrayed his fear.

How could I not see that?

"Yes," I responded, not hiding my own fear any better. Before us, maybe one hundred feet or so away, was something I can describe only as demonic. Roughly the height of a dinosaur and entirely made of fire, it resembled some kind of hybrid between a man and a dragon, complete with a reptilian head and a tail. Upright on hind legs, it sprayed fire as it swept its head back and forth in large half circles.

The heat and the noise were intolerable. I lifted up my hands and tried to visualize myself being able to push the beast back—but nothing happened. I wasn't surprised.

"It's going to burn down everything!" I had to shout just to be heard over the roar of the fire.

Henry started to yell something back at me, but I couldn't make it out.

Suddenly, there was a loud explosion. We jerked our heads toward the beast to find that there were now three of them instead of just one. It had split itself into pieces.

We were clearly in over our heads here. Two seventh graders against a self-multiplying fire monster . . . the odds just weren't very good. There wasn't any doubt any more, at least with regard to Finch's claim to be able to wield multiple powers at once. He may as well *have* been Elben himself because the threat was just as huge in our eyes. He seemed to have more than enough powers to destroy us easily.

"We gotta get out of here," Henry shouted, rolling as quickly as he was able.

I agreed. Instinct kicked in, and I whipped around as Henry grabbed my arm to guide me to his chair, and we took off in the opposite direction.

But we were already surrounded.

It's difficult to grasp how hard it is to race through a cornfield pushing a wheelchair—all while mostly blind—until you've actually tried it, which I understand most people will never get the opportunity to do. We made it only a few paces before the fire demons started slamming into the ground around us, making up the distance with a single jump. The earth shook and quaked and knocked us off balance. There were six of them now, and we had nowhere to turn.

The commotion seemed so immense that surely Mr. Charles would have heard or felt it by now, even if he'd somehow missed the sound of Finch's goons digging an enormous cavern. Or one of the other neighbors. Surely someone was calling for help, right?

We're dead, I thought. *This is it. What were we thinking?*

Henry thought the same thing.

"You're going to regret doubting me," the head demon snarled.

"No! Don't hurt us!" Henry screamed, falling forward onto the ground, no longer the least bit defiant.

The demon's voice rang out again. "Thanks for playing, little heroes." In my mind, Finch was a distant memory. This current enemy resembled him all of zero percent. All six of the fiery figures started closing in. I covered my head with my arms and collapsed in a ball, wishing I could will myself away from this place to somewhere safe.

Just then, a flash of a memory hit me. And I did what I should have done several minutes prior . . . what any normal kid probably would have done at the first sign of trouble: I called for my mother.

As with every other time I'd tested the tiny metal disc my father had given me in this very cornfield prior to the start of school, Mom appeared almost instantly.

"Oh God," she screamed as she took in her surroundings. She was startled, but her adrenaline kicked in quickly. She wrapped her arms around me, placed a hand on Henry, and lowered her head. I lost my signal of Henry's images and got ready to be teleported to safety.

We were going to be saved. Everything was fine now. Mom was going to whisk us away to some warm, safe place, and this living nightmare would end. I was beyond relieved.

Until I realized we weren't gone yet. Nothing had happened.

"Do you like that, Mrs. Sallinger?" It was Finch—from the roar of the flames I could tell he was still in fire-demon form but now using his normal voice once again, his doppelgänger fire demons encircling us but holding back. "That's a localized NPZ, controlled by me. And it's completely dynamic. I can make it as big or as little as I want, and right now, it's keeping you and your young heroes there from making use of your God-given abilities. At the same time, it's small enough that I'm allowed to continue using my powers, as you can plainly see."

Most NPZs were much larger than what Finch was claiming. Only a handful of heroes in recorded history had such focus to allow for zones smaller than a house or a small building. And that must have been why I'd lost Henry's images—because he couldn't send them to me once the zone was established. It was a terrible time to go blind again.

Mom, for her part, was as brave as anyone I'd ever known. I felt her place her body between the main fire beast—the one that was speaking—and us kids, and then she told him off as though her powers were fully operational. "Do you have any idea what you've done? Do you have any clue what kind of town this is, you idiot? What have you got against a couple of children?"

"Oh, I haven't got anything against them, ma'am," he said, his voice now completely back to its original, seductive state. Henry would tell me later that the fire also melted away, and Finch actually resumed his normal appearance, his duplicate monsters disappearing into a mist. "I was just negotiating their silence."

"Their silence?" My mother was incredulous.

"Yes, ma'am. I'm not quite ready for all my intentions and efforts to be public knowledge. I need them to keep quiet about what they've seen here tonight—going to need the same from you at this point, I'm afraid." He paused slightly. "And I've just realized your unexpected appearance has provided me with the perfect way to guarantee what I want."

I heard a noise I'd never heard before—a loud, sustained buzzing sound that lasted for about two or three seconds. When it was done, my mother's body fell limp to the ground.

"No!" I shouted, not having any idea what had happened but knowing that Finch had just done something terrible to my mother. I fell to her side and shook her arm. "Mom! Mom!" Her body was lifeless. I screamed at him, "What did you do?"

"Remember, boys," Finch said evenly, "Mum's the word." He cackled as he said it, like he was delivering the world's greatest punchline. And with a soft *ooph*, he disappeared.

The moment was just too much for me. My mom was lying lifeless on the ground, and that's about all I could manage to get my head around. I threw myself on top of her and began to cry.

In the distance a brilliant blue light approached rapidly, lighting up the sky around us. But I wasn't paying any attention to that.

PART 3

WINTER

17

MOVING ON

Winter came suddenly, with a weeklong chill that went straight to the bone. One day it was fifty degrees and the next, twenty. One day we were playing in the yard outside—or pretending to, at least—the next we were lighting a fire in the fireplace.

Dad had always been good about going out early to warm up the car, and I had always been thankful for it. The vents on the dash blew warm gusts of air over my face as we drove. I wasn't used to riding in the front seat for family outings. In the back seat, the vents are down on the floor, so the air comes up at you from below. In the front seat, though, there are vents everywhere—on the dashboard, under the seat, in the center console. You're surrounded by a constant blanket of heat from head to toe.

The comforting heat did little to take away the sting of why I was able to ride in the front seat in the first place. We were going to visit Mom.

It had been several weeks since the incident in the cornfield, and though the three of us had managed to form some measure of a new routine, we were far from ready to live without her.

It was hard on Patrick, I could tell. He didn't speak much at all anymore, and his hyperactivity had totally vanished. He was on autopilot, and it was obvious that Dad was getting worried about him too. If Patrick knew what had really happened—his shock would be even worse.

Dad seemed to be driving slowly, but it could have just been the traffic. After making this trip several times now, I had the route down cold, but I could never account for other cars on the road. I wondered if maybe it just seemed slower because . . .

I mean, all three of us wanted to go, on some level. But none of us really enjoyed it. It's not easy seeing your mother in a coma.

There's no way to say this without sounding like a jerk, but it was incredibly hard to go into that room. Every single time. No matter how many times we visited, it never got any easier. I wanted to visit my mother for certain, but it was just . . . hard.

Henry had accompanied me on an early visit—so that I'd be able to actually see her—and those images would pop up again in my head again every time we went. I had insisted he come, against my father's advice, because I wanted to be brave. I wish I'd never done that.

Mom lay on her bed, motionless and silent. Machines stood guard all around the head of the bed, beeping and whirring. The breathing machine was the worst one, and the sound it made would appear in my nightmares for years. In . . . and out. In . . . and out. It was mechanical, droning, and awful.

Dad sat down on the side of the bed and started to talk to her. He usually just told her about our day and what had been going on at home. The doctors said there was a pretty good chance she could hear it, given the unique nature of her condition.

Mom's coma wasn't common because it wasn't natural. It was caused by the use of a superpower.

There are powers that, even in our fantastical world, sound so horrible as to seem fictional. Teachers would speak about them in hushed tones, as though someone wielding that power lay just outside the door. There were many of these kinds of powers, and they almost always belonged to terrible people. One man we learned about in Custodian Studies, named Caleb, had the ability to point with his index finger and stop a person's heart cold.

Finch had used a similar power—called linking—on my mother. It literally gives the user absolute power over their victim's mind and is most often used to instantly remove their consciousness, resulting in death. As the name implies, it creates a link between the two minds. For reasons that were unknown to

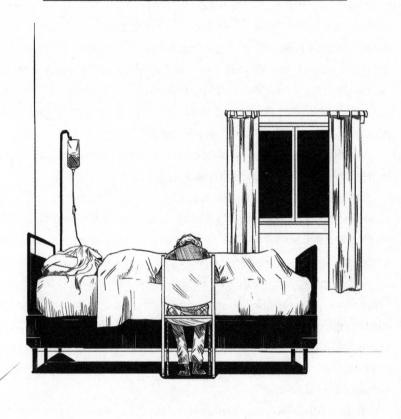

me, the doctors, and everyone else, Finch had chosen to keep his link with my mother open, which left her in a state of "linked coma."

The doctors said there was technically nothing they could do to fix or even sustain her coma. Someday, they said as kindly as they knew how, the man who did this would just decide to sever the link, and she would either die instantly or regain consciousness completely. It all depended on Finch's whim and his unique power. The "linking" ability was so rare, medical information about its consequences was scarce.

That helped make more sense of the old man's parting words in the cornfield: "Mum's the word." He was buying our silence with my mother's life—or implying it. But he had to know by the time he disappeared that our silence alone wouldn't keep his actions secret.

For our part, Henry and I had said nothing initially. Unfortunately for Finch, there had been more witnesses than just the two of us.

Donnie hadn't been hurt or killed by Finch; he'd run off on his own and somehow managed to find my father. They arrived—along with a pair of Dad's buddies from work—just in time to see Finch zap Mom and disappear. It shouldn't have surprised me that Donnie would do something selfless and heroic in a crisis, but it still kind of did. What I hadn't expected, though, was Dad's report that Donnie had moved with unusual speed that night. He was a speedster, like my brother Patrick. That was the flash of blue light behind us, which Dad had seen firsthand as Donnie literally picked up all three men and raced back to the scene. Dad's exact words were, "I've never seen anyone move that fast, Phillip. Never."

So, in addition to being faster than other kids while just running normally, Donnie was apparently also gifted with the ability to move at superspeeds. That was his power.

Mr. Charles hadn't come outside to inspect the commotion because, apparently, he'd sworn to never use his powers again, no matter what. Which, in my mind, changed him from a simple old man to a coward. But even without him, Dad and his partners had seen enough to turn Finch into a wanted man.

Nothing Henry or I said could stop them from talking about what they'd seen. My father told the authorities—his bosses. Patrols around town were doubled. Special scout teams had been dispatched to try and track down the first man to attack Freepoint in over three decades. The rash of kidnappings in the custodian community around the world already had the adults spooked, and this new threat only ramped up the state of alert.

There was no way to stop the story, and soon the whole town knew what had happened to us out there in the cornfield. The fact that many of them now finally believed our earlier story about the library break-in was of little comfort to me.

If Finch really was serious, he would surely follow through on his threat and sever the link, killing my mother, as soon as he learned the story had leaked. But he hadn't yet. Maybe he hadn't killed my mother because he knew there'd been other witnesses—maybe he knew we hadn't been the ones to say anything. Or maybe he just didn't know exactly how high profile he'd become in Freepoint.

Ultimately, it didn't matter. We were powerless. Mom was powerless. And it was the worst feeling in the world.

The routines at home continued: family meals, game night, homework, etc. But despite the forced normalcy, everything changed without Mom around. Dad did his best to try and keep us distracted, but it was an impossible task. His footsteps were heavier and slower, and even his words seemed to come at a labored pace. However terribly I felt about Mom's condition, I had a feeling Dad was taking it even harder.

Finch didn't just put my mother in a coma, he put my whole darn family in one, and it felt like it would last forever.

"I'm still not sure about this," I said, standing on the sidewalk, certainly looking like the guiltiest kid in history. My hands were shoved in my pockets, and I tried to look casual.

Bentley, on the other hand, didn't appear the least bit worried about getting caught. He shimmied up one tree and then down the next. He was a pretty good climber for a kid with untrustworthy legs. I guess he used his arms mostly.

"Look, Phillip, I'm telling you it's not cheating. It can't be cheating if there aren't rules being broken." It was Henry. Once Henry made up his mind about something, he might as well have been standing in superglue.

"I know it's not against the rules," I said, "but that's only because they don't think any of us are stupid enough to do this."

"Correction," came the word from Bentley, ten feet above our heads in a bushy maple. "They don't think we're *smart* enough to do this. And I'm sure they don't think any twelve-year-old has a hundred microcameras lying around either."

Thud. Bentley landed out of the tree, and I heard his three-pronged gait—foot, cane, foot—as he shuffled down to the next tree on the block.

"I just think we're on pretty thin ice, don't you? I'm not sure how many more times we can ask this town to forgive us." My moral center wasn't completely gone. But I wasn't even arguing from a place of morality. I was mostly concerned about my dad and what he'd think about all this. I knew Henry was right—there wasn't any rule against it. But I also knew that the nagging feeling in the back of my throat was a sign that, even though there weren't any regulations, what we were attempting was still somehow . . . wrong. Or at least it would be perceived that way. After the near-murder of the kindly old school board lady, the first SuperSim story about Finch, and then the cornfield incident, I'd had my fill of being the talk of the town, and I'd been living here only five months.

"We won't have to ask for forgiveness," Bentley singsonged from the branches of the next tree down, "because we're not going to get caught." He was certainly chipper, and his voice had a light and playful tone.

"Doing it in broad daylight probably isn't the best way to keep it a secret," I grumbled, still nervous that someone would see us.

Henry continued looking up and down the block, as he had been all afternoon. He was acting as our lookout, Bentley was doing all the work, and I guess I was the doubting Thomas. I didn't seem to have any other task to fulfill.

"Do you see anyone around?" Bentley asked petulantly. Of course he knew that I didn't; the street was empty. "I think every adult in this town is at that caucus, Phillip. Seriously . . . it's a ghost town out here."

The caucus was a pretty big deal, at least if my dad was to be believed. It's an annual event where the adults of the custodian world gather in Goodspeed to vote on all kinds of things—new officials, new rules, and stuff like that. I had to admit that Bentley was right; our town was eerily quiet.

It was also cold as the dickens. Christmas was only two weeks away, which meant that even in the middle of the day, Freepoint was a chilly thirty degrees. I shivered from the cold and thought about the hot chocolate that would await us back at Bentley's house.

"Man, I hope the bad guys never decide to attack us on the day of the caucus," I said with a chuckle. "We'd be screwed."

"If the bad guys attack on caucus day, they'll be attacking the actual caucus," Bentley reminded me. "You know, where all the heroes will be holed up together in one building?"

"I suppose," I agreed, with none of Bentley's confidence.

"How do these things even work? Man, they are so tiny!" Henry was examining one of the microcameras, which was the size of a pencil eraser.

Another *thud*, then more scampering sounds as Bentley continued making quick work of this street. We ambled down the sidewalk a few feet at a time with every successful camera planted.

"All these cameras are networked together wirelessly. Like a net," Bentley explained.

"What do you mean?"

"I mean they are all satellite parts of the same system, which I can control from my computer. They can be used independently of one another, or . . . they can work together."

"How can cameras work together?" scoffed Henry. If he hadn't heard of it, then it didn't exist.

"They're programmed to," Bentley explained patiently. "If one camera picks up something interesting, the other cameras in the network that are nearby will turn and focus cooperatively with the first camera, which will give us a much larger picture of whatever action is going on."

"A better question is to ask if it's legal," I muttered, voicing my reservations for the thousandth time.

"I'm telling you—it's legal, Phillip. These are public streets! If you and I are walking down the sidewalk and we stop to take pictures of some skateboarders doing tricks, we don't need permission from them to take their picture, because they're in public." I was tempted to argue, but I also knew that Bentley had spent part of last summer studying copyright law—for fun.

"Yeah, yeah," I said, signaling that I wasn't interested in repeating the exact same argument we'd had over breakfast. "You may have found a technical loophole or excuse, but I'd bet good money the bulk of these townspeople would be bothered to know they're being recorded."

"That's just it, Phillip," Bentley said excitedly. "We're not recording a thing!"

Thud. Bentley walked over to Henry and me, breathing a little heavy from all the climbing.

"The camera system is designed to be live. It's recording capabilities have been disabled. This network will never be used for anything but live images, which should be all the advantage we need to keep the next competition more even."

"I don't know, Bentley. A hundred cameras is a lot, but I'm not sure it's enough to guarantee we'll see anything on them come the next SuperSim. For all we know, the crimes will take place in locations where we don't have coverage."

"Then what are you so worried about?" he said, smiling in response. "Besides, it's worth it to try. Considering the number of fake crimes they had prepared for the first challenge—and we can assume they'll have the same amount or more for the next one—we're bound to catch something on camera. And if it's enough to get us into the action instead of falling behind, then we just might make a respectable showing this time. Plus," he said with a devious grin, "I just ordered a thousand more of these puppies from a Chinese distributor."

I had to admit, the upside was attractive. We'd been embarrassed in the last SuperSim—annihilated, actually. Almost every team helped apprehend a criminal or scored some points. We did neither, and there was no getting around the reason: our disabilities. We'd gone into the challenge with two blind kids, two crippled kids, a mentally challenged boy, and an asthmatic. With those kind of handicaps, we never stood a chance.

"Come on," Bentley said, zipping up his duffel bag. "Let's head over and get some coverage of the high school."

⚡

The weekend of the caucus was notable for one other reason: the return of Chad Burke, my old lunchroom nemesis. Chad's father, the head of the board, had obviously gone to Goodspeed for the caucus with the rest of the Freepoint adults. Apparently, Chad had completed enough banishment time that his father decided he'd earned a second chance, so he brought him back home.

We didn't know any of this until that next Monday at lunchtime, of course. We were in our usual spot—a rectangular table in the far back corner of the cafeteria—just munching on snacks and chatting about Bentley's cameras, filling in the rest of the gang on the plan.

"Is the image quality any good?" It struck me as an odd question for a blind kid like James to ask, but it definitely made sense. How would we make use of the cameras if the picture was too blurry?

"These things transmit in crystal-clear high definition, guys. It'll look better than your television. I'll show you a demo on my smartphone after school when they aren't blocking Henry's powers, okay?"

"Okay. Sounds good to me," said James, appearing to be convinced by Bentley's description alone.

I decided to seize the temporary lull in conversation to squeeze in a topic that I'd been concerned about for a while. "I'm still worried about who we're going to get to join our team." We had always been one man down compared to other teams. We had Bentley, Henry, Freddie, James, Donnie, and me. That made six. But we were allowed seven.

We thought about trying to recruit Penelope, but Bentley said her parents were too strict to let her compete in the SuperSim. We also briefly thought about recruiting Darla. Bentley was confident that Henry would be able to supply her with audio the way he now regularly supplied me with "video," but we never got the chance to try.

So we were ultimately still a team member short of an entire roster, not that we technically needed to have the full number. But it had been nagging at me for weeks, because there didn't appear to be any solution, and I felt like we were already a team with natural disadvantages. Having fewer members than other teams would only make it worse. There didn't appear to be too many other options. No one else in the special education class could do it, and no one outside the class was likely to stoop to joining our team.

"Who needs another teammate?" Bentley asked. "It'll just be the six of us guys."

"Did I just hear you say you're looking for a new teammate?" The voice coming from behind me was unmistakable. It was Chad Burke. The last time I'd heard it, it was followed almost immediately by physical pain and public shame. The voice was burned into my brain, and I wouldn't ever forget or mistake it.

For a split second, everything froze. It was like déjà vu. I was here—in the same seat, in the same cafeteria, with the same friends. It was happening all over again.

But Donnie must have sensed my trepidation—and must have also had far better hearing than I realized. Before I could even decide what I wanted to do or say, Donnie whirled around with lightning speed and socked Chad Burke right in the gut as hard as he could.

Chad went flying back with a surprised yelp, the linoleum squeaking as he slid on the floor.

It was a shocking object lesson on the protectiveness of Donnie, despite him being the one who really needed protecting from us. Before I could find myself in a situation where I might get hurt or embarrassed again, Donnie stepped in to act as my protector. He'd probably been carrying a grudge against that kid since the last incident. I had no idea Donnie's hearing (or memory, for that matter) was that exceptional.

Pandemonium ensued. I stood there in the cafeteria trying to make sense of Chad's return and Donnie's reflexes, but I couldn't. Teachers came rushing into the fray determined to break things up before any more fighting occurred, and poor Donnie got hauled off to the principal's office.

It would be several more days and a few conversations with Chad one-on-one before I would really be able to understand what had just taken place.

18

THE BREAK-IN

I was listening to the television. The news was on. Even with Mom in the hospital, Dad still kept his same routine. He watched the same shows at the same times, but he wasn't paying attention to any of them these days. Maybe he was on some passive level, I guess. They were still talking about superheroes after all, and this was the national news.

The incident in Central Park that had been caught on film had ignited a massive story across the country—as though an alien flying saucer had crash landed right on the White House lawn. Who was this man? Are there more like him? The public was rabid for information, so the news kept finding a reason to talk about it. There were several reports of similar incidents around the country, but none had produced any evidence to date and were considered by the mainstream media to be hoaxes or attention-seekers.

I heard the phone ring. Since Patrick and I got so few calls, Dad always still got up and answered, taking a few more rings to make his way over to the counter than he used to. I paid more attention to the news anchor's voice than to Dad's phone conversation, so I was surprised to feel him tapping my shoulder with the phone.

"Here, it's for you." He dropped the receiver into my open hand and slowly ambled back to his easy chair to continue sitting in silence. He thought that because I was blind, I wouldn't know that he'd taken to simply doing nothing but staring and thinking.

"Hello?" At this point I knew it was Bentley or Henry, as they were the only two human beings on the planet who ever called me.

"I'm ready." It was Bentley.

"Ready for what?" I quickly scanned my memory banks for some forgotten appointment or plans but found nothing.

"It's time to go back to the library, Phillip."

"Wait . . . what?"

"It's time for us to stop reacting to Finch and start being proactive."

I still didn't understand, and I guess my lack of response communicated that fact.

"We're going to find out what he was after. Tonight. Midnight. Be in your room, ready to go." The line went dead.

I was naturally intrigued by the cloak-and-dagger nature of Bentley's message. Short, concise phrases in a hushed tone, followed by a surprise hang up? Who wouldn't be intrigued? And despite the fact that the plan called for us to sneak out of our homes at midnight—something we'd all surely be punished for if caught—I didn't even think about *not* going.

The wait for Christmas morning has nothing on the wait I endured that evening.

Long after I'd pretended to go to bed, I heard Dad shuffle down the hall and shut the door to his bedroom. A few seconds later, I heard the click of the light switch being turned to the off position.

I reached down to my watch—braille, of course—and found it to be 11:45 p.m. Only fifteen minutes. Would Dad even fall asleep that fast? Would Bentley be quiet enough? I assumed he was bringing James, but what if he started throwing pebbles at my window or something?

I was such a neurotic kid; I managed to kill the last fifteen minutes just frightening myself with all sorts of scary possibilities. I was actually surprised when I heard the unmistakable sound of a teleporter's arrival.

Ooph!

"Phillip?" I heard Bentley whisper.

"Yeah? Be quiet! My dad just went to bed!"

"You ready?"

"For what?" I asked cautiously.

"You'll see. Come on."

I crawled over the foot of the bed and reached out my arms, feeling for James or Bentley. I found Henry—the left wheel of his wheelchair, to be exact. "Oh," I whispered, as politely as one can whisper, "hi, Henry."

"Hey," he said back. "Oh, I guess I can let you see now."

I received a very grainy image of my completely darkened bedroom about one-tenth of a second before we jumped.

Ooph!

Man, am I ever going to get used to that? I wondered.

"Are you kidding?" Henry asked incredulously. "It's like a roller coaster!" He put his hands above his head. "Woo-hoo!"

"Shh!" Bentley urged.

"Why?" Henry asked. "We know they don't have any kind of security or anything, now don't we? Learned that firsthand, I believe."

"You don't think they maybe thought about upgrading since then?"

"No, actually," Henry said, "I don't think they did, because I don't think they believed us, remember?"

"They believe us now," Bentley said quietly. "Phillip's father saw Finch in the cornfield. The kids at school may still be jerks, but the people who matter in this town—the grown-ups—they believe us now, Henry. So I know it's a long shot, but just in case . . . just in case someone in this town is wondering the same thing we are about what Finch was doing here . . . will you please keep it down or shut your trap entirely?"

"Okay, okay," Henry protested, hands out in front of him. "You win." He lifted up his right hand and pretended to zip his mouth shut. Then he looked around a little while Bentley started unloading his gear.

We were in the main hallway of the library. It was as quiet as the last time we'd been inside after hours. Actually, it was quieter since there wasn't a crooked old geezer in the references section tossing things around. It was also colder than ever, with the building's heat turned down for the overnight hours.

"Hey," I said, thinking out loud. "Where's Freddie?"

Bentley pulled a long cardboard tube out of his bag. "Oh," he said, pausing to look up and explain. "No one answered the phone when I called his house. I tried a few times. I guess they were out or something. I didn't exactly think it was the wisest idea to just pop into his room at midnight unannounced."

"Ah," I said. "Makes sense. Too bad," I added.

Bentley popped the top off one end of the tube and removed a few rolls of blue paper. He set them on the ground, and with a smooth motion, unrolled them on the marble floor and began to examine them.

"What is that?" I asked.

"The blueprints of this building," he said, not looking up from the paperwork.

"Where did you get that?" I asked in surprise.

He looked up at me, smiled broadly, and said, "The resources section of the library, of course."

Now *I* was smiling. Henry was just chuckling with appreciation.

"You got the plans for this building . . . inside this building," James said, double-checking.

"Yup," Bentley said. "Kind of . . . poetic, isn't it?"

"That's outstanding," James agreed.

"You just checked them out like a normal book?" Henry asked.

Bentley glanced up a moment, then looked back down at what he was doing. "I didn't say anything about checking them out."

"Look at you, you little lawbreaker," Henry said. "First the cameras, and now this."

A thought hit me. "You don't really think whoever built that room and is protecting it was dumb enough to put it on the blueprints of the building, do you?"

"No," he responded with confidence. "But there will definitely be other clues."

"What do you mean?" Henry asked, now a bit more intrigued than before.

"Well, what do we know about NPZs?" Bentley was a natural teacher, even down to asking questions to spark discussion.

"They suck," Henry said.

"Right. But what do we know about how they work?"

James gave it a try. "They're a result of a custodian—a blocker—using their power."

"That's correct," Bentley said. "So if we're going on the assumption that there's an NPZ under that rotunda in the Archives Room, then we're also assuming there's a person down there." He paused to let us catch up. "A person with the superpower of blocking."

I hadn't thought about that before, but he was right. NPZs were only a result of powers. Despite many attempts by some of our brightest engineers—and probably even Bentley—no one had yet invented a machine or device that could block the use of a custodian's abilities.

"Think about it," Bentley continued, bringing more knowledge to the discussion than most educators. "If there's something in that room that's so valuable, so worth protecting, that they'd build a secret room with no door and use an NPZ to guard it . . . then it's worth guarding around the clock. This is no come-and-go blocker. This is a permanent resident of that room . . . forever. All just to protect something so important that Finch deemed it a worthy target."

"Okay," Henry said, "but how does that help the blueprints make sense?"

"Because a person needs water, Henry, and almost certainly electricity. Just by looking at these blueprints and seeing where the main water and electrical lines are, I can get a good idea of the position and size of the secret room."

Henry looked at me as though I knew what that meant and then vocalized his confusion. "I still don't understand how that gets us in the room, Bentley."

"Well, we're going to teleport in, of course. But not until we have more information about that room—size, position, and, most importantly, escape routes. In addition to water and electricity, a person also needs air. Oh, and it's not going to be us going into the room at first. First . . . we send in the robot."

The robot?

Bentley reached into his shirt pocket and pulled out a small rubber ball, roughly the size of a golf ball.

"That's 'the robot'?" Henry asked. "That thing?"

"Exactly," Bentley said with enthusiasm. "This is one of my simplest inventions ever, but it's perfect for this task. It's just a rubber ball with a homing beacon inside. See?" He pointed at the blueprints. "This air duct goes all the way to the rotunda, runs under the floor, and then stops abruptly. Now, if I'm right, in reality that duct continues on into the secret room, providing fresh, temperature-controlled air to whoever is controlling that NPZ.

"We put the ball-bot in the AC duct here in the main library and send it on its way down toward the room. If the ducts don't go all the way into the secret room, the ball will bounce back in our direction, which I'll see here on my computer. But if the ball keeps going, then we'll know they go straight through, and we're in business."

"What do you mean?" I asked.

"Those ducts are twenty-eight inches wide, Phillip. We can fit inside them."

"It's almost there," Bentley said with a giggle, watching the bot's progress on his monitor. All he could see was a little red dot blinking as it slowly moved its way across his screen. But that was enough to tell him all he needed to know.

"Guys, it's well past the spot I pegged as the boundary." Bentley looked up at us, resolute. "That's it . . . it's gotta be in there. We can go in now."

"Now, Bentley," I cautioned, "just because we can prove the air vent goes all the way into the hidden room doesn't exactly prove we can get out."

"Why not? It proves the air conditioning ductwork runs clean through whatever wall is there, all the way into the secret chamber. We already know from the blueprints that it's big enough for us to fit inside, and it runs along the ceiling. So all we'd have to do to get out is climb up and crawl for a while."

"Yeah, Bentley," I argued, "but that's assuming whoever is in there creating the NPZ is going to just let us leave."

"Well," Henry said, joining the conversation, "if they're creating the NPZ, they won't have any other powers to throw at us."

"Right. Tell that to Finch," I said, winning the battle, if not the war. "Not to mention they could simply have a gun or something."

"If they were protecting it from Finch, that means whoever is down there is on our side. Why are you so sure there's something or someone dangerous down there?" Bentley inquired, with a hint of an edge to his voice.

It was a decent question since I was really the only person dissenting on this decision, at least vocally.

"I'm not sure. But you know what I am sure of? That we don't know what's down there! It could be a secret treasure room full of superhero gold. Or it could be a bottomless cave to the center of the earth."

"If you want me to break out my snake-cam, I can, and we can run that cable all the way down into that room and prove to you it's not a bottomless pit."

"Jeez, how long will that take?" Henry whined. "Screw that, let's just do it."

"Come on, now, Henry." I tried reasoning with him. "You can't seriously want to go teleporting into some unknown space, do you?"

"How do you know what I want anyway," he shot back, a little snotty. I hadn't realized we were even at odds on the issue.

"What about James?" I asked. "You're acting like he's just going to go with you whether he wants to or not. Doesn't he get a choice?"

Henry started to fire back at me, but James spoke first. "Actually, I want to go."

I turned to face him, shocked. "But you won't be able to teleport out!"

"Well," he said, as calmly as if we were debating what to eat for lunch, "Bentley, here, says we can crawl out through the ducts. And that sounds reasonable to me."

"I can't believe this!" I was honestly surprised, not that my friends would disagree with me but that they'd all be so risky all at once. "This is crazy. There's no way we're doing this." I started walking away, hoping to pull out a victory through forfeit.

"*We're*," Henry spat, putting the emphasis on first word to hammer home how far apart we stood on the issue, "going to do what we want. *You*," he continued, "are going to do whatever the hell you want. Because *you*," he sneered, as if the point hadn't been made already, "are not the boss of us. Got it?"

I didn't know how things had gone from a disagreement to an argument in such a short time span. I was speechless for a moment. Henry was downright mad at me, and thirty seconds ago, he'd just been bored.

"I . . ." I stammered, legitimately unsure of what to say. "I'm sorry," I said, probably sounding a little more pouty about it than I should have.

"I say we take a vote," Bentley said, grabbing the reins. "All in favor of throwing caution to the wind and going into the secret chamber of unknown contents, raise your hand." Everyone did except for me.

"All opposed?" Bentley asked.

Hanging my head, I raised my hand with a spectacular lack of confidence and conviction.

"You're outvoted. We're going in. You're welcome to stay up here if you want," Bentley said.

"Right. I'm going to stay up here while my friends fall to their deaths at the earth's core."

"Well, don't bring the attitude with you," Bentley said flatly. "If you're coming with us, I don't want to hear about how annoyed you are about it the whole time, got it?"

I simply nodded, suddenly wary of any little move or comment potentially drawing more ire from my friends. *Have I been acting too negative? Am I too much of a naysayer?*

"Okay," Bentley said. "Everyone in."

He and Henry immediately reached out and grabbed James's shoulder, and then they all turned and looked at me expectantly.

Help us, Jesus, I thought, very intentionally. *Help us not to die. Amen.*

"Thoughts count too, jerkwad," Henry scolded.

I reached out my hand.

Ooph!

Upon arriving in the secret chamber, it was immediately apparent I would soon be saying "I told you so," at least if we got out of this place alive.

It turned out to be a room the exact same size as the rotunda above it, as Bentley had predicted. It was dimly lit by two slowly dying fluorescent lights in the ceiling.

We were standing on one side of the circular room. In the center of the room was a pedestal, roughly three feet tall. On the pedestal sat a very old book, completely encased in a glass security case. It was easily the oldest book I'd ever seen. It was handmade, obviously sewn together, with a cover made of some kind of leathery animal skin.

None of that was immediately alarming. But what sat behind them was.

There were two upright cushioned chairs, side by side on the far wall—

the kind of chairs the Founding Fathers probably sat in while they toasted their declaration. Between the chairs, on the wall, hung a picture frame which displayed some kind of old-looking group portrait.

In the chair on the right sat the clothed skeleton of some poor soul who was very dead . . . and probably had been for some time. His clothes were mostly intact, but instead of hands and a head, there were only bones showing.

The chair on the left might as well have been a throne of fire, for on it sat the now-notorious Mr. Finch. His right leg was crossed over his left thigh, with his stupid double-billed hat resting on his knee. His head was leaned against the tall back of the chair, and his eyes were closed. His arms were crossed, and his right hand held his pipe. It looked like he was sleeping.

"I knew it," I said dejectedly. "I freaking knew it."

Finch's eyes sprang open, and a smile slowly crept across his face. It soon faded. "You know," he began slowly, "I was beginning to wonder if you boys were ever going to muster the courage to come down here."

We said nothing. I assumed the others were frozen in fear, but I was mostly frozen in anger.

"But look at you. Do you guys understand how monumental a moment this is for you? You just boldly leaped into a room you couldn't even prove was there!" He sounded impressed, almost proud.

"If you're going to kill us," I said stubbornly, "just do it already, okay? I'm not playing any more of your games."

"I am not playing a game either, Phillip," he assured. "I'm merely . . . following a plan." He stood. "Do you know where you are right now?"

I did not, and he knew it, so he did not wait for a reply.

"This is the clubhouse used by the original founding members of the Believers. You see, back when we founded it, your grandfather and I and our friends"—he threw his right hand over his shoulder, thumb-pointing at the portrait on the wall—"the Believers wasn't actually a serious outfit."

"You knew my grandfather?"

"Yes, Phillip. Try and keep up. See, we were just college students looking for a way to rebel, and Elben was just as much of a hush-hush topic back then as it is today, maybe more so. What better way to act out—secretly, of course—than to start a society dedicating themselves to the return of Elben?"

He leaned forward and quieted his tone slightly, as though letting me in on a secret. "Mostly we just did drugs and waxed poetic about social issues, like most college students. Little did we know how seriously we should have been taking it."

I was growing impatient with yet another unasked-for history lesson. "Why are you keeping my mom in a coma?"

"Well, see," he said, feigning shame, "now, that was unplanned. If you hadn't surprised me with that little gizmo there in your pocket, that wouldn't have happened. Frankly," he said, suddenly no longer ashamed, "I'm surprised you had to call your mommy to come and rescue you."

I seethed.

"I mean, I wasn't ever going to actually hurt you. I have bigger fish to fry, Phillip."

I wondered why Henry wasn't popping off at him like usual.

"Then just give her back her mind, and let her go," I shouted.

"I'm afraid I can't do that, Phillip," he said with a phony sadness. "I need her, you see . . . as a bargaining chip, should certain contingencies . . . occur." He uncrossed his legs, placed his cap on his head, and then crossed his legs again in the reverse position.

"We didn't have to say anything. My father saw you."

"I know. But you've blabbed plenty since then, haven't you?" He smiled. "I'm not angry. But still . . . let's try and keep *this* little meeting to ourselves, okay?"

I nodded.

"Now then," he continued politely, "I hope we can move beyond this thing with your mother for now, because I have more pressing matters to discuss with you. In particular, that book you see before you. That's for you. Go on now and take it."

"What is it?"

"Just take it," he said kindly. "It's a gift, from me to you."

"I don't want your gifts," I snarled.

Finch looked at me for a moment, cocking his head. "You know, you could have it a lot worse, Phillip. I could just kill you. Instead, I'm not only letting you and your friends live, but I'm also offering you a present. The least you can do is accept my gift and be polite about it."

"I don't want—"

"Take it!" he screamed. "Take it now!" His tone had shifted dramatically, as to suggest this would be my last warning. After the echo of his voice subsided, he straightened his tie and vest and settled himself back into a proper gentleman's temperament.

I hated this man for what he'd done to my mother, but I was far from ready to die, at least not as long as she was alive. If he was trying to frighten me into submission, it was working. I slowly stepped forward toward the pedestal. As I made my last step, Finch's hand waved in front of him, and the glass security case popped into the air above the ancient book, hovered a moment, and then disappeared into nothingness with a poof.

I reached out my hands, grabbed the book, and walked backward, retracing my steps.

"My use for this room has come and gone, and I've already taken everything I need. However, that book," Finch said, like a teacher beginning a lesson, "contains the original prophecy of Elben's return, the prophecy as foretold and written on those very pages you now clutch in your arms by the visionary Malea."

I looked down at the cover. It was plain—no words or pictures.

"This is what you broke into the library for during the SuperSim?"

"Don't be silly," he said dismissively. "I broke into the library during the SuperSim so I could steal some other things that were in this place, things I needed very badly. Then I broke back into the library again tonight so I could be here when you arrived."

I'm sure my face showed my confusion, but he didn't stop to explain himself any further. "Please be sure to study that book with care. I believe it will help you understand . . . what I'm trying to do here. Hundreds of historians have written about that book, but most of them have never touched it or even seen it. The Believers have been guarding it since they took possession of it thirty years ago. Preston, here, gave his life to protect and hide this book and many other documents and treasures from anyone outside our order. His no power zone kept it secret for years until I no longer needed him. So tell me, Phillip," he said, "are you ready?"

"Ready for what?"

"To know what the prophecy really says," he softly whispered.

I never believed what it says anyway, I thought to myself.

"I know," he answered. "What's it going to take to get you to believe that it's all real—'the one who can do all'? That his followers, like me, are more powerful than any being you've ever encountered? Haven't I demonstrated my multitude of abilities already? Perhaps you hadn't noticed, but I'm keeping your mother alive while also reading your mind and keeping an NPZ active in this room—all at the same time." He sounded a little too impressed with himself. "I bet you didn't even stop to wonder how you were receiving images in a place covered by an NPZ, did you?" he taunted.

He was right. I hadn't.

"Do you not remember the fire? How many demonstrations do you need before you understand that your fabled Elben is real, and his return is imminent?" He leaned forward, and a deep anger flashed. "Do you need another one right now?" he asked, both politely and menacingly.

I shook my head back and forth, feeling totally helpless. Finch was the ultimate bully—nice one moment, terrifying the next—and he had me completely at his mercy. "There is more left to the part you have to play in this affair, young Sallinger. Perhaps you'll wake up to the truth."

I looked down and closed my eyes, hoping to will the entire experience to simply go away.

Surprisingly, it worked. I suppose the timing might have been coincidental, but that was the exact moment Finch banished us from the secret chamber, teleporting us with a flick of his wrist to the more familiar surroundings of the cornfield.

For a few beats, we all just stood there in silence.

I was a stunned, pitiful mess. Part anger, part shock, part blubbering baby. I dropped the archaic manuscript to the ground and felt it bounce off my tennis shoes. "Well . . ." I said with a sigh and a healthy dose of bitterness, "thanks a lot, guys." If I'd known their silence had been due to Finch's powers, I might have gone easier on them. Maybe.

I turned and walked all the way home by myself.

19

APOLOGIES

"I'm sorry, Phillip."

They were words I definitely wanted to hear—and even expected to hear—but not exactly like this.

Chad Burke was wrapping up a very heartfelt soliloquy. He'd talked for almost fifteen minutes straight as he and I sat on the picnic table in Mr. Charles's cornfield. He'd stopped by my house on a Sunday afternoon unexpectedly, starting right off with an apology for everything and asking if I would be willing to hear him out. My dad was standing right behind me when I answered the door, so I knew I had to do the "mature" thing. If I'm honest, I was also a bit thankful to have some social contact outside my family; I hadn't seen or spoken to any of the guys all weekend, since I was still upset about the way things had gone at the library.

To hear him tell it, Chad's last few months had been even rougher than my own. First, his father had apparently beaten him before sending him off to Goodspeed after the cafeteria incident—not because Chad had done something bad, but because he'd tarnished the family name. I have to admit, an abusive father is so far from the reality I personally had known that it was hard to get my head around.

Then, as soon as he'd gotten to Goodspeed, his father had arranged for Chad to join the custodian equivalent of a military boot camp. They took young superpowered individuals on the verge of turning evil and beat the good back into them with a three-month regimen of running, rock climbing, team activities, and lots and lots of push-ups.

And it sounded, for a while, like the story might go exactly as I expected: That Chad had learned what it felt like to be bullied by his drill sergeants. That he'd come to regret his behavior toward me and other students. That he really had changed. And indeed, that's the story Chad was telling. But the unexpected wrinkle was his missing arm.

On a weekend field training exercise, Chad had been involved in an accident, and it had cost him his arm. One of the other soldiers in the camp, a kid named Rodney, had bumped a vehicle Chad was changing a tire on, dropping the two-ton auto onto Chad's left arm. The doctors told him they had no choice but to amputate, and he didn't even find that out until after he'd woken up in the hospital with the surgery complete.

"It didn't take long for me to start getting frustrated by the normally simple tasks I could no longer do myself," he said honestly. After a long pause, he added, "I even got a taste of my own medicine . . . you know, with the insults and bullying and stuff."

Chad Burke—the biggest bully I'd ever known in my short life, at least until I met Finch—was apologizing to me and asking me to forgive him. He'd turned from his former ways. It was surreal yet real. It was too good to be true, and yet it seemed true. I wasn't sure I'd ever heard a more sincere apology speech in my life, which is saying something considering Patrick's history of apology speeches. Either Chad was being honest or he was a better actor than he'd been a bully.

"If I'd known what it felt like, I never would have said or done those kind of things to you. I know it will take time and that you understandably have some reservations about me . . . but I hope you can find a way to forgive me."

Truthfully, I guess I'd already forgiven him. I had bigger fish to fry than a kid who punched me three months ago. I had servants of "the one who can do all" after me now, for Pete's sake. Forgiveness wasn't a problem.

"Maybe we can even be friends," he added softly.

That . . . will probably take more time.

I told him I accepted his apology and that I was willing to start fresh with a clean slate together. But I also told him I'd come to master my powers a lot better since he'd been gone, and if he ever tried any funny business with me again, I'd use my abilities to make something sharp fly at rapid speed into his crotch.

⚡

"Phillip, I'm sorry." It was Bentley this time, sitting down beside me in the cafeteria.

I'd been ignoring the guys all morning throughout class, trying my best to maintain my grudge. It was difficult; everyone in school was buzzing about another teacher having gone missing, and I really wanted to talk to them about it.

"You were right," Bentley continued. "We never should have gone down there without knowing what we were up against, and it was a huge mistake. And I just hope you can forgive us."

"Yeah," Henry added, wheeling up to the other side of the table. "All that stuff he said goes for me too."

I took a few seconds to ponder it. I wanted to hold onto my anger. I wanted to stay bitter. But I'd never really had a group of friends before, and the temptation to get back to our old ways was too much for me.

"It's okay," I finally said with a sigh. "All is forgiven."

"All right," Bentley said happily, as Henry and James rejoiced as well.

"But no more teleporting into unknown places, okay?"

"Done," James agreed.

"Promise," Bentley added.

"I really want to get that guy," I said, betraying how much I'd let him get into my head. "Even if he lets my mom wake up tomorrow and then disappears forever, I want to get him."

"Hey, Phillip," I heard behind me, recognizing Chad's voice. He had apparently been passing by.

I turned around to acknowledge him. "Oh," I said awkwardly, "hey." I heard his feet shuffle away, so I turned back around.

"What in the heck was that?" Henry said, unable to hide his amusement.

Bentley thought I might have made a mistake. "You do know that was Chad Burke you just said 'hey' to, right?"

"Yeah."

"It's a good thing Donnie wasn't here," he added, still a bit confused.

"Oh yeah," I said, "how is Donnie doing? Does anybody know?"

"He's good," Henry said. "I think he gets to come back to school next week."

"Good."

"We'll have to have a talk with him about how you're apparently not enemies with Chad anymore," Bentley said, thinking out loud.

"Just Phillip, though," Henry said, stuffing a chicken nugget in his mouth. "I'm still considering Chad an enemy."

"Well," I said, deciding to explain things a bit further, "Chad and I had a little talk the other day. He, uh . . . wanted to apologize." I let it hang there in the air, though it received nothing but stunned silence in return. "For being such a bully and for making fun of me and punching me." Still no response. "And . . . he hopes we can be friends someday."

There was a sizable pause. "What?" Henry was incredulous.

"And you believed him?" Bentley asked.

"I did. It was . . . honest. I don't know . . . I could be wrong . . . but I usually have a good sense about when people are being truthful. And . . . I mean . . . he even cried. You know, his life hasn't been so easy, particularly since he got shipped out of town. He lost his arm and has had to endure some pretty crappy bullying himself."

Henry was always quick to add his own opinion. "I don't really care what he says. I still wouldn't trust him."

"I agree . . . that guy gives me the creeps," said James.

Since Chad had turned over his new leaf, his old friends had quickly shut the door on him. He wasn't popular anymore and had been cast out of their ranks. Steve Travers was the new head bully at Freepoint High, and Chad was just a rung or two above complete outcast status.

"I'm sorry to hear you say that," I said. "I was actually thinking of asking him to join our team."

"What?" Henry again.

"I'm not sure that's a good idea at all," Bentley said. His words fired off in several directions as he spoke, indicating he was shaking his head back and forth. "Even if this guy's no longer a bully, that doesn't mean he's going to mesh well with our team."

"Don't look now, Bentley, but none of us really meshed that well in the first SuperSim either. And we could use the experience from a guy like that—he's a senior, for Pete's sake!"

"I don't know," he replied, obviously on the fence.

Henry was less on the fence. "I don't care how old he is. I don't trust him!"

The debate raged on from the end of lunch all the way through to our team meeting that evening. We were still deliberating even after Dad had cleared the empty pizza boxes from the table. Patrick was spending the night at a friend's house, which allowed us the rare opportunity to discuss our powers openly at my house.

"Once a bully, always a bully." Henry had now uttered that phrase roughly fifteen times in the last few hours.

"You don't think losing an arm like that changes a person?" I asked in Chad's defense.

"It might very well change someone, Phillip," Bentley explained, "but that doesn't mean we have to be the guinea pigs who find out firsthand if he's really different. I mean, we're trying to do well and show that disabled kids can be just as good as regular heroes. We don't need the drama."

"You're right, Bentley," I said, seeing my chance. "We are trying to do well and show that disabled kids can be as good as regular heroes. And . . . how exactly did that work out the last time we were in a SuperSim?"

"Pretty bad, actually," he allowed.

"Right! Pretty bad. Heck, since this school year started, the six of us have probably done more harm than good to the reputation of disabled heroes. We're certainly not making our case very well. So don't you think we could use someone with his abilities on our team? Basic math tells us that seven is better than six."

"Unless seven punches the six of us in the stomach and runs away laughing," Henry said.

"He's not going to do that, Henry," I said. "Even if he doesn't end up helping our team, he's not a bully anymore."

"So says Chad," Henry scoffed, clearly not ready to buy Chad's story. "Like I said before, once a bully, always a bully."

"You guys don't think a person can change?" It was Dad, who'd been reading his paper in the other room, and as it turns out, eavesdropping.

"Well, Mr. Sallinger," Henry countered, "my dad says you should always trust what you can see with your own eyes. And I've never seen a bad guy turn good."

"Me neither," James chimed in, giggling.

"Well, I have," Dad replied knowingly. Without us having to prompt him, he knew we wanted to hear him continue. So he did. "How many of you have heard the story about my dad, Thomas Sallinger?"

We all raised our hands because we'd covered it in Custodial Studies earlier in the school year. It had been only the slightest bit awkward for me.

"Who can tell me what happened? You don't need to include all the details. Just give us a refresher." He leaned forward, folding his paper and laying it aside. It was the most engaged he'd been with the real world in weeks.

Bentley, of course, was the first to respond. "Your father was killed in the Battle of New York, right?"

"That's correct."

Bentley continued. "He was betrayed by his best friend, Luther, who used his powers to keep Thomas from defending himself against Artimus."

"That's correct. Very good. My father, Thomas Sallinger, was killed by Artimus Baxter, a notorious killer and villain who was attempting to take over New York City entirely." We shuffled a bit from our seated positions, turning to face Dad and inching closer. "Artimus was a cold-blooded killer, an electro with an attitude, you might say." An "electro" was a slang term for someone whose powers involved the use of electricity. In Artimus's case, he was a modern-day Zeus, hurling lightning bolts at will to destroy his enemies.

"Near the end of the battle, the heroes had things well in hand and had cornered Artimus, who leaped to the top of the Empire State Building and began firing electric bolts in all directions. He was desperate and out of options. His armies were defeated. It was only a matter of time." Mrs. Crouch hadn't given us anywhere near this level of detail.

"Luther and my father were sent up to bring Artimus in since they were partners and had hunted the villain together for years. But on top of that building, in the driving rain, Luther turned on my father unexpectedly, encasing Thomas in a no power zone temporarily. That allowed Artimus to kill my father easily . . . one final act of villainy and mayhem. He fired his lightning only once at my dad—a direct hit—sending him flying off the building and down onto the rain-soaked street one hundred stories below.

"Luther felt so guilty that he immediately turned and used his power on Artimus and then shoved him off the top of the skyscraper to his own death. Still . . . Luther stood trial for his heinous act. And he even served time in Sperrington." Sperrington was the name of the remote custodian prison facility, located somewhere north of inhabited Canada.

"Now," Dad continued, "here's the part of the story you probably haven't heard. After Luther was released from prison, he went on to live a healthy, productive, and crime-free life. And he never chose evil again. So you see, a tiger can change his stripes. A villain can become good again, and a bully can change his bullying ways."

"But how do you know Luther never turned evil again?" Henry asked. "He could be out killing people right now for all we know."

"Ah, but he can't do that. He can't. Because if Luther was out killing people . . . who would look after his corn?"

It probably took about five seconds for me to begin putting together what Dad was saying. I didn't understand the reference to corn when the entire previous story had been corn-free. By the time it dawned on me, I could tell the others were having moments of realization as well.

I turned toward my dad in shock and surprise. "Dad?" I asked hesitantly.

"Yes, son. Luther's last name is Charles. The infamous criminal who murdered a hero and the quiet old man who comes to dinner every month are one and the same."

"Dad?"

It was later the same night. All my friends had gone home, and Dad had let me stay up late to read and listen to the TV. I'd spent most of the time mulling over the revelation that old Mr. Charles had killed my grandfather. I wanted to know more about why this evil man was allowed in our house . . . and in our town. Was he truly no longer evil? Was he a prisoner of some kind?

But more than any of that, I wanted to know about my grandfather.

"Yes, Phillip?"

"Tell me about Grandpa's power."

"What's that?"

"His power. That day in the cornfield you told me it was absorption, right?" *Just like Finch's.*

"Yeah."

"Well, tell me more about how that works." No need for Dad to know my ulterior motives for asking, at least not yet.

"Well, Phillip," Dad said with a sigh, looking up from his newspaper, "people with the power of absorption are incredibly powerful. The power is basically like a sponge, soaking up the powers of any other superhuman people in the vicinity. It's one of the rarest powers around. They say it shows up only a handful of times in each generation."

I thought about that a moment. "So . . . he had every power?"

"Well, probably throughout his entire life . . . yeah. I guess he probably did have every power at one point or another. But they weren't permanent. He possessed the powers of others only while he was close to them."

"How close?" I'm a stickler for details; it helps build the mental pictures I use to "see" things. Plus, this was information I sort of needed to know in case I ran into Finch again.

"I don't really know, son. Maybe fifty yards? It's not a very large distance. But while within that distance, he could make use of any power nearby. He could be fast, he could fly, he could even shoot lasers out of his eyes—if he was close to someone else who had that power."

This made the next question all the more pressing to me. "So if he could do that, then how did he get killed? I mean, couldn't he just use the power of his attackers against them?"

"Sure could. Yep. But my father didn't really see his attacker coming."

"Mr. Charles," I murmured.

"Correct. You see, Grandpa and Mr. Charles were partners. But more than that, they were lifelong friends. They'd defeated hundreds of villains together throughout a long career, and they were virtually inseparable. Your grandfather never expected Mr. Charles to betray him. He was supposed to use his NPZ against Artimus, but instead, he used it on my dad and killed him."

"Well," I said, playing devil's advocate, "technically it was Artimus that killed him." I think I was searching for reasons not to hate Mr. Charles completely.

"Isn't it really the same thing, son?"

"Yeah, I guess it is." I was dejected. "Then why do you treat Mr. Charles like such a good friend? Why don't you hate him or kill him or something?"

"Mr. Charles paid his debt to society long before I met him, Phillip. He served twenty years in prison. And while inside, he was a great resource for the custodian police forces in tracking down some of the last remaining old-generation supervillains. The entire hero population has deemed him rehabilitated."

"That still doesn't explain why you have to invite him over for meat loaf."

"Phillip, something I hope you learn one day is that forgiveness is far more powerful and fulfilling than anger and revenge."

I was instantly skeptical anytime an adult told me that I would agree with them later on in life. "That doesn't make any sense at all," I responded honestly but not argumentatively.

"Well, someday it will, son. Someday it will."

20

HAPPY HOLIDAYS

Christmas came entirely too quickly, most likely because I was dreading it so much. It comes too slowly any other year, when I'm a normal kid and I just want to open presents and stuff my face with homemade food. But this Christmas, I wasn't a kid anymore; I was a young man, growing up too quickly as a result of his mother's coma.

I tried for weeks to ignore the coming holiday, instead telling myself that Mom would wake up in time to take on her usual array of holiday-cheer responsibilities. It was almost as though Christmas without her would end up being some sort of morbid milestone. A note of finality to her damaged state. I couldn't imagine the season without her, so I simply pretended as though it wasn't upon us. A Christmas version of denial.

Believing that she would be fine and back with her family for Christmas was the only way I was able to make it this far without falling apart.

But two weeks prior to the big day, I had a total change of heart. The holiday was going to come, whether I wanted it to or not. So I went the other direction. Instead of putting on blinders, I became obsessed with Christmas. I convinced myself that—somehow, despite all logic to the contrary—if I were able to keep Mom's vision of the season alive for our family, perhaps God would let her come back to us. It wouldn't be the last time I would try to force the hand of fate with my own insignificant actions.

It started small. A piece of tinsel here, a little snowman figurine there. With Henry's help I was able to find the spot in the garage where all the decorations were stored away each year and bit by bit began to unwrap the knickknacks and place them throughout the house.

But once I started, I couldn't stop. I lost myself completely in the pursuit of recreating what this time of year was supposed to feel like when Mom was around. Within a day or two, I was keeping Christmas music playing on the stereo around the clock—something Mom always enjoyed during the holiday season. The little village—which Mom used to put together one day at a time over the course of the month of December—I assembled in one hour flat, complete with the artificial "snow" and all the little townspeople figurines.

By day three, I had gone through all the decorations in the house and began looking for other ways to bring the spirit of the season into the house. I lit cinnamon-scented candles and put out little glass jars of Hershey's Kisses. I even hung an Advent calendar, though it was from 1995.

I found out when all the usual yuletide specials were set to come on television and made sure to have them on when I was home, even when no one was watching them or when I was home alone.

I spent an entire Saturday baking—a first for me. Probably a last, as well. Between my inexperience in the kitchen and my lack of sight, it was challenging, to be sure. I forced Henry to come over to be my eyes and read me all of Mom's recipes and tried to follow them to the letter for holiday treats like candy-cane-shaped cookies, zucchini bread, and apple pies. I baked for five straight hours. When Dad got home from work, the kitchen looked like a culinary battle zone, with delicious shrapnel strewn all over the counter, floor, and table.

He set his coat on the back of one of the dining room chairs as he walked slowly toward the kitchen. His mouth was hanging open a bit, and he rubbed his temples furiously.

At first, I thought he was going to be mad at the mess I'd made. He just stood there, wide-eyed, looking around the room over and over again. He looked at me with an expression I'd never seen before, which I now know was concern. At the time, I just thought he was in shock at the mess. "I'm going to clean it up," I promised cheerily as I continued banging the pots and pans around.

"It's okay," he said, still staring at me.

It's easier now, long after the fact, to look back and understand my father's unique position. He had to have been just as upset about Mom as Patrick and I were, if not more so. This was his wife, his best friend, and his true love.

And yet, he also had two kids to look after, which included things like getting us fed and off to school every day. But it also had to include concern and worry for our mental well-being. Seeing me go from zero to "Captain Christmas" in about forty-eight hours probably caused Dad to think I'd lost my mind. Maybe I had.

He didn't know what it meant or how to handle it. It's not like there are guidebooks for how to cope when your spouse is in a superpower-enhanced coma. He was making it up as he went along. I've always regretted not being more mature and alert to his struggles during that time. I could have tried to make things easier for him.

But to his credit, he didn't get mad or show frustration about any of it. He didn't get mad about the mess in the kitchen—though I definitely had to clean it up that night. He didn't get mad about the decorations, the insomnia, or Patrick's newly emerging nightmare problem. He just went about his duties as a loving father, all the while shielding us from his own worry and pain.

In fact, I'm not sure my father got upset with us boys a single time in the weeks after Mom's coma. To our credit, we didn't do too much to rock the boat during that time either. Whether it was our own trauma or just an instinctive sense that Dad didn't need misbehaving boys to deal with on top of everything else, we were little angels for the most part.

Christmas morning, we loaded up a picnic basket and several presents into the car and went to the hospital to celebrate with Mom. The ride wasn't nearly as difficult as usual. It was the first and only time that visiting that room felt like a good thing.

The nurses and staff on duty greeted us warmly, and dad told me that the hospital hallways had been decorated with wreaths and holiday greens. I think Mom would have appreciated that.

The clunking machine noise in her hospital room faded quickly into the background, drowned out by the little radio I'd brought to play carols on. We sang carols while Dad clumsily strummed his old acoustic guitar. I sang the harmony part that Mom usually sang, though I missed several of the notes. We ate sticky bread and licked our fingers clean. It was almost a regular Sallinger Christmas.

Almost.

We took only a few presents to the hospital because of time and space, so there were still presents under the tree when we got home. And it was when we sat down on the living room floor to open the rest of the presents around the tree that I realized how poor a substitute that hospital room had been.

As Patrick tore open a transforming robot—it also turns into a boat!—a realization hit me: this was the real Sallinger Christmas . . . the one at home . . . and Mom wasn't around. The hospital celebration had been a mirage. Artificial. An approximation of the real thing but so far from what it should have been. This second celebration at home is the one that was meant to be. The one we deserved. The one we were stuck with.

Christmas had come and gone, and fate had not restored my mother's health. It was over, and there had been no miracles. Finch's coma wasn't bound by the traditions of family. It wasn't bound by the emotions of a boy who missed his mother. It was bound only by his own selfish needs.

How many more family moments would this man's actions rob me of?

It was the first time I considered a future where Mom never came out of her coma at all. I'd been operating under the assumption that, no matter how difficult or awkward life without Mom might be, it was a temporary situation— that someday, probably soon, she would wake up and come home to us, and life as we knew it would just pick right up from there. But sitting there watching Patrick squeal with glee as he leaped up to bear-hug Dad's neck as a thank-you, I realized exactly how bleak things had become.

And I started to cry.

Christmas break typically goes by at breakneck speed. Long before you're ready, you're headed back to school.

That was not the case this year, though it had as much to do with simple boredom as it did anything else. I was going absolutely crazy with the complete lack of things to do.

It was Bentley's fault, really. And Henry's. Actually, it was their parents' fault. They'd gone away for Christmas vacation. Superheroes apparently have friends and family scattered across the globe, just like normal folks do. So Henry's family was down in Georgia. He said Christmas was a pretty big deal in his family and that over fifty relatives would be gathering on his uncle's farm.

Bentley, on the other hand, had gone to Goodspeed with his family. They had relatives there in the custodians' capital city—cousins, I think—but Bentley's dad also had some official board business to attend to, even during the holidays.

So I had two weeks off of school with my two best friends nowhere to be found.

I quickly got bored. Almost out of necessity, I started spending more and more time with Donnie. He didn't have anywhere to be for Christmas break, and I needed someone to hang out with who wasn't part of my family. I also still felt bad about how much trouble he had ended up in after trying to protect me from Chad.

Most days, we just walked around town and talked. Or I should say, I talked. Donnie spent about 99.9 percent of Christmas break the same way he spent the rest of his life: quietly listening. I think that's what I enjoyed about our one-on-one time, at least in the beginning. It was me getting some alone time to work out my thoughts without actually having to be alone.

Around the house, I was much quieter than normal. I wasn't sure about anything anymore. About Finch, Mom . . . none of it. I spent a lot of time thinking, and I mostly just kept my thoughts to myself. But Donnie offered me a chance to verbalize some things without fear of reprisal. He almost never shared an opinion on anything. It was perfect, really. I had a sounding board for all the wildly changing thoughts and emotions I was experiencing, and it came with virtually zero risk.

"I think maybe he knows more than he's letting on," I said, jamming my hands into my winter coat pockets. I was talking about Dad. "I mean, if the doctors told him there was no chance Mom would ever come out of her coma, do you think that's something he would share with me? 'Cause I don't."

Even though Donnie didn't offer much in the way of feedback, I still always paused to give him a chance to participate in the conversation. Seemed like the polite thing to do.

He said nothing, as usual, so I just continued my stream of consciousness rambling. "I think maybe if Patrick wasn't so young, Dad might shoot straight with me more often. But mostly I feel like he's just trying to shield me from the whole ordeal. Isn't that ridiculous? I mean, I was in that cornfield and watched Mom get zapped!"

I wasn't really mad. Just frustrated. I was a little kid who wanted adult answers, but no adult in their right mind was going to give them to me.

"I just want her to be okay. But the only way that's going to happen is if Finch decides to let her live. Or maybe they catch him somehow and keep him from being able to sever the connection to my mom. But Dad won't talk about the investigation at all! He said he's not allowed to talk about it because of work, but I'm not sure I believe that. I think he's just trying to keep me away from the details."

Donnie grunted—something he did often. I wasn't ever sure if it was his way of responding or if it was just a thing he did involuntarily to clear his throat. I chose to believe it was the former.

"He has to be keeping her alive for a reason, right?" I was back to talking about Finch again. I didn't know if Donnie followed my sporadic ranting. "It just doesn't make any sense at all to devote time or resources to doing that unless there's a reason, you know? But I can't for the life of me figure out what it would be. What possible reason does he have to keep her alive now that he knows the entire protection agency is after him?"

I thought about that for a moment, letting it hang in the air. Was my mother somehow important to Finch's plan? Or maybe it was my father who was? Regardless, something didn't add up. Spending time with Bentley had taught me to examine the logic behind things, and in this case, Finch's logic didn't work. Something was missing, and it was something Finch knew that I did not.

We reached the center of downtown Freepoint—a fact I knew only because the sidewalk under my feet had changed from concrete to brick. That meant Jack's was only a block away, which gave me a sudden craving for cheesy breadsticks.

"You feel like having some breadsticks?" I asked Donnie. He didn't respond with a statement, but I heard him grunt, which I took as a yes. "Come on, then, my treat."

Donnie's legs are quite a bit longer than mine, and there was a noticeable pep in his next few steps. I could tell he was excited about the unexpected treat, and I did my best to keep up. The thought of Donnie being so happy made me smile. "You know," I said, as much to myself as to Donnie, "I can't believe I haven't talked to you about this before now, but I heard a rumor about your superpowers."

Silence.

"I was thinking . . . it wasn't a very long time that you were gone. You took off and then found my dad and brought him back to the cornfield in an incredibly short amount of time. The blue light flash? And I talked to my dad about it too."

Still nothing. We strode on. Jack's was only a half block away.

"And then there was that time when you went racing around Bentley's guesthouse, remember that?"

Donnie grunted again.

"You know what I think, Donnie?" I asked with a playful tone. "I think you run fast. In fact, I think you run really fast . . . like, superhumanly fast. I bet you can do other things fast too, right, Donnie?"

"Yeah." It was the simplest of admissions, with no real emotion attached to it at all. He sounded almost sad, even. Like a kid whose mother just asked if he had any homework he needed to do before playing his video games.

I was astonished. I'd known Donnie for almost four months, and I'd heard him speak only about four times. Anytime you got a word out of Donnie was an occasion to mark in some way.

"I think that's your superpower, Donnie," I continued, "speed."

We'd reached the sidewalk in front of Jack's Pizza. The little bell on the door gave a ring, and a couple shuffled past, carrying on whatever heated conversation had begun at their dinner table. I grabbed the door to hold it open as they went by.

I finished my thought, whispering, "You have the ability to be extraordinarily fast, don't you, Donnie?"

Donnie just stood there for a minute. I assumed he'd returned to his normal self, and I'd gotten all the spoken words there would be out of him that day. But he must have just been contemplating things, because suddenly, he spoke again. "Yeah . . . Donnie is fast."

And with that, he took his large frame inside the restaurant, leaving me to deal with the open door . . . and my open jaw.

21

SPILLING THE BEANS

Ordinarily, I wouldn't be allowed to have a sleepover so spontaneously, especially on a night that Dad was working. Even the regular weekend sleepovers required planning and pleading that began weeks in advance. But we were fairly desperate. The next installment of the SuperSim was upon us, and we felt we needed one more night to plan and prepare.

Much to my surprise, Dad didn't bat an eye; he gave me permission right there on the spot. I couldn't believe it. I guess maybe he was giving me extra leeway because of the situation with Mom. Actually, everyone seemed to be giving me extra leeway lately. I was even getting grades on schoolwork that were better than I deserved, of that I was certain.

The gang and I gathered at my house for one more powwow session before the second SuperSim. Dad had the night shift at work, off looking for Finch or patrolling for danger somewhere. He rarely told me any details about the cases he worked on, and when he did, it was always long after they'd closed.

Thanks to stupid custodian traditions, we were forced to wait for Patrick to go to bed before we could discuss superstuff. And that proved difficult any time all his older brother's friends came over for a sleepover. After all, it's the little brother's job to try endlessly to horn in on an older brother's social gatherings.

Even Chad was present, having been officially inducted as a member of our team after a tense debate and vote only the night before. Henry had voted no. He continued to cast his wary eye in Chad's direction every now and then, looking him over suspiciously and not being the least bit inconspicuous about it. For his part, Chad stayed quiet and mostly just tried to observe and not rock the boat.

When I asked Patrick what time it was, he started stalling, giving excuses for why he wasn't tired yet. Asking him for the time was my way of letting him know it was bedtime, and he hated it.

"I had too much caffeine at dinner, and I'm not even a little bit tired," he whined.

"Whose fault is that?" I shot back.

"But I'm just going to be lying there looking up at the ceiling."

"Then maybe next time, you won't drink two Cokes with your dinner." *Sheesh, kids.* I heard Henry snort a little bit.

Eventually, after much more lollygagging than Dad would have put up with, I lost my patience a bit and yelled at him. "Would you freaking go to bed already so that the adults can play?"

He shot me that snotty look he'd earned medals for and stomped off to bed like the eleven-year-old he was.

"Finally," I exhaled. "Sorry about that, guys."

"No problem," Bentley said. "But we need to get to it if we're going to get any decent sleep tonight. And we need decent sleep."

"All right, let's go over the plan again," I began. "Bentley's cameras are now all in place, right?"

"Check. All one thousand two hundred thirteen of them."

"Holy crap, that's a lot of cameras," Henry said. "You didn't say you were going to put up that many!"

"Wait, what?" It was Chad, the only member of the team too new to have been told about the camera plan already.

"We put up a bunch of cameras—" I began before being cut off.

"One thousand two hundred thirteen of them to be exact," Bentley repeated, quite proud.

"One thousand two hundred thirteen cameras, all around the city," I continued. "And we're going to use them to get an advantage in finding the crime for the SuperSim."

"Isn't that, like, against the rules?" Chad inquired, just as I had originally.

"You would think," I muttered, "but Bentley says it's not."

"Every camera is in a public place, filming public activities. And none of them are actually recording anything. They're just streaming a live feed that only I can pick up."

"I don't think that means it's legal, but whatever," I said, not wanting to have the same argument with Bentley yet again. "Regardless, it's not against the SuperSim rules."

"Wow," said Chad, sounding impressed. "That sounds like quite an advantage, indeed."

"That's what I'm talking about," Bentley said, awkwardly attempting to give Chad a high five. It didn't go very well, but I was pleasantly surprised to see him accepting enough of Chad to even attempt it.

"Okay, Bentley, give us a rundown on the cameras," I said, getting us back in gear.

"All right, gentlemen," he began, opening his laptop. "Through the miracle of modern wireless technology along with a dash of my own creativity, we can use this laptop to access any camera's feed." He clicked a button on the computer, and a grid came up showing small video boxes. There were about a dozen or so on the screen. One showed a view of Freepoint Circle, and we could see people from town walking about, enjoying a Friday evening. "Now, it's a little impractical at this point, at least in terms of knowing where to look. I can fit only twelve feeds onscreen at once, and with over a thousand, well, you can see the massive amounts of data we'll be trying to sift through."

Bentley was an egghead. Nothing got him talking more excitedly than his own inventions and creations, and it was fun to watch.

"But," he continued, "I have compensated for that by grouping them together by their location." He flipped through the various grids onscreen, showing how the camera feeds were arranged in geographical order.

I thought I heard a noise coming from the hallway, which is something I was always hyperalert for on these sleepovers since I definitely didn't want to see how angry Dad got if I spilled the beans to Patrick about his superpowers. "Keep going, Bentley," I said quietly as I got up and excused myself.

I crept down the hallway. Patrick's door was shut, so he definitely couldn't have been eavesdropping. I stopped by his door and put my acute hearing to work, listening for any sign that he was up to mischief, but there was nothing. He probably was just lying on his back staring at the ceiling, practicing his snotty face.

Since I was nearby, I popped into the bathroom really quick to relieve myself. In the process, a funny thought occurred to me, one that kept me giggling to myself all the way back into the living room.

"What's so funny?" Henry asked, the way a prosecutor asks a murder suspect what they were doing on the night of the murder.

"I just had the strangest experience," I said, still smiling. "I went down to make sure Patrick was still in his room, and then I went to the bathroom. And I'm standing there in the bathroom, you know . . . doing my business . . . and while I'm doing that, I'm still getting Henry's pictures and audio of him looking at Bentley's cameras. It's like I don't have to miss out on anything, even if I'm gone, as long as good old Henry's around. I saw you zooming in and out on the bank camera while I was washing my hands," I said, probably a bit too amused and impressed.

No one else seemed amused except for Bentley, who chuckled. But his smile quickly turned to a frown. It was one of those good frowns, where his brain was mere seconds away from putting something together. "Wait a second," he said. "Phillip, you just gave me an idea."

All the heads in the room turned to face him, waiting for his next nugget of brilliance. He stared at the computer, deep in his thoughts, clearly trying to work through something in his mind. He looked up at me, then at Henry, and then at the computer screen. "Phillip, I think you might be a genius," he finally declared. "Hang on one minute and I'll show you what I mean. James . . . give me a quick lift home?"

"Why, sure," James chirped. He placed his hand on Bentley's shoulder, and a second later—

Ooph!

They were gone.

And that's when I heard my brother, Patrick, say his first phrase involving a swear word, one slow syllable at a time. "Ho. Lee. Shit."

Indeed.

⚡

I completely forgot about Bentley and his grand idea because I immediately lost myself in the verbal flogging of my little brother. It was an instinctive reaction. I just launched into him for having snuck out of bed, ignoring the fact that Dad and I had been hiding the facts from him. "What are you doing? You're not supposed to be out here!" But as soon as I started shouting, he hightailed it back to his bedroom and slammed the door.

I stomped right after him, but reality kicked in by the time I reached his door, and I knew it was pointless to be mad at him. The damage had been done. I collected my thoughts, took a deep breath, and walked into Patrick's room.

"Patrick, I'm sorry I yelled—"

Patrick cut me off, rambling incoherently and quite excitedly. "What in the heck just happened, Phillip? I mean, did you see that? That was unbelievable!" He was speaking at an incredible rate of speed. "B-b-b-Bentley just up and disappeared! And James too! What the heck is going on? Are they aliens? Are they magicians? This is amazing! I can't believe you didn't tell me your friends were aliens. Or superheroes!" His eyes managed to get even wider. "Oh my God, like on the news!"

I just let him go for a bit until he was done since my attempts to interrupt him were unsuccessful anyway. Finally, he began to get tired and sat down on the edge of the bed and flopped on his back.

"Okay, Patrick," I began, having never planned any kind of speech for this moment. "First things first. You cannot tell Dad, okay? You cannot tell anyone in the entire world that you know about this. No one can know that you know, do you understand?"

He didn't respond, and I didn't wait for him to.

"I don't have time to tell you everything tonight. I won't have time to tell you everything for a long time because we're going to be able to talk about it only when nobody's around, okay?"

Again, I required no input from him.

"Freepoint is a town almost entirely populated by superheroes. Dad and Mom are both superheroes. Every kid in that room"—I pointed toward the living room—"has a superpower. Bentley has a superadvanced brain. Henry can read minds. James can teleport to anywhere in the world in the blink of an eye. Chad can turn invisible. And Patrick . . . I can move things with my brain. I have telekinesis."

At this, Patrick burst out laughing, as though all of it were possible in his mind except for his brother having a cool power. That part was apparently ridiculous.

"After what you just saw, are you really trying to tell me you don't believe me?" I asked wearily.

"You can move things with your brain, right," he said dismissively. "You can't even see, Phillip!"

"I can still use my power," I said flatly, "but I also get to see things around me because of Henry's power."

Patrick folded his arms in defiance and merely said, "Prove it." It was the quintessential challenge from a little brother—and one I didn't waste any time accepting.

"Yo, Henry!" I yelled into the living room. "Can you come here?"

Patrick and I remained silent, stuck in a game of knowledge-based chicken while we waited.

"Hello?" Henry said as he pushed the door open with his hand. "Um, did you call me?" I could tell Henry didn't really want to get involved, but it was too late for all of that.

"Yes. Thanks. Okay, Patrick, I want you to hold up your fingers, however many you want. Because I'm blind, I won't be able to see, right?"

I waited a moment. Through Henry's vision, I was able to see Patrick think long and hard before finally holding up two fingers on his left hand and the thumb of his right hand.

"Two fingers and a thumb. Try again."

Patrick looked at Henry, then back at me, then bit his lip in determination, and held up two closed fists.

"That's no fingers. Zero fingers. I can see you, Patrick. What do I have to do to prove it to you?"

"But that's impossible," he said in disbelief. "You're blind."

"I am, but Henry's mind reading ability works in both directions, so it lets him share what he sees with my brain. So whenever he's around, I can see just fine . . . sort of. It's a work in progress." In my mind, the lesson was over. We were already short on practice time, and I wanted to get this over with as soon as possible so I could begin strategizing on how to best keep it secret from Dad. "Now, I believe you also scoffed when I told you what my ability was, correct? Please name something in this room . . . something that you don't think I can move with my brain."

Patrick glanced around the room, his eyes still wide as his mind continued to process an enormous amount of inconceivable information. Finally he said, "My football." Back in New York, Patrick had been quite a Jets fan. He still was, actually. He'd even gone to games with his best friend's family a few times. And his prized possession in all the world was an official NFL football signed by the entire team. It sat in the far corner of the room on a little shelf my dad had made as a present during his woodworking phase. And within about 1.2 seconds of him saying the word "football," it was in my hands.

And that's when Patrick fainted, which is something I definitely did not see coming—pardon the pun.

My brother woke back up within ten seconds of passing out. And after several more minutes of him peppering Henry and me with questions, he finally seemed to be accepting this new reality that had been thrust upon him earlier than anticipated. He nearly fainted again when I told him that he, too, would develop a superpower. And he got downright giddy when I told him it was superspeed.

We worked out the terms of our pact of silence: Patrick would keep his mouth shut about knowing any of this, or I would kill him. In exchange, I had to promise to answer questions and give him more information any time we had the opportunity to be alone. Oh, and I had to let him sit and watch the rest of the evening's SuperSim planning session.

He didn't realize it yet, but he had all the power in this situation. He could squeal on me to Dad, telling him everything he knew, and Patrick himself wouldn't face any discipline. I, however, would either be grounded for a century or sold at auction to the highest bidder.

And yet, strangely, despite all that, I didn't really care that he knew. I was so tired of keeping the secret that it felt good to let it out and finally be myself around my brother. In a way, I welcomed it.

When we returned to the living room, Bentley and James were back, and they'd brought some more of Bentley's equipment with them. A lot of it, actually, including some tools. Bentley was holding some kind of plastic contraption in his hand, and I couldn't quite make it out. It was black and shiny, and he seemed to be holding it with a lot of pressure—as though he'd just glued it back together and was waiting for it to set. Which is exactly what had taken place.

"Here, Phillip," he said, not skipping a beat from his earlier epiphany. "Put these on." He held out his hand with the palm up, revealing a pair of bulky black sunglasses. I used my telekinetic abilities and pulled the glasses into my hand.

"I'm never going to get tired of seeing you do that," Bentley said, shaking his head in wonder.

"You aren't kidding," Patrick said from his position on the couch.

I looked the object over. There was a small black cylinder, about the size of a tube of lipstick, crudely attached to the arm of the sunglasses that hook over the wearer's right ear. I was looking at the glasses from Henry's perspective, of course, which made it tough to see the exact tight angles I wanted.

"Put 'em on," Bentley urged.

I decided to go with the flow and opened the glasses, placing them on my face. It was the first time I'd ever worn any kind of glasses except for dark sunglasses, and I hated those things so much I barely wore them. They felt weird on my face, and Bentley's glasses did as well.

"Okay, Henry, you come sit over here." Bentley was getting excited again. "Okay, now. Phillip, reach up with your right hand, and flip the little switch on the outside of the glasses."

I felt along the lipstick tube until I came to a switch. When I flipped it, it made a little clicking noise.

"Henry, stop sending Phillip what your eyes are seeing." Henry did so, and my "vision" disappeared. Bentley continued, "Now look here." A pause. "And now send Phillip your vision again."

And suddenly, I was looking at the most accurate "first-person" perspective I'd ever seen from Henry's images.

It was obvious right away what Bentley had done. The lipstick tube was a camera that was sending its images to the laptop, which is what Henry was looking at. Instead of seeing Henry's perspective of my surroundings, which, frankly, sometimes made it difficult to gauge depth and distance, I was looking at what the camera on my glasses was recording. And that was almost exactly in line with the perspective my eyes would give me had they functioned like everyone else's.

The inventor explained his creation. "The camera on the glasses records your first-person view and sends it to the computer, which is light and portable, so Henry can take it with him. Actually, remind me to mount that thing to your wheelchair arm before tomorrow's event. We'll put it on a nice sturdy swivel arm. So now, Phillip, you can see what . . . you know . . . you should be able to see, if you could see. Got it?"

"Do I ever," I marveled. "Bentley, this is incredible! You're a freaking Einstein," I gushed.

"You're the one who figured it out with your little trip to the bathroom. All I had to do was put it all together."

"How far will the signal reach?" I asked hopefully.

Bentley grinned. "One hundred yards on that camera, and I can probably get a camera off the internet that'll reach even farther. This is just a prototype, obviously. We don't have time to make a proper version before the Sim, but we can definitely improve on this moving forward. For now, though, it should allow you to see a more accurate version of what a sighted person would see in terms of perspective, which should, in turn, give you greater control with your powers. And it also frees you up from having to have Henry and his wheelchair at your side in order to see."

"How far will Henry's ability reach, though?" I wondered aloud. The camera could send its feed one hundred yards away from the laptop, but we'd yet to test the distance limits on Henry's little vision-sharing trick.

Bentley smiled again. "I think maybe now is a good time to find out. Who's up for a field test?"

Patrick's hand was the first one up.

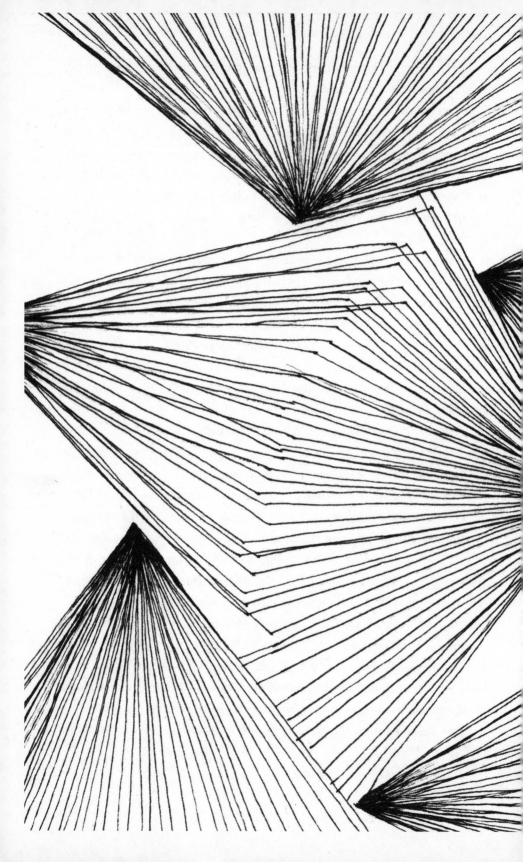

22

THE BOOK

Bentley had played right into Finch's hands. He was simply too eager to soak up any new knowledge that he could. And he had a particular weakness for learning about historical custodian-related information. He'd dove headfirst into researching Finch's creepy prophecy book, and he finally had some theories to share.

We gathered at Jack's, taking up residence in the back corner booth between the row of arcade games and the hallway to the restroom. Books were strewn about of every color, size, and age imaginable.

"All of this is starting to add up, is all I'm saying." Bentley was wrapping up his summary of his research so far, much of which had been unimportant, but Bentley was thorough. "I think this guy not only truly believes in the prophecy," he said, and then paused and swallowed, "but after looking over all this material, I'm actually starting to think he may be right."

"What?" Henry said through a mouthful of calzone. Bentley was, in fact, the only one not currently stuffing his face. "Mr. Science-Loving Guy is buying into mystic prophecies now?" It was a valid question, and one I would have asked myself if Henry had given me a chance, though I would have been more polite about it, of course—and waited until I stopped chewing.

"It's not mysticism, though, that's the thing. The further you dive into this prophecy and especially McKenzie's theory of mathematical recurrences in DNA cycles, it's science. It's math. It's a formula."

"Awesome. And I'm so good at math," I said sarcastically.

"That's the thing, Phillip—he's already done all the math for us." Not even a chuckle out of Bentley, that's how focused he was. When he was on a roll, he was difficult to distract. "Actually, several folks have. Grankage, an early seventh-century philosopher, was the first one to speculate that Malea's prophecy wasn't religious in nature but scientific. Then, a few centuries later, came Cray and his gang. They're the ones who actually started laying down the track, doing basic calculations on when the conditions of the planet and human evolution might again allow for an all-empowered individual."

Henry looked at me, giving me a glance at my own confused face. "Are you getting any of this?"

"Me, no," I said immediately. "I'm waiting for the CliffsNotes version."

"Me neither," Chad chimed in before slurping at his soft drink. "Get to the point, Smart Phone." Smart Phone was a nickname Chad had assigned to the uber-bright Bentley, one that he generally detested.

Bentley sighed. For a moment, I felt sorry for him. It truly must be difficult to be able to reach and understand conclusions long before your peers. "It's this year, okay? Every person who's ever run the numbers in an attempt to decipher the prophecy's end-date has come up with the same year—this one. I don't think Malea was making a prophecy. I think he was offering up a mathematical proof that, sooner or later, the odds demanded another all-powered being show up."

"Okay, but that doesn't mean Finch is right, right?" It was James, but it could have been any of us because we were all thinking it. "So the math suggests the return of Elben will be this year, but that's only if you believe in the prophecy, right?"

"Well, sure," Bentley agreed. "But it doesn't really matter whether or not we believe. It only matters that Finch believes and that, for some reason, he seems intent on including us in the event."

"Okay, this is all a little too much for me. I'm taking a pinball break." Henry threw up his hands briefly and then scampered down the arcade line to his favorite machine. I was at once mad at him for bailing and jealous that he'd get to skip the next few minutes of science lessons.

"Because the pepperoni break wasn't relaxing enough," Bentley shouted after him hopelessly.

"Forget him for a moment," I advised. "What's your point, Bentley? What are you saying, that the prophecy is real?"

"I don't know. I may never know," he admitted. "I'm just saying we should take it seriously, if only because Finch does."

"So Elben is going to return this year, that's the basic premise, and we should consider that a possibility?"

"Actually the prophecy isn't calling for 'the one who can do all' to do anything specific except manifest . . . realize his or her own powers."

I wrinkled my face, which had become a universal signal with Bentley that he should continue explaining things. So he did.

"You know how I know Finch himself isn't the reincarnation of Elben?"

I did not and shook my head accordingly.

"Because he's old. He's grandparent age."

I still didn't understand. If Henry were still at the table, I'm sure he'd have the perfect barb to tell Bentley he was still being too vague.

"Powers manifest between the ages of eleven and fifteen. We all know that, obviously. This person the prophecy is talking about? Their powers would manifest in the same age bracket, not later in life."

"You're saying it's going to be a kid?"

"I'm saying if this prophecy stuff is true in the least, it *has* to be a kid."

"I still say we should be trying to figure out who this Finch guy really is." It was Henry, beginning his sentence a few feet from the table, having already blown through his small stack of quarters on a game at which he was terrible.

"I agree," Bentley said, nodding. "Which is why I pulled all the yearbooks from the time he claims to have been a student at Freepoint, school records, birth records, and anything else I could get my hands on."

"And?" Chad inquired.

"Nothing. No records whatsoever."

"How is that possible?" I was instantly dejected.

"I think it's safe to assume at this point that Finch is a pseudonym."

"A what?" Freddie interjected.

"A fake name."

"Well, wonderful," I said, sighing. "So basically square one, then, right?"

"Not exactly," Bentley countered. "We know he's an absorber, right?"

"Right," came Henry's reply, again partially concealed behind the chewing of a rather large bite of calzone.

"Well, that's a pretty rare power, actually. So I managed to dig up the names of all custodians with that power who ever lived or attended school in Freepoint in the last sixty years." He produced a piece of paper from his binder. "It's a pretty short list." He flipped the paper so it would be facing us and proceeded to go down the list. "First, there's Phillip's grandfather, Thomas Sallinger. He's deceased. Then, there's Rodney Milner, from Goodspeed. In 1965, he died in a training incident. But he was in Freepoint for only six months during his father's job transfer anyway."

Henry's thoughts invaded my mind unexpectedly. *I'm going to fall asleep if he doesn't get to the point soon.*

Bentley continued, oblivious to Henry's impatience. "Grady Ball was a teacher here during the 1980s but has the cleanest service record I've ever seen. He also died in the early 2000s in a car accident."

"Are all these guys dead?" I wondered aloud.

"Actually, yes," he replied. "At least, all the ones with any connection to Freepoint. There are two living in the world who are from the right generation—one in Russia and one in Brazil. Neither has ever been to Freepoint, much less attended here as a student."

"Well, what are we supposed to make of that?" James asked.

"That either Finch is not the absorber he claims to be or his backstory about founding the Believers is a lie. Regardless, I think it's safe to assume we can't truly trust anything this man says."

"But we still have to take it seriously," I said, echoing his earlier words.

"Right," he allowed cautiously.

"Right. So in other words, square one," I said for the second time this conversation.

"I think we've actually learned a lot," Bentley countered. "We know he's not who he says he is and probably doesn't have the ability he claims. We know he's sincere in his stated desire to bring about and witness the return or reincarnation of 'the one who can do all.' And we know that person, if they actually exist, is more our age than Finch's. And the name Finch itself is phony." He paused, taking stock in the facts. "That's not nothing," he concluded.

"Fair enough," I allowed. "We've learned a few facts. But in terms of being better equipped to face him or defeat him somehow, we're actually not any closer, right?" My frustration was starting to show, and I regretted not masking it better.

"I'm saying I think the thing worth investigating maybe isn't the prophecy anymore. Maybe it's the man himself."

Ten minutes later, by virtue of our pal James, we were once again standing inside the hidden basement of the rotunda. This time, there was no Finch, though I'll admit to having been more than a little concerned about that possibility.

"Okay. Now, he said he'd broken into the library that first night for some reason other than this book."

"But we can't trust him to be telling the truth about even that," I reminded him.

"Yeah, sure." Bentley placed the book back on the stand in the center of the room.

"What are you doing?" Henry asked. "You're giving it back?"

Bentley, momentarily confused, responded, "Oh, well . . . I sort of memorized it."

"Isn't that thing written in a dead language?" I followed up.

"Yes," he boasted, "Claret, the original custodian language." He paused, perhaps realizing how much of a nerd he sounded like. "I took a class last summer."

"You took a class on a dead language during the one time of year you're not required to take classes?" Henry was in shock.

I merely shook my head in a mixture of amusement and wonder.

Bentley just continued his original thought. "Look around, everyone. It's not a big area. We're looking for anything you think might even remotely pertain to Finch or this prophecy, okay?"

We spread out as best we could in the small space. There was a main round area under the rotunda, roughly fifteen to twenty feet in diameter, and also a small side room that was part office space and part kitchen. Chad and Freddie started opening cabinets while Henry began pulling up the cushions on the chairs lining the rotunda wall. James and I were mostly left to watch and wait. Blind kids make terrible private detectives. Only slightly better than Donnie, who also stood in the center of the room helplessly.

I was mostly monitoring what Henry was seeing since he was still sending James and me his images. He was striking out, finding nothing in the chair cushions but dust and a few pennies. He looked up at me briefly. *I don't know, man.*

"What do you got in the kitchen, Freddie?" I shouted hopefully.

"I don't think anything useful," he answered, pausing briefly. "Mostly just kitchen stuff, actually." He puffed his inhaler. "Why would they need three muffin pans?"

I sighed heavily. Henry stopped his search and looked around the room. As his gaze panned over the far wall of the rotunda and into the kitchenette, something caught my eye. "Wait, go back," I said sharply.

Henry was used to this kind of thing by now and merely reversed his gaze back over the wall. When he passed over the framed portrait, I stopped him. "Right there! Grab that picture, would you?"

Henry merely cocked his head sideways, silently willing me to remember he was a crippled kid who couldn't stand up out of his wheelchair. I got the message.

"Freddie, can you come grab this picture for Henry, please?" Henry enjoyed sarcasm and laying blame, but I was all about solutions. Freddie scampered over, nearly tripping on Bentley's cane as he darted out of the side room. He jumped up onto the chair Finch had occupied during our last visit, grabbed the frame, and then stepped back down and took a puff from his inhaler.

Henry grabbed the picture and tossed it to me. Unfortunately, it's not easy to catch something thrown at you when you are seeing it from the perspective of the guy doing the throwing. It smacked me in the stomach, knocking out my wind for a moment and doubling me over.

"Oh crap! Sorry, Phillip," Henry blurted sincerely, but still too late.

"Dang," I wheezed. "Do try and remember that I am a blind person, okay?"

"Oh man. Sorry," he replied.

I reached down and picked up the framed photograph. "Besides, I can't see a thing in this picture if your eyes aren't looking at it." I flipped it right back at him, half hoping it would ricochet off his forehead like the woman at the school board hearing, but he caught it fine. He then laid it in his lap, facing up, and looked down at the picture to allow me the view I needed.

The photo gave me instant déjà vu as I remembered that first night I'd seen it. But I hadn't paid close attention to it that night. "Someone in this photograph is Finch," I said aloud.

"Well," Bentley cautioned, "that's if you believe he was telling the truth."

"We're going to play that game forever, aren't we? And do you not think he was telling the truth?"

"Actually, no, I do. I think he's in this picture."

"Well then, let's identify everyone we can and see who's left," I suggested.

"That's fine, Phillip. And we should do that." Bentley was already a step ahead of me, as usual. "But if we assume Finch is a false identity and add in the fact that his present-day facial scarring makes it impossible to match him to anyone in this photo, we still might come up empty. I mean, if we had a picture of his current appearance . . . maybe I could write a program to do some photo altering to see if we could match him to any of these people. But his scar is just too dramatic. He could be any of these people." He gestured at the photograph in frustration.

"Maybe your dad knows some of your grandfather's old friends," Henry pondered. "I mean, if Finch was an absorber and was running in the same circles as your dad's dad, also an absorber, by the way, then doesn't it make sense they'd know each other?"

"Bentley already basically proved that's not possible, though," I argued. "Right?"

"There were no other absorbers in Thomas Sallinger's social circles at that time," Bentley concurred before offering a caveat, "on record. Again, it's always possible someone was lying about their powers or is doing so currently."

"You think Finch isn't actually an absorber?" Chad pondered. "After all you've seen him do?"

"Well, to play devil's advocate," Bentley countered, taking on one of his favorite roles, "it's entirely possible that Finch is merely a one-power custodian flanked by unseen associates—Believers, perhaps—doing the heavy lifting for him."

Henry had some questions about that theory. "How are they unseen, then?"

"One of them has Chad's invisibility power, and he keeps them all hidden."

"And so the rest of the powers he demonstrates would be . . ." I said aloud, honestly just working through the theory.

Bentley finished for me. "Controlled by others."

Everyone took a beat to consider that before Bentley added his usual qualifier. "It's just a theory, a logical possibility that would, at least in part, explain the gaps in Finch's story. I'm not saying it's definitely happening."

"So, again, I feel compelled to ask," I said reluctantly, "what concrete facts have we actually learned?"

The collective silence served as all the answer I needed.

"All right, let's go home, everyone. We have a SuperSim to get ready for."

Everyone shuffled in toward the center of the room.

"Henry, bring that picture, okay?" Bentley asked. "I want to examine it further."

"Sure thing," Henry said, sliding the frame in the pouch on the back of his wheelchair. "So, anyone want to hit Jack's before we all head home?"

"We were just there, man," Chad exclaimed. He was the one among us that was the least used to Henry's appetite. "Honestly!"

"What? A guy's gotta eat, right?" Henry smiled, slapping his hand on top of the pile.

Ooph!

We were gone, having once again unknowingly done precisely what had been expected of us.

James dropped me off in the garage as usual, and I slipped into the main house expecting darkness and silence. Instead I smelled coffee, a telltale sign that Dad was still up. And it was probably more than a little late for me to be waltzing in casually.

"Hey, son," he said, not seeming remotely angry. The trajectory of his voice told me he was sitting at the kitchen table.

"Um, hey," I responded, not sure if I was in trouble or not and therefore not sure how to behave.

"Kinda late, no?"

It was definitely kind of late. "I guess we lost track of time."

Dad was usually either still at work or already in bed by the time I returned home from my too-late practice sessions with the guys. I'd grown accustomed to him not really monitoring my actions the last several weeks since Mom's coma, and I guess I'd let things go too far.

"You know, your brother sat here at home watching TV for five hours this evening . . . alone." The picture of my current situation began to clear up, and it wasn't good.

"I don't know, Dad. He likes watching TV." Some things sound wrong as soon as you hear yourself say them. "I mean . . . I didn't realize how long I'd been gone," I said quickly, hoping to head him off at the scolding pass. "I'm sorry. It won't happen again."

"I'm not mad, Phillip," he sighed, sounding sincere. "I'm really not. I'm more thrilled than you could know to see you making friends and exploring your abilities. I just . . . this thing with your mom . . . I'm really worried about your brother, Phillip. He's still young enough that . . ." he trailed off, though I could guess fairly accurately where he'd been headed with that thought.

"I know, Dad. I'm sorry. I haven't really been thinking about anyone but myself." It was true, actually. I just wasn't as sorry for it as I was pretending to be.

"When your mom comes back, she's going to need this place to run as normally and as smoothly as possible, you see?"

"Yes," I agreed.

"I need you to be there for your brother, even if it means you have to give up a few hours a night of practice time with your friends. He's not dealing with all this stuff too well. You may not have noticed."

If only you knew, I thought to myself.

"Your mother . . ." he began before trailing off. "This is exactly the kind of situation I would normally turn to her for . . . to find out what I'm supposed to do as a father." It was a shocking display of honesty, every bit as touching as it was surprising. "I'm kind of lost without her, son," he allowed. "And until I figure out what I'm supposed to be doing . . . I am sorry, but I have to ask you to grow up a few years for just a bit and help me."

"Yeah." I wasn't sure what else to say, or even if I should be saying anything right now.

"I understand the SuperSims are important to you, but your family is more important. I'd rather have you be a good big brother these days than a good custodian, and that's not taking anything away from being a good custodian, you know?" He cleared this throat. "I guess what I'm saying is that . . . I am not sure I know what I'm doing here, son." His voice cracked ever so slightly. "And until I do, I need your help with Patrick, because he's in a very fragile place, okay?"

"Okay," I nodded.

"Okay," he repeated, as much for himself as for me. He took a long sip of his coffee. "So, what adventures did you have this evening? Anything exciting?"

"Nope, just Bentley's research. Thrilling stuff," I said, hoping to cheer him up a bit.

"No more sightings of this Finch, right?" He probably told me three times a week to let him know if I ever heard from Finch or saw him again. It was borderline paranoia, but I was equally concerned about it myself.

"No, sir."

"Good. The less I hear about him the better. Besides, your grades should be your main focus, am I right?"

That was below the belt since there was no denying my grades had started to slip. Dad was pulling the ultimate parental trump card.

"Right. I got a B-minus on my pop quiz this week," I offered meekly, hoping he wouldn't remember that I'd already told him.

"I remember."

Dang.

"Were you studying tonight?"

"Not really. I mean, a little bit. But mostly we were just talking and hanging out."

"And planning for the upcoming SuperSim, no doubt." Like most parents, Dad's default position when receiving information from his children was "skeptical."

But I decided the truth was a can of worms best left unopened on this night, so I lied. "Nope. Just pizza and video games tonight."

Dad shook his head as he spoke. "I hate thinking about how much money I've given that man."

"Jack? Oh, it's worth it, Dad. It's worth every penny, believe me."

23

THE SECOND SUPERSIM

"I don't think he's going to stop, Phillip," Henry yelled over the noise of the attack. "We're going to have to take him out somehow!"

Henry, Chad, and I were pinned down behind a dumpster in the supermarket parking lot. Thirty yards away, ducking between the cars, was one of the simulation's bad guys—a particularly aggressive fake villain who was also a fireballer.

We'd caught him breaking into the town's grocery store on one of Bentley's security cameras, and James had zipped us over to confront him before zipping right back to the other side of town to help Bentley and the rest of the gang.

James was part of a unit with Bentley, Freddie, and Donnie, who were across town at the car dealership checking out another crime in progress spotted on Bentley's cameras. Since Henry couldn't be around for both of us, Bentley had given James my old Personal Navigator—with some custom Bentley modifications, of course. He'd downloaded the latest 3-D satellite imagery from an online maps service, which meant the Navigator was able to give James detailed audio information about his surroundings even when he was outside of the school. It wasn't the same thing as getting pictures from Henry, but it was a step up from total blindness.

"You are standing twenty feet outside the front door of the Freepoint Grocery," I heard faintly from his earpiece after we arrived.

After he'd deposited us on the front side of the grocery store, we'd come around the corner to the side parking lot and stopped dead in our tracks. The villain was just a few rows in front of us. He already had one fireball loaded up in his right hand; his left arm was wrapped around the neck of an unhappy female hostage. And he was just standing there like he was waiting for us. Instantly, he started shooting baseball-sized firebombs at us, and we were forced to take cover behind the nearby dumpster.

The bombardment had been going on for almost three full minutes at this point and showed no signs of stopping. This guy was clearly trying to keep us pinned down until he could either make a getaway or at least stall long enough for a buddy to come help him. He'd already taken one hostage—we assumed she'd been a shopper from the supermarket—and we didn't currently know her status because we were too busy cowering behind a dumpster.

I began to realize that being a true hero was all about reacting in the moment and wondered if the real adult heroes ever felt the panic that was currently gripping me. The typical superhero/criminal scenarios were so unpredictable and fluid that even in a simulation, planning didn't seem to do any good.

I took off my new pair of glasses Bentley had given me and slid over to the corner of the dumpster. I reached out my hand, peeking the camera around the edge so I could get a look at what we were up against without taking a fireball to the face.

The man was now standing in the middle of the street, about fifty yards away. We were pinned up against the grocery store's exterior brick wall, with a couple rows of cars between us and the bad guy. With his left arm, he held his hostage tight to his body while his right hand dished out punishing fireballs lofted in our direction. So far, there weren't any other student-led SuperSim teams in the vicinity, which meant we could have the points all to ourselves if we could apprehend him somehow.

Of course, with the kind of fireworks show he was putting on, there was enough light and sound to ensure we wouldn't be alone for long. That meant we needed to act fast.

And then, a thought hit me. *He's not going to hurt us! What are we afraid of?* I pulled the camera glasses back, returned them to my face, and addressed my teammates.

"Okay, check this out," I said to Henry and Chad. "This man, whoever he is, is not going to hurt us."

They both looked at me blankly, probably wondering when I'd become fireproof.

"I mean . . . he's an adult. Probably a protector or a teacher." They still didn't get it. "It's the SuperSim! No adult, however much they're pretending to be a supervillain, is going to hurt a kid during this thing. It's an exercise! He's not trying to hit us with the fireballs. He's probably just positioning them carefully to keep us pinned down! What are we afraid of here, guys? We're superheroes!"

"Just because he won't want to hurt us doesn't mean he can't accidentally do it . . . or that he's not still trying to stop us," Chad reminded me.

"Sure, sure," I said, only to continue my own argument, "but he's trying to stop us in nonlethal ways. This isn't a real supervillain. He doesn't want to put any of us into the hospital or anything like that."

"So then, what should we do, Mr. Not Afraid Anymore?" Henry asked dryly. "What's your big plan to get us out from behind this thing, stop his fireballs, save the hostage, and arrest the adult villain?" When he put it that way, maybe I did sound a little crazy.

"I don't know. But when we're real heroes, we're going to have to learn to think on our feet. We won't always have time to make a plan." Another thought hit me. "Use your powers and see what he's thinking."

Henry heard me but didn't *hear* me. "What?"

"Use your powers—read his mind and see what his plan is or whatever."

"Oh yeah," he said, just now remembering he could read minds.

A few seconds passed, and a few more fireballs smashed into the wall above us.

"Okay," Henry said, exhaling. "He's thinking, and I quote, 'Oh God, don't let me hurt these kids. Oh God, don't let me hurt these kids.'"

There was something chilling about that, but I let it slide because it also proved my point. "See, he's not only *not* trying to hurt us, he's actively attempting to keep us safe!"

"He actually sounded more scared than we are," Henry allowed.

I nodded. "Then let's do something here, okay?"

"Yeah," he agreed. "But what?"

I stretched the camera back around the dumpster again, relaying its image to Henry, who saw it on his wheelchair-mounted laptop and sent it to me.

I looked for anything I could control with my powers. There were cars all over the place, but I knew I wasn't ready for that yet. My telekinesis wasn't focused enough to move something that large and heavy.

There were trees all around the bad guy, but like most of the trees in Freepoint, they were ancient and giant—way too big for me to budge. I considered trying to move the branches but ultimately thought that any branch I was strong enough to move would probably be harmless if it fell on or near the villain. I couldn't be known as the kid who tried to win the SuperSim through the use of projectile twigs. Besides, branches are quite flammable.

There were a few loose shopping carts in the parking lot. But again, I wasn't positive I could get something of that size up in the air, let alone force it to fly across the sky. Maybe I could, but until I was sure, I didn't want to risk it.

"Whatever you do, Phillip, you'd better do it soon, man," said Henry alongside a chorus of fireball explosions on the other side of our shelter. "Sooner or later, he's going to catch one of those cars on fire, and then we're all screwed."

Ah, Henry, I thought, knowing he could hear me. *You've always got the worst-case scenario in mind, don't you?*

"Yes, I do," he replied verbally. "Somebody has to."

"Henry, I don't think we need to worry about the cars catching fire, okay? This man is a professional. I'm sure he has better control of his powers than that. And besides, if those cars started exploding, he'd be in just as much danger as we would."

I stopped cold. Had I really just stumbled onto my own solution?

"How much do you think those fireballs weigh?" I asked Chad.

"I don't know," he said. "They do a lot of damage, but they're not very big." He was right. They were the size of softballs.

"Okay," I said to myself, working through my plan. "Okay, guys, I think I got it." And then I went into field-general mode.

"Chad, I need a fire extinguisher."

He just looked at me blankly.

"Use your power," I explained, a little impatiently, "and duck back around into the grocery store and bring back the fire extinguisher. There should be one near the front desk, okay? Can you do that?"

There was about a four-foot length of wall from where we were positioned to where the building's front corner was. Chad would have to get past that four feet of exposed air without getting hit by a fireball in order to dash around the corner and into the store. He could turn invisible, but he wasn't invincible, so he took a moment to glance at the wall while considering my proposition.

"Yeah, yeah, I can do that," he finally said, not sounding wholly confident.

"Okay, listen for the next round of fireballs to crash, then go on my signal."

Chad nodded, then disappeared into thin air. We all waited a few seconds until another wave of ammo hit the front of the dumpster.

"Go!" I yelled.

It was a little anticlimactic for me. Since Chad was already invisible, I didn't get to see him take off running. Heck, I wasn't sure at first that he'd even gone. "Chad?" I asked, as another fireball smashed into the wall above us. There was no response.

"I hope he makes it okay," I said aloud.

"I hope you know what you're doing," Henry said skeptically. I'm sure he'd read my mind enough to have an idea of what I was planning.

"Me too," I agreed.

We sat there waiting silently for what seemed like fifteen minutes, though I'm sure it was only a few. And suddenly, as though he'd never been gone, Chad appeared before us, beaming and holding a fire extinguisher under his one good arm.

"One gently used fire extinguisher," he said politely, like a butler fulfilling his millionaire's most recent extravagant request.

"Awesome," I said, unable to hide how impressed I was. I turned to Henry, smiling. "Didn't I tell you he'd come in handy?"

"Yeah, yeah," Henry reluctantly agreed, shaking his head.

"Okay, now I'm going to go out there. I want you to go invisible again and dash around behind the store. Cut over into the neighbor's backyard, and come in around behind this guy, okay? I'll keep him busy long enough for you to get into position."

"Okay," Chad nodded, understanding my words but still sounding uneasy.

"Stay invisible. You're everything in this thing. When you see the distraction I create, Chad . . . you're going to have to get in there and grab that woman and get her to safety while he's not paying attention."

"Oh God," Chad said, feeling a bit more nervous now that he knew what he'd have to do.

"You can do this, Chad. He's not going to have that good a grip on her. Remember—they're just acting. This is all just pretend. Some part of them probably even wants us to save that woman and succeed, okay? I don't care how you get her away from him. Tackle him, maybe. Heck, tackle her if you have to, but as soon as she is free of his grasp, you turn both you and her invisible again, and get the heck out of there. Got it?"

"You make it sound easy," Chad said. He'd lost some of the confidence that he'd had as a bully and as a person with two good arms.

"Wait until you see what *I* have to do," I responded.

Chad thought of one more question. "What's the distraction?"

"Believe me, you'll know it when you see it," I responded, still not 100 percent sure I could actually do what I had planned.

"What about me?" It was Henry.

"You?" I asked, smiling. "Why, you get to do exactly what you want to do, good sir. Stay here behind this dumpster, and make sure you keep your eyes glued to that screen so I can see what I'm doing."

"Phillip, I commend you on having such a smart plan," he said, smiling. "I will be happy to stay here in relative safety while the two of you risk your necks."

"Thanks a lot," Chad said sarcastically.

"Okay, boys. This is it. Wish me luck," I said.

"Good luck," they both said.

"Go, Chad. Go *now!*" He disappeared, and this time I heard his footsteps tear off around the corner of the building. And with that, I turned and once again reached my glasses around the edge of the dumpster.

From that angle, I could see about six or seven cars that were mostly between our position and the position of the bad guy. There were many more off to the right, but they wouldn't come in handy.

Of the six cars, three were parked at the angle that I needed—one that allowed me a direct sight line to their gas tanks. I focused in on the first one, a giant pickup truck. Concentrating the way my father had taught me, I reached out my hand and visualized the gas tank door popping open. I was still completely behind the dumpster, using Bentley's camera as a way to "see" the vehicles well enough to use my powers.

One by one, I opened all three gas tank doors and mentally unscrewed the gas caps, dropping them to the blacktop.

I turned my attention back to the pickup truck, which I'd noticed had a gas can in the bed. I took a deep breath, knowing my plan was out the window if that gas can was empty. Then I reached out my hand again, concentrating on the gas can while also watching it through Henry's screen-vision. The truck was parked facing away from us, which meant that as long as I was careful, the fireballing attacker wouldn't see what I was up to.

With little effort, I got the plastic can up into the air, hovering a few inches off the bed of the truck. Gently turning my hand the way one turns a doorknob, I caused the can to tip up toward its front, spilling out a tiny bit of gas. I felt a wave of relief come over me knowing there was gasoline in it.

I knew I had to work quickly, so there wasn't time for self-congratulation. Using subtle movements, I guided the gas can around the truck bed, spilling out a small trickle of fuel as I went.

"Jeez," Henry said breathlessly, in shock at actually seeing my plan in action.

Once the truck bed was pretty well covered, I pulled the can back in my direction off the back of the truck and maneuvered it around the cars nearby. Without raising the can above the car roofs, I was able to pretty well coat a wide area with gasoline without our adversary even knowing we were up to anything at all. He just kept smashing fireballs into the wall above us to keep us pinned down.

Then came the hard part—the part where I had to actually go out there and do some things with my powers that I wasn't even sure were possible.

I turned to Henry. "You think Chad's in position by now?"

"He better be," Henry cried. "He's missing an arm, not a leg."

Nice, I thought sarcastically. But Henry was right. It had to have been long enough. Trusting that Chad was ready, I stood to my full height, turned, and strode out into the parking lot to face the villain.

He noticed me right away, and for a moment, time sort of stood still. He just stared at me. It was as though he couldn't believe what he was seeing. Not wanting to jump into battle any faster than necessary, I was willing to return the stare down. I even briefly considered that maybe I could talk my way out of this.

That thought died in seconds as he snapped back to the present by shaking his head and immediately firing three fireballs on a medium arc toward my current position.

I knew what I wanted to do. And I knew that, in theory, it was entirely possible—likely even—that I would be able to do it. But because I'd never done it, I still wasn't completely sure. I wasn't even close to sure. And yet, when you're staring at three softball-sized fireballs hurtling through space at your body, instinct kicks in and pushes fear and doubt off to the side just long enough for you to act.

Without moving, I looked up at the three fireballs, tracking them with Henry's eyes. I reached out my left arm, hand outstretched, and concentrated on the lead fireball. Suddenly, I "felt" something. It wasn't a physical touch, and yet, it kind of was. I don't quite know how to explain it, but it was as though the fireball had locked into my control. And I just knew it instantly. *I've got it!*

I flung my arm down toward the ground like a football player spiking the ball after a big touchdown. To my opponent's horror, the lead fireball raced out of the sky, jerking out of its arc trajectory and plummeting straight down to ground level, where it made contact with the bed of the pickup truck.

Immediately, the truck burst into flames, and half a second later came a sound like a sonic boom as the truck's gas tank exploded.

I'd initially planned on taking any additional fireballs and sending them straight into the gasoline-soaked parking lot as well, but I ultimately didn't need to. The explosion of the truck ignited the rest of my trap, and two more cars exploded.

Clearly, my distraction was going to be a lot bigger than I'd intended, and I started to worry about the fire spreading and blowing up more cars. But one thing I knew for certain: there was no way the attacker was worried about what

was behind him. His eyes were giant ovals, and his grip on the hostage seemed to loosen as he stared in wonder at the destruction this twelve-year-old kid had just rained down on him. He was dumbfounded, exactly as I'd hoped he'd be.

But after a few seconds, I began to wonder why Chad wasn't making his move. The villain still held the woman in his clutches, even as he gaped at the destruction.

"Chad—go! Go now!" I said into the microphone that Bentley had added to my camera glasses. Everyone else on the team had earpieces, but mine was attached to the camera. It was a party line, which meant we all heard what was said any time someone spoke into their mic. It was a much better communication system than sending James teleporting around town delivering messages.

There was no response.

"Chad?"

Nothing.

I shouted. "Chad! Chad, you have to go now!"

But all I heard in response was silence. Either Chad was gripped with fear to the point of turning to stone, or something had happened on his way around the grocery store.

I panicked as the villain shook off his amazement and got back into character. He fired six more fireballs in rapid succession over the raging fire, right at the spot where I was standing. This time, they came in on less of an arc and with a lot more velocity. *See, I was right. He was taking it easy on us.*

I knew I wasn't accomplished enough with my powers to handle redirecting six of those things, so I did the next best thing I could think of: I held up my fire extinguisher and started spraying. There was far too much fire coming from my impromptu car bonfire for me to spot the individual fireballs flying toward me. So I mostly just sprayed in front of my face, strafing the nozzle left and right to add coverage.

And then I felt . . . nothing. I saw nothing.

I had expected the fireballs to be doused, but I thought they'd still hurl in and clobber me in the head like stones. I didn't know anything about how fireballs worked, but I imagined them having a solid center mass surrounded by flame. Instead, despite the massive force with which they crashed into their targets, it turns out there's nothing but fire inside those things. So the ones doused by my extinguisher merely dissipated into thin air.

I grinned and lifted my head up to look at the bad guy. He seemed rather annoyed, so much so that he instantly sent off another round of ammunition, this time ten fireballs in one volley.

It was clear that the extinguisher, while effective, would not last long enough for me to keep this up.

I tried one last time. "Chad? Can you hear me?"

"Where the hell are you, Chad?" It was Henry, sounding just as scared as I was, despite being in the relative safety of his secured position.

And that's when a new idea hit me.

"Bentley, can you hear me? Come in, Bentley."

"Yeah, Phillip, we can all hear you. Are you okay? What's going on with Chad?"

"I don't know. But I need James. I need James right now!" I figured with Chad out of commission, James could simply teleport in and grab the hostage lady. There was an urgency to my voice, and Bentley could tell I wasn't kidding around. But that didn't mean he could give me the answer I wanted.

"Um . . . that's going to be a little tough, Phillip."

"What? Why?"

"Well, James sort of got captured."

"How in the—" I realized I didn't have time for follow-up questions. "Crap!" I said in frustration.

"What now, genius?" Henry shouted, his voice dripping with his signature sarcasm and a touch of fear.

The fireballs reached the peak of their orbit and started back down toward my position. I lifted the extinguisher again, firing constantly for at least seven or eight seconds. At that point, it was empty, and the remnants of white goop spat out of the nozzle with a hiss. I'd survived the second volley, reducing the ten fireballs to vapor, but I was out of my own ammunition and a sitting duck for the next round.

"It's going to have to be Donnie, then," I said to Bentley over the radio, realizing that the big guy was indeed my only remaining option.

Bentley sounded confused, like he'd misheard my request. "Donnie?"

"Yeah, he's our only chance now."

"Sure, Phillip," he said cautiously. "He's listening. Go ahead."

"Donnie, can you hear me? I need your help, buddy. I need you to use your power—remember when we talked about that? I need you to use your power and run really, really fast over here to the grocery store. There's a man in the street, and he has a woman in his arm he's holding hostage. I'm in the parking lot of the grocery store, and I'll keep him distracted so you can swoop in and grab that woman and take her to safety, okay?" Mr. Villain decided to stop playing games and tossed about twenty-five fireballs my way, which sounded like a machine gun. "Donnie . . . I need your help, buddy. Go fast—go real fast! Please, buddy, I need you to go now . . . hurry!"

I paused a moment. "Is he coming?"

"Are you kidding?" Bentley asked. "He took off before you were even done talking."

I knew that Bentley's team had been at the car dealership, which was on the opposite side of town. And I had no real idea how quickly Donnie was able to run, so I wasn't sure how long it would take him to arrive. But if I'd ventured a guess, I would have been wrong.

Almost as soon as Bentley had ended his sentence, I both heard and saw Donnie approaching from several blocks away. Audio-wise, it sounded a bit like a military jet soaring far above. Visually, it was a tiny but powerful blue light that started as a dot five blocks down the street from where I stood. But I still knew it was Donnie. He was coming to my rescue to help me . . . as I knew he would.

It took only a fraction of a second for Donnie to go from five blocks away to right upon us, that's how quickly he was moving. I'd never seen anything like it.

But before relief could flood my soul at his arrival, something awful happened.

We know now that it was Chad. Or I should say, Chad's body. He was apparently lying unconscious in the middle of the road. And he was somehow still invisible, which meant that Donnie couldn't see him.

With Donnie's speed and size, the crash after he tripped over Chad's body was colossal. Donnie went hurtling forward, bouncing and sliding across the pavement of the street, yet still traveling at extraordinary speed.

He plowed directly into the SuperSim villain, sending the man and his hostage flying into the air as though a grenade had exploded nearby. The sound of the impact was sickening.

When it was all over, they found the fireballer on the roof of a house three blocks over. It took them an hour more to find the woman hostage up in a tree on Fifth Street.

Donnie himself had careened straight down the road like a rock skipping over a smooth lake. He came to a stop seven blocks away in a pile of clothing, blood, flesh, and blacktop. It's an undeniable miracle that he didn't die. The doctors said he had more broken bones than unbroken ones.

Never before had I experienced such a drastic last-minute shift from near-success to abject failure in anything I'd ever done in my life. One moment my ingenuity was about to score us a major SuperSim victory, perhaps redeeming the reputation of the Ables entirely. The next moment, that same ingenuity was nearly getting several people killed.

It was a shock to the system, and I wanted to puke.

24

CONSEQUENCES

Donnie, Chad, and both adults were taken to Freepoint Hospital, where most of them would stay for a month or more. The woman who had been playing the role of the hostage was actually unconscious for a day and a half. Chad was on a breathing machine; his lungs had collapsed. We still didn't know what had happened to him, and it would be some time before he would be able to talk.

Mr. Howard, the fireballing SuperSim villain, was in pretty good shape, actually, considering how far he'd flown. He had six broken bones, a dislocated shoulder, and second degree burns in patches all over his arms; the impact of Donnie crashing into him had been so severe that it had spontaneously caused Howard's power to go off, burning him as he soared through the air.

Donnie was the worst off of the group. After a twelve-hour surgery to regraft his skin and seal up his wounds, his broken bones were set and he was placed in a full body cast in the ICU. His condition was officially listed as "stable," though it had been "critical" for the first couple days after the accident. He almost died.

Henry and I were fine, of course, and I couldn't have felt guiltier about it.

There were some serious consequences to our actions that night—*my* actions that night. Some of them hurt.

The Ables were disbanded, first and foremost. An emergency board meeting had been called in the days following the tragedy, where it was decided that disabled hero kids were too big a danger to themselves and to others and would henceforth be barred from participating in the SuperSim exercises. It had been a closed meeting, but Bentley said his father had told him it was a unanimous vote, which did nothing to improve their strained relationship.

No public hearing to make our case. No eleventh-hour rescue from Mrs. Crouch. No chance for appeal. As heroes and crime-fighters, we were basically done, at least until we finished high school.

It's not hard to imagine how popular I was with the rest of my team after that little proclamation. Both Henry and Bentley went out of their way to say it wasn't my fault, but I could tell that on some level, they still thought it was. And I couldn't blame them, because I agreed. It was totally my fault. All of it.

If I hadn't opened my big mouth or executed my idiotic plan . . . if I hadn't told Donnie not to let anything get in his way . . . if I'd realized he wasn't ready to actually use his powers in a combat setting or understood exactly how much momentum he could create . . . everyone would still be okay, and my team would only be mildly depressed at not having scored points in another SuperSim. Instead, four people were laid up in that hospital, and it was a direct result of my actions.

There were some other people who suffered because of my actions as well—namely, the owners of one SUV, two pickup trucks, three Hondas, and an Acura, all of which had been reduced to charred-out vehicle frames after my little ballet of fire in the parking lot. Turns out they weren't very happy to have had their cars unexpectedly pulled into the action, and I know my dad had to field several phone calls from angry citizens who wanted full restitution.

Of all the mistakes I'd made, this one seemed to bother Dad the most. He seemed bewildered that I could be so cavalier about destroying others' property. He kept saying, "We raised you better than this, Phillip. What's wrong with you?" And I had nothing to say in response. With the gift of hindsight, it was obvious that blowing up the cars was wrong—I mean a-few-miles-over-the-line wrong. Super wrong. But I was at a loss to explain my actions to my father, because in the heat of the moment, my decisions had seemed perfectly natural and logical. I hadn't even stopped to think about the consequences of my actions.

But according to Dad, I would be feeling them for the next ten years since that's how long he decided to ground me. And even though the city's insurance covered damage related to the SuperSim so those people would get reimbursed for the damage to their cars, Dad swore I would be working my tail off to make it up to the victims.

I didn't care anymore. I was somewhere between angry, ashamed, and aloof. Didn't these people know that we all had disabilities? And that maybe we'd break a few eggs on our way to making a superhero omelet? Did they expect perfection? Did the able-bodied kids even attain perfection in their first year?

The one victim I couldn't make amends to was Donnie. I figured I would never be able to repay him for the pain I'd caused him. And it wasn't just physical pain. The entire town had turned on Donnie as though he was some kind of Frankenstein monster, something to fear instead of nurture. The locals had branded him a menace, and there was even some early talk of shipping him off to some kind of mental hospital. Thankfully, that had died down within a few days. But the whispers continued.

They didn't know him, and the more they demonized him, the angrier I got about it. This had been my fault, not Donnie's. Donnie was just a sweet kid who had honestly been trying his best to help. It wasn't his fault that Chad had been in his way.

I gave the order, and he followed it loyally. And now he was bearing the brunt of the punishment for actions that had been my own. I was sick to my stomach about it. The committee's decision to ban the Ables from future competitions didn't even upset me all that much. To be frank, I didn't know if I deserved to be a hero anymore, and I wasn't even sure I wanted to be one. But Donnie didn't deserve this.

I visited Donnie every other day. It was easy; I had pretty much nothing to do anymore. Most of the team had forgiven me or pointed out how the whole thing was really no one's fault because it was just a freak accident. But their parents weren't so forgiving. Bentley's dad, always concerned with the family's reputation, advised him to steer clear of me for a while, at least until things blew over. James's parents weren't exactly happy about him spending time with me anymore either—though he was free to give me rides around town as part of his teleporting business.

Some days at the hospital, Donnie was alert and wide-eyed. Other days he was groggy and tired. The nurses said it would be months before he would even begin to get back to being himself. So I usually just talked to him about mindless stuff like schoolwork or the science fair or even my comic books. I was used to doing most of the talking with Donnie anyway. I guess I just felt like I owed it to him to be there for him. I couldn't think of any way to repair the damage I'd done, so this was sort of my penance. And Lord knows no one else in town was willing to show him pity.

On his good days, when he was able to look around and had energy, he was his usual self, aside from the injuries. To his credit, he didn't seem to blame me for what had happened and appeared to hold no ill will toward me whatsoever. I'm not even sure he remembered the events of that night. The poor guy didn't understand much about the world and might never know how bad a friend I had really been to him.

I told him all the time, of course, but I'm not sure he ever understood. I tried to apologize several times. I just kept saying, "I'm sorry, Donnie. I'm going to fix this. I'm going to make this all better." I said it every time I visited him, but I never once actually felt better after saying it. Several times I promised him I would never put him in harm's way again no matter what occurred.

One night, I stayed really late at the hospital. The nurses were so used to me by now, after all my visits to Mom's room, that I think they took pity on me and looked the other way on the whole visiting hours thing. Dad was working, and I knew Patrick was at a friend's house.

Anyway, I didn't want to be at home alone, so I put together a comic-reading marathon for Donnie. It was a greatest hits of my own personal collection, the very best of the best. I even did the voices and the sound effects as I read them, which Donnie seemed to enjoy. Around the seventh comic, Donnie fell asleep, but I kept reading silently to myself.

Until I heard someone clearing their throat. I lifted my head up toward Donnie but could tell he was still asleep. I turned my body around, assuming the nurse was about to finally kick me out. But instead of a nurse, I heard Finch's voice.

"What a fine mess this is you've created, young Sallinger. A fine mess, indeed." He sounded like a disgruntled principal looking over the latest batch of hooligans that had been sent to his office. "You know, this one you can't pin on me . . . for once."

I instinctively lifted my arms and tried to use my powers to throw the old man back against the wall, but nothing happened.

"No power zone, son. Did you forget?" My arms dropped in defeat. "I can do all, even if I'm not him, remember?"

For a moment, I thought about just rushing him and running out the door, but some part of me knew how fruitless that would be. He'd never let me get even two steps before incapacitating me somehow. And if he had come to kill me . . . well, I was just emotionally exhausted enough not to care anymore.

"What are you doing here?" I asked with a healthy dose of disdain in my tone.

"I feel our relationship has become entirely too adversarial, particularly when our goals and life paths overlap so much. So I've come to suggest a peace accord between us. And I've come to ask for your help, Phillip."

"Right," I uttered, my words dripping with bitter sarcasm. "Why don't you just leave me alone?"

He paused to consider my request. "Interesting that you should say that, Phillip, considering this is actually the first of our meetings that I myself have instigated. You entered the library and surprised me that first night. Then you followed me through town on Halloween . . . that's hardly my fault. Finally, at the library again, I was merely catching a nap and minding my own business when you and your friends burst in to kill the quiet. So maybe you should be asking . . . why don't *you* just leave *me* alone?"

He had a point. Even though I viewed him as the aggressor in this relationship, technically, he wasn't. I was.

"Of course, we both know that's just a technicality, though, right? And there is something . . . special about you, isn't there, Phillip? You've felt it, surely. I noticed it the first time I met you. And it's the reason I'm here right now."

Donnie grunted a bit in his sleep, shifted positions, and drifted back off to dreamland.

"This world is changing, Mr. Sallinger. More than you know. Soon, people who have long been content to be bystanders are going to have to choose sides as the power shifts fully from the humans into the hands of the custodians."

Is he talking about the thing on the news?

"I am," he replied. "Exactly! Now, I doubt your young friends have stopped to wonder what it might mean if the rest of the world found out about us, but it is going to happen. There is now no stopping it. The pendulum is swinging with full momentum, and it cannot be unswung. Soon, there will be no line of demarcation between heroes and villains, Phillip. It will only be us . . . and them. Empowered people . . . and the rest."

"You make it sound like there's going to be a war."

"There *will* be a war, son. Human nature will not allow any other outcome. The question is when will the war begin, and when will it end? And, perhaps most importantly, where will you be standing when it does?"

"On the side of good," I said, feigning confidence.

He laughed hard. "It's been so long since I was your age, it's easy for me to forget how noble and conscientious children can be." The smile in his voice faded. "Neither side is good, Phillip. That's the entire point of what I'm trying to tell you. The world is not a black-and-white place. I know they tell you it is in school. I know you're taught to believe there's a right choice in every situation. But there's not. Life is a muddled, screwed-up mess of secrets and motives, and everyone's out for themselves. You're going to have to make your choice on something other than nobility. Something other than morality."

"My father says the board is negotiating with the government."

"Sure, sure they are. And I'm sure the esteemed members of the board have only selfless goals in mind with those negotiations."

"What does that mean?"

"The board, Phillip, is just another oppressive government looking out for its own interests. You're going to leave it up to two groups of billionaire politicians to ensure custodians get a smooth transition into public life?"

I began to feel like I'd finally found someone with more innate pessimism than Henry. "You're wrong. People are inherently good."

"Bah," he barked. I felt a small gust of wind from his dismissive hand-waving. "Obviously, you're not ready to have this conversation. You're still clutching too tightly to your security blanket." He sighed, clearly frustrated. "Listen, you're going to have to speed up the timetable of your maturation, young man. Before long, the prophecy will be fulfilled, and there will be a war at that point whether or not anyone is ready for it. You're going to have to grow up while still being twelve. I don't envy you that. The learning curve is going to be steep." He paused for a deep breath. "And it begins now."

I rolled the silver disc around in my pocket. I knew what I was supposed to do as soon as Finch showed up, but I was hesitating.

"I want you on my team, Phillip. Now, the rest of your gang, they're okay kids. I'll take them too, if it means I can have you. But you're the one I really want. I've seen your DNA charts, son, and there's something special about your abilities. You know this. Surely you've felt this!"

Sure, Dad had said it was rare for a son to inherit his father's power, but other than that, there definitely didn't seem to be anything special about me. Not anything good, at least. But there had been the raid at the DNA facility, where most of the records were stolen. Did Finch know something about me that I didn't?

"Phillip," he said rather unceremoniously, "you are the one we've all been waiting for." Then he went silent while I processed that information.

I was close, but I hadn't put it together yet.

"Let's take another look at that prophecy, shall we? 'He will return an outcast, one who does not see the world as others do. "The one who can do all," an unexpected hero with a terrifying rage.' I wonder if you see how much that description fits you? Blind, shamed, outcast . . . does not see the world as others do . . ."

Again, I said nothing, still not ready to believe he was suggesting what I was now sure he was suggesting.

"They could put that under your yearbook photo, so perfectly does it describe you."

He wasn't wrong, but in my mind, those words also described several other people in this town.

"I have studied this text for decades. I've gone over every translation, every analysis. I've done the math. I've examined the genetic sequences of thousands of potentials. No one knows this prophecy as intimately as I do, Phillip. Elben got his start on the soil this town was built on, and thanks to my research and efforts over the last twelve months, he'll have his return here as well. Soon. And he'll look a lot like a certain blind telekinetic we all know."

He might as well have been Darth Vader telling me he was my father because that probably would have been more believable. I simply couldn't find the words to explain how wrong it seemed he was about me.

"But the prophecy goes on. 'This one shall not know of his own true depth of power until he suffers great loss and injury, and he alone stands as the last protector between the world and a great evil. Only then shall he truly see. Only then shall he embrace his true purpose.'"

Despite everything I'd experienced this year, I wasn't sure I would call any one event a great loss or injury. Others had certainly been injured greatly because of me, but me personally? Finch's argument was losing steam.

As though sensing my attention waning, he continued, "Your mother . . ."

I stiffened.

"She is going to die tonight, I'm afraid."

A sharp intake of air, which my lungs held onto for dear life.

"You see, there is a man, a man I believe you're aware of. He alone has long been responsible for the custodians' ability to remain hidden from the public view. It took us a couple tries, but we finally have him in our custody, and I need to use the linking ability on him to put him in a coma. We'll need him in the future, but for now, we can't have him protecting the protectors anymore."

I was still processing his statements slowly, but he didn't slow down to let me catch up.

"I can use it on only one person at a time, you see. I waited as long as I could, Phillip. I do hope this won't keep you from considering my offer to join my team. You being who you are, you'll be joining it one way or another anyway. I can promise you that."

"I would never join your pathetic evil henchmen society," I blurted out. "All you've done is mess with me over and over again. Why would I join you? What the hell is wrong with you, old man?"

For a few tense seconds, he said nothing. Finally, he said, "I suppose I could make an exception just this once—find some other way to keep Weatherby powerless, and leave your mother in a coma for a little while longer—if you were to come with me now and join the Believers."

"Why can't you just let her out of the coma?" I demanded.

"Oh, I can. I just won't. She is, first and foremost, leverage. If that fails, then she is something much more powerful."

My thumb rested on the disc's button; I was losing patience with Finch's latest game.

"Join me now, or your mother dies," he said with mock sadness, as though he had no choice in the matter.

"You forgot about the third option," I replied with confidence. I pushed the button on the disc three times—the predetermined signal.

Finch's entire demeanor changed. "I like you, Phillip. I really do. That's not a lie. I wish you hadn't done that."

"Done what?" I said nervously, already sure he knew what I had done.

"Little outcast . . . meet great loss."

Ooph!

I heard another *ooph!* outside in the hallway, but I knew it was too late.

Dad wasn't a teleporter, so he wasn't able to respond to my signal personally. But he had a contingency plan all worked out. He'd given Mom's receiver to his teleporter buddy Harry Warren, reasoning Harry would be able to respond faster should I run into Finch again. In fact, the entire protector force had been briefed on the plan. They had been pretty sure that Finch would try to make personal contact with me again, and they were right.

The plan had been simple: If Finch ever showed up again, I was to click the disc's paging button three times in a row. Harry and his partner, an NPZ-enabled custodian named John Hampton, would then leap to a spot twenty-five yards away from my location.

See, they couldn't teleport straight to my location, or they'd risk the same fate as Mom—jumping into one of Finch's patented localized no power zones. They'd be rendered harmless immediately. Instead, they planned to teleport just outside the range of Finch's zone so they would arrive with powers intact.

After the telltale teleportation sound in the hallway, they ran in. Harry had teleported in with John's no-power-zone ability turned on. There was a lot of shouting—the kind typically heard on a cop show on TV. "Hold it right there!" "Freeze!" "Hands in the air!"

But Finch was already gone. He'd been one step ahead of us the whole time and probably had read my mind enough to know about the disc in my pocket. As the adults loosened up and put their weapons away, I kicked myself mentally for being so stupid. Of course he was going to outsmart me. Of course I was going to lose.

I just didn't realize in that moment exactly how much I was going to lose.

There was a sudden flood of noises outside Donnie's room. Footsteps raced past the doorway, accompanied by the urgent voices of medical professionals. Faintly, in the distance and nearly buried by the commotion, I heard a long, sustained high-pitched beeping noise.

I started to go numb, as though my body understood what had happened before my mind could process it. I ventured mindlessly into the doorway as more doctors and nurses rushed by in the hall outside, barking medical commands at one another that sounded like some kind of secret language. There were too many voices for me to focus on what they were saying.

In the room behind me, Donnie was probably still the picture of serenity and rest. But in the hallway it was the complete opposite. It was pandemonium.

I don't know if it was childhood innocence or morbid curiosity, but my feet began to move, leading me down the hallway to the right. I followed the sounds of emergency, leaving the drama of Finch's attempted arrest far behind me mentally and physically. I made two steps outside the room into the hallway, the people speeding past me barking out orders I was too dizzy to comprehend.

Ooph!

Dad appeared in front of me along with a teleporter friend and nearly got trampled by the medical stampede. "Phillip?"

Finch's words echoed between my ears: *"Little outcast . . . meet great loss."*

I heard Dad turn toward the room at the end of the hall that the doctors and nurses were all running to . . . a room he'd immediately recognize. He turned back to me. "Phillip?"

Suddenly, I knew exactly where I was and where the doctors had all been rushing to—and that my life would never be the same.

"Mom?"

25

REBELS

The next month passed like a day. I didn't leave the house at all except for the funeral, and I don't even remember that day much at all. I was a zombie, and my memory banks certainly weren't turned on. My life just became a repeating cycle of sleeping, refusing to eat, vomiting, crying, and sleeping.

Dad didn't make Patrick or me go to school, and while he tried to keep it together, it was obvious that he was just as lost as we were. He was beating himself up pretty badly.

Strangers in our house became a common sight. Dad's coworkers, their wives, people from the neighborhood church, and neighbors all took turns as guests and caretakers. They cooked us meals, cleaned our messes, and generally looked after us. Honestly, without them, I'm pretty sure we would have self-destructed, wallowing in our own sadness and guilt until we withered away forever.

I had killed my mother. I was sure of it. And it wasn't even open for debate. It wasn't an opinion but a fact. Had I not pushed that button, she would still be alive. In my eyes, it was as black and white an issue as there had ever been, even though nearly every person I knew kept trying to convince me it wasn't.

Of course, Dad felt pretty much the same way about his own inability to protect Mom. None of us were ourselves.

Patrick would have had plenty of depression and angst on his own just from the experience of having his mother taken away from him forever. But to have his remaining family members so lost and despondent made it so much worse for him. As I look back now, I wonder how he avoided a complete and total breakdown. There's no way we could have known it or stopped it from happening, but boy, did we ever let him down in those weeks after Mom's death. We were just too self-absorbed with our own grief and guilt.

I began to plot how I might seek retribution by killing him—Finch, that is. I wasn't serious about it, I don't think. But in that month after Mom's death, it was one of the things I spent the most time thinking about.

And did I ever do plenty of fantasizing about it. That's all I could do, really. I wasn't sent to school—not for five weeks anyway. I wasn't planning for the next SuperSim, playing with friends, or doing homework. I was in a house with plenty of people, constantly surrounded by my father, my brother, and a host of community members coming and going, but I had never been more alone.

Mostly I thought about the past. So much had changed in the last twelve months. A year prior, we had just been a normal nuclear family living in New York City. But since learning of my true lineage and my family's real role in society, it had been nothing but mistakes and tragedies.

All through the months of Mom's coma, I had never allowed myself to believe it could be permanent, that any outcome would occur except a complete and full recovery.

Dad, though, was different. I think some part of him knew all along it was possible—maybe even likely—that we'd never see her awake and alive again. In some ways, I think he'd already done some mourning, steeling himself for the possibility.

Which is not to say he was anything short of crushed and hopelessly lost. Late at night, when I couldn't sleep, I would sneak over to my closet and listen to him crying on the other side of the wall. There's no more hopeless feeling in the world for a twelve-year-old kid than to hear your dad bawl like a baby. It makes everything in the entire universe feel like an oppressive, threatening evil. It's easy for a kid to forget that his parents aren't just authority figures and partners but also true loves and best friends.

But he did start to resume his normal life far earlier than Patrick and I. Maybe it was because he didn't have any other choice. Someone had to get this family headed in the direction of recovery. And Finch was still at large. So, after two weeks off, he started going back to work. He didn't push us to resume our normal activities for another three weeks. If he'd waited any longer, it might have been too late.

$$\huge\lightning$$

When I did return to my old routines, I found the city of Freepoint to be happily humming along the way it always had. I remember being offended that the rest of the town wasn't completely heartbroken and in mourning like we were. I was insulted that they could just carry on with the status quo.

The third and final SuperSim was the talk of the town, especially with the new restrictions put in place after Finch's attack in the hospital. The adults were worried about Finch but even more concerned about their children getting some kind of training—any kind of training—in the face of the threat. The Ables, of course, were still barred from participating, thanks to my wonderful decision-making skills.

But most of the tension with my friends and classmates around that matter had faded. I think they felt too sorry for me to stay bitter. In fact, they were downright giddy to see me and far too affectionate. Henry even hugged me—*Henry*, of all people!

Chad was back at school, and I was pleased to see that my friends had continued involving and accepting him in my absence. He had some memory loss, though, and still had no idea what had happened on the night of the fateful SuperSim. He didn't remember the grocery store, the fire extinguisher, or what had occurred in the street. The doctors said that kind of memory loss wasn't uncommon considering the head trauma he'd suffered in the collision with Donnie, and his memories were expected to return over time.

Donnie was finally healthy enough to have been discharged from the hospital, they told me. He'd been there eight weeks, poor guy. But he was not allowed to return to school and probably wouldn't be for the rest of the year. While I was out of commission grieving the loss of my mother, several parents in town had led a charge to get Donnie ruled ineligible for regular schooling. They reasoned that his brute strength and newly discovered superspeed, along with his inability to truly control either, was a danger to the other kids, and they'd successfully convinced the school board to agree. Scaremongers.

He was still a long way from recovering enough to return to school anyway. Bentley said Donnie probably had months of physical therapy ahead of him before he could even walk again.

I tried to act normal at school, which is difficult to do when everyone keeps going out of their way to be overly nice to you. They meant well but served only as a reminder of how things would never really be normal for me again.

I'd overheard a conversation my father had on the phone with Principal Dempsey and had gathered that I would basically be given a free pass on the year's schoolwork. I'd missed so much time that, under normal circumstances, I would be destined to repeat a year. But since my absences were caused by something so tragic, and because everyone felt so bad for our entire family, the teachers had all decided to give me passing grades and allow me to progress with my classmates.

And, like a jerk, I took full advantage. I basically just stopped doing any of the assignments we were given, from reading to worksheets. I took all the quizzes and tests like the rest of the kids in class, but I would guess I did no better than 25 percent on any of them. On one multiple-choice test, I simply marked the first choice for every single answer. Mrs. Crouch never gave me any of my tests back for the rest of the year.

My selfishness didn't end with schoolwork. I let my friends do simple tasks for me, even though I was totally capable of doing them myself. They just offered out of pity, and I just kept selfishly accepting. They fetched my lunch, carried my backpack, and opened doors for me. And I just let them treat me like a prince, because it was easy. And I was too angry and sad at everything to say no. I guess I was pretty lazy too.

It's easy to diagnose my depression now, looking back. Dad would have caught on to it, too, if he'd been able to spend more time with me or had been even a little bit less depressed and distracted himself. But as a kid in the moment, I had no idea how much the recent events had changed me and altered my character for the worse. I felt like I deserved it all. I deserved to be waited on hand and foot. I deserved to get out of homework and tests. After all, I was a victim of extraordinary hardship. The world had battered and bruised me, cutting me down and leaving me broken. The least it could do was even things out with a little privilege, right?

Out of everyone in my life, only Mrs. Crouch had the courage to tell it like it was. "You're really letting yourself go, Mr. Sallinger," she said one afternoon. School was over and the final bell had rung, and I was the last student left, making my way toward the exit.

"Excuse me?" I said, feeling entitled and offended that she should speak to me so bluntly.

"I know you've been through a lot this year, but you're really pushing it now."

"What do you mean?"

"I mean that it's time to grow up, young man." She was grading papers and, judging by the direction of her voice, hadn't even looked up from her red pen. "You've milked this special attention for all it's worth, and if you're not careful, you're going to turn into a horrible human being."

I was pretty shocked to hear her say these things, even while some part of me knew she was right. And I was about to scoff and defend myself when she continued.

"You're not the only kid to ever suffer a tragedy, Phillip. It happens every day all around the world. What you have to decide is whether you're going to let your depression define you or if you're going to rise above it." Finally, I heard her put down the pen and raise her head to look at me. "I'm so sorry you lost your mother. I really am. I cannot imagine how hard it's been for you, and I wouldn't even dare to try. But you've let the bitterness and the sadness grip you for far too long. Look at Chad. Look at Donnie. Look at the rest of your friends. Henry's in a wheelchair. Bentley will never be able to walk properly. Poor Darla can't see or hear. Mr. Brooks spent the better part of three months in the hospital."

"What's your point?" My voice was a bit softer, not as defiant, but I was still not letting down my guard completely.

"My point is that people suffer," she continued. "It stinks. It's not fair, but it happens. And there are only two kinds of people in this world, Mr. Sallinger—people who rise above that suffering and people who let it define them. I just don't want to see you become the latter."

"Why do you care?" It wasn't half as snotty as it sounds. Her harsh words had actually penetrated my defenses. Maybe some part of me had just been waiting for someone to grab me by the shoulders and shake some sense into me, literally or figuratively. And now that it had happened, I was genuinely curious why this old woman would show such interest in my personal development. The teachers in New York certainly never seemed to care that much. They would have just shaken their heads in pity at the little boy who lost himself in his own grief.

"Because you're the future, Phillip. You and your friends. In the coming years, you're all that stands between evil and the rest of the world. If you don't snap out of this, if you don't grow up to be the hero I believe you can be, then we're all doomed. There's plenty of selfishness in the world's villains. We don't need our heroes adding to that problem." I could tell by the sound of her voice at the end that she'd gone back to looking at the papers in front of her.

I brushed her off and headed for home, where her words spent the evening echoing through my head.

All the other kids' chatter about the upcoming third simulation had given Bentley and me the superhero bug again. Which was a terrible thing, because we were effectively blacklisted from all future SuperSims. It was like taking a dog to the public dog park but leaving him chained to a tree.

So we decided to hold our own SuperSim. It was just one of our old practices out in the charred-out cornfield, but it was the closest we were likely to come to real action for quite some time. So James, Bentley, Henry, Chad, Freddie, and I all met one Friday evening. We split up into two teams and basically created a glorified game of capture the flag on the spot.

Chad's invisibility gave him obscene advantages in a game like capture the flag, though I did my best to counter that for my team by repeatedly moving the flag with my powers. It wasn't very fun, mostly because it was so fake. Like trying to play baseball with three people. And while even the SuperSim was, by definition, not the real thing, it still felt a lot closer than what we were going to be able to recreate on our own.

"This sucks." Henry was always the best at summing up the entire group's emotions succinctly.

"Yeah," everyone agreed. We'd played two rounds of our fake little game, and exactly no one was having any fun.

"Maybe this was a bad idea," Bentley suggested. "Maybe we really are screwed. Maybe we'll have to wait until we get to college to be heroes again."

Everyone hung their heads at these words, as no one wanted to go back to being a normal kid, not after what we'd experienced. Most of us agreed with Bentley, but no one wanted to say so because it would feel like the final nail in our coffin.

But I had been spending time thinking about this very issue, and I had the perfect solution to the town's ban on disabled hero kids: we would be heroes in some other town.

"Maybe we don't have to wait," I said enticingly. "Maybe all we need . . . is a change of scenery."

⚡

Central Park had never looked so gorgeous.

Of course, technically, I'd never seen it before, which might explain why I thought it was so gorgeous. The lights throughout the park were all sparkling. And because it was a Friday night, there were lots of people around.

It had taken a full fifteen minutes to convince the group that we should go on a real-world reconnaissance mission and another fifteen after that to convince James that he could get us to Central Park even though he'd never been there. In the end, we used Bentley's computer to show James some maps and photographs, and he finally agreed to try. He'd gotten us there on his first try, which I was sure would be a huge boost to his confidence while also expanding the services his business could offer.

Even though there were lots of people around, there were pockets of deserted park area as well. Central Park is ridiculously big—way bigger than you think it is until you've been there.

On my direction, we fanned out to try and find some place to sit and observe the park. We settled on a cluster of oak trees near a dirt path. It was relatively low lit, yet it afforded us a nice wide view of the park. I scanned the park using my specialized sunglasses. After a few minutes of silently waiting, some on the team began to get restless.

"Phillip, are you sure about this?" Bentley asked. "With Weatherby gone, our abilities won't be hidden."

"Relax, Bent," I assured him. "We aren't going to be using any abilities people will see, okay?"

"So what are we supposed to do, Phillip?" It was Henry, of course. "Just wait for a crime to happen?"

"Yeah," I said, trying to sound confident enough to shut him up. "That's what the real heroes do."

"That could be like looking for a needle in a haystack," he continued. "We could be here all night and not see a crime."

"Henry," I said calmly, with my best condescending tone, "this is New York City, my friend. There's so much crime here, we probably won't have to wait twenty minutes to find someone to apprehend."

Almost as though I'd planned it, there was a loud scream at just that moment. It came from our left, partway down the jogging path.

Everyone looked at me in awe for a few seconds before I snapped them out of it. "Okay, gang. That's it. Let's go. James, advance us down the path in that direction," I ordered, pointing. Everyone scurried in close and put a hand on James. "Okay, James. Let's go."

Ooph!

We appeared 100 yards up the path in the direction of the screaming. Another 150 yards up, there was a woman and two small children. She was shouting and pointing in our direction. "He's got my purse!" Only then did I see the man running straight toward us, still 100 yards off or so but moving quickly. We weren't under a streetlight, so he probably hadn't seen us yet.

"Everyone off the path!" I scampered to my right into a small grouping of trees and shrubs, and everyone else followed.

"What do we do now, Phillip?" Bentley asked, sounding excited but nervous.

My mother would have killed me for being in the park at night. She'd said it was an incredibly dangerous place to be after dark, and I surely would have been grounded. And once upon a time, I believed her enough to actually be scared of Central Park—even in broad daylight.

But now . . . I wasn't remotely scared. I'm not sure if I was being cocky or had simply lost enough innocence over the previous several months to no longer care. Surely any criminal I encountered in the park would pale in scariness to the people I'd been bumping into back in Freepoint. I'd faced off with a man in possession of nearly every power, for crying out loud. What could a purse snatcher do to compete with that? Besides, we were a bunch of superheroes. This man was just a human being.

I walked out of the brush with a firm step, stopping just off the path's edge. The man was only fifty feet away at this point, still running hard. The poor woman was still shrieking in the background.

I glanced up the path about ten feet from my position and found the kind of tree I was looking for. It was a crooked old maple with two or three very low-lying branches. I reached up with my right arm extended and pulled one of the away-facing branches toward me with my powers. It creaked as it swung out over the path—about chest high on an average adult. I could tell it was building up pressure because I had to concentrate and focus more as I pulled it backward toward me.

When it had completed a 180-degree arc, it was pointing straight at me. I simply held it in place mentally and peeked out around its leaves to see the purse snatcher approaching. Twenty feet away. Then fifteen. Then ten.

When he was five feet away, I finally made my presence known. "Boo," I said sharply, simultaneously releasing the branch from my control. It whipped instantly back around to its original intended position, smacking the burglar in the chest with a loud *thwack* as it went by. It stopped him in his tracks and reversed him, sending him flying backward.

I walked out onto the path as he tumbled through the dirt. He'd lost control of the woman's purse in the fall, and it was lying just off the far side of the path in the grass. I concentrated for only a second before it levitated off the ground and zoomed straight across the walkway into my outstretched hand. I turned immediately and threw it straight into the bushes where my teammates were.

The criminal was far from incapacitated and had begun to rouse himself just in time to see me throw his prize into the trees.

"Why you little . . ." he sputtered. He stumbled back a bit, losing his balance, only to suddenly return to a proper upright position again, this time brandishing the gun he had tucked in his pants.

Oh crap!

I hadn't considered the fact that he might be armed, which was pretty foolish. I'd assumed that taking him to the ground and relieving him of the purse would be the end of it. As though he'd be so shocked, he'd just give up and leave. I was too stunned to even think of the obvious solution: using my powers to disarm him.

He didn't have any idea what had hit him, and he was still a little dazed. But he'd regained his sense enough to point the pistol straight at my head. I knew I had to run, and that I had to run right away, but my legs wouldn't respond as quickly as my brain was processing things. There's no way around it . . . I froze. Choked.

Right around the time I heard the sound of the gun going off, I heard two lightning-quick, distinct little sounds.

Ooph!

Ooph!

And I was in the bushes again.

James had saved my bacon, thinking quickly and getting me out of the bullet's trajectory just in the nick of time.

"Hey!" I heard the burglar yell behind me, no doubt wondering where his assailant had disappeared to. That was followed quickly by more yelling, this time from much farther away. It was the police. The victim of the purse snatching had finally managed to wrangle some more help. I leaned down and looked through the brush and saw two figures running full speed in our direction. I turned and looked at the robber, who still needed one or two more seconds to process his situation.

Eventually, he decided to cut his losses and took off running down the path in the opposite direction of the cops.

"He's getting away," Bentley said, sounding disappointed.

"No, he's not." It surprised me to hear Chad's voice. He sounded calm and confident. "Come on, James," he said.

Ooph!

I jerked my head to the left, wondering what Chad was up to. I became a spectator this time. I saw nothing, of course, because Chad had gone invisible. At least, I assumed he had. All I could see was about a hundred yards or so of path, with the burglar moving away, getting smaller and smaller as he ran.

Ooph!

James returned. "Hi, guys," he said, smiling. "I'm back. What's he doing?"

"Nothing yet," I said anxiously.

Not knowing what to expect, we watched, the intensity building as we waited for Chad to make his move.

Turns out he'd already made it, turning himself invisible and then getting down on his hand and knees in the center of the path. The robber never saw it coming, obviously, and ran full speed into the invisible obstruction.

Chad had lowered himself at the last second to ensure the burglar's shins would be the point of impact, which sent the man tumbling into the air in a series of rapid cartwheels. He landed flat on his back on the dirt and instantly let out a loud groan.

The cops came racing up the path just as Chad made it back to our position and turned himself visible again. The group let out a small cheer as everyone raved about how impressed they were with his quick thinking.

"Good job, Chad!" Henry said, now seemingly completely over his original suspicion of the reformed bully.

"That was amazing!" James cried. "He never saw it coming!"

There were many pats on the back for Chad, and he deserved them. Some part of me—the selfish part—wanted to point out that I'd originally subdued the criminal and reclaimed the purse, but I said nothing. Even though a little praise of my own would have been nice, Chad definitely deserved his.

I grabbed the purse out of Bentley's hands and tossed it quickly back into the open path. The police had cuffed the burglar and had begun leading him back down the path the way they'd come. They were searching alongside the path for the victim's belongings and found the purse easily.

And that was that. The criminal was apprehended, and it was all because of us. While our classmates were practicing to face pretend criminals, we had already helped bust our first real one. And I'm not gonna lie: it felt awesome.

26

THE BULLY

After the lopsided victory over criminal activity, the Ables began to increase the frequency of their unsanctioned field trips to the park. About once a week or so, we would go back to New York and attempt to find and stop a crime. We told our parents we were practicing and honing our hero skills on our own, and shockingly, they all bought it every time. We'd assemble in the cornfields, which still bore the scars of the fire that destroyed them, and then hop off to the big city to play heroes.

It was mostly small stuff: a lot of purse snatchers or muggers. Henry had once found a car illegally parked in a handicap spot and called the police anonymously. He beamed while we watched the traffic cop write the ticket. "Sometimes," he boasted, "we don't even need to use our powers to stop crime."

But I was quickly growing tired of the little fish. My thirst for adventure—for danger—grew, even though I wasn't sure where it was coming from. Park hoodlums were easy targets, and honestly, something the cops could easily take care of without us. I wanted a real challenge. Someone more our equal . . . or at least more worthy of our powers.

James, Freddie, Chad, Henry, Bentley, and I were now fairly inseparable. No one else at school was all that friendly to us as a group, not even the other disabled kids. We knew we'd probably carry the stigma of our fall from grace for years, so we might as well go through it together.

After our weekly Thursday evening trip to Jack's Pizza, we were on our way back to my house, warm cheesy breadsticks in our bellies. Along the way we stopped for James to run into a little shop right on the edge of the downtown area of Freepoint. A few moments after entering, he returned, beaming and holding a small rectangular box.

"My new business cards," he declared proudly, shoving the box out in front of him, arms outstretched.

He carefully opened the box and removed a small stack of the cards. "I want each of you to have one," he said as he began handing them out one by one.

"I already have one," Henry said half politely. "Thanks."

"No, that's the old one," James assured him.

"What's the difference?"

"There's a new contact email address on these specifically for emergencies," he explained as he went around handing out the cards. Then, as an afterthought, he said, "I charge two dollars more per trip for emergencies. Plus, these also are printed in braille as well as regular typeface."

"Why do you print them in braille?" Bentley asked curiously.

"I can't read it by myself if it's not in braille," he said, closing the box on the remainder of the cards.

"Why do you need to read it, though?" Bentley was still confused.

"Well, for one thing, I can know it's printed correctly," James offered.

The group started walking again while the conversation continued.

"That still doesn't answer why you paid extra to have the braille printed on there." The logic-driven computer inside Bentley's skull wouldn't let him give it up until it made sense to him. "Who else needs the braille but you?"

Henry jumped in. "Yeah, if the cards are for your customers . . . I mean, your customers aren't blind, right? Aren't blind people rare? How many blind people do you even know?"

"I know Phillip," he countered, making a fairly convincing point.

But Bentley was still searching for logic. "Right, sure. I get that. But you *know* Phillip. Like, he's you're friend. You see him almost every day. You give him a card once, like tonight, but then you still have a bunch of braille cards left over. You don't give Phillip one every day."

He said it casually but confidently. He wasn't asking; he was telling. But he was wrong.

I cleared my throat a bit. "Um. Yes, he does."

Bentley couldn't believe it. "He does?"

"Yup," I confirmed. "Every day I see him, he gives me one. He's quite the little self-promoter."

James just smiled ear to ear and said, "It's called marketing."

"I also get his"—I cleared my throat, mostly by coincidence—"email newsletter."

"Jeez Louise, dude," Henry said, my vision shaking side to side along with his disbelieving head.

Bentley and I just chuckled in amusement.

"Showmanship," James explained further. "Like Finch," he added, stopping everyone in their tracks for just a beat before we all continued. "That guy has some showmanship, is all I'm saying. Very dramatic. He'd be excellent in marketing."

Now that we were a superhero unit again—albeit an unofficial one—and the dust had settled a bit since Mom's death, the topic had begun to turn toward Finch more and more. Almost any conversation we had would eventually make its way back to him as we tried to get to the bottom of the mystery.

Bentley had been breaking out the books again and studying all the angles of what he found as we collectively tried to piece together the mysteries surrounding this man. In between the nights we'd sneak away to fight real crime, we'd meet or sleep over at someone's house and do research and planning.

"Are we sure it's only showmanship?"

"What do you mean, Phillip?" Bentley asked.

"I mean . . . what if he really is planning to usher in the new Elben and unleash hell on Freepoint? What if all the nonsense he spouts . . . he really believes?"

"Even easier for us, then, I'd say," came Henry's reply. "Crazy people are easier to defeat than logical people."

"Fair enough," I allowed. I hadn't told the rest of the gang about Finch's belief that I was actually the one he was seeking. In addition to seeming terribly unlikely, it was also the kind of thing I thought might cause some of my friends some concern. "But, just for the sake of argument . . . what do we do if it's all true?"

No one had an immediate answer, but it didn't take Henry long to find one. "We're screwed."

Freddie agreed, saying, "Yeah, screwed." He sucked on his inhaler nervously.

"If it's all true, Phillip," Bentley said, "then Finch is the least of the real worries."

"Well . . . if it isn't Captain One Arm and his band of screw-up friends." The voice belonged to Steve Travers and had come from our left. There was an alley running down the middle of this block, and he'd called out to taunt his former friend as we passed. We took the bait, as we all stopped and turned down the alley.

"Oh, hey, Steve." Chad tried going with friendliness to start.

"Oh, hey, Steve," Steve said in a mocking tone. "What, are we buddies again now? Are we friends?"

"Look, dude, let it go, okay? I wish you knew how stupid you sound when you talk like that." Chad was standing in the middle of our little group, with Bentley and me sort of out in front. Steve had two friends with him—members of his SuperSim team. I briefly wondered why so many hooligans hang out in alleys.

"I see, I see. Now that you're part of the special crowd, you're above all that bullying nonsense, right?" Steve took a few steps forward, stopping just a couple feet from where we stood.

"Yeah, I guess so, yeah," Chad agreed.

"So I suppose if I was going to mess with your little friends here . . . you'd try and stop me, then?" Steve reached out and poked Henry in the chest.

Henry didn't have the patience to be treated that way and do nothing. "Man," he started to warn Steve. But before he could finish, Chad darted between his old friend and his new one.

"Mess with them and you mess with me," he said.

Steve wasn't the least bit scared. It was strange seeing how much the relationship between them had changed in just a few months. He fired right back in Chad's face. "What makes you think I'm scared of you?" Steve's eyes began to glow, signifying he was gearing up to use his eye-beam powers. At the same time, his right arm went back in preparation for a punch.

But before he could make another move, Chad disappeared.

Steve punched anyway, aiming for the spot where Chad had been standing, but as his fist came forward, his arm suddenly stopped in its tracks. Chad reappeared, standing one step to the side of his former position, his one good arm holding Steve's in place. "Not quite fast enough, Steve," Chad said, disappearing again immediately as Steve and his buddies darted their eyes around frantically. We heard the scattering of Chad's footsteps as he took off running away down the alley.

"Screw this," Steve spat, placing his fingertips along the edge of his temple. His eyes began to glow again. He quickly spun away from us and fired off a stun-beam blast down the heart of the alley. As Steve's laser reached the middle point of the alley, we saw it smack into the back of a retreating Chad, negating his invisibility and sending him sprawling forward onto the blacktop with a grunt.

Steve merely laughed and began walking toward the spot where Chad had fallen. "My powers have always been superior to yours, Chad. You know, honestly, I'm not sure why I ever allowed you to be in charge of me, like I was just your little lackey. I've always been stronger than you." He reached the spot and stopped, looking down with his hands resting on his hips. "And now I'm going to show you." He reached up his right hand to his temple, but just as his laser was about to discharge, his body flew up violently into the air, and he dangled for a second like a limp puppet. Suddenly, his body careened to the left, smacking into the wall of a building lining the alley with a dull thud. He slipped down the side of the wall and collapsed with a wheeze.

It wasn't a surprise to see it. At least, it wasn't a surprise to me. I made it happen. With nothing more than a flick of my wrist, I'd lifted the bully off the ground and tossed him into the wall like a rag doll.

I stood there, breathing a little heavy, my arm still outstretched. Chad looked up from the ground at me, his face suggesting shock or surprise. Steve's friends took off running. The rest of the guys were all just standing there in nervous silence, looking at me like they'd seen a ghost.

"Damn, Phillip," Henry finally said. "That was . . . intense. I didn't even know you could do that."

"I didn't either," I said, a little surprised at my own strength.

Chad rose to his feet, went over to Steve, and leaned down to inspect him. Then he started walking back toward the group.

"Is he . . . okay?" I asked.

"He's fine. Just got the wind knocked out of him, from the looks of it." He looked around, wondering if anyone had noticed our little scuffle. "We'd better get out of here, though. He's going to be out for blood when he comes to."

On the walk back to my house, I lagged a bit behind while the others led the way, mulling over what had just occurred. I was mildly impressed with myself for having shown such a leap in the use of my powers. But I was also a little freaked out by it. Because I hadn't known I could do that, or at least I hadn't ever done it before, it ended up feeling a little out of my control.

Immediately in front of me were Bentley and Henry, and their silence spoke volumes.

"I hate it when you do that," I said quietly.

"What?" Bentley asked innocently.

"When you think about me without including me."

There was an awkward pause and at least one stammer.

Henry took a shot at responding. "We're just a tiny bit worried about you, is all."

"Worried about me?"

"It's nothing," Bentley said, trying to dismiss the issue. "We just didn't know you could do that, and that . . . was maybe a little more violent than we expected. That's all."

"Yeah," I admitted. "I'm in the same boat."

"Well, just . . ." Henry said, pausing to word things correctly before just giving up, "just don't kill anyone on accident and stuff, okay?"

I got to visit Donnie again, finally. After weeks of his parents being understandably overprotective, they finally agreed to let me stop by. He was still bedridden, but he seemed happy to see me.

Or maybe he was just happy to see the breadsticks he adored, which I'd brought along to share with him. While he ate, I told him about some of the latest news. I filled him in on how we'd verified that Finch had been a founding member of the Believers. And when I told him about the run-in with Steve Travers, he made a few happy-sounding noises when that story was over.

It was hard to visit him in that state. Donnie was effectively a prisoner in his own home—unable to go to school with us, play after school with us, or even head to Jack's Pizza for a slice and some conversation.

Most of the town either hated him or feared him, and some were actively trying to pass laws against future Down syndrome kids entering the school system. Stupid adults . . . as though Donnie's Downs had caused the real damage at the last SuperSim rather than my own foolish actions.

I still felt completely responsible for Donnie's situation; that feeling would never go away. Donnie, for his part, didn't even seem to remember it.

I felt around in the pizza box and realized he'd already eaten half of the breadsticks. "Man, Donnie, you must have been starving! You sure ate those breadsticks awfully fast."

"Yeah," he murmured, "Donnie is fast."

How do you make things up to someone who doesn't even know that you wronged them? It's not easy. All I knew to do was keep promising I'd try.

"I know, buddy. I know. You're very fast. Listen, I'm sorry I told you to run fast that one night and that people got hurt. I'm going to make it up to you, Donnie."

"Yeah," he allowed, sounding like he was agreeing that it was a nice day outside.

"I'm going to fix this whole mess somehow."

27

THE FINAL SUPERSIM

Shut out of the final SuperSim, the team was gathered at my house for the evening. Since I had to watch Patrick, we didn't have any extracurricular hero activities planned for the night. I was getting rebellious and reckless, sure, but not stupid. I wasn't going to put Patrick in harm's way.

But we'd managed to avoid having to have an adult chaperone for the evening. Most every adult in town was involved in the SuperSim in one way or another, and I think most of our parents had begun to trust us again. They wouldn't have if they'd known what we'd been up to lately, of course. But we figured what they didn't know couldn't hurt them.

We rented a few movies with the intent of keeping ourselves distracted so that we wouldn't dwell on the SuperSim going on without us. The first movie had been going for about twenty minutes, and the popcorn was well-consumed, when we heard the initial air horn rip through the air outside. The Sim was beginning.

Everyone looked around grimly at one another, all of us thinking the same thing: *wish we could play too*.

"Okay, guys, okay," I said, trying to defuse the tension a bit. "It's happened now . . . the SuperSim has started. We knew it would. Now let's just go back to our movie and rest easy in the thought that we've defeated more real criminals than any of those kids out there have." I thought that was a pretty good pep talk, and the group seemed to agree, as they lightened up right away and went back to joking and commenting about the movie.

A few minutes later, there was a loud boom outside, like the sound of nearby thunder, followed by a loud crash. We all tried to ignore it, but I saw Bentley's eyes look up and widen in surprise.

It sounded like the adults had saved the best for last with the final SuperSim and were pulling out the big guns—perhaps literally. It was excruciating to be shut out of the action.

Another loud boom, like the sound of an explosion, the echo reverberating throughout town. "Whoa," I said.

"I know," Bentley agreed.

The explosions and other loud noises continued off and on, getting progressively louder. It sounded as though the SuperSim had turned into a real battle for the ages. And that's exactly what it was, even though we'd yet to realize it.

Finally, one of the crashes of thunder was so close that it shook the house on its foundation, rattling my rib cage. That sound was followed by several audible screams of panic in the distance. And it sounded like adults doing the screaming.

Something wasn't right. I wrinkled my brow to try and piece it all together. *These people sound entirely too frightened for a simulation. And why are the adults . . .*

It was then that a very frightening thought hit me, one that I instantly hoped was wrong.

"Bentley," I said, "did you bring your computer?"

"Yeah," he replied, just as the character in the movie tripped over a stick and fell to the ground. The rest of the group roared in laughter, ignoring Bentley and me completely.

I waved my hand, signaling Bentley to join me at the kitchen table. We left the rest of the group watching the movie, but Henry had seen us slink off and had gotten curious. It was just as well, as I wanted to be able to see things for myself anyway.

Bentley sat next to me and opened up the computer.

"You've still got your cameras set up, right?"

"Yeah, of course."

"Let's see what's going on out there," I said.

"Sounds like the most serious SuperSim yet," Henry said, rolling up to the table to join us.

Chad looked over from the living room floor and saw the three of us at the table. He stood up, which got the attention of Freddie as well. Soon enough, we were all crowded around the laptop, waiting for Bentley's camera feeds to boot up.

Once they did, we knew instantly that something was dreadfully wrong.

The first camera angle we saw showed the Freepoint Circle . . . on fire and reduced to rubble. There were people on the ground here and there, and some of them looked to be badly hurt. Some weren't moving.

Bentley clicked a button and changed the view, and a picture of City Hall appeared on the monitor. "This camera's on the flagpole," he explained. Three of the giant stone columns were gone, scattered in pieces on the steps below. A section of the exterior wall looked black and charred. There were more bodies on the ground.

Click.

Another angle, this time of the Freepoint Bank. In the parking lot of the bank was a group of students—that team with the horrible all-green uniforms, the Vipers. They were under attack. One of them had a force field up in front of them, and it was currently protecting them from a barrage of fireballs.

"I bet that's the same fireballing bastard from the last SuperSim," Henry said bitterly.

The Vipers' attacker was still off camera. I was going crazy with just one angle to view. "Don't you have another angle?" I asked Bentley.

"Why, yes," he bragged a little, "I do."

Click.

This angle was from twice as far away, but the image came from a camera mounted on the bank itself, giving us a wider view of the parking lot. The fireballer was not, in fact, the one who had attacked us in the last SuperSim.

"Dang," Henry said, disappointed. "Not him."

I looked at him a moment, then glanced back to the screen. The fireballer attacking the students was tall and skinny, with an entirely black outfit and long black cloak. *One of Finch's Believers, no doubt.*

More men in black outfits walked into the camera's view. A lot more. There were at least thirty. One of them said something to the fireballer, and the man stopped firing at the Vipers.

"Can these things zoom?" I said anxiously.

"You bet," Bentley said, punching another button on the controls.

The camera angle lurched forward, quickly focusing in on the villains in question. The fireballer was facing the camera, but the other man—the one who told him to stop—had his back to us.

"Come on . . . come on . . ." I urged, willing the man to turn around and confirm what the pit in my stomach had already determined to be true.

Finally, he did just that. He turned to look at the students he'd spared, giving us a great look at the right side of his face.

It was Finch.

Before we could say anything, Finch raised his hand, and a flash of brilliant green light came from his palm and quickly disappeared off camera.

"Zoom out! Zoom out!" I commanded.

Bentley did just that, just in time for us to see the last of the Vipers' bodies hit the pavement. They looked dead, and I immediately knew that they were. Zapped with the same mind-controlling power Finch had used on my mother, only in this case . . . no coma. He'd removed their consciousnesses in a nanosecond. For all the scary moments I'd had involving Finch, this was by far the most horrific and brutal thing I'd seen him do. Here, he was finally the killer I'd always feared him to be.

Onscreen, Finch was hovering above the ground by a good ten feet, gesturing and speaking to a large group of the black-outfitted villains as though giving marching orders. Flames came out from his fingertips as he talked, like he was moments away from turning back into the fire monster from the cornfield.

"You know, you wouldn't think an all-powerful bad guy would have much use for henchmen," Bentley said in disgust.

"He needs their powers," I remarked, "or else he's not all powerful."

"Well, for a while he is, though, right?" Henry said.

"Whatever his goal is for all this . . . he's going for it tonight." I was talking to myself as much as the others. "This is it. He said he was going to take the city of Freepoint. This is it, Bentley."

Bentley turned to face me. "If you're right, Phillip, that means we aren't safe here, because he darn sure knows where you live."

"Why is that?" James asked.

Just then, a phone rang, and nearly everyone jumped through the ceiling. It took a second ring for me to figure out that it was the phone in my pocket. I jammed my hand inside, pulled it out, and flipped it open.

"Hello?"

"Phillip?"

"Dad." I exhaled, relieved. I'd half expected it to be Finch.

"Get out of the house, Phillip. You hear me? We're under attack. The city is under attack, and you're not safe there."

"It's him, Dad."

"I know, Phillip. That's why I'm calling you. Get your brother and the rest of those kids, and get out now. Go somewhere where you know you'll be safe . . . someplace random and far away. I'll call you when this is done."

"But, Dad, what about you?"

"I'll be fine, Phillip. Just go. That's an order. We don't have time to argue. Go now."

I heard the sounds of battle raging behind his voice, and then he hung up.

I looked up at the rest of the group, each of whom had turned several shades whiter upon hearing my side of the conversation; I think they heard the explosions too.

"The city is under attack. We have to get out of here." Something snapped and I sprang into military mode. "Everyone come over here—you too, Patrick. We're leaving right now."

No one was in any position to argue with that plan. We gathered our things, huddled around James, and popped off to Central Park and relative safety.

I felt guilty the moment we arrived in the park. Even though my father had given me explicit instructions, we had effectively just run out on our city, leaving them to fight a massive evil on their own. I felt like a terrible hero for deserting them.

Bentley's camera feeds were still accessible. Since he'd hooked them all up wirelessly to his home computer, he could access them from anywhere there was an internet connection. So we found a picnic table in a Wi-Fi hot spot and sat down to watch our parents defend our city in a movie that was all too real.

I was sick to my stomach as we watched camera angle after camera angle, each showing either tragic destruction of property or horrific brutality against the townspeople.

Finch and his massive army of cloaked Believers—there had to be at least one hundred of them—looked set on destroying the city completely. There were several people injured or killed, but a great many could be seen being led away in chains.

"They're taking prisoners," I exclaimed, pointing at the screen where three Freepoint citizens were being led away by Finch's soldiers. "Do you have a better angle? They're moving offscreen!"

"Hang on," Bentley said, punching a couple buttons.

A new angle came up onscreen, slightly closer to the action but with a view from the opposite side of the street. The prisoners were more centered in the picture on this angle. They came to the intersection, and the street lamp threw light on their faces.

"Oh my God, Phillip, isn't that your dad?" Henry gasped.

I instinctively reached out and pulled the laptop on the table into my hands, tilting it toward Henry's face and focusing on the image of the screen he was sending me.

My father had been taken prisoner along with the two men from the hospital the night Mom died. Three of the bad guys were serving as guards, but I had to assume they were also under an NPZ, because otherwise, I think my father would have been letting them have it. This was Finch's reason for kidnapping heroes with certain powers—like NPZs—so he could use them to mount his siege against Freepoint.

A sinking feeling came over me . . . a moment of despair. I nearly had a panic attack, I think, before something unlikely came along and saved me: anger.

Just as I was about to lose hope completely upon the sight of my captured father, anger swooped up from the pit of my stomach and brought things sharply back into focus for me.

And that was all it took. Once I allowed my rage to take over and settle me down, I was all business. It was "kill Finch or bust" at that point. I simply didn't care anymore. I was going to take this man down myself or die trying, because if I failed . . . well, that was a world I couldn't bear to live in anyway.

I sent the laptop gently back down into Bentley's waiting grasp.

"We have to find out where they're taking them."

I think the guys expected a more emotional response from me, because they seemed stunned at first and said nothing.

"Bentley, what can you tell me? If they're taking prisoners, they have to be taking them somewhere, right?"

I heard him clicking through the camera angles already, but I don't think he was finding much.

"I'm not sure, Phillip. I don't seem to have an angle that shows that."

"Well, how is that possible?" I demanded, displaying a flash of the anger that had saved me from blacking out under the pressure.

"I'm sorry, Phillip," Bentley said, sounding genuine. "I know I have a lot of cameras, but they're not infinite. Finch must be taking them somewhere that I don't have coverage on."

"Unbelievable," I muttered, frustrated by technology's inability to help me for even one quick moment.

"They could be taking them to Arkansas, for all we know," Bentley continued. "There's no guarantee they're even in Freepoint."

"No, they're there," I said, almost sounding as confident as I felt. "He's not going to start ferrying groups of prisoners through some makeshift teleporter network. He's going to get them out of the way and continue to ravage the city. It begins and ends in Freepoint tonight. I can feel it." As usual, I didn't have any idea how right I was.

"Well, unless you think it'll work to give your dad's cell phone a try, I'm not sure there's any other way for us to know."

"I'm sure they'll let him answer it, Bentley," I said with a fair amount of sarcasm. I knew he hadn't been serious in his suggestion, but I still wanted him to know how little I appreciated it.

Everyone got quiet. No one wanted to say what we all feared. No one wanted to admit we had no way of finding where they were taking my dad.

I shoved my hands in my pockets—at this point, a typical thinking posture for me. I liked to roll the communication disc my mother had given me around in my fingers. It helped me concentrate and think. On this one occasion, it helped me do more than think; it presented itself as a solution.

"Bentley, do you know anything about these?" I asked, holding out my palm containing the disc.

He cocked his head, as though confused, but then seemed to realize where I was going. "Yeah, sure," he said, picking up the disc and examining it. "They developed these about ten years ago. It's a personal GPS communicator."

"Right," I said. "I click it, and whoever has the corresponding receiver knows where I am in the world, right?"

"Right. And vice versa." And as soon as he uttered those words, Bentley's eyes lit up. "It's both a receiver and a transmitter." He continued explaining, growing more excited in his speech, all the while pulling out tools and gadgets from his backpack. "Have you ever seen the other unit, Phillip? The one your dad has?"

"Yeah, sure. It looks just like this one," I said, pointing at the disc, which he had placed on the table.

"Exactly," he confirmed. "Because it is just like this one. They're identical. They're not transmitter and receiver sets . . . they're sold as pairs of identical devices that both send and receive a signal so that the bearer of either could instantly know if their partner or loved one was in trouble."

"Are you kidding me?" I didn't really think he was kidding, but the expression came out before I could stop it.

"Nope," he said, taking a pair of pliers to the disc. "Your parents probably just didn't tell you . . . didn't ever intend to push their device's button to signal you, because . . . well, they're parents. Since when do parents need rescuing by their kids?"

"Since now," I said somberly.

He kept working and had the device in two pieces in no time.

"Wonderful," I said sarcastically. "You've broken it."

"It's made to come apart, Phillip. Calm down." He set the cap down and held the remaining half in his hand, bringing it up to his face. "They're still pretty simple devices. They can't carry much data in their signal."

While Bentley tinkered with the device, most everyone else went back to watching the computer screen, which displayed a grid of camera feeds four across and three down. In the middle square, a firestarter stood in the center of the street, shooting twelve-foot flames at the Freepoint gas station. Suddenly, it exploded. Bentley's cameras took outstanding video, but there were no microphones. But even without the audio, the explosion caught everyone by surprise, and we all gasped.

Then we all turned to Bentley. "Work fast, buddy," I said.

Bentley simply nodded and went straight back to work. With a few twists of his screwdriver and a spliced wire, Bentley was satisfied, and he carefully put the device's two pieces back together again.

"I boosted the signal," he said, like it was the easiest task ever. "Now it'll be more clear, to help him differentiate."

"Differentiate?"

"It means to tell the difference between things," Bentley said.

I know what it means. "Differentiate what?" I asked, unable to hide my confusion.

Bentley wrinkled his brow but then shrugged and said, "The beeps."

I felt like I was in the Twilight Zone, as Bentley's answers produced only more questions.

I sighed. "What beeps?" I asked.

"For Morse code, obviously."

The picture had finally become a bit clearer. "You want me to send my dad Morse code?"

"Well, I didn't imagine that you knew Morse code."

"I don't!" I was growing frustrated.

"It's okay, Phillip," he said, smiling, "I do."

"But what makes you think my father knows Morse code?"

"Well, doesn't he?"

"How should I know? He's certainly never talked about it. What if it's all just a series of beeps to him?"

Bentley took a moment to ponder that question and then made his decision. "I'm pretty sure any former crime-fighters or any Freepoint protector, like your dad currently is, would know Morse code. It's one of the fundamentals of military and police training."

It was my turn to think for a minute.

"Okay, so . . . we send my dad a bunch of beeps, hope he understands it and maybe can tell us where they're being held. Or . . . he doesn't understand it and thinks I've lost my mind."

"Or maybe he doesn't even have the other receiver, and it's in a guard's pocket . . . or a dog is chewing on it," Henry offered unhelpfully.

"There's not really a downside to giving it a try," Bentley argued, making a lot of sense, actually. The worst-case scenario was that Dad either didn't know Morse code or didn't have the device on him as a prisoner. We'd be no worse off in those cases than we were now.

"Okay," I said. "Let's give it a try. Let's send my dad a bunch of beeps."

"What do you want to say?" Bentley asked. "But keep it short. Morse code can get pretty long."

"I don't know," I said. "Do you think 'Where are they holding you prisoner?' is enough, or do I need something more?"

"Love, Phillip?" It was James, offering his two cents. I cocked my head at him in complete bewilderment, and he said, "Well, I imagine he probably already knows you love him."

"Plus," Bentley added gently, "they're a pair. He'll know that it's Phillip's signal because the two devices work only with each other. I think 'Where are they holding you prisoner?' is a fine message."

Bentley then set about tapping out the Morse code sequence on the disc's button. There were short taps and long taps and virtually no discernible pattern or meaning to them at all, to my ear. Though I certainly trusted that Bentley knew what he was doing, Morse code struck me as a needlessly complicated affair.

It seemed like he was tapping out beeps for several minutes, but finally, he finished. "Sorry," he said. "You have to punch out the symbol for each letter separately, so I had to spell every word, and some letters have a bunch of beeps just for that one letter."

"I'm not sure I could remember all that if my life depended on it," Henry said.

"So, now what?" I asked.

"Now we wait and see if he responds," Bentley said, holding the disc in the palm of his outstretched hand.

Everyone sat silent and still, eyes and ears honed in on the device, as we waited to see what would happen. Would my father still have his device? Would he understand the code and respond? It was an agonizing wait. The crickets in Central Park were droning in the background. In the distance I could hear the faint sounds of the city traffic. But none of us made a peep.

After several quiet seconds, the shrill beep of the disc device cut through the silence like a screech. It took only seconds to realize the beeps were continuing in the same stilted short-long formats as Bentley's.

"All right," I cheered, in complete awe of Bentley's genius. Everyone celebrated and high-fived.

Bentley had a pencil out and was scribbling down the message, one letter at a time, as it came through.

"Wait a second," Henry said, interrupting our jubilance. "How do we know this message is coming from Phillip's dad?"

"What," I said with disdain, "you think that Finch's goons are going to go to the trouble of responding to a Morse code message, assuming they even confiscated it?"

"I'm just saying—"

"Shut up! I can't concentrate!" Bentley chided, silencing us immediately. He continued transcribing the message until the beeping finally concluded. It seemed like a lot longer a message than Bentley's had been.

"That's it," he said, scrawling the final letters. "Here's the message: 'School basement. Don't be stupid. If want to help, contact Goodspeed.'"

We all soaked in the content of Dad's message but quickly got into battle-planning mode.

"Okay, gang, you heard him. They're holding prisoners at the school, in the basement. That could be an advantage for us," I said. "And that's where Finch's soldiers are holding our parents and the rest of Freepoint's adults and students . . . the ones who are still alive, at least," I added rather grimly. "So that's where we need to go."

"Why would he keep any of them alive?" Freddie asked cautiously, hitting his inhaler before continuing. "I mean, we saw him kill the Vipers without any reservation at all. Why keep some of them alive?"

"Their powers," I said, realizing the answer as it came off my lips. "He's building an army, even if they're unwilling participants." With hundreds of Freepoint citizens held prisoner, Finch would have access to nearly every power known to our kind. He'd be unstoppable. "Which is why we have to stop him!"

"But your dad just said not to come," Henry argued.

"I don't care what he said. You know as well as I do that if we do nothing, Freepoint is going to fall to Finch. Now, which one of you wants to let that happen? What falls next, after Freepoint, if we let that happen?" I turned my head from person to person, daring each of them to tell me they wanted to let the city fall. None of them did, of course.

"Well then, what do we do?" It was Chad, a bit more eager for battle than I'd expected.

Chad's question forced me to face the fact that I wasn't at all sure what we should do, where we should start, or how a band of tiny super-misfits should go about attempting to defeat an entire army of villains. "I'm not sure," I answered honestly.

"Guys," Bentley gasped. "You'd better take a look at this."

We all scurried over to Bentley's side so we could see what he was watching. It looked like the field in front of the high school. We could see the school's entrance on just the right top corner of the image, but the rest of the screen was grass.

"I don't see anything but grass," Henry stated, still sounding impressed with himself despite his rather obvious findings.

"Hang on a second . . . I think you will. He was spraying some kind of liquid all over the grass a second ago."

We all watched intently, with nothing happening for thirty seconds or so. Until, finally, a figure strode out from the left side of the picture. It was Finch; I could tell by his measured, practiced steps. He looked small—he was a good fifty yards from where the camera was placed—but there was no doubt it was him. When he was almost exactly in the middle of the video picture, he stopped, whirled, and faced the camera directly. It was almost as though he knew it was there.

Finch's arm went up into the air, and a tiny flame burst forth from his fingertip, flickering like a star on the tiny video monitor. He lifted it to his face and drew from his pipe for a moment. Then, with a flash, he threw the flame to the ground. Instantly, sections of the grass around him came ablaze.

He'd used lighter fluid to spell a message in the grass, and it was a message to me. We all saw it, plain as day. There, in the front lawn of my high school, were horrific flaming letters arranged to say "Phillip. It's time."

I cursed under my breath—but everyone still heard me.

"Jesus," Henry said, exhaling in disbelief. "He wasn't kidding. This whole thing really is about you, isn't it?"

"I guess so." I was dumbfounded. "I thought he was just . . . you know . . . messing with me. Inviting me to be on his 'team' and whatnot." Before I could recover from the shock of the fire message, a new thought occurred to me. *How does he know about the cameras?*

A new thought, one I hadn't had before but that made perfect sense even as it chilled my bones.

Henry, can you send a message to Bentley for me . . . privately? I mentally asked my good friend.

Sure, he responded.

Ask him why a man who has every power—or at least access to them—is so obsessed with recruiting a kid who has only one power. What does he need me for? I still hadn't told Bentley and the others about Finch's suggestion that I myself was the prophesied one.

A few seconds went by, and then Henry sent me another silent message. *He said he doesn't know. That's a good question.*

Another pause, and then Henry followed up with another message from Bentley. *Unless he thinks you're the next Elben.*

What do you mean? I responded directly to Bentley, even though I knew Henry still had to relay the message.

He's looking for the one in the prophecy, right? He told you as much. It's obvious why—because then he'd need only that one person around and he'd have every single superability at once. If he finds the real Elben . . . well, then he can get rid of them. He's talked of nothing else. What if he's convinced, for whatever reason, that you are that person?

It was a pretty obvious explanation. No matter how silly or untrue, Finch was convinced that I was Elben's reincarnation. It made so much sense, it seemed obvious. I mean, it was ludicrous, to be sure. I had all the powers just about as much as I had sight. But if you accepted the premise that Finch was already kind of crazy just to be devoting so much time and effort to the myth of Elben and factored in the number of times he'd mysteriously bumped into me . . . it made all kinds of sense.

If Finch truly believes that I have every power and if he really did set up this entire attack on Freepoint as a way to get to me . . . he's not going to rest until I show up. He'll kill everyone.

You can't go out there, Phillip. It's suicide. You'd be walking into his trap.

Maybe. Maybe not. Maybe we can spring a trap of our own.

The silent mission planning went on like that for several minutes as Henry, Bentley, and I laid out each person's role. It would be the mother of all long shots, but we had to try. The way I saw it, either everyone I loved was going to die, including me, or everyone I loved was going to die, leaving me alone in New York with my festering guilty conscience. Or maybe, just maybe, we could pull off a miracle.

"Okay, listen up, everyone. Here's what we're gonna do . . ." I finally said aloud to everyone. The others gathered in to listen to the details of the plan, though they didn't know how much of it I left out.

28

RESCUE PARTY

Before putting any plan into action, we first tried to follow my father's instructions. We called Goodspeed . . . on the telephone. We knew there were a few emergency call buttons in Freepoint, but it still seemed worth a shot to literally call them first. We phoned several businesses and homes using Bentley's computer to look up numbers—he'd long ago hacked his father's personal and official board email accounts—but seeing as Goodspeed was having their own SuperSim that night, no one was answering.

"Why don't we just *go* to Goodspeed?" Freddie asked.

"During a SuperSim? Anyone that even paid attention to us would assume we're part of the Sim," I explained. "They might even try to fake-arrest us. By the time we convince them who we are and what's going on is real, it could be too late. We also can't be sure Finch's crew hasn't attacked Goodspeed as well. Might have an NPZ up, and then we'd be out our transporter. It's just too risky."

"This is getting us nowhere," Henry complained.

"He's right," I said to the group. "We're wasting time."

Bentley thought for a moment, which would count as several dozen for most people in terms of productivity, and finally announced his findings. "I'll set the computer to search through all his messages and dial each phone number it finds automatically. Maybe someone will answer before we get to the panic button."

"Okay," I agreed. "Do it. Let's get going."

He rattled the keyboard a few times, punctuating it with one demonstrative keystroke. "Okay, ready," he said.

"Cool. Henry? James?" Both reached out a hand, which I met with my own in the center.

Ooph!

We'd decided to use the cornfield as a staging ground for our delusional rescue mission. It was the closest thing this group had to a headquarters, and we hoped it would be safe out there on the edge of town. We were counting on the presumed fact that Finch had gotten everything he needed from that field on Halloween.

Henry, James, and I went on a brief scouting mission. We wanted to make sure—I wanted to make sure—we had some idea of whether or not it was safe before we all went. Chad had wanted to go as well and actually seemed to be itching to get involved. But I needed him in the park to protect Patrick; Chad's invisibility was really the best power in the group for taking cover from potential danger.

The scouting mission quickly revealed the area was secure, and then . . .

Ooph!

We returned to find the rest of the group gone. Completely gone, without a thing left behind to indicate they'd been there in the first place.

Henry looked around the park frantically once he realized we were alone. There was no sign of them.

"How long were we gone?" I asked.

"No more than fifteen minutes," Henry answered.

"Are we in the right place?"

"Absolutely!" James said, his pride wounded a bit that I would even ask.

"What could they have gotten into in that amount of time?"

"Hang on," James said. "Let me look around the area. Come on, Henry," he said, slapping his hand on Henry's wheelchair so he'd have eyes.

Ooph!

For the next few seconds, I heard faint versions of the familiar popping sound that accompanied James's teleporting. The noises came from all around me and at various distances as he quickly hopped here and there, surveying the surrounding area.

It startled me when he suddenly reappeared in front of me.

Ooph!

"Phillip, grab on!" he said excitedly.

I did so right away.

Ooph!

We were only a few hundred yards from our previous position, near the edge of a small batch of trees next to a clearing. Another hundred yards or so beyond the clearing, I saw Patrick, Freddie, and Bentley being placed into the back of a police van.

"Oh no," I murmured, immediately fearing the worst. Central Park, while huge, was still the site of the only public sighting of a superhero using his powers in generations. And now, with Weatherby completely missing and presumed dead, any custodian activity in public was subject to eyewitnesses, cell phone cameras, and a general lack of the privacy and anonymity my people had enjoyed for generations. People around here, including police officers, were probably a little more sensitive to odd circumstances, but I didn't have any idea what could have led to them being arrested.

"Where the hell is Chad?" Henry barked.

"Where *is* Chad?" I reiterated.

"Right here," Chad replied, his voice coming from several yards behind us. We all turned around in time to see him appear out of thin air as he came jogging up. He was clearly out of breath. "We got separated."

Henry wasn't buying it. "How did you get separated?"

"The cops were on us out of nowhere, man. We all split in different directions out of reaction. I didn't have time to get everyone together and hide."

We watched the cops slam the rear doors on the van. "What are we gonna do?"

Everyone turned to look at the van. The officers were climbing into their seats up front, slamming the doors behind them.

"We can't use our powers," I muttered.

"Why not? Why not just let James and Mr. Invisible here jump over and pull them out?"

"Because there's already been one superhero who was seen using his powers in this park, Henry, and it's still national news months later, okay? We can't exactly go prancing around flashing our abilities for all to see, especially without Weatherby's protection."

"Phillip, Freepoint is on fire. To hell with the special rules about using your powers in public, man! We need to get those guys out of there if we're going to have any chance."

"Whatever we're going to do, we need to do it fast," Chad interrupted as the van began to slowly pull forward.

"Oh, damn," I said. "Now I'm really in trouble. First I let my brother find out about his powers, and now he's getting arrested."

Suddenly the van stopped dead in its tracks with a terrifying screech. The metallic roof and sides shredded into pieces with a deafening roar as out of the rear of the van rose an enormous giant. All in the span of mere seconds, the vehicle had essentially exploded as Freddie went from normal size to three stories tall, ripping away their metal prison with incredible strength.

As he reached his full height and bulk, he let out a roar like a lion after a kill, only to instantly stagger, bracing himself against the ritzy apartment building nearby and gasping loudly.

Cars on the road slammed on their breaks, and a great commotion rose out of relative silence as people opened their windows and rushed out their front doors to see what had happened.

"Holy crap," Chad said.

"Well, that's going to be on the news," I said matter-of-factly.

"So much for not using our powers, eh, Phillip?" Henry added.

"Yeah. I guess so," I said, still in shock at seeing the raw destruction Freddie had caused just by turning on his power.

Giant Freddie stumbled again and then quickly started to shrink in size, disappearing from our view behind the crumpled van.

"Do you think," Henry said, "maybe now is a good time for us to get in there and—"

"Yeah," I said immediately, cutting him off. "James, Chad, go get 'em."

"Right away," James said as Chad reached out and clasped his hand like a handshake. They both disappeared.

Ooph!

Henry and I immediately turned our heads back toward the van. The crowd was growing by the moment, and who could blame them? Seconds later . . .

Ooph!

The first thing I looked for was Patrick, and he was standing there grinning as though he'd just spent a day at the amusement park. Then I did a quick head count to make sure everyone else was present. Freddie was sitting on the ground, puffing on his inhaler. James stood over him, rubbing his shoulder and encouraging him to breathe. Chad and Bentley stood behind them, smiling.

"Oh my God, Freddie," Henry gushed. "That was amazing! Do you have any idea how amazing what you just did was?"

Freddie puffed once more and then looked up. He barely got out a quick smile before being compelled to hit it again. For a few seconds, I grew a little worried he was going to have an asthma attack, but he eventually evened out and started breathing a bit more normally.

"Are you okay?" I asked desperately.

"Yeah," he said, taking an oversized breath. "I'm fine. Whenever I get big like that, nothing really seems to hurt me." He looked down, then back up. "I am naked right now, though."

We all laughed pretty hard at that, but it began to feel awkward when we realized it was basically true. There were a few shreds of his pants left on his body, but not much.

"Here," Bentley said, offering up a pair of pants he produced from his backpack. "They're rain pants, but they'll do the job."

"You carry rain pants in that thing?" Henry asked in surprise.

"Sure. You never know when they'll come in handy."

Henry shook his head.

"We need to get out of here before the cops come back this way," I said. "James, can you take us over to the other end of the park?"

James stepped forward, holding out his arm. We all latched on.

Ooph!

Henry moved his head around a bit, taking in the surroundings. He lingered on Bentley a moment, because Bentley was looking right at Henry and me. He lifted his head a bit, with an inquisitive look on his face. He was asking how our scouting mission had gone.

I gave Bentley a thumbs-up, and he nodded. *You're not gonna believe it*, Henry said mentally to both Bentley and me.

"Bentley," I said aloud. "Pop open that laptop, will you?"

"Sure thing," he said.

"All right, everyone. There's too much to do and too few of us to do it. So we're going to have to split up. Bentley, you take Freddie, Patrick, and James and head to your house." One of the three emergency call buttons in Freepoint was actually located in Bentley's home since his father was one of the higher-ranking members of the board. We'd seen it that first sleepover at his house. The button, when pressed, notified the leaders of the other hero cities that Freepoint was in trouble.

"Henry, Chad, and I will go after Finch."

"I can't tell you how excited I am about that," Henry grumbled.

"Sorry, buddy. I gotta see somehow. We'll all jump to the cornfield together, and then, James, you can take us to the spot Bentley picked, okay?"

"It's just two blocks from the school, someone's backyard," Bentley explained. "But there hasn't been any activity on that camera whatsoever, so it should be a good spot to get you in close."

I continued. "James, then you'll go back to the cornfield and grab the others so you can head off to Bentley's house."

"Wait," Chad interrupted. "Do you have a plan? Are you just going to waltz up to Finch and tap him on the shoulder?"

"Not at all," I said, smiling, trying to act completely calm. "In fact, your power is going to help us sneak right past him."

"We're going past him?" He was confused.

"At least to the front steps of the school, yeah. See, he's out here . . . in the east field . . ." I pointed to the spot on the main camera angle, which showed Finch doing nothing but standing and surveying. Several of the Believers scurried around here and there, wrapping up skirmishes with the last few remaining Freepoint resisters. "But if we can get past him without him knowing we're there . . . we just might have a shot."

"A shot to do what?" Chad must have thought I was crazy.

"To turn the school's NPZ against him. At least, that's the hope."

"This has to be the craziest thing I've ever heard, Phillip. You think you can turn the school's NPZ against Finch? How? No one knows who the hero is that controls it."

"But we do know how the principal activates and deactivates it," I said with a bit of pride.

He thought for a minute. "Chelsey?"

I nodded.

"Don't tell me you're going to—"

"That's right," I interjected. "Bentley hot-wired my radio to imitate the school's walkie-talkie frequency."

Bentley smiled broadly at this but said nothing.

"You're going to sneak past the most powerful villain in our lifetimes and then say a woman's name into a walkie-talkie in the hope that whoever controls the school's NPZ isn't already a prisoner—and is willing to follow orders from the voice of a twelve-year-old instead of the principal?"

I smiled at how ridiculously perfect it all seemed. "Yeah. Yeah, that's exactly what we're going to do."

"And what if it doesn't work? We'll be sitting ducks!"

"Only if Bentley's team fails, Chad. Because if they succeed, then we're nothing but a distraction anyway, because the good men and women of Goodspeed will swoop in at the last minute and save our behinds."

"Either that or the Freepoint prisoners we bust out," Bentley added.

"Wonderful," Chad said in mock happiness. "You're sending a cripple, a blind transporter, a dude with asthma, and your little brother to rescue all the prisoners?"

I had my own doubts about the plan, for sure. But I wasn't about to let them show in front of the rest of the group and definitely not in front of Patrick. Besides, we had to do something. Doing nothing would have been unbearable. I couldn't take much more of Chad's dissenting opinion, though. We didn't have time for it.

"Chad, you know what?" I used a gentle, friendly tone. Casual even. "Let's not worry about that. Okay? Now, unless you want to bow out here, which nobody would blame you for doing . . ."

He wagged his head side to side, indicating he wanted to stay.

"We've got enough to worry about. It's basically going to take a miracle for us to come out of this alive, let alone victorious. So . . . I figure . . . if it's fate, if it's out of our hands, then either everything will go wrong or everything will miraculously go right. Either way, there's probably not a lot I can do to impact it beyond my own job. Let's let Bentley and them worry about Bentley and them, you know?"

He nodded. "Okay. Yeah." He wiped his hand on his knee and shook his whole body as though shaking off a dizzy feeling. "Okay. I'm with you. I'm with you. What's my job?"

I smiled. "Keep Henry and me invisible, man. That's all you gotta do."

"I can do that," he said with a grin. "I know how to do that."

"Okay, everyone . . . hands in." I put out my hand first, palm down. One by one, everyone else gathered into a small circle, adding their hand to the pile in the center. When we were all in, I turned to James. "If you don't mind, good sir?"

"Why, not at all," he said in a terrible British accent.

Ooph!

The cornfield was still peaceful, but there were distant noises coming from the heart of Freepoint, maybe a mile or two away. An explosion, a few loud banging noises. Fires raged here and there all over town, their light and smoke collecting over the city in a terrible glowing dome of death and destruction. None of us could really believe it. We stood there, hands still clapped together, staring at what seemed like a simple nightmare, even though we knew it was all too real.

What had happened to our city? Our parents? Our friends? How many had died? Were there even any left to save?

I snapped myself out of it, if only so I could snap the others out of it as well. "Okay," I said sharply, pulling my hand back. "We know what we have to do, everyone, right?" They all nodded. "We don't have time for any big speeches or anything, but I just want to say that we're all going to be fine. We're going to get through this because we have to. If we don't, we die."

There was a group pause as the weight of the situation came crashing down on everyone. We were about to seriously risk our lives on a long-shot plan. If we failed, we might not live to see tomorrow. Deep down, we all knew our history of mission planning and execution was spotty at best.

I turned briefly back toward the farmhouse, wondering what Mr. Charles would be up to. Henry looked from the computer screen back up at the orange halo around our city; it was a mesmerizing sight.

Turning back at the group, I couldn't resist trying to find the perfect thing to say to wrap up what we were all feeling—which was, of course, impossible. "There's nothing I could say or do to let you guys know how much you all mean to me, you know? But . . . you've been like a second family to me in a year when my real family has been turned upside down. And I appreciate it. I wish I could show you how much I appreciate it.

"I know we face tall odds. We have a flimsy plan, and the enemy probably has a lot of NPZ coverage. In a way, if you think about it, it's a lot like the original Ables. Outnumbered and having to rely on our smarts . . . our ability to be more clever than the opponent. The Ables faced incredible odds too, guys, hundreds to a handful, just like us. And just like them, we're going to defeat the enemy with our teamwork and ingenuity . . ." I trailed off, struggling to find a good way to wrap up my speech. "I'm not sure how to end this thing to be honest, guys . . ." I trailed off again.

Everyone looked around at each other, all feeling a range of strong emotions but none really sure what to say or how to behave. This could be the end for some of us and almost certainly the end of the Ables. We might not see each other again, depending on how things went.

"We could hug," James offered meekly.

Everyone turned and looked at him. He'd always been so friendly and polite, it probably shouldn't have surprised us that he would be the one to suggest a group hug.

"You know . . . if you want. We don't have to," he backpedaled, shifting his gaze to his feet as he realized the awkwardness he'd caused.

I looked at Bentley, who was smiling but trying to hide it. I glanced at Henry, who was choking back a laugh. And then I looked at Patrick, who looked back at me with these honest eyes that seemed to genuinely need a hug. And I gave in.

"Okay. I guess."

James lit up. He stepped forward and wrapped me up with a surprising amount of strength as everyone else piled in on the group hug around us and started to laugh. It was a really nice moment. Sometimes, you don't realize how much you've grown to care about people until something threatens to take them away from you.

It made me really miss Donnie too.

"Okay, okay," I said, backing out of the scrum, trying to get us back on task. "Let's get serious now, guys. We don't have time to waste. At all. Okay?"

Everyone settled themselves down and tried to focus.

"Henry, Chad, James? You guys ready?"

"Yeah."

"Let's do it."

"Yes, sir!"

We formed a tight square, and the four of us placed a hand inside. "Good luck, Bent," I said to my friend. "Patrick, you do whatever he says, you hear me? Dad's going to kill me if you get killed, so don't die. And if there's trouble . . . run, and don't stop running till you're three states over." I turned to James. "Okay. Let's go."

Ooph!

Henry immediately looked down at his laptop screen at what my camera was capturing while I scanned my head back and forth looking for movement. There was none. I glanced at James and silently nodded.

Ooph!

He was gone.

We were in the corner of a residential backyard. It was surrounded by a tall wooden fence, and James had plopped us in perfectly, tucked right into the corner where two edges of the fence met. The lights in the home were off, and we appeared to be alone in the yard.

On the other side of the fence was school property. The home's land backed right up to Freepoint High's east side lawn, which was mostly used for band and soccer practices. It was a huge amount of distance to cover between our current position and the front steps of the school, easily two football fields.

We peeked through the slats of the fence. It was tricky for me to line up the camera properly, but once I straightened that out, Henry got a pretty good picture to send me. The camera was night-vision capable now, thanks to another round of tinkering by Bentley.

For about a hundred yards or so, roughly half the distance we needed to cross, there was no one. There were two men, Believers in their full robes, standing and talking at the halfway point, then we saw three more of them walking toward the school another fifty yards in. I briefly wondered what kind of chitchat Believers would be making on a night like tonight. About thirty yards from the main entrance of the school, where we needed to go, stood Finch. His arms were crossed, and there was no movement in him at all. He could have been a statue. He was waiting. For me.

And by golly, I was going to show up. Just not the way he planned.

There were about ten to fifteen other robed sentries scattered here and there, some near the front of the school and others toward the back. But that was all we could see.

The earpiece in my ear crackled to life. "Phillip. Come in." It was Bentley.

"Go ahead, Bentley," I whispered in reply.

"Listen, man. Bad news."

Uh-oh.

He continued. "They've been here. They must have known about the emergency communication system to Goodspeed. The entire house is trashed, and the device is destroyed." He paused. "I'm sorry, Phillip. I'm sure they know about the other similar devices in town and have already destroyed those as well. I think we're on our own."

That was a blow I didn't expect and one I didn't need. With the activation of that device—one push of a button—our chances for success would go up in a big way. Goodspeed forces had plenty of teleporters on their payroll, just as Freepoint did. They could be here in seconds, but not if they didn't know we needed their help.

"Bentley," I said.

"Not now, Phillip." His voice was suddenly hushed and carried a new sense of urgency. "There's someone in the house. I think there's someone in the house, Phillip!"

"Oh crap." It was Henry. It was a party line, so everyone on the team could hear.

"Bentley!" I whispered, not sure what else to say. But there was no immediate response. I swallowed hard.

"This is bad, Phillip," Chad whispered, off radio. "This is very bad."

I nodded, my face surely portraying panic. My heart began to pound a nervous beat. "Bentley!" The silence was killing me.

"I'm here, Phillip. But I gotta be honest." He'd never spoken more quietly in his life. "I think we're in trouble here. We can't use our powers. NPZ. There are several men in the house, Finch's men, I'm sure. They're coming up the stairs now and—" he went silent again, but that wasn't because he had stopped transmitting. My ears were more than strong enough to still pick up the crackle of the open radio connection. He was still broadcasting, just not talking.

I tried to listen more intently. I could hear breathing—no doubt Bentley's. It was fast and heavy. Without warning, there was an incredibly loud bang, like the sound of a door being kicked in. Then voices. "All right! On your feet!" "Now, now, now! Get up! Get up!" There was a lot of commotion, rustling, and muffled shouting. I couldn't tell what was going on.

"You move and you die, you hear? I have no compunction about killing you just because you're kids, okay?"

I looked up at Chad again. Even with the night vision, it still looked like he'd turned a few shades whiter.

More voices. "Call it in. Four more prisoners."

I dropped my head in defeat, exhaling a lot of held breaths at once. Bentley's team had been captured.

"What in the hell is this? Is that a radio?" There was a sharp popping noise, and the line went dead.

For several seconds, none of us said anything. We were all processing what these new developments meant. Prior to that radio call, we were going out to face a fierce and evil enemy, but we had hopes that either rescued Freepoint citizens or emergency troops from Goodspeed would come to our aid. Now, with Bentley, Freddie, James, and Patrick captured by Finch's goons . . . there would be no aid.

We were truly on our own. The three of us against the world. Things had gone from mostly hopeless to totally hopeless, which feels like a bigger drop than I expected.

"Why didn't James just jump them out of there?" Chad wondered aloud, shaking his head in disbelief at what he'd just heard.

"They had an NPZ," Henry said.

"Geez, how many does this guy control anyway?" Chad said in frustration. "Aren't they in limited supply?"

"Yeah," I confirmed. "A few of the heroes in Freepoint with that power disappeared this year, though. I'll bet you anything it was Finch, and he's somehow using their powers against us."

"You know, now that you say that," Chad said slowly, "I think there was an NPZ hero kidnapped or something when I was in Goodspeed."

"He was probably picking them off one by one," Henry added.

"So we're going up against a guy who has every power in existence and also controls most of the world's population of blockers? We're screwed," Chad said. He didn't say it angrily or argumentatively but rather as a matter of fact.

"We *are* screwed," Henry agreed. I was surprised he hadn't said it first.

"We were already screwed," I offered.

Both of them looked at me at once.

I explained. "Like I said in the cornfield, we had pretty slim odds to begin with, right? This is like going from having a five percent chance of success to having a three percent chance of success. It's not that big a difference, if you think about it."

Neither of them appeared to be swayed by my logic, which I knew was flimsy at best. Bentley would have been more persuasive.

"Look," I tried again, "all we need to do to defeat this guy is trap him in an NPZ. That's it."

"You make it sound easy," Henry scoffed.

"I admit the Chelsey plan is a long shot. But it's the only thing I've got, Henry. Unless you know a better way to find an NPZ we can control, we have to try the one method we've seen work before."

"There'll be no cavalry, Phillip," Chad warned. "No rescuers. Bentley couldn't call Goodspeed, and now that he's been captured, he can't rescue your dad and the other prisoners. It's just the three of us."

"It only needs to be one of us," I said somewhat angrily, "if we can get his ass in an NPZ. I'll take him down myself if I have to." I softened a bit, but only a bit. "Now, you two can stay here if you want. But I've had it. I'm done. If this is all about me, then it ends with me out there, win or lose. I'm not going to turn and run after all that this jerk has put me through. Either I'm going to defeat him, or I'm going to die trying. I can't ask you to make that same decision, but if you're going to go . . . you go now, okay?"

They looked at each other, both a bit surprised at the edge in my voice.

"I'm staying, Phillip. I'm with you to the end, buddy." Henry smiled as he said it, and so did I.

"I'm in too. I've got nothing better to do," Chad said. He smiled too, but it was a nervous smile, and I could tell he wasn't completely sure of himself. But he'd been given a chance to back out. And besides, I needed him for my real plan to succeed. He was kind of essential to it, actually.

29

SHOWDOWN

We had to walk all the way around the interior fence line to the other side of the yard to find a gate we could push Henry's wheelchair through. But after that, the terrain before us was all grass.

Chad turned on his invisibility as soon as we closed the gate behind us. Slapping a hand on each of our shoulders, he turned Henry and me invisible too. It was maybe the ninth or tenth time I'd seen him do it, and it never got any less cool. If I was a normal kid, I would dream about using that kind of power to sneak out of the house or pull off some other mischievous task. Instead, I was using it to try and take on maybe the most powerful evil to ever exist. I wasn't a normal kid, not anymore. There would be no going back to a normal life after what I'd been through.

We made our way across the field without a problem, going in a wide arc around Believers standing guard on the perimeter. Soon enough, we were nearing the area where Finch himself stood. As it turned out, we would have to go right by him in order to get to the school's entrance. This was, in part, because of the arrangement of his Believer guards and henchmen, but it was also because of the terrain. The shortest and safest route—the quietest route— just happened to take us very close to the one guy we were currently trying most to avoid.

We were invisible, but not silent. So we couldn't hurry. We couldn't make much noise at all. And as dangerous as it was to go near Finch, it was probably still safer than trying to push a wheelchair past a grouping of six men without one of them hearing a noise. It was just basic math: better odds. But it sure made for the most nail-biting fifty steps of my entire life.

We practically tiptoed through the grass, moving at roughly one-sixth the speed of a normal person's walk. We drew closer and closer to him until we reached the closest we would be while passing him—about twenty feet. We stared at him as we passed, searching his body for some sign that he could see us, but there was none. He really could have been a statue. There was no movement at all in his eyes or his posture. He was totally still.

Behind him, there were burning embers and charred soil from his challenge to me spelled out in the grass.

Whatever emotions had propelled me here in the first place—anger, revenge, heroism—they were all gone now, replaced by a suffocating fear. Fear of being discovered too soon and fear of failure and death.

I'm not sure any of us breathed at all as we inched slowly by, covered only by Chad's camouflaging power. We didn't want to make a peep.

After a near eternity, we finally passed Finch's position unscathed and began moving away from him. The main entrance to the school was only a few yards away, with no bad guys in between. We were almost home free, at least temporarily.

I glanced back at Finch again, but he remained unchanged. *Did he really think I was just going to waltz up to him out in the open?*

A bit of my nervousness faded with each passing step. There was an entire list of things that needed to go right for us to prevail, and getting by Finch unseen was just the first one. But we'd done it successfully, so I mentally crossed it off the list. One challenge down, one success in the books. It built a little confidence in me, and it was probably just the amount I needed to do what I had to do.

But my welling pride was harshly interrupted by the sound of Chad tripping on a rock. A dull, loud thud. Then came the physical contact, as Chad lurched forward into my left shoulder and Henry's wheelchair. I was knocked to the ground, and Chad tumbled after me. His contact with us severed, his concentration broken, Chad's invisibility simply quit working for all three of us.

We'd just gone two hundred yards in the quietest manner possible, only to trip all over each other and cause a scene within sight of our goal.

Instinctively, I turned to look at Finch, but all I saw was the ground—Henry hadn't yet recovered enough from the jostling to put his gaze back on the computer screen. He started to move his head to look around, still not remembering how badly I needed his eyes.

"Well, well, well," came an all-too-familiar voice. "It looks like we have some unexpected visitors. Or should I say, expected visitors. I did write your invitation in fire, after all."

"Henry!" I shouted.

It worked, jogging his memory and snapping him back to reality. He looked at Finch, then turned sharply to the laptop and my camera's video feed.

I jerked my head to my left and finally saw my enemy. He was dressed the way he usually was, the way he had been on the night we'd first encountered him. A long tweed jacket. His customary matching hat. His cane. He was as distinguished looking as ever.

"I knew you'd come," he said gently. "I knew you'd see my message. You know, Phillip," he continued, bringing his left hand out of his pants pocket to gesture with, "you will have to give my regards to your pal Bentley for me. Those cameras of his have been a godsend." He pulled his cane out from under his right arm, placed the tip in the grass in front of him, and stacked both hands on top of the handle. I'd wager it was the most casual evil-villain pose in history. "They were very easy to spot and even easier to hack. And I cannot tell you how much they helped us plan this very mission to take over and destroy the mighty hero city of Freepoint."

He looked out over the huge field. "We knew exactly where everyone would be, you see. I mean, sure, we would have taken this ridiculous little town either way. The cameras just made it easier."

My heart sank a bit at his words. To know that a system we'd put in place to give ourselves an edge had helped lead to the death, injury, and imprisonment of hundreds was a weight I was not prepared to feel.

"But no matter," Finch continued. "You're here now. Which is all I really wanted anyway. The rest of it is just . . . icing on the cake, I suppose. Fringe benefits. You're the real reason I ever came to Freepoint in the first place. And

I think you're ready to embrace your true destiny."

Finally I couldn't stand it any longer, and the twelve-year-old in me just had to have his say. "Are you crazy, old man? Do you somehow seriously think I have all the powers in the world?" It was the stupidest-sounding sentence that had ever come out of my mouth, of that I was sure.

"I don't *think* you have all the powers in the world, Phillip," he said softly, almost lovingly. "I *know* you do. There's not a shadow of doubt in my mind."

I hung my head, wondering how to go about reasoning with an obviously crazy person.

"I know you've heard the prophecy," he said. I didn't give him the courtesy of an answer; he didn't give me the courtesy of waiting for one. "And by now, you have to have read the original texts I gave you." The cane was flipped up onto his right shoulder now, another in his seemingly endless supply of cane poses. "I have it memorized, as you might presume. 'He shall return again, an outcast, one who is not like us, who does not see the world as we do, and he shall have all abilities. Where once he used his gifts for death and destruction, his second life shall see them used for life and protection. This one shall not know of his own true depth of power until he suffers great loss and injury, and he alone stands as the last protector between the world and a great power. Only then shall he truly see. Only then shall he embrace his true purpose.'"

He'd given the whole speech like it was an audition for a play, with plenty of gesturing and emotion. I had to admit, the rest of the prophecy did sound a bit like me. I had recently suffered great loss. And here I was—basically, the lone protector between the world and this great evil.

And yet those things were all Finch's fault, all the work of his manipulative hand. Several emotions spun together inside me like a tornado: anger, sadness, pity, confusion, and finally rage, as a new revelation hit me. "You killed my mother just so your stupid prophecy could fit me?" I was shouting and nearly sobbing. "You killed all these people here tonight . . . all this misery . . . just so I'd be a better candidate for your little utopia? You're sick, Finch! You're a sick bastard, you hear me?"

I was enraged. I wasn't the second coming of Elben. I wasn't the one who could do all; I'd known that before. All this time Finch had just been delusional to the point of forcing real-world events into his preconceived visions to try to force me to fit the role.

"To be fair," he said in his own defense, "the prophecy doesn't really say anything about the specifics of how these tragic events come about . . . merely that they do. And now they have. Can't you see it, Phillip? You're the one. It's all there. There's no one else alive that text could be talking about at this point. All you have to do is embrace it . . . know it deep down within your being. Believe in yourself, and you will see how little limit there can be to our power!"

This villain was starting to become less scary by the second. The crazier he grew in my eyes, the less frightened of him I became. "Our power, eh?" I scoffed. "Our power? I know what you are, Finch. I know what you are, and I know why you need me to be 'the one who can do all' . . . because without 'the one who can do all,' you can't do all, can you? You're just like me, a one-power hero. So you may have a hundred invisible henchmen behind you, each one feeding you another amazing or impressive power, but that's all you got. You top out there. You don't have them all, you never did, and you're completely reliant on the loyalty and service of other empowered individuals to do any single thing!"

His smile had slowly faded during my speech, uncurling into a sinister straight line. "You think you know me, kid?" A new edge had appeared in his voice, and his volume began to increase. "You think you know who I am, what I'm about? You don't know a thing, you little punk!"

I looked at him square in the eye, lifted my right hand to the side of my glasses where the radio button was located, and said, "Let's find out."

I pressed the special button Bentley had created for me, which mimicked the school's frequency, gave a deep breath, and then said, "Chelsey."

But nothing happened. I glanced at Henry, who looked up at me in return. He looked nervous.

After several seconds, Finch broke the silence. "Was something supposed to happen there, little Sallinger? Who's Chelsey, your girlfriend? Is she supposed to show up with the cavalry and save the day?" I'd been around twelve-year-olds who were more mature than Finch was in that moment. "Let me teach you the first lesson you need to know as a hero, young man," he carried on, taking a few steps forward. "Never go into battle without knowing something about your enemy's plans." He stopped walking and leaned again on the cane. "Isn't that right, Mr. Burke?"

I jerked my head toward Chad, but Henry had done the same, so instead of my angle of Chad, I saw Henry's. Chad's head hung low, and he refused to look up at either of us.

"You see, when I heard about a brash young hothead hero who'd been in a fracas with the blind kid at Freepoint High, newly sent to Goodspeed as punishment . . . I started cooking up my little surveillance plan right then and there. See, I knew that if I could make you feel sorry for young Chad here, you'd welcome him into your group with open arms—you have a big heart like that, don't you, Phillip? And then, once he gained your trust, he could relay back to me everything I'd need to know to stay one step ahead of you.

"And it worked, too, didn't it? Because I knew about your foolish little Chelsey plan. It wouldn't have worked anyway, though, son, because we killed her a couple hours ago. And I knew your plan to walk past me using Chad's invisibility. And I know your poor little friends were unable to place a call for help and were eventually captured by my men. How do I know all this? Well, because you're just gullible enough to believe that the biggest jerk in school could turn over a new leaf just because he lost his arm." He turned his eyes to Chad, who was still looking at the ground. "You see, Chad? I told you it would be a sacrifice worth making."

A shiver ran through my body as Finch's words were processing in my brain. He had taken Chad's arm off . . . and Chad had gone along with it!

"So, now what?" I asked, only a trace of defiance left in my voice. I'd been betrayed, my plans laid bare.

"Now you spend a few seconds making the biggest choice of your life. Do you want to join me? I'm willing to wait for your powers to blossom and show themselves, and you can pick some of your friends to join you if you want. Or do you want to choose willfulness . . . stubbornness . . . doubt? Oh, and certain death. That's it. Those are your two choices—join me or die. I can give you a few seconds, but honestly . . . it's been a long night, and I'm tired."

"You might as well go on home and get some rest," I said. He looked up at me with a hint of optimism on his face. It didn't last long, as I continued, "Kill me first, though. 'Cause I'll die a thousand painful deaths before I join you for anything other than a fistfight."

His expression flashed with anger, and his face became a few shades darker. "You know, Phillip," he stammered, holding back the brunt of his rage, "I always pegged you for a smart kid. Bright . . . intelligent . . . intuitive. It's in your blood. But now I see how wrong I really was." He started walking toward me again, this time more briskly.

"Oh, I don't know about that," I said. "I was smart enough to figure out your little game with Chad over a month ago. Which means I was smart enough to make you believe my only plan here tonight was to say a woman's name into a radio."

Finch stopped walking and looked up at me.

Oh God, I said in thought, *please let this work.*

Amen, Henry silently finished my prayer for me.

"Now!" I shouted.

30

THE REAL PLAN

The truth is, we'd been onto Chad for a while. In the end, it was his own thoughts that truly did him in, but not before other signs had begun to spring up.

Even though I'd defended him to the rest of the group when he'd first reappeared, I never quite bought it completely. Sure, I basically fell for it, but a few strings of lingering doubt had always remained. After all, how do a couple months in boot camp change a bully into a hero? It didn't seem possible. In the end, it was the arm—or lack of one—that made the story believable to me. It was a powerful piece of evidence to support his story: that he'd experienced the same world of disability as the ones he once tormented.

But at the time, I think I wanted to believe him. I wanted his conversion to be true and his intentions pure. So I believed him, defended him, and befriended him. For a while.

The first embers of suspicion stirred during the second SuperSim, when he'd so strangely disappeared right when we needed him most and ended up decimated by a two-hundred-miles-per-hour Donnie. And then, somewhat conveniently, he couldn't remember a thing about any of it. It was subconscious, but I think that's when the sheen started to wear off of Chad, and I began to wonder if he was what he appeared to be.

But I still carried that hope. Optimism is a funny thing, and I may never understand how it so easily trumps reason.

Then came the extracurricular activity I'd gotten us involved in on the sly, our own real-world SuperSim—a Super Not-Sim, if you will—where we actually discovered, chased, and apprehended real-life criminals in and around Central Park.

During our encounter with the very first guy we caught, the purse snatcher, things moved from subconscious to conscious. A light bulb went off as Chad went to his invisible knees to trip the fleeing robber. It was like déjà vu. I didn't even realize what it meant until the next day, but I felt very strongly that I had almost lived through that moment before.

Of course, I had. Chad had tripped Donnie that night during the SuperSim. He tripped him on purpose, causing himself terrible injuries in the process, and then lied about it afterward.

A week or two after the tripping capture in the park, Henry came to Bentley and me one day after school to share a concern.

"He's just acting strangely, is all," Henry said.

"Like, what do you mean?" I didn't really do well with vague concepts. I needed specifics. What, exactly, was strange?

"It's hard to describe. But he's not telling the truth, I can promise you that," he explained.

"About what?" This time it was Bentley's turn to ask a fair question.

"I have no idea."

Both Bentley and I looked at Henry, cocked our heads, and then looked at each other. We were lost.

Henry tried again. "You know how you'll be talking to him about a mission or whatever, and he'll reply to you?"

"That's called having a conversation." I was beyond confused and not entirely sure Henry should have bothered interrupting us to mention whatever vague thing he was trying to say.

"Right, but his thoughts don't match all the time."

"How so?" Bentley asked.

"Like, sometimes he'll be talking about a one thing or another, but his thoughts are about unrelated things like homework. Sometimes there aren't thoughts at all while he's talking."

"Are there usually thoughts at the same time a person is talking?" This was news to me; it was actually pretty interesting.

"Sure, but they always match the physical words being said. It's sort of like the brain acting like one of those teleprompter things the president uses. Unless the person is lying, and then the thoughts are usually the opposite of what's being said. But in Chad's case, sometimes there aren't any thoughts at all. Almost like he's somehow blocking them from me or something. I know that sounds crazy."

"How much time do you spend concentrating on listening to Chad's thoughts?" Bentley asked, sounding a little like a disapproving teacher.

"More than I should, probably," Henry said. "But someone has to stay wary of that guy."

"Do you . . . spend a lot of time listening to my thoughts?" I asked, suddenly embarrassed at the thought of what he might have heard throughout the months.

"Not really, no. I try to be respectful of other people's minds as much as possible, especially my friends."

"Except for Chad," I muttered.

"Yes, except for Chad," Henry fired back with snappy sarcasm.

"I wonder what it means that you can't hear his thoughts?" Bentley asked. "That's really interesting."

"You know as well as I do that I can really hear only complete thoughts, like sentences in the brain when a person is actively thinking through something like dialogue. It's the way most people think, by default. But maybe he's just concentrating really hard on *not* thinking that way."

"Interesting," Bentley repeated.

"The real question you need to be asking, though . . . is why would he do that unless he had something to hide, huh?"

From that point on, all three of us had a healthy skepticism regarding Chad.

Henry decided to keep eavesdropping on Chad's thoughts to try and discover more evidence. Bentley, meanwhile, went to work on the technical side of things. His first step was to create a simple tracking device. He didn't even need to order anything because he had all the spare parts he needed to build it in his workshop. But because it was built by Bentley, it was deluxe. It didn't look pretty, but it didn't have to. It carried powerful GPS technology to allow us to easily track Chad's movements from anywhere in the world.

Planting the device was easy enough. We had numerous practice sessions as a team, and then there were the "field trips" to Central Park. All I had to do was wait for a good moment when Chad and I could "accidentally" bump into each other. It was simple.

What was difficult was deciphering his movements once we started tracking them. Within just the first few days of having the tag in place, Chad's travels proved to be much wider than we ever guessed. He went to Goodspeed three times, LA, Canada, and the Bleeding Grounds twice. The Bleeding Grounds was the place where the original Ables fought their battle with the Haladites, a miles-wide stretch of barren land with a huge rock in the center. We'd learned about it in class, though none of us had ever been there—except Chad, obviously.

It didn't take someone with Bentley's superbrain to see that the first obvious conclusion was that Chad was leading a secret life. The second conclusion, which was a hard pill to swallow, was that he was likely working for Finch.

It made perfect sense, actually. If Chad was a spy, he had to be a spy *for* someone. And I had only a small number of enemies at twelve years old: one. Well, two, I suppose, if you're counting Steve, but honestly no one was counting Steve as an enemy at this point in the game. There was no one else Chad could be working for other than Finch.

Somewhere in the midst of monitoring Chad's movements, Bentley hit upon a scary notion: if we could use technology to help learn more about Chad, Chad could be doing the same thing.

It was a shiver-inducing thought, and Bentley, Henry, and I frantically checked ourselves for homing devices or bugs. Thankfully, we found none. But Bentley wasn't satisfied yet.

So he set up a scanning device—he called it a "digital net"—in the cornfield and monitored an entire practice session. That's how we found out Chad was bugged. There was a small device somewhere on him, probably very well concealed, recording audio of everything that went on in our practices, conversations, and adventures and uploading it all to a private server.

That was the domino that set the whole plan in motion—the plan to use Finch's spy against him by pretending not to know he was a spy.

We obviously fed Chad—and, by extension, Finch—a phony plan. Never in my wildest dreams did I intend for the "Chelsey" gimmick to work. I just wanted them to believe that I thought it would.

So the plan we spoke of aloud in the park was just a show. We'd hashed out the real plan silently, using Henry's abilities to ferry messages back and forth between Bentley's mind and mine.

In reality, I didn't know who Chelsey was or if there was even a real person by that name controlling the school's NPZ. But I'd seen enough heroes with that power disappear over the past year to know that Finch would know who it was and would probably already have kidnapped or killed them.

It's apparently easy to believe that a kid my age would think that plan would work, because both Chad and Finch played right into my hand.

No, there was only one hero with the NPZ ability that I was pretty darn confident would not have been kidnapped. Unfortunately, he was also the least likely person on the planet to help me. But that didn't mean I wasn't going to try.

So when Henry, James, and I did our "sweep of the cornfield," while Chad and everyone else were back in Central Park getting arrested, we actually went to pay a visit to Mr. Charles. I had maybe said fifty words to him in my entire life, and now he was my only hope.

I'd known him to be exceptionally quiet, sometimes short and cranky, and generally mean-spirited, so I knew it wasn't going to be easy. He'd left us on our own to die in a fire in his own backyard, so he wasn't exactly the volunteering type.

"We need your help," I said once we were standing in Mr. Charles's living room. He sat in a rocking chair that did very little rocking, from the sound of it.

He said nothing in response to my statement.

"Did you hear me, Mr. Charles? We need your help. I need your help . . . my dad needs your help!"

"Heck," James chimed in, "the whole city of Freepoint needs your help."

We waited a few seconds again, wondering if this was going to be the shortest and most one-sided conversation ever, when suddenly, the old man spoke.

"No."

It was a fairly simple statement, just the one word and all, and its meaning seemed pretty straightforward. And yet I could not help myself. "What do you mean 'no'? Like, 'No, the whole city of Freepoint doesn't need your help'? . . . or 'No, I won't help you'? Which one is it?"

"Both of them," his crackling voice replied. Everything about this man was old. His house, his face, and even his voice. I wondered if I might even see dust come out of his mouth with every word if I hadn't lost my ability to see as soon as we'd walked in the door. Yes, this was clearly the man we needed because he definitely had NPZ powers, and they were still functioning just fine—and finely tuned enough to encompass just the interior of the house and nothing else.

"You won't help us?" I asked, sounding deflated.

"No. I can't."

"You can't, or you won't?" Henry had very little patience on an average day and even less in a crisis. He'd been brought along to talk to Mr. Charles for precisely that reason.

"Does it really matter?"

"Yes," Henry shot back defiantly.

"Fine, then. Won't." Mr. Charles was a man who didn't like to waste any words.

"Why not?" I asked, taking on more of Henry's tone than I really intended to.

"I made an oath. I don't expect you kids to understand. But I . . . made decisions in my past that I'm not proud of."

"We know all about that, old man. You killed Phillip's grandfather, your partner, in cold blood. We got it. Whoop-de-do. We heard about it in school, and then we got the unabridged version from Mr. Sallinger. So quit wasting our time." Henry was on fire.

Mr. Charles seemed legitimately surprised, maybe even stunned, but for only a flash. "You may know the facts, young man, but God willing, you will never know the pain."

"Pain?" Henry asked.

"The pain of living with your own selfish, evil choices. Now, leave me alone."

I finally started to get it. "That's why you live out here alone and never do anything or talk to anyone." I felt James and Henry turn and look at me, no doubt anticipating my conclusion. "It's your penance, isn't it? This farm . . . this town . . . it's like an extended prison to you, right? You're just riding out the rest of your life trying not to do any more harm."

I could tell he was nodding as he began to respond because his voice slowly raised and lowered through his first several words. "On the day I betrayed your grandfather, I felt instant regret for my actions. Split seconds after I'd completed them, I wanted to take them back, but I couldn't. It was too late. After a lifetime as a hero, I'd cast myself in the history books as a villain forever. I then used my powers to neutralize Artimus and throw him off the roof. I swore then and there that I would never use my powers again for evil or for good. And that, children, is why I can't help you."

"That's a lie," I said flatly. No raised voice, no outrage, just a calm statement of fact. "You want to know how I know that's a lie, you old grump? Because I lost my ability to see what Henry's eyes can see the moment we walked inside your home, that's how. You're using your powers right now, you freaking liar. And what's worse, you're using them for self-preservation. You won't lift a finger or use your powers to help this city, or us when we're facing a fire-breathing monster in your cornfield, but you'll do it to help keep yourself safe. Pathetic! So don't give me any of this crap about vowing not to use your powers, because it's bullshit!" I didn't swear very often, and it was usually a sign of me losing control of my temper. "If you don't want to help, if you're too scared, then say you're too scared. But don't make yourself out to be all noble and holy, so guilt-ridden that you can't bear to use your powers anymore," I singsonged in sarcasm.

And that was the first glimmer of hope I'd had, because when I said this, he lowered his NPZ, and I was able to see again.

"Jesus," Henry said under his breath, shaking his head and marveling at the old man's stubbornness.

Mr. Charles obviously felt guilty, which is why he lowered the NPZ when I mentioned it. And I hoped that was the opening I needed.

"You know what I think, Mr. Charles? I think you're just scared."

He said nothing and resumed staring at the floor.

"I think you're scared of everything anymore. Scared to be a good guy, scared to be a bad guy . . . just scared to have superpowers in general. And you know what? Right here in front of you are three little kids, man. Three freaking twelve-year-old kids. You don't think we're scared? Scared to get hurt or die or fail? Because we are, mister. We are. But you don't see that stopping us, do you?"

He looked up at me, which I took as a sign that maybe I was getting through to him. So I continued.

"There's a very good chance we could all die tonight. But you know what? Some things are more important than life. And I think you're going to learn that in a very real way if you choose not to help us and instead sit here inside your stuffy old farmhouse, too afraid to be a hero. You may still be alive, but you'll never be free, and you know it." I paused, getting ready to make my pitch. "Now, will you please help us?"

His eyes never wavered from mine, but he took several moments before answering. It appeared to me that he was on the fence about helping us, and maybe he just needed a little push. But he was very conflicted, it seemed.

He finally spoke, but I didn't let him finish his first sentence. "I'm sorry, Phillip—"

"Come on, man, what the hell is the matter with you? Do you want evil to win?" I was aghast.

"No."

"Do you want my friends and me to die?"

"No," he said, a little more emphatically than last time.

"What about my dad, the only guy in this whole freaking town that has shown you nothing but kindness and friendship, even though he's the guy in this town with the best reason to hate your freaking guts?"

"Your father is a saint and a friend."

"Then get up off your ass and help him!" I screamed. Trying to change Mr. Charles's mind was quickly beginning to resemble a typical argument with Patrick. I just couldn't understand his logic.

"Do it for my mom," I continued yelling, with a few tears beginning to spring forth, "who cooked you hot meals with her own two hands, invited you into our home, and treated you with grace and respect even though you deserve neither, and who's now lying under a mound of dirt in the Freepoint Cemetery because of this man." I started to sob. "Do it for her!"

"I can't!" he shouted back at me.

It was probably the most honest moment I'd ever witnessed. He obviously wasn't saying he was incapable of helping physically. He was admitting he was too scared. Too immobilized by fear and years of regret.

I sighed. "James, hand me the picture."

James reached into his backpack and handed the framed photograph to me, and I turned and plopped it on Mr. Charles's lap. "Someone in this photograph has been terrorizing us—and me, personally—for the whole year, and now he's killed or imprisoned nearly every other soul in Freepoint. Now, you may be a miserable, gutless jerk, but we're going to go out there. I am going to go out there and face this man. And probably die. Since you're the only person alive who ever knew him, maybe you can tell me something that might be useful to me, even if you won't lift a finger to help!"

He was looking over the photograph intently, memories rushing back.

"His name is Finch. He's got a huge scar down the center of his face. That's all we know. I can't even tell you which guy in the picture he is."

"Martin Finch?" he responded quizzically. After a pause to think, he answered. "Well, he's a blocker, and well, yeah, this is a . . . a club, I guess, that we started in college." His voice lowered as he added, "It became something much worse after that."

"Was Finch the leader?"

He scoffed. "Are you kidding? That man was a sniveling little mouse."

"Are you saying this isn't the birth of the Believers?" Henry asked, joining the questioning now that the man was opening up a bit.

"No," he said flatly. "Not really. We were just college kids playing around. We took the photo at a party after a little too much wine and philosophy, and that was it, as far as I remember."

"Well, then Finch must have been the one who turned it into an honest-to-goodness evil cult," I concluded.

"I have no idea," Mr. Charles said. "I never saw him much after that second year of school."

My shoulders sagged and I sighed. With my final attempt to gain some advantage over the enemy, we'd hit another brick wall.

"But I doubt the man you've been dealing with is Finch," he added as an afterthought.

"What makes you say that?"

"Because Finch is dead. Has been for a dozen years or more. In fact, everyone in this photograph is dead except for me."

He suddenly tore into the frame and pulled out the photograph, bringing it close to his face and tilting it sideways. Then, without warning, he abruptly ripped a three-inch tear in the photo, again pulling it close to his face for examination.

"Well, I'll be damned," he said as realization dawned upon him.

31

REUNION

"Now!" I shouted, praying with all my might that Mr. Charles could hear me from his position.

And thankfully, he could. About one second after I yelled, Mr. Charles slipped from the tree line along the east edge of the school property and turned on his NPZ.

Now, what I didn't know from the textbooks and legends was that Luther Charles had one of the most powerful and flexible NPZ abilities in the entire world. Much like Finch—or the man who called himself Finch—Mr. Charles could create an NPZ of any size and place it where he wanted with pinpoint accuracy.

As planned, his NPZ covered Finch and all his men, but not Henry or me. As you might guess, this pretty much instantly changed the balance of power in our direction.

Behind Finch, nearly four dozen men suddenly appeared. They'd been there all along but were finally visible to our eyes thanks to the NPZ.

Before I could speak, Luther Charles decided to say his piece.

"I knew it was you," he shouted, still roughly a hundred feet away from us. "As soon as he showed me that damn photograph, I knew it couldn't be anyone else."

"Luther?" Finch asked, sounding cautious. "Luther, is that you?"

"Yes, Thomas. It's me."

There was clearly a history involved, though I was just doing my best to keep up with all the new information flying at me in rapid succession.

"I . . . I . . ." Finch stammered. He'd gone so long being known as Finch that my brain didn't yet know how to refer to him in any other way. "I didn't know you were still around. I assumed you withered away and died off like the rest of them."

"It has been a while since my last Christmas card," Mr. Charles said sarcastically.

And that barb of sarcasm seemed to jog Finch from his surprised stupor, and he came back with a jab of his own. "Back to finish the job, then, eh? Fifty years later?"

"I was wrong, Thomas. I should never have tried to hurt you. I should never have betrayed you," he said, sounding sincere.

And it hit me like a ton of bricks. "Thomas . . . Sallinger?" My mouth blurted out the words before my brain could stop it.

My grandfather turned suddenly, as though he'd forgotten I was even there. But Mr. Charles beat him to the explanation.

"I'm sorry, Phillip," he called. "This piece of filth is your grandfather, and he's a real son of a bitch. I couldn't risk telling you, or you would have been too distracted to fulfill your portion of the plan."

"Phillip." It was Finch—my grandfather, Thomas Sallinger—speaking now, trying his best to sound grandfatherly. "Phillip, my boy. Now do you see why you're so important to me?"

"I thought it was about my supposed powers," I argued, not ready to believe everything I was seeing and hearing, "not a chance to reconnect with your long-lost grandson. You want my power for the same reason you want everyone else's powers—you're useless without them."

"But I know you, Phillip. We are of the same blood, and even in just our short time together, I can see so much of myself in you . . . of your father in you. It's why I know for certain that I'm right about your abilities . . . because we're family."

"Leave the boy alone, Thomas," came Luther's voice. "You're finished. Whatever little fantasy you've been planning, it's over. You know I'm not going to let you out of my zone."

"Well, Luther, you're definitely the man you always were. So quick to rush into battle that you don't really think through things too well. You see . . . here I stand, with fifty of my most gifted Believers . . . and while you may have me in a no power zone, you're all the way over there." He paused and smiled, shooting his eyes right at me. "And we have guns."

The next few seconds happened quickly, and I relied heavily on instinct.

Finch's men drew firearms. Though I don't read minds, it was clear that they all intended to fire on and injure Henry and me. I also instinctively knew in that moment that Mr. Charles couldn't help. Even if he was standing right next to us, he was a frail old man whose power was already being used to its highest effectiveness. Guns aren't affected by NPZs. It took about a nanosecond for me to do the math and realize we were going to die. And then something happened.

A switch somewhere in my head flipped, and I somehow skipped ahead a few years in the development of my powers. Instantly I knew—I just *knew* it to the very core of my being—that I could stop them and could control their weapons with my powers. Never mind that I had never come close to that kind of telekinetic strength at any time over the previous year. Never mind that I had never even controlled multiple items at once before. I just knew it, and I may never be able to explain how.

I raised my right arm, hand outstretched toward Finch and his men. I really didn't even need the hand; I learned not long after this incident that my powers are 100 percent mentally controlled. Holding out my hand toward an object I want to control just looks cooler, I guess, because I still do it to this day.

With my mind, without moving a muscle, I took control of every single gun—all fifty of them, one from each of the henchmen. My eyes closed, I suspended them all in the air and turned them one by one to face their owners. It was like synchronized swimming, an operatic ballet of coordinated dancing guns. After holding a gun in each man's face long enough to feel sure they were sufficiently scared, I brushed my arm from left to right toward the school, and every gun but one soared over the school's roof and flew hundreds of yards beyond where the goons stood. It took very little effort on my part.

I zipped the final gun over to Finch's location, leaving it hanging there six inches from his face. I jutted my left arm out low and slowly raised it. As I did, Finch and all his henchmen were slowly lifted off the ground about a foot each.

I had just disarmed fifty Believers of their guns, gotten rid of the weapons, and lifted every opponent into the air in a suspended physical prison, all without breaking a sweat. It was easy, in fact. Child's play. If I hadn't been so high on adrenaline, I would have been impressed with myself.

Something about the prospect of imminent death had awoken a deeper level to my powers than I had ever suspected existed. Something had changed in me, and I could feel an increased strength in my abilities. It was as though my abilities had matured years in the span of a few minutes.

My grandfather noticed and began to laugh as he dangled there just above the charred grass. A few staccato chuckles quickly turned into a more sustained belly laugh.

"Look at you, son," he said, holding out his finger to point at me. "Look how powerful you are!" he said in wonder. "I told you there was more to you than you thought there was. You just disarmed my entire army with a casual gesture. Do you realize what that means?"

I had to admit he had a point. With only the faintest of effort, I'd wiped out a fifty-man threat. I barely even had to concentrate.

"It means he's a telekinetic, Thomas. Stop feeding the boy lies. He's not your man."

Thomas raised an eyebrow at that and turned toward his old friend. "You know about the prophecy?"

Mr. Charles just nodded. "It's not him. It's not Phillip, I promise. Is that why you're messing with this kid? Jeez, I thought it was because he was your grandson. I should have known there'd have to be a more selfish reason. You think this boy is Elben?"

"I know he is," Finch said, seething. "There's no doubt in my mind at all. It's kismet . . . fate . . . predestination."

"Let me save you the trouble," Mr. Charles said. "If that's what you think, this is going to end badly."

"Oh, I'm counting on it, Luther. I'm counting on it."

The "Chelsey" plan wasn't the only lie we'd told Chad. We had pretty much decided we couldn't trust him at all since we figured Finch was listening in on everything, and so every branch of our plan had some element of fiction in it.

Such as Bentley's capture . . . which had never really happened.

In a performance deserving of multiple Academy Award nominations, Bentley, Freddie, James, and my kid brother had put on a spontaneous old-time radio show for the ages, complete with sound effects, gunfire, and deeper voices. The whole thing was a ruse, all for Chad's benefit.

So while Finch was led to believe they'd been captured, they were instead carrying on with their secondary mission to rescue the other Freepoint prisoners.

That didn't mean their job was easy.

The prisoners were being held by two of Finch's henchmen in the school's basement. The detention hall was in the very center of the basement, with a hallway all the way around it and smaller classrooms and closets along the outside. Having been built to corral adolescents with superpowers, it was no ordinary classroom area. The outer walls were reinforced steel, and when all the thick plexiglass detention doors were shut, it was more secure than most state prison facilities.

With Mr. Charles throwing down his own NPZ, though—over both the school's massive yard where I was facing off with my own grandfather and the school itself—the two guards had come under an NPZ.

"What just happened?" the fat one asked the skinny one.

"What do you mean?"

"My powers are gone."

"What?"

"My powers . . . they're gone."

Both men wheeled and looked at the prisoners, none of whom were escaping.

"There appears to still be an NPZ over the prisoners."

"Well, it must be coming from the big man, because it's not mine."

The skinny one looked worried. "Wouldn't he tell us if he didn't need us down here anymore?"

"You want to go ask him, feel free. I'm content to just sit here and play babysitter to these do-gooders here. No sense joining a fight when I have a perfectly good safe-zone seat right here." He plopped his butt down on the folding chair again and crossed his legs.

The skinny one nervously reminded his buddy, "This ain't no safe zone, Harry. You forgetting what's down the hall there?"

"Oh yeah," the big one chuckled. "Well, that's still a ways off. For now, I'm not going anywhere. I've seen what he does to people who disobey."

Bentley, Freddie, James, and Patrick watched from around the corner at the end of the hall. Most of the lights were off downstairs except in the detention area itself, where the prisoners were being held.

"Okay, guys," Bentley whispered. "Looks like Phillip's plan worked. There's an NPZ over the whole school now, and now we have to get these two idiots out of the picture. Remember . . . no powers. Just four kids against two adults . . . We ought to be able to handle that, right?" He grinned, and the others returned the smile.

They crept back away from the corner and into the nearest classroom so they could plan their assault on the guards. But as soon as they were inside, they stopped dead in their tracks.

"What is that?" Patrick asked nervously, referring to the giant foreign object in the center of the classroom.

"Um," Bentley replied, still processing.

"Is that what I think it is?" Freddie said. "I mean . . . is that a . . . a . . ."

"Bomb?" Bentley offered.

"Bomb?" Patrick asked, hoping he'd heard wrong but knowing he had not.

"Um . . . yeah," Bentley said, sizing up the coffin-sized device in the center of the room. "I definitely think . . . that this is a bomb."

"Like . . . a *bomb*-bomb?" James asked politely.

Bentley bent down and looked at the control panel of the bomb. "Yes, James. It's a bomb."

"Holy crap, guys, we gotta get out of here," Patrick suggested urgently. "We gotta go!"

"Calm down, calm down," Bentley said, dismissing my brother's worries. "It's not on a timer or anything. It's not counting down. It looks like there's a remote switch back here," he said, pointing, though doing so from a good foot away. "I think it's just dormant for now."

"You do realize, don't you," Patrick said, in his patented sarcastic tone, "that your assessment doesn't make me feel any safer, right?"

"Is it . . . you know, nuclear?" James asked, wanting to gather as much information as possible before freaking out.

"How should I know?" Bentley countered, giving no comfort whatsoever to the other two.

"Aren't you, like, the gadget wizard?" It was Freddie chiming in.

"Gadgets? Yes. Explosives? Nuclear warheads?" Bentley shrugged. "I mean, this casing is pretty solid, so there's no real way to tell what's inside there."

"That doesn't sound like a good thing," said James.

"Probably safe to assume the worst, I guess, given this guy's track record." Bentley seemed concerned but not panicked. "Look, guys, if we don't get those prisoners out, a bomb may be the last of our worries, okay? Now, if it said two minutes on it, and it was counting down, then yeah, I'd say we get the hell out of here. But it's not. And we have a job to do. Don't you wanna save your dad?"

"Yeah," Patrick agreed. "Definitely."

"Okay then, let's just pretend this thing isn't here and figure out how to take care of those two guards."

"Don't you think we ought to warn Phillip?" James wondered. "About the bomb, I mean?"

Bentley shook his head. "No. We have to maintain radio silence, that's the plan. Finch might have equipment or abilities that could pick up our transmission, and for now, at least, he thinks we've been captured. The bomb doesn't matter unless everything else goes right. Otherwise, it's just a bomb that goes off after we're already dead. This must be his endgame, though," Bentley added, mostly to himself, "to blow everything up."

"Then . . ." Patrick asked timidly, "tell me again why we aren't panicking?"

Bentley turned and looked at my brother with a smile. "Because it isn't the end yet." He put his hand on Patrick's shoulder. "Which means we've still got time to stop it."

"Jesus, Thomas, was that your plan?" said a tired-sounding Mr. Charles. "Force the prophecy to come true by manipulating this boy's life?"

"The prophecy doesn't say anything at all about how things come about, just *that* they come about," Thomas/Finch argued. "'He shall return again, an outcast, one who is not like us, who does not see the world as we do.' Now tell me, Luther . . . how does that not describe our little friend here?"

"He's not a little friend, Thomas. He's your grandson. He's your flesh and blood!"

"All the more reason I should want him on my side," he continued. "'This one shall not know of his own true depth of power until he suffers great loss and injury, and he alone stands as the last protector between the world and a great evil. Only then shall he truly see. Only then shall he embrace his true purpose.'" He spread his arms out wide, like he was preaching the gospel. "It's all come true now. It's all happened, and here we are, the great evil," he gestured toward himself, "and the last protector." He gestured at me. "All that's left is for him to embrace his true purpose."

"He already has, Thomas, by simply showing up here. Unlike you, this boy has courage."

Finch's eyes flared, and he seethed as he barked back at Mr. Charles, "I had courage once too, Luther! All my life I did the right thing . . . the good thing. I was the ultimate hero, Luther! Do you remember that?"

For the first time, Mr. Charles seemed to lose confidence a bit, and his head lowered to the ground.

Finch just kept right on with his verbal offensive. "And do you remember how I lost my courage, old friend?"

The frail old man, eyes still facing downward, merely nodded.

"That's right," Finch gloated, almost giddily, despite the fact that we now had the upper hand. "I was betrayed by someone I trusted, handed over into tragedy by my best friend."

Bentley, James, Freddie, and Patrick hid in a classroom just down the hall from the prisoners and Finch's guards. The gang had moved the teacher's desk to a new position. The classroom door opened inward, and the desk now stood behind the door.

One by one, they each climbed up on the desk.

Patrick looked over at the bomb in the center of the room, trying to find a way to put it out of his mind.

"Are you sure this is the best idea?" Patrick asked, relatively new to crime fighting and definitely new to the genius of Bentley Crittendon.

"Look, this was the plan all along, Patrick—put the guards on a level playing field with us with the no power zone, and then we take them out old-school style."

"It feels more like Scooby-Doo style," Patrick said, picking up the sarcasm responsibilities in Henry's absence.

"Well, if you have a better idea . . ." Bentley said, knowing full well that Patrick did not have a better idea. It was almost like Bentley had dealt with little brothers before, though he had not.

Still, Patrick took a moment to think, only to come up empty. "No, I don't," he said dejectedly.

"Okay then. James, you ready?"

"Ready, indeed!" he chirped.

"Freddie?"

Freddie held out a thumbs-up.

"Patrick?"

Patrick rolled his eyes but agreed anyway. "I guess."

"Okay then, guys . . . here we go." Bentley grabbed two large books off the surface of the desk at his feet and hurled them across the room. One of them smacked hard into the bookshelf next to the window while the other one found the window itself. The concussive impact of the books and the unmistakable sound of shattering glass echoed down the hallway outside the classroom.

"Well, that ought to do it," Bentley whispered, startled by the level of noise he'd managed to create.

I imagine the fat guard and the skinny guard bickered for a moment about whether they should go check out the strange noise, finally deciding to do it together after realizing their prisoners were still captive, whether they stayed or not.

Bentley held a finger to his mouth as the four boys heard the guards slowly shuffling down the hallway.

James and Patrick had raided the room's potted-plant collection on Bentley's instructions, and each kid stood silently, holding a large pot high above their heads. They looked like wound-up little human rubber band guns, cocked and loaded, ready to spring into action. They just needed a target. Patrick helped get James aimed in the right direction while Bentley held a slightly smaller plant up over his own head.

And about a minute after Bentley tossed the books, two targets appeared exactly where Bentley had said they would: in the classroom doorway, on the opposite side of the door from the four hiding kids.

Bentley looked at the two men through the frosted glass of the door's window and found they were definitely larger up close than they'd appeared from far away. Bentley shouted, "Do it!"

"Imagine how easy your misunderstanding would have been to avoid." My grandfather was lecturing his old partner, twisting the knife. "When Artimus knocked me off that roof, it might have been prudent for someone to go and check to make sure I was actually dead, don't you think?"

"No one ever survived a direct hit from Artimus like that, Thomas, and you know it. There was no reason to doubt."

"Right," he spat back at Mr. Charles. "Because you and Artimus had a pact, right? Tell me, Luther," Finch droned on, "do you feel bad? Do you . . . have any remorse about what you did to me?"

Mr. Charles said nothing and continued looking down at the grass. A lifetime of shame, regret, and self-loathing was bubbling to the surface, and the man couldn't even bear to look his former friend in the eye. I didn't blame him.

"Luther!" Finch's voice rumbled, louder than I'd ever heard it. "Tell me, *friend* . . ." The word was layered with a poisonous tone. "Are you sorry?"

"I was," Luther responded, with a surprising amount of conviction. "For almost fifty years I was sorry, Thomas. I've devoted my life to self-loathing since betraying you. But now that I see what you've become—what you truly were all along . . ." he paused, swallowing. "Well, I wish I'd pushed you off that roof myself."

Finch smiled, as though he'd just earned a trophy he'd been chasing for years. "You know, I've been warming myself for years on the hope that you had a festering wound of guilt for turning on me."

"You were changing," Charles argued in his own defense. "We could all see it, but I saw it most of all. You were growing power hungry and losing your grip on reality."

"We should be greater than mere public servants to these humans. We should be more than just cops or soldiers. We should be their gods!" he bellowed. "And soon, we will be."

$$\lightning$$

James and Patrick let their projectiles fly according to the plan, and each boy scored a direct hit—one on each guard's head.

It probably would have been a total success if the pots had turned out to be ceramic instead of just a heavy-grade plastic. Alas, they bounced off the thugs with a hollow thud. Instead of two guards slumped to the ground with tweeting birds circling their heads, the end result of Bentley's plan turned out to be two very ticked-off guards turning on the kids in anger.

Patrick was the first one to leap into action. Even though the NPZ prevented any of his supernatural speed from kicking in, he was still a quick little bugger. He jumped off the desk, bounced off the back of the bent-over skinny guard, landed on the floor in the doorway, and took off down the hall to the right.

Bentley had wisely prepared a backup plan in case the old "potted plant to the head" gag failed, and it mostly consisted of "everybody run."

Bentley was second to move from the desk. He tried diving under the fat guard's legs to get through the doorway, but he was too slow. Freddie tried to follow Patrick's example, but the guards were too quick; the fat one grabbed Freddie by the leg and then reeled him in.

Poor James, without Henry's sight, was forced to choose between standing there waiting to be captured and running away without knowing where he was going. He chose the latter, and it was a poor choice. He jumped off the desk and took off running. Two steps into his flight, he tripped over the leg of a chair and careened across the linoleum floor into the concrete wall.

"Wait a minute," I said softly, mostly just to myself. Watching the two old men pick back up a half-century-old disagreement had given me time to think and reflect on some of the things I'd learned throughout the evening. And something didn't add up in my head. I almost had my finger on it.

They either didn't hear me or didn't care, as Finch and Luther continued their argument.

"You think you're just going to convince this kid to be evil? Join the man who killed his mother?"

That comment triggered something in me. We were just chess pieces to him. He'd used his own flesh and blood, killing his daughter-in-law and taking her away from his own grandsons, and had felt nothing. No remorse. He wasn't truly my grandfather, and in that moment I began to realize he wasn't even human.

Thomas smiled, becoming almost completely calm, nearly looking the part of the kindly old grandfather he should have been all along. "You push someone up to the edge, you'll see what they're made of, Luther. All I'm trying to do is find the unlikely hero that was foretold. All I'm trying to do is get him angry."

"It worked," I said, loudly and firmly. That got their attention, as both men abruptly turned to face me. "You're a murderer," I calmly declared, keeping my rage back for just a moment or two more.

I was staring him down, trying to let him sense how furious I was. But he simply responded by pushing my buttons to get me even more riled up. "I'm sorry, Phillip, but I'm afraid I'm going to have to ask you to be more specific. I've killed far too many people in my life to have any idea which one you're referring to."

"My mother!" I snapped, no longer able to keep the bubbling anger at bay. "Tell me, did you think of her as a human being? As a person? As your own son's wife? Or did you just view her death as a statistic? Did you pause . . . even one second . . . to consider your actions? Or was it an easy decision to kill my mother?"

I was almost totally overwhelmed with some of the darkest and most powerful emotions I'd ever experienced.

"Was it easy?" I asked, a bit more forcefully. "Was it?" I shrieked. I'd never been more resolute in anything in my life. I was about to kill a man, but first he was going to confess the truth about his actions to what few witnesses were present.

Finch casually answered, "I thought about her exactly the same amount of time I've thought about any of the bugs I've squashed beneath my feet on my way to my goal."

If getting me angry was his goal, it had worked. My left arm reached out and lifted slightly, and I used my powers to lift my grandfather up off the ground another ten feet. The rest of his men remained in place suspended a few feet off the ground, but I didn't even have to think about them to keep them in check. My powers had grown considerably, so much so that I began to wonder if he might even be right about the prophecy referring to me. If the telekinesis had this much extra power lurking below the surface without my knowledge, what else might I be capable of?

"You know how you could have gotten me to join you, old man? Do you want to know what would have worked? How about being a grandfather, you bastard." I took both my arms, starting them way off to my left, and swiped them quickly across my body to my right, sending my enemy flying twenty-five yards through the air toward the school's exterior wall. His body smacked into it with the sickening sound of bones breaking.

"Phillip!" Henry screamed in shock. He hadn't expected that level of violence. I wasn't really myself anymore at that point. I probably hadn't been for weeks, if I'm honest. The violence was new, but the outburst had been building for a while.

I nudged Finch back away from the building—still dangling in the air, fifteen feet off the ground—and then mercilessly slammed him back into the concrete wall. Henry shrieked again in alarm.

"This is for my mom!" I said, pulling him back away from the wall again just as quickly as I'd thrown him into it.

"Phillip!" Mr. Charles shouted, just as horrified at my actions as Henry was.

"This is for my dad, who never got to have a father because you're such a selfish asshole!" I sent him into the wall again.

"Phillip, no!" Henry wailed, openly crying at the raw horror of what he was seeing.

"And this is for me!" One last time, I fired his body at the wall, battering the old man even further. I didn't have much practice in beating a man into submission, but I reasoned he was very likely well past that point by now.

He hung there, powerless and possibly passed out, like a rag doll. Four hits. That's all it took for a kid to take down the most powerful bad guy in the world—that's how quickly fortunes change in the world of empowered individuals.

"Any last words?" I asked. I was on the edge of the cliff, about to jump. There is no doubt in my mind I was ready to kill this man—my own grandfather—had it not been for Henry.

I suddenly lost my sight. I could tell right away, though, that my power—my hold on the enemy and his men—was still intact. It's almost like I could *feel* them . . . their location . . . my connection to them. I wasn't sure how long that would last, though, especially if I actually needed to move them.

Phillip, Henry said with his thoughts, *you have to stop. You have to stop this now. I can't be a part of this.*

Fine, then—go, I responded in kind. *You don't have to be a part of it.*

Phillip . . . this isn't you, buddy.

What do you know about me, man? Nothing, that's what!

If you kill this man, they're never going to let you be a hero, Phillip. You'll be a villain for life . . . no going back. No more SuperSim, no more Freepoint, no more Ables. Forever.

Who cares? The Ables don't matter, Henry, can't you see that? They're already going to make sure we don't get to be heroes. The Ables were doomed from the start! The whole town hates us. They think we're liars even when we tell the truth. We have no mentor or leader. We're just a bunch of kids with half-powers and no idea of what to do with them.

"Is that what you think?" He was speaking now with his actual voice. "You really think that?"

"Yeah," I said, surprised to find him so surprised.

"*You're* our leader, Phillip. *You* are!"

I wrinkled my face in confusion, so Henry just continued.

"*You* suggested we form a team for the SuperSim. *You* chose the name and even the story that would serve as the historical significance of that name. *You* fought for our rights to participate and found a place for us to practice. You thought of the plan to trick Chad. You thought of going to Mr. Charles. I mean, damn, Phillip! I know you're blind, but can't you see anything? Without you, there are no Ables—period!" He took a few deep breaths and then wrapped it up. "So you see . . . if you kill this man, you'll be killing the Ables forever. I'm sorry, Phillip, but this is about more than just what happened to your mother."

I hadn't turned to face him the entire lecture because I didn't want him to get through to me. I wanted to dismiss his words so I could go back to killing the man who killed my mother. But he *had* gotten through to me.

"But Henry," I protested weakly.

He read my mind and answered before I could finish the sentence. "He does deserve to die. And you know what? You probably deserve to be the one to do it. But you know what else, Phillip? Being one of the good guys means that sometimes, you don't get what you deserve. Things aren't always going to go your way, and sometimes you have to give up what you want for the greater good." Henry didn't know how closely his words echoed those of my mother.

"But he killed my mother," I said, as tears formed in the corners of my eyes.

"I know, Phillip. And while I didn't know your mother for long, I do know this for a fact—she would never, *never*, want you to seek revenge for her death in this way."

I slumped to my knees, letting go of my grip on the body of Thomas Sallinger, who fell fifteen feet to the ground and crumpled on the grass, clutching to life by a thread.

But I wouldn't have let him go at all if I'd been paying much attention to my surroundings while Henry and I had been talking.

The stakes were so high. For me, this was about my mother and revenge and honor. For Finch and Mr. Charles, this was about history and good versus evil and settling old scores. There were so many huge story lines, I just simply forgot about one of the smaller ones: Chad Burke.

Chad had been standing near enough to me to remain outside Mr. Charles's NPZ. I hadn't given Chad another thought since learning Finch was actually my grandfather, and neither had anyone else. He managed to activate his powers and slip away unnoticed.

It was easy for him to sneak up behind Mr. Charles, but I still don't know where he got the gun.

The four rescuers in the school basement were being dragged through the hallway, right past the prisoners' area. The guards had caught up with Patrick when he mistook a classroom door for the door to the stairwell. The fat guard had a hold on Bentley and James, dragging them both by their arms toward the same closet.

"Why don't we just throw them in there with the grown-ups?" the skinny one asked.

"Because, idiot, the boss said not to open that door for any reason at all, okay? Besides, as long as the big man's NPZ is covering us, those kids are just as powerless in a closet as they would be anywhere, you dig?"

The skinny one smiled but obviously still did not understand.

Something silent occurred, and Bentley was the only one who noticed it. And while it meant good news for the near future, it was a terrible omen for the long-term success of the Ables' mission.

"James," Bentley said as he shuffled. "I feel smarter."

A single gunshot rang out, and I whirled around in time to see Mr. Charles fall to the ground face-first with Chad standing behind him, a trickle of smoke twirling up into the air.

All of Thomas's men fell to the ground, and I spun back around to see them all staring directly at me. And then I lost my sight.

Henry gulped audibly.

I merely whispered, "Oh boy."

We were in trouble, and we knew it. Our powers were neutralized, and those of the enemies had returned. It was several dozen against two.

But nothing happened, at least not right away. I waited for someone to speak or simply blow me up with a laser or something. There was nothing.

"What's going on?" I asked Henry in a hushed tone.

"Um . . . nothing, really. They're all staring right at you, but none of them are moving."

It was my turn to gulp.

"Wait a minute, Phillip," Henry said softly. "One of the guys is walking."

"Toward us?" I asked in stark fear.

"No. Toward Finch—toward your grandpa."

I concentrated and could hear footsteps. He was walking on grass, but he was the only person moving in the entire field. He was walking from my left to my right, not quickly, but not slowly either. Finally, the footsteps stopped.

"He's bending down toward your grandfather," Henry announced. "He's putting his hand on his shoulder." The narration stopped, and there was silence for several seconds.

"Oh God," Henry gasped.

"What?" There was no response. "Henry, what's happening?"

"He's a healer," he whispered. "He's healing him!"

While it was obvious we didn't stand a chance against the remaining henchmen, I at least assumed we were done dealing with Thomas Sallinger. But if there was a healer in the mix, then all bets were off. My heart sank. Healers were among the rarest of all superheroes, like blockers or those with the ability to manipulate memory on a large scale. He'd planned so carefully for all contingencies to this point, it made perfect sense that my grandfather would have had a healer in his crew. But it was still a surprise to me, one that threatened to send me into a tailspin. We'd thrown our best at the enemy—heck, I'd broken nearly every bone in his body myself—but it was all in vain.

Suddenly, I got my vision back, only it wasn't quite the same as it usually was. There was more clarity, and the colors were more vivid. "Henry? Are you doing that?"

"Doing what?" he snapped back.

"I'm doing that, Phillip," my grandfather interjected. "I want you to see everything that's about to happen. Because it's time, son. It's time for the end."

$$\frac{\quad}{\quad}$$

"I *said*, 'I think I feel smarter,'" Bentley repeated, with a distinctively slow delivery to emphasize each word.

James didn't know what Bentley meant, so he just smiled a polite smile in response as they continued to be pulled down the hallway.

"James," Bentley tried again, as the guards neared the closet. "All of the sudden, I feel smarter. Do you have any idea what that could mean?"

"That . . . you're . . . getting smarter?" James asked. He couldn't figure out why Bentley was making small talk at a time like this.

The skinny guard whipped out a key and unlocked the closet door. Time was running out.

"James . . . do you remember what my power is?"

The fat guard tossed both boys into the makeshift cell with Patrick and Freddie and started to close the door.

James answered Bentley excitedly. "Supersmarts," he said, with a point of his finger for good measure. And as soon as the words were out of his mouth, he realized what Bentley had been trying to tell him: the NPZ had gone down.

$$\frac{\quad}{\quad}$$

"I've pushed you pretty far, young man," Thomas said, with a bit of his standard Finch charm now missing. He'd finally abandoned the Finch persona completely. "I've pushed you about as far as possible, and you're still resisting your true nature." He smiled. "I guess that stubborn streak runs in the family."

I turned toward Henry, and the image I was receiving followed. I was somehow receiving a video feed of what my eyes would actually see if I weren't blind. I wondered briefly which of the many men and women behind my grandfather was providing that little talent.

He continued, "There's only one thing left to do, my boy. Only one way to find out if you're truly made of . . . what I think you're made of. And that's to push you out of the nest completely to see if you really can fly. It's time to fly, Phillip. It's time to choose. Are you going to be the most powerful superhuman ever, or are you going to settle for being a blind telekinetic little imp?"

He started walking toward me slowly. "Which is it going to be?" He took another step. "Actually . . . the choice is much more final than that, I suppose," he said as he stopped walking. "It's either embrace your destiny as 'the one who can do all' or die."

"You're going to kill me if I don't suddenly sprout a million different powers?"

He chuckled. "No, son. I'm not going to kill you." He reached inside his jacket and pulled a small black box out of his pocket. "This is going to kill you. Providing, of course, that you don't dig down deep and find a way to stop it."

He turned and waved at the school. "This building is pretty impressive, don't you think?" He didn't wait for an answer. "It's state of the art—hell, a lot of things in Freepoint are, am I right?" He looked around with a fake sense of nostalgia. "I think it's going to be sad to see it all decimated."

I looked at Henry and then back at Grandpa, a nervous pit growing in my stomach.

"In the basement of that school, actually, just a few yards away from where your dad—my do-gooder son—and all the other prisoners are being held, is a special plan I saved as a last resort in case you wouldn't listen to reason. Always plan for contingencies," he added as a twisted bit of grandfatherly wisdom. "My contingency plan is a three-ton atomic bomb, Phillip, with enough power to wipe out the whole city and kill a few hundred thousand citizens around the state with radiation poisoning as well."

The pit began to grow rapidly.

He kept going. "And when I push this button right here, you, Phillip, will be the only thing that can save them. And I'm willing to bet, when you're faced with certain death and tragic loss for that many people, you'll find something inside you that you didn't know was there. You're the unlikely hero after all, don't you know? I should have made this my first plan instead of just trying to talk to you, because the prophecy basically calls for you to have your coming-out party by saving the day."

"I don't have these powers! Please," I begged, "you don't know what you're doing."

"Shh, shh, shh," he said, like a mother trying to calm down a screaming child. "We're about to find out, Phillip."

$$\frac{}{} \lightning$$

"Go! Now!" Bentley shouted.

James reached out his hands, corralling the wrists and fingers of everyone in the closet, until he was sure he was touching everyone.

Ooph!

They all disappeared and then reappeared together in the hallway.

"What the—" The guards were startled, but my friends leaped into action too quickly for them. Patrick, showing his own remarkable jump in ability to use his newfound powers, sped into the supply closet, grabbed a rolled-up garden hose, and wrapped it around the two guards dozens of times by circling them—all within two seconds time.

That left enough time for Freddie and James to push the two stumbling goons into the supply closet and lock it as Patrick finished securing the hose.

High fives were exchanged as the group took a moment to savor their spontaneous little victory. As reality set in, each of them slowly began to turn their heads until they were all looking at the detention room door and the trapped heroes inside. Dad stood at the front of the pack, his face contorted in shock at what he'd just witnessed.

"Oh yeah," Bentley said sheepishly. "Who's got the key?"

32

THE UNEXPECTED HERO

Finch had been too cocky to consider any kind of prison break a possibility and had therefore activated his own NPZ over only the field, ignoring the school completely. In a flash, a small army of Freepoint's finest heroes, including my father, appeared behind me.

"What's this?" Thomas asked no one in particular, somewhat startled by the sight. It was already too late for him to use his power against them; there'd been one NPZ hero confined with my father in the makeshift prison—his partner from the ambush in Donnie's room at the hospital—and he'd activated his ability the moment he arrived.

I lost the images my grandfather had been sending me but instantly regained the ones from Henry. I looked around to get a feel for things. Behind me I saw a large number of my city's adults—we easily outnumbered the enemy two to one now. About twenty yards behind me, on my left, was my father. He was staring straight at the man who had tormented me for eight months.

"Dad?" he asked, well beyond confused.

The old villain looked up and locked eyes with my father. "Hello, son." There was a kindness and warmth to his voice, which vanished immediately on the next sentence. "You've raised an interfering little bastard here, you know that?" He gestured at me.

Dad smiled nervously with a combination of concern and pride.

"What are you . . . doing here . . . alive?" Dad was bewildered.

"Dad, Finch is Grandpa. He's been the one behind it all along," I said rather urgently, hoping to get him acclimated quickly to the situation. We didn't have time to stop for every new arrival and retell the story to this point.

"Phillip," Bentley blurted out, unable to control himself. "He's got a bomb."

"I know," I said, pointing at the black box my grandfather held in his hand. Quite cooperatively, he held it up in the air for all to see.

"Everybody freeze," one of Dad's protector buddies yelled. "Nobody moves an inch!"

"I'm willing to stay put," Thomas said playfully, "but I don't really think you're going to play by those rules yourself if I do. And you've got all those superpowers over there on your side, while I have only this little black box. So I think I'll keep my thumb right here on the trigger for a while and do damn well what I please."

He turned and looked straight at Dad. "Son," he said, "I'm afraid we'll have to have our own reunion later, after your son saves the day. Right now, I have more pressing issues to deal with than a trip down memory lane. Now, I'd appreciate it if you'd hush up for a while and let your son and me talk, okay?"

Dad was stunned, still reeling from the new knowledge that his father was even alive. He looked at me, then at his own father . . . then back at me.

"Phillip," said Thomas in a tone that was almost chipper, "what your friends discovered down there in that basement is part of a three-stage bomb. That means there will be three separate steps to the process. There is, of course, no added advantage to using multiple explosions—the end result will be the same level of devastation. But I wanted something visceral to trigger your powers."

"I don't—"

He cut me off. "The first stage is your basic dynamite, and that'll just blow out the windows and doors. Sure, it'll make a pretty gigantic thump in your chest—I mean, you'll know it's for real at that point." He smiled the way someone does who is telling a favorite story they've told a million times. "The second explosion, well, that's C-4, and that'll wipe out the school . . . probably send plenty of debris here into the field . . . might even hurt someone. That explosion is designed to really sock it to you—you in particular, Phillip. If, somehow, the first wave doesn't kick in your instinctive God-given abilities, then we'll have to wait for the second. And it will do the trick, I'm sure. You've been through a lot in the last year, but you've never been this close to a few dozen pounds of C-4. That kind of explosion will make Navy SEALs soil themselves."

And then he just stopped, almost as though he was waiting for something.

"And the final stage?" I finally said, remembering that this was all a carefully choreographed and scripted affair for my grandfather, almost like a play reenacting his grand vision for this moment.

"Well, if it comes to that, there's no going back. That's the nuclear option— literally." He took a few steps toward me and was now only a few feet away. "Phillip, if those first two explosions don't wake up the powers I know to be inside you . . . then I don't want to live, and none of you deserve to . . . so we'll all die. Together. But," he chuckled, "I am not remotely worried about it. You are the one I've been searching for these last forty years, Phillip. I know it as strongly as I've ever known anything in my life.

"Of course," he said, as though he'd just remembered something, "I have only the one trigger. Once I push this button, there'll be no turning back, son. And at that point, if you can't save us . . . no one can." He leaned down, smiling knowingly. "You sure you don't just want to tell us the truth about your powers?"

I lifted my head so I was looking directly at his eyes. "I have told you all the truth I know about my powers."

"Ah," he said, following it with a sigh.

"Please don't do this," I said, figuring it was worth one more shot to try and talk this maniac down from the fiction he'd built in his mind. "Please, I promise you . . . I don't have the powers you think I do."

"But you do, Phillip! You do have them! Just like the baby bird who inches up to the edge of the nest, never really sure that his wings will keep him airborne until his parents push him out, and he faces the cold, stark reality that he is, indeed, *falling*. It is I, Phillip, who promise *you* . . . you do have them. And as soon as you realize it, I'll have them too. *Then* let's see them try to stop us."

I looked down to the ground, trying to make peace with the fact that I was about to die.

"At least let these people go," I said, grasping at straws. "You don't need to put them at risk when all you want is me."

"Ah, but I do! I do have to. You see, this"—he gestured to the field around him—"is your *nest*, young man. And I can tell you've already made your peace with the fact that death is a possible outcome of our little standoff here. That's why I need these people here, so that you'll have a motivated reason to want to flex your muscles and stop my bomb. Your friends . . . your teachers . . . your father," he said, and looked at Dad and then right back to me, "they'll all be dead in a few short seconds if you aren't able to save them."

"Dad," my father said softly with a noticeable quiver of emotion in his voice. "Whatever this is . . . don't do this."

Thomas looked at my father, not as a father looks at his son, but as a police officer looks at a deadbeat criminal: with disdain. "If your sad puppy-dog eyes didn't keep me from turning my back on you when you were a kid, what makes you think they're going to work now? Don't be so weak, John. It's *always* been your biggest flaw."

He lifted the black box with his left hand and moved his thumb over the button.

"No!" I yelled.

"Dad!" My father shouted.

"If I'm right, we'll see the real you in a few moments, Phillip. If I'm wrong . . . well, I'm going to be pretty upset that I wasted all this time on you." And with that, he depressed the button.

Almost immediately, there was a large, rumbling explosion. It shook the ground on which we stood and was followed immediately by the ear-piercing sound of a thousand panes of glass shattering as each of the school's windows blew out in spectacular fashion.

"You'd better hurry up and do something, Phillip. I can't stop it now!" Thomas cackled. He was genuinely enjoying the carnage.

The second explosion came only a few short seconds later and made the first look like a child's firecracker.

The force of the blast knocked me to the ground and sent me tumbling as the school walls burst into thousands of pieces. Debris flew everywhere. Finch had guessed right, and hunks of concrete and metal smacked into some of the custodians on both sides of the battle, sending them flying and knocking some of them unconscious.

I'll remember the sound of that second explosion forever. It started with the roar of a jet engine but was quickly replaced by silence as the sheer decibel level of the blast momentarily deafened me. When it returned, it did so in a pulsing scream.

I looked up from my prone position in the direction of my grandfather. My images had changed again, and I instantly could tell I was receiving pictures from him and not from Henry. The blast must have incapacitated Dad's partner who had been holding Thomas and his men at bay with the NPZ. I whipped my head to the right, only to find Henry's empty wheelchair tipped over on its side. Henry was twenty feet away, passed out, with flaming chunks of school property set around him like sentries.

I looked left to where my father was and saw him facedown on the ground. Behind him, most of the rest of the hero force had been wiped out or knocked clear by the explosion. Even most of Thomas's men were out of commission.

Twenty yards away, I saw Freddie grow rapidly to his full-empowered size—probably out of instinctive reaction—and then immediately shrink again, gasping for breath.

I turned back to look at the school only to see a horrific, charred shell of a building. A few support walls still stood, and the building's foundational outline was intact. But it was otherwise leveled, burning, and in pieces.

I had been correct; I did not have all the powers in the world. Hidden abilities had not been awakened by Thomas's final, violent catalyst. I was just a regular old blind kid with some fairly cool telekinetic powers. But I was no Elben.

Frankly, it was a relief. I'd rather face death than the prospect of joining forces with such an evil person . . . or being his prisoner for the rest of my life while he milked my powers for his own gain.

I looked at his eyes and slowly rose to my feet, my gaze never wavering. I said nothing. I did nothing. My silent fortitude conveyed my message entirely: I cannot stop you, but I will not yield to you.

Screw you, Grandpa.

For a moment, he seemed surprised. His eyes widened. Fires raged throughout the treetops above us, dropping ash and ember all around us. I knew what came next, and I knew I couldn't stop it. I wasn't even going to try anymore.

My father's father looked around, surveying the damage and taking in all he'd lost in his pursuit of what he thought was a sure thing. He looked back to me. His eyes flashed with defiance. Suddenly, he was directly in front of me, having teleported inches from my position. More than half his face was mangled in raised, discolored scarring. Artimus must have hit him square in the face with that lightning bolt on that night so many years ago. He shook his wiry, wrinkled finger in my face, silently scolding me. Then he leaned down quickly to my ear. "I'm very disappointed in you, grandson."

Then *ooph!*, he was gone. And yet I was still able to see. No Henry, no grandfather—yet I still had some kind of images being sent to my brain, with a faint blue tint behind them. I didn't get to enjoy it or analyze it much. I looked up to find every one of my grandfather's soldiers was gone. I've never felt more dread and misery than I did in that one moment as I realized I was about to die.

I briefly thought about Mom. I wondered if there would be an afterlife and if it would be such a paradise as to at least let me be together again with her there.

But I thought no more about winning or living.

I turned back to the school just in time to see the flash of light from the atom bomb, the third and final explosion.

Honestly, that's where things should have ended. That white-hot light should have been the last thing I ever saw.

But it wasn't.

Time slowed down to a crawl for me in that moment. What I witnessed over the next several moments should have taken place in a nanosecond, completely invisible to the human eye. And yet I saw it all . . . I heard it . . . I got to experience every bit of it in a dreamlike state.

As the blinding white light emanating from the school began to slowly grow in size, another light appeared. It was moving much faster than the explosion, and it was blue, and it more resembled a line than a ball. It zipped left and right, high and low, zigzagging all over the field, leaving a trail that created a spiderweb pattern in the sky. It was moving at lightning speed, even with this bizarre slowed-down perspective I was enjoying.

The explosion, meanwhile, continued to inch forward, chugging along like a snail, with the white ball of light growing by minuscule amounts—but definitely growing.

Having already resigned myself to certain death, I was more bemused by what I was seeing than shocked. I was living in the middle of a slow-motion nuclear explosion with bright blue lights in the sky . . . I was more in awe than anything.

The line of blue light shot here and there out above the field, and I began to notice that some of the heroes were missing. And that's when I realized what the blue light was; it was a person trying to save us!

The lines in the sky were like tracer rounds on bullets, marking the trail like bread crumbs where this mystery savior had been. Whoever it was appeared somewhere on my left, and I wheeled to try and see, but the person was already gone again—with my father in tow—leaving only a brilliantly colored loop in his or her wake. Though the real world was moving at a tiny fraction of its normal speed, the blue-light hero was still moving too fast for me to see. And I still didn't even have any clue as to *why* I could see.

I turned my head back to the right just in time to see a trail of brilliant blue light dance away from where Henry's body had been lying.

One by one, this person was pulling us all away to safety, all while the nuclear bomb continued its glacial explosion. I don't know if time was really slowed down or if it was merely something I imagined to help me process what I saw.

The explosion grew and began to climb up into the sky, and the shock wave from the blast formed a circle parallel to the ground, which began to quickly expand outward.

Soon there were enough blue tracer lights above and around the school property to create a faint glow over the field, and it seemed everyone had been lifted and taken away but me. I spun around to try and catch the light I saw coming toward me, but it was already upon me.

In a flash, I felt myself lifted up off solid ground and into the sky, with the rush of air around my ears telling me I was moving at speeds I'd never fathomed, though it still seemed slow, like in a dream. I turned my head slightly during the flight, stretching to try and see who the mystery hero was, but I couldn't get my bearings right; we were moving too quickly. I was facing down—looking toward the earth below as we streaked through the air—unable to see the identity of my rescuer.

For a brief flash of a moment I felt at peace, flying through the air at speeds defying logic, racing over the decimated Freepoint landscape below. It was the strangest, most serene feeling I've ever encountered. For a moment, I wondered if I had actually died already and was being ferried to heaven in the most brilliant way possible.

And then, just like that, I felt solid ground beneath my feet again. And the light dimmed as the savior of Freepoint stood before me, a faint blue hue glowing around him.

It was Donnie.

He looked completely healed, as though he'd never had even a scratch on him. He gripped both my shoulders and leaned down, like a father teaching his son a lesson on the Little League diamond. He smiled—the warmest smile I'd ever seen—and said softly, "Don't worry, Phillip. Donnie fix."

And just like that, he was gone, with nothing but the vapor of blue light in his place. I looked up to see the chaser round headed back toward the explosion, which I could still see off in the distance. I looked left and then right and saw all the others had been brought to the same location—Henry, my father, Patrick—all of them.

We weren't that far away from the bomb. Donnie had deposited us all in Mr. Charles's cornfield near the outskirts of town. It wasn't remotely far enough to escape death from the explosion, and I momentarily wondered if Donnie's mental handicap had doomed us all to die anyway—rescued . . . just not rescued quite fully enough.

But then I saw the trail of bright blue, growing wider and more pure in color as it streaked straight toward the now ballooning mushroom cloud, picking up speed. Even with the effect of time being slowed, I struggled to keep up with the new information my brain was processing.

I stood there, completely still, dumbfounded, as I watched my friend race at freakish speeds toward certain destruction. Even in shock there were obvious conclusions I could draw. Donnie was definitely fast; we already knew that. But Donnie was also flying. Heroes didn't get two powers—other than the occasional Jekyll-Hyde I'd heard about, but those were always more like split personalities, with two variations of a similar power.

There was only one hero in the entire history of our kind who had more than one root power, and that was—*Wait . . . is he . . . ?*

"The one who can do all"?

It was Donnie, not me. Had Finch—my grandfather—been right all along about the prophecy but merely picked the wrong disabled, downtrodden kid?

One who doesn't see the world as we do!

I'd been so deceived by Finch that the prophecy had begun to seem written for me—the blind kid. But it was a perfect fit for Donnie as well. There had also been great suffering for him, and now he was showing up in our time of need to save the day. The last man standing. The unexpected hero.

A mix of emotions flowed over me; relief blended with sorrow and happiness with sadness.

Donnie's blue trail made a beeline straight for the looming explosion like an expertly thrown dart sent to pop a balloon.

"Donnie, no!" I yelled helplessly.

Just as he neared the explosion, the slow-motion effect dissipated, and time seemed to right itself, fast-forwarding again to a normal speed. It was jarring. When Donnie reached the point of impact, there was a gigantic sonic boom loud enough to make me cover my ears and knock half of us onlookers to the ground.

Just at the point where he made impact with the mushroom cloud, a shiny black sphere appeared, rapidly growing in size. It was accompanied by the sound of intensely loud static, not unlike an improperly tuned radio, only a million times louder. It was a terrifying sound.

As the opaque black ball continued to grow in size exponentially, the explosion from Finch's bomb seemed to weaken as the light and smoke and debris were all slowly pulled toward Donnie like a magnet.

The black hole power!

Within seconds, the black orb had grown rapidly, hovering over our heads and the entire city like a small moon. The bomb's effects—debris, fire, smoke, and radiation—were all being sucked into Donnie's black hole, which fed off the added energy and continued growing exponentially in size.

Soon he'd gobbled up every bit of light and smoke from Finch's bomb, and all that remained was Donnie's black circle of energy, hanging over the city like a dark and twisted moon. The deafening static continued a few seconds.

Then the sphere began to shake, shiver, and vibrate. Suddenly, the edges of the circle raced inward with intense speed as the entire ball collapsed in on itself. When the edges reached the center, there was an audible but faint—and ultimately anticlimactic—popping sound. And then it was gone. Disappeared. Evaporated, along with every ounce of danger and destruction from the bomb.

Half a second later, my vision disappeared as well, and the survivors of the Freepoint Massacre were left to gape and stare at each other in confused relief.

33

SUMMER

The recovery efforts took months—and not just the physical rebuilding of Freepoint. There were emotional scars, in many cases more damaging than the physical toll Thomas Sallinger's attack had taken. It would be a long time before Freepoint would be able to trust anyone completely again, hero or not. One of the city's most decorated and celebrated heroes of old had come back to wipe it off the map. It would take some time before anyone in town could feel 100 percent normal again.

There was mourning to be done, to be sure. One hundred seven citizens— mostly custodians, but several human support as well—had been killed. Four hundred twenty-five more were injured in some way, from the superficial to the serious.

Many of the casualties were people I knew. Steve was one of them, wiped out with the rest of his team by the same power that had been used to put my mother in a coma. Coach Tripp was another casualty, struck down defending the hospital from a dozen of my grandfather's men.

Everyone knew someone who'd been hurt or killed. It was a tragedy that impacted literally every single citizen of Freepoint. There'd been memorial services, tributes, and candlelight vigils. And the footsteps of everyone around town seemed a bit heavier for quite a while.

It was hard for me to come to grips with the fact that my own flesh and blood had been behind such atrocities. He'd escaped, of course, along with several of his men, and hadn't been seen or heard from since. Dad said he was the most wanted man in the world among custodian forces and that he'd have to be the stupidest criminal in history to ever show his face around Freepoint again. It didn't make me sleep any better, and yet . . . at least I found comfort knowing that I ultimately didn't have anything he wanted.

It had been Donnie all along who did. And now he was gone too, though most of us Ables were reluctant to pronounce him dead and gone forever. The truth is, none of the adults had ever seen the kind of power Donnie displayed that night, particularly the fabled black hole ability, which some had written off as a myth. No one could say for sure whether he had died or simply transported somewhere else in time and space. But I couldn't help thinking if he were alive, he would have come back.

Still, I held out hope that somehow my friend had lived and was out there somewhere in the universe, leaving a brilliant trail of blue light wherever he went.

The town erected a monument in Donnie's honor, but only because Bentley harassed the city council with legal filings to get them to do it. Left to their own, I don't know that they would have done anything. It was a complicated issue. It didn't help that I was the only one who saw Donnie's rescue in real time. For everyone else involved, it had all happened faster than the blink of an eye, and none of them could truly confirm Donnie's appearance was anything other than the hallucinations of a traumatized kid. I guess it was just hard for some people to admit that their salvation had come from a kid like Donnie, especially the ones who'd been the most outspoken against him earlier.

The monument, which I visited at least once a week, was in the memorial gardens the town had built on the school grounds to commemorate all the victims of the attack. There were lots of monuments there, some big, some small. Donnie's wasn't a statue or anything like that, just a nice plaque noting his contribution to the city's survival. I guess I thought it was a little insulting to deprive Donnie of the full measure of credit and praise he deserved. But considering the prejudices I'd seen over the last year, I tried to focus on the positive—the fact that the town had done anything at all to honor him.

I'd been fairly well exonerated for my previous shortcomings, as had Bentley and Henry. Whatever distrust the town held for us over the trouble we'd caused throughout the year was now erased. We were the disabled kids they found acceptable to call heroes, while Donnie was the one they preferred to remember differently. Local history would probably end up glossing over Donnie's role in the battle. It felt wrong, but we were definitely glad to no longer be complete outcasts. Now everyone loved us.

The school was being rebuilt. They'd started construction only six weeks after the explosion. It obviously wouldn't be done in time for the next school year. So even though the summer had only just begun, the board was already holding public meetings to debate and discuss a solution on educating the town's kids in the meantime.

"I don't see why we can't have school right here," Henry said, taking a massive bite out of a breadstick.

"At Jack's? Get serious," I said. "No way. I can't concentrate on anything but video games and pizza in here."

It was a Tuesday in mid-June, and we were having a bite to eat at our favorite spot before heading out to practice a little bit. Patrick was with us. He'd become an honorary member of the Ables after playing a role in the rescue of the prisoners. The guys really seemed to like him, though Patrick kept pretty quiet and smiled almost constantly. I couldn't tell if he was subdued with us because he was nervous hanging out with the Ables or if he was still somehow scarred from the trauma of the previous six months. But Dad said there wasn't much point in keeping him away from the superhero life anymore. He'd even begun to practice using his powers, which were still developing and often used to annoy me.

"There's no building in town big enough to convert into a school," Bentley said matter-of-factly. "They're going to have to split us all up."

"You mean there's no such superpower as 'instant school creator'?" I asked playfully.

"Sadly, no." He smiled back, tolerating my joke.

"I, for one, wouldn't mind just having a year off from school," James added.

"Ha! Yeah," I said sarcastically.

"Good luck with that one," Henry said, dabbing a napkin on his face. "They'll make us sit out in the street for classes before they cancel a school year."

"I hear they may be sending us all to Goodspeed," Bentley said. And he would know, his father being on the board and all.

I shook my head at that notion. "All of us? Where would they fit us?"

"What, are they going to make us all hold hands and teleport there every morning?" Henry said, giggling.

"Yeah, actually, that's one of the suggestions they're talking about."

"Oh, good grief," I blurted out. "Freaking adults."

Bentley scooted his chair back away from the table. "We better get going if we're going to make use of the daylight."

"Freddie," I said, pointing at the table, "don't forget your inhaler."

We all pushed back from the table and started standing up. Henry hurriedly stuffed a few more pieces of breadstick in his mouth. He didn't bother chewing before speaking. "Tell me again . . . why are we practicing in the summer when there are four more months before another SuperSim?"

"Because we want to get better, dummy," I answered, slapping him on the top of the head playfully. We headed outside and took a right, heading in the direction of the cornfield.

"But we saved the day," Henry objected. "We're the big heroes now, right?"

"Donnie saved the day," I corrected him. "Not us."

That brought the group to a momentary silence, as everyone thought about our friend. We'd barely talked about it with one another, and I figured it would be a long time until we did. It was still pretty fresh.

"Besides," I said, determined to get us back to cheerier subjects, "even though we played a part in saving the day, our track record in SuperSim competitions is still pretty awful."

Henry had to agree with that one. "That's for sure."

We rounded the corner of Ashbury Street, heading west. There were blue tarps patching up holes on the roofs of the houses all around Freepoint, and construction crews were everywhere, sawing and hammering and drilling. Tree limbs, even entire trees, were stacked along the side of the street in nearly every neighborhood. Everywhere you looked there were signs of the recent destruction but signs of recovery as well.

"Did you end up getting in any trouble over those cameras after all?" I asked Bentley. The authorities in Freepoint, my father included, had been pretty shocked to discover that Bentley had a network of cameras covering 30 percent or more of the city. I believe my father referred to it as "unconstitutional" and "really, really, very illegal" when he'd learned about it.

"Heh," Bentley chuckled. "Actually, no."

"What? How is that possible?" Freddie asked. Bentley definitely had a knack for getting away with things.

"Well . . ." he replied, "I'm not really supposed to say."

"You can't leave us hanging like that," Henry said. "That's cruel. You can't tease us like that."

"Well," he said, weighing whether he should tell us, "I was going to get in lots of trouble—until the chief of the protectors came to my house to see the whole operation. And once I started showing him and my dad how all the feeds worked, they got real quiet." He smiled. "Turns out the citizens of Freepoint are pretty adamant that the board and the protector force find a way to keep something like what Finch did from ever happening again. So instead of punishing me for the cameras . . . they bought 'em."

"You've gotta be kidding me," I said, clearly impressed.

"Yup. They actually ended up purchasing the cameras to use as their own security monitoring system to protect and patrol the city."

"Unbelievable," Henry muttered. "It's illegal if a kid does it, but if the adults do it, it's totally okay."

We continued on across Baker Street, only a few blocks from the cornfield.

"Too bad, really," I said. "Those things came in pretty handy that night, you know? Would have made a killer edge in SuperSim competitions."

"You're not kidding," James said.

"All I said was that I sold them the camera system, not that we wouldn't be able to use it anymore."

"You got them to give you permission for us to use it?" I was beyond impressed.

Bentley just grinned that grin he had when he knew he'd outsmarted everyone. "Who said anything about permission?"

At that, we all shared a smile and a laugh.

"I mean," he continued, "I did build the system after all. I think if anyone would be able to tap into it without getting noticed, it would be its creator, don't you?"

We could see the cornfield now, only two blocks away. And I could see it more crisply and clearly than ever now that Bentley had made some modifications to my camera. He'd even created a special pair of glasses for Henry with a computer screen built into the clear lenses. It didn't obscure Henry's own vision if he needed or wanted it. But once activated, Henry was able to see my high-def camera feed without carrying around a laptop.

"So . . ." James said, his usual optimism shining through again, "what are we practicing today?"

"I think it's time for Phillip and Henry to start learning a new ability," Bentley replied.

"What?" said Patrick, in one of his rare breaks of silence.

"Yeah, I'm with Patrick," I said, scoffing. "What are you talking about?"

"I think we pretty much proved that Phillip has only the one power, Bentley," Henry reminded us, "as impressive and, frankly, as scary as it turned out to be."

"I said ability, not power," Bentley said with a smile. He turned to look at me as we walked. "I was rewatching the footage from that night again yesterday," he continued.

"I don't know how you watch that stuff," I said. I knew I would go to my deathbed without ever watching the video feed of the showdown with my grandfather. It would be too painful, too emotional, for me to relive it.

"I thought you said those cameras didn't record anything," Henry remembered aloud. "They just streamed live video, right?"

"Well, that was true. Up until the moment we left Central Park for Freepoint." He grinned devilishly.

"Why am I not surprised?" I asked.

"Anyway," Bentley refocused the conversation, "something *huge* stood out to me. You, Phillip, have been holding out on us."

"Here we go again," I said. "I promise I'm only a telekinetic."

"Oh, I know," Bentley countered, "but you can do things with that power that you didn't tell us about." He had a playful edge to his grilling, but I had no idea where he was going.

"What are you talking about?" I asked a bit more pointedly.

"Well, you can move objects with your brain, right?"

"Duh!" Henry chimed in. Bentley just ignored him, politely waiting for my reply.

"Yeah, of course. You know that."

He kept going. "And human beings . . . well, they're made up of matter and atoms, right? They're objects, wouldn't you say?"

As usual, I couldn't quite figure out where Bentley was headed. "I guess so."

"And you had those guys, Finch and his men—"

"His grandfather, actually," came Henry's voice in its correcting tone. "Thomas Sallinger, if we're going for accuracy."

"Sorry," Bentley said, not missing a beat. "Your grandfather and his men—I'm not sure if you remember this or even know this—but you had them suspended up off the ground for a long time, just using your power."

"And you threw your grandpa into the wall a few times too," Henry reminded us. He was likely to never stop reminding me.

I did remember all of it. I was on a seven-week streak of recurring nightmares that relived the most traumatic bits of that night, and it was turning me into an insomniac. But I still didn't get his point. "So I can move people. What's your point, Bentley?"

"If you can move objects, and people are objects, and *you're* a person . . . well, then I don't see any reason why you shouldn't be able to fly."

That shut us all up pretty quickly as we contemplated what Bentley was saying.

"You mean 'fly' fly?" I asked.

"Why not? If you can lift another person into the air twenty feet and toss them through the air using your powers, why couldn't you achieve a similar effect to flying by using your powers on yourself?"

We stepped up onto the curb, crossed the sidewalk, and found ourselves in our favorite spot—the cornfield.

"Throw myself into a wall?" I asked, showing my skepticism.

"Throwing yourself into the air," he said emphatically. "And then . . . around. I don't know how it works. I'm just saying you should think of yourself as an object you can move, and move yourself in a motion that makes you fly through the air. *You* have to figure out how to do it. But you know it's possible."

I looked at Bentley with a mixture of disbelief and intrigue. I had to admit, he made a fair bit of sense. I smiled. "I guess maybe that *could* work."

"It *will* work, Phillip!" he added exuberantly.

"It's going to take me forever to learn how to do it."

Bentley just looked at me with that puppy-dog expression, and I caved.

"Okay, we can try it," I said cautiously.

"And Henry," Bentley continued, "I want to start playing around with your ability . . . seeing what you may be capable of that we haven't considered. You have the ability to place a thought or an image into someone else's mind. That ultimately means that for a short period of time, you take control of their image-rendering processes."

Henry waited all of three seconds to get impatient. "And?"

"It's time to see what else you can control in other peoples' minds."

I looked back out over the city, its appearance forever changed by the events of that night. But there were no more sounds of crackling fire or explosions. No more screams.

I thought about Donnie and the sacrifice he made to save us all. I thought about how he probably didn't even realize all that he was doing. Protecting his friends was just instinct for Donnie . . . part of his DNA. I wondered if he ever even knew he had all those abilities until he needed them.

I thought about my mother and how unfair it was that she was gone from me. I knew that if she were alive, she'd chastise me for dwelling on her death instead of moving on with my life. But it didn't change anything. I kept on dwelling.

And I thought about my own actions and how little I'd managed to do right in the year since learning about my powers. It didn't feel good, but I knew that I wasn't half the man Donnie had been. I knew I probably wouldn't have been able to sacrifice myself blindly the way he did to save others. I would have been too scared.

But that's the point of Freepoint, I suppose—to help foster heroes for the future. And after the carnage caused by my own flesh and blood, there were going to be a whole lot more disabled heroes in the special ed class next year. They would need someone to look up to. A leader.

One thing I knew for sure: I was no hero, not yet. Not compared to Donnie. But I would be someday soon.

I looked back at Bentley and smiled. "Okay, let's do it," I said. "Besides, what's the worst that could happen? We're custodians," I said, beaming.

"Ugh." It was Henry, unsurprisingly. "Can't we change that name while we're at it? I hate being a freaking janitor."

"Words have the meaning assigned to them by current culture," Bentley said without expounding.

"What?" Henry asked.

"Custodian means janitor only in this current culture. As recently as one hundred years ago, the word meant merely a guardian or protector of something important. The word once had strength, and it will again."

"It will," I added, "as long as we have anything to say about it."

THE END.